DRE

Jake slipped the glove from under ——— ——— d offered it to Brenna. "This is a pitcher's glove."

She took it. The leather was still warm. The shape of dreams. "So, you think this game will catch on?" she asked.

"Catch on? It caught on before the Civil War. Why, I've heard tales that during the war itself, ball playing became a mania in the camps, North and South. Some say baseball is already the symbol of America."

Brenna stroked the glove one more time, noticing how the spread of the palm and the slight bend of the fingers conformed so intimately to Mr. Darrow's hand. Suddenly aware that he had been watching her, she felt the heat of her blush.

In that one awkward moment, nothing felt more natural than to be standing near this man. Tentatively, Jake touched her cheek. Craving more, she tilted her head. The movement of his mouth to hers was slow, their shared breath delicate. His gentle kiss silenced the sounds around them, causing all thoughts of danger to vanish.

"With homespun magic on every page, *Just a Miracle* is the perfect prescription for what ails the heart. A warm, memorable read."
            —Sharon Ihle, author of *The Marrying Kind*

"*Just a Miracle* is a spellbinding, sensuous tale of the magic of romance and the healing power of love. Zita Christian's gift for storytelling will leave readers enthralled."
            —Carla Neggers, author of *Finding You*

Books by Zita Christian

Band of Gold
First and Forever
Just a Miracle

Published by HarperPaperbacks

Harper Monogram

Just a Miracle

ZITA CHRISTIAN

5/7/96

For Kim —
To the fulfillment
of your dreams!
Zita Christian

HarperPaperbacks
A Division of HarperCollinsPublishers

This is a work of fiction. The characters, incidents, and
dialogues are products of the author's imagination and are
not to be construed as real. Any resemblance to actual events
or persons, living or dead, is entirely coincidental.

HarperPaperbacks   *A Division of* HarperCollins*Publishers*
10 East 53rd Street, New York, N.Y. 10022

Cover illustration by Aleta Jenks

First printing: May 1996

Printed in the United States of America

HarperPaperbacks, HarperMonogram, and colophon are
trademarks of HarperCollins*Publishers*

❖ 10 9 8 7 6 5 4 3 2 1

For my father
C. C. Winterberg, HMCM, U.S. Navy (Ret.)
who, from the time I was five years old, shared his
world of pharmacy with me
and
In memory of my mother
Jeanne Marie Lumadue Winterberg
who gave me her own kind of magic

1

**Coventry, Montana
1890**

    "I cure fits."

    The crowd gasped. Walking slowly enough to conceal his limp, he made his way across the makeshift wooden stage, tugged on his red brocade vest and scanned the plainly dressed men and women gathered before him on the corner of another wide dirt rut called Main Street. They'd been cooped up all winter on farms throughout the Flathead Valley and on this cool Saturday evening, the last day of May, they had lingered in town, eager to spend at least a little of the profit they had eked out of last fall's harvest. Yes, indeed. This was a velvet crowd if ever he'd seen one. The only problem was knowing he was stuck here for a while. Weeks. Maybe months. He had to be careful about what he promised.

*   *   *

He was back.

The small pharmacy was empty except for the feeling of dread that gathered strength every time Brenna McAuley pressed her clammy palms to her black silk apron and glanced out the large, unadorned front window. In her twenty-four years, this was only the second time such anxiety had gripped her heart. There proved to be good reason for her fear the first time. And now?

She closed her pharmacopoeia and neatly wedged it between the other reference books she kept on the back counter. She didn't need to look up the formula for tincture of gentian. She knew it by heart, as she did the formulas for mercurial ointment, liniment of lime water, and dozens of other preparations she had reviewed in the last few hours. But the exercise had bought her time to think.

She had caught a fleeting glimpse of him when he had driven through town several weeks ago. She had been standing in the open doorway of her shop. He waved. She remembered his bright blue wagon painted with yellow moons and stars and the tall, red letters that proclaimed it the home of the Amazing Amazon Traveling Medicine Show. She remembered thinking how odd it was that he hadn't stopped for a day or two, suspicious behavior for a man who makes his living off crowds. She remembered his charming smile. Contorted to an ominous snarl, it was that very smile that haunted her dreams that night and every night since, leaving her gasping for air and drenched in sweat. She prayed he would never return. Now, nearly a month later, he was back, his wagon parked at the end of Main Street. As Coventry's only medical professional, she knew it was her duty to investigate him.

All afternoon, excited citizens had stopped by to share their impressions of the snake oil salesman. The men said he talked like he knew his business. The women said he was ever so handsome. The children said he was fun. He had invited them all to come back at sundown for a show they would never forget.

Brenna had cautioned her neighbors to be wary, but she knew that right this minute every man, woman, and child in Coventry would be gathered around the stranger, willing to give up their hard-earned money in exchange for a worthless, and possibly dangerous, bottle of promises. But in the three years she had lived here, not a single show of any kind had come to town. She couldn't blame people for being curious.

Standing on the raised platform behind the black walnut prescription case that dominated the back of the store, Brenna lined up her meager collection of mortars and pestles, smallest to largest, two Wedgwood, one glass. She ran her finger along the walnut base of the two-plate precision balance, straightened her collection of spatulas, then rubbed a few drops of lemon oil on the counters, looking for dust she knew wasn't there.

The raised platform was to afford her a full view of the store, from the cracked-glass case on the left containing toiletries and shaving equipment, to the floor-to-ceiling, slightly warped shelves on the right containing sewing machine oil, household cleaners, leather soap, and sickroom supplies. The items in the case were neatly arranged and the shelves were tidy, although Brenna lacked the funds to keep either fully stocked. Unfortunately, despite all the people who had stopped by to ask if she had met the snake oil salesman, she hadn't had a single paying customer all afternoon.

Through the window she saw two young women laughing as they hurried in the direction of the medicine show, leaving the hollow echo of their heels against the wooden sidewalk. Everyone wanted to see him.

Everyone but Brenna.

Knowing she couldn't put it off any longer, Brenna lifted her heavy gray shawl from the pitted brass coat tree, grabbed her gloves, and turned down her kerosene lamps. Coventry was still too small and too remote for gas lines, but that would change soon if Lord Austin Halliwell decided to make Coventry his home. It would hardly matter that the growing depression had already made Montana's mining business all but worthless, that the state's infant lumber industry was idle, and that most of the cattle from here to Texas was dead as a result of the harshest winters people had ever known. With Lord Austin's patronage, Coventry would once again thrive.

While the vision of tomorrow might be bright, that of today was dismal. Brenna stepped outside. Three days of cold drizzle had washed the dust from the storefronts, but left the untreated lumber smelling damp and turning gray. Only the rounded, dense green mountains and the silver, snaking Flathead River brought relief.

She shivered and drew her shawl closer. At the end of the street, the crowd was growing. Like candles on an altar of sacrifice, the flickering homemade torches of the medicine show summoned her too, especially her. Heart pounding, she headed down the street.

The more optimistic proprietors had given their shops a coat of gray paint. Ralph Newton's once ramshackle barber shop now boasted the tallest red-and-white-striped pole in all of Montana, or at least that's what he claimed. A hand-lettered sign in the sparkling glass window offered a free shave with every haircut. From Inga's Bakery spilled tantalizing aromas of buttery shortbread, frosted sweets, and cinnamon scones. After years of neglect, even the library, formerly the Bullion Saloon, bustled with activity. Just yesterday, Sarah Zimmerman, the volunteer librarian, had bubbled with excitement about the growing wait list for *The Plays of William Shakespeare.*

From the other side of the street, Brenna's best friend, the owner of Miss Amabelle Sweet's House of Recovery for Consumptives, waved as she called out, "Cheerio!"

Relieved to see her friend, Brenna waited as Amabelle lifted her skirt and hurried across the wagon ruts that patterned Main Street.

"I see you're headed for the show," Amabelle said.

"I'd rather muck stables, but yes, I guess I am."

"Brenna dear, don't look so glum. It's just a bit of harmless entertainment, that's all." Amabelle looked over her shoulder and then pressed her white-gloved hands to her cheeks, a contrast to the natural pink that gave her a perpetual blush. "And he *is* about as handsome a man as ever rode into this town. More handsome than Lord Austin, if you ask me."

Brenna knew the implication of her friend's words. When Brenna first moved here, not a week went by that some well-meaning customer didn't mention someone's handsome son or eligible brother or prosperous neighbor as the perfect husband for her. But as time went by, she let it be known that she was content with her life just as it was. Amabelle respected that. When Lord Austin Halliwell came to town and told Brenna he would enjoy having her show him the sights, it was Amabelle who lectured her, saying she mustn't feel obligated to keep company with the man, no matter how much Coventry needed his business.

"When did you see his face?" Brenna asked.

"Oh, well, when he . . . when he stopped at my place."

"I heard he came in from Whitefish. That's north. Your place is west."

"Oh heavenly days, dear, not today. I meant when he drove through earlier this month. Yes, that's what I meant. He thought I ran a hotel. A common mistake. You know that."

"Well, he certainly made an impression on you."

"Yes, he did. Now, let's go. I can't wait to hear what you think of him."

Brenna longed to confide in her friend. But how could she explain the disturbing image that had robbed her of sleep every night this past month? How could she explain the feeling and growing fear that with the arrival of the medicine show, the phantom of her dreams had finally come to take revenge? How could she do all that without admitting the guilt she had hidden all these years?

They reached the end of the sidewalk and stepped down into the street. Though Amabelle was fifty-two, more than twice Brenna's age, the two shared a common bond. Neither had ever been married. Amabelle once said she was waiting for the right man, one who could see into her soul. Brenna couldn't imagine anything so terrifying.

Gathering twilight carried a pine-scented breeze down from the mountains. Like it or not, change was on the wind. Though her heart raced, she slowed her steps and walked bravely down the center of the street. The moon would not be up for hours, but when it did rise, it would be nearly full. It would hang low in the southwest sky, right behind the man on-stage.

*   *   *

He could sell this crowd the moon, and he knew it. Jake Darrow relished that feeling of control as he smiled at the spellbound men, women, and children at his feet. "With your own ears you've heard the unsolicited testimonial of hair restored to the bald. With your own eyes you've seen the pain of arthritis eased at an instant. All by the ingestion of the elixir known far and wide as Cosmos Clarion's Curative Compound. But fits? Good people, you know as well as I that just the thought of being so afflicted can fill the healthiest person with fear. And rightly so."

"Amen," said someone in the crowd.

The stiff, white collar of his shirt was beginning to chafe despite the chilly evening air, but this was no time to be concerned about comfort, not when there was money to be made. He ignored the impulse to loosen his black silk tie and instead took the framed and tinted sketch from a small table and held the picture up for all to see. Some cringed and turned away. Others stared.

"This drawing was made by an eyewitness," he said as he calculated the number of bottles he still had to sell before the night was over, "hired by the government of the United States of America to document, for men of medicine such as I, the horror of one whose mind is seized by insanity. Look at her. Go ahead, look. Ladies, weep if you feel the need."

He waited for the curious men and the frightened women to inch closer. "How tragic a fate for one so young and beautiful, for no doubt you can see from the delicate structure of her features that she once possessed the face and temperament of an angel."

Clenching his jaw to hide the annoying pain in his leg, he bent down and held the sketch in front of three girls, barely over the age of twelve. "Note the wide blue eyes, sunken as they were in her last days, for yes, these were her last days, each minute filled with unspeakable agony." The girls flinched, just as he knew they would.

"We'll take one," the tallest of the girls said, accepting money from each of her friends and handing it all to him.

"You young ladies have taken the first step in protecting your future," he said, handing them a bottle. "And from my years of experience, I can guarantee you that right this very minute there are three handsome young men out there somewhere who are saying to themselves, 'I just hope that the woman I marry has a sound mind.'" The girls muffled their giggles with their hands and looked at one another while he raised the sketch again and held it high for all to see. Oh, this was going to be a profitable evening. He could just feel it.

"Excuse me, Mr. . . . ?"

He turned toward the woman's voice. Women were always so concerned about whether or not the elixir had cosmetic application. An easy sell.

"Or is it 'doctor'?" she asked.

Well, well, well. "It's Jake," he said as he gave the points of his vest another tug. "Jake Darrow."

He knew he was staring, but couldn't stop. Despite the way she pursed her lips and the superior way she lifted her chin, the woman was nothing short of beautiful. She couldn't have been in the crowd all this time. He would have noticed. Her hair was black and shiny. She wore it pulled back as so many women did, but not tightly, giving her a softness that didn't match the edge to her voice. Her skin was the color of cream, except for the spots of pink high on her cheeks. But it was her eyes that captured him. Not only were they large and fringed with thick lashes as black as her hair, they were pale, pale green. The color enticed him to linger, despite her cynical glare.

Those beautiful eyes bore no hint of flirtation as she moistened her lips. He guessed her to be nervous, definitely nervous.

"Then you don't claim to be a doctor?" she said.

He caught the trace of anxiety in her voice. Good. He broke his gaze and addressed the crowd. "Ladies and gentlemen, we have a skeptic." He looked back at her, enjoying the sudden outline of curves as she folded her arms across her chest, crushing her shawl and the bib of her black apron against her white blouse and clearly ample breasts.

"Well, if you're not a doctor, Mr. Darrow, you must have some proof of your claims. Without it, how can you stand up there and sell to these hardworking people a bottle of what could be nothing but sugar water or, far worse, alcohol or opium?"

"She wants proof," he said to the men in the audience, and smiled. "Proof." When their only show of empathy was a sheepish grin or a shrugged shoulder, Jake grabbed a rolled-up handbill from the back pocket of his black trousers and, in dead earnest, read aloud. "'My husband was ill for fourteen long years after a distressing cough settled on his lungs. But after only eight bottles of the Cosmos Clarion elixir, he now enjoys renewed health and vigor.' That was from Mrs. M. McCoy of Richmond, Virginia."

She gave him a withering look. He read again. "'The Cosmos Clarion elixir restored my health and beauty. I rejoice that I found this miracle before it was too late.' Miss Fiona Prew of Boston, Massachusetts." He let the handbill curl back on itself and tucked it in his pocket. "There. You asked for proof. You have it, Miss . . . ?"

"I had assumed you would produce written testimony by true men of medicine, men whose names others in the field might recognize. Not strange women whom you might have enticed by one means or another to endorse your product."

A man in the audience shouted, "Come on, Miss McAuley, give the man a break!"

McAuley. So that was her name. Jake extended his arms in a show of innocence and said to her, "Miss McAuley, do I look like a man who could entice someone into doing or saying something untrue?"

"Appearances are often deceiving," she said, her gaze unflinching.

This time there was no show of support from the crowd. Needing a quick ally, he gave the women in the front row a big smile. They lowered their eyes. Who the hell was this McAuley woman who could change things so quickly?

One of the three young girls held her bottle of elixir for the woman to see. "He said it would get rid of pimples. What do you think?"

"I think you've wasted your money," she said.

Just as Jake was about to protest, he heard one of the other girls ask, "Can you make up something like this for me in your pharmacy?"

Her pharmacy? So this was the woman Amabelle Sweet had told him about. Beautiful. Smart. He should have known. "So you're the druggist," he said. He forced down a familiar feeling of contempt and bowed slightly. "I'm always pleased to meet a fellow of the profession."

"You *will* give the girls a refund, won't you?"

Those full lips didn't form anything close to a smile, but then, knowing who she was, he didn't really expect one.

"The Cosmos Clarion Curative Compound comes

with a money-back guarantee. Always has. Always will. Of course, the girls are welcome to try the elixir first."

"Yes, well, before they take that risk, why don't you tell all these good people exactly what goes into your elixir."

He brushed aside the wave of brown hair that always fell in his eyes, and flashed his best smile. "Vegetables." Copies of the handbill he'd passed around earlier lay scattered all over the stage. He bent down, grabbed one, and handed it to her. Her hands were small, her fingers long and graceful. "See? Carrots, beets, red and green peppers, a little sassafras—"

"Then how do you justify these miraculous claims?" She cleared her throat, then read from the handbill. "'Toothaches cured without extraction. All manner of liver ailment relieved with one dose.' Really, Mr. Darrow?"

He didn't like seeing how readily the others in the audience deferred to her. "Ah," he said, "but as with fine cooking, the proportions are key, as is the blending." He detected slight nods of agreement from several women. "I would be less than truthful, however, if I didn't admit the presence of a secret ingredient."

"I might have known."

"Yes, and though I would not hesitate to confide it to you, another professional, I must respectfully refuse, for it is not mine to reveal." He gestured with pride to the traveling wagon behind the stage and the ornate red letters that proclaimed it the vehicle of the Amazing Amazon Traveling Medicine Show and the home of the one and only Cosmos Clarion, lately arrived from consultations with the crowned heads of Europe.

Miss McAuley extended her arms across the backs of the two girls who now stood on either side of her, reminding him of a mother hen gathering her brood. "If that elixir is laced with either alcohol or opium, you give these girls their money back this instant."

"They're both useful drugs."

"For medicinal purposes, yes. But not for a daily tonic. You should know that, Mr. Darrow, since you're a professional."

He knew that pompous attitude so well. "You're absolutely right," he said, hiding his own disdain. "And rest assured, there is neither alcohol nor opium in the Cosmos Clarion elixir, not one drop, not one grain."

A few men and women to whom he had already sold the elixir looked with uncertainty at the bottles they held. With the profit already spent, he wasn't prepared to make good on his money-back guarantee. He made eye contact with several others in the crowd to be sure he still held their attention as he said, "Trust me. The secret ingredient in this elixir is perfectly safe for human consumption. Why, Cosmos Clarion himself takes the elixir on a daily basis and he's in fine health, especially for a man past seventy."

He heard the usual murmurs of amazement and wondered what would happen if these trusting people ever knew the truth. He glanced toward Amabelle Sweet. She had the good sense to look away quickly.

Grabbing a bottle of elixir from the table behind him, he squatted down and jumped off the stage, gritting his teeth at the ever-present pain in his leg.

She took a step back, clearly uncomfortable at having him so close. "Please, Miss McAuley, give me a chance. It's obvious you enjoy the respect of your neighbors. Before all these people, I swear to you on everything I hold dear, the Cosmos Clarion elixir is as harmless as it is helpful. Try it yourself. You'll see."

She looked around at all the people who held bottles in their hands. "I intend to do just that."

"Free." He handed her the bottle. "I insist."

She took the bottle and glanced at the label. "You have the nerve to charge a whole dollar? Why, that's robbery."

"Wait till you try it. You'll say it's worth ten dollars. Certainly those suffering with all manner of illness and disease would find a dollar a pittance to pay for relief. Wouldn't you agree?"

Miss McAuley's hand shook slightly as she fished in the pocket of her long black apron. Maybe she wasn't as confident as she pretended to be.

"It's free," Jake said. "From one professional to another. I insist."

"I prefer to pay for it," she said, holding out the bill. "I insist."

"As you wish." He reached for the bill and tucked it in his pocket. "An open mind. That's all I ask."

How could a woman look him straight in the eye like that and at the same time seem so far away? He had learned the hard way how to read people, but she was a puzzle indeed. He was sure of one thing, however. For all her challenging rhetoric, the tightly controlled look in her pale green eyes and that trembling hand said she was concerned over something far more threatening than his elixir. "So, you'll try it," he said.

"After I analyze it." She slipped the bottle in her pocket. "And girls, don't you take one drop until you hear from me."

"Yes, ma'am."

She gave him that look again—not so much at him as through him. "Good night, Mr. Darrow."

"I'll be in touch."

The air stirred with the scent of cloves and eucalyptus as she turned and walked away. She didn't sway her hips the way a woman will do when she knows a man is watching. She didn't stop and do that little primping motion to her hair. In fact, the whole time they'd talked, she hadn't returned his smile. Not once. But those eyes . . . even without the usual demure glance or not-so-innocent flutter of lashes, those pale green eyes made Jake want to get closer to the woman. Instinct warned him to tread lightly. Well, he'd just have to be careful. Because if she was the only medical professional in town, then getting close to Miss McAuley was exactly what he intended to do. For Cosmos's sake, he had to.

Jake calculated the cost of the untouched food on the lace-covered table next to Cosmos Clarion's bed. "What's the matter? You take a sudden dislike for pot roast and mashed potatoes? That's not like you." Jake stuck his finger in the rich brown gravy and drew it to his mouth. "Still hot."

Cosmos rolled to his side, his once thick white hair now an unruly crown of thinning spikes on his pink scalp, his wrinkled red flannel pajamas falling from one pasty white shoulder. "She's been keeping it in the oven."

"Why? You know better than to wait for me. You know how long some of those shows last."

"I just wasn't hungry."

"Your teeth bothering you again?"

"No, I just wasn't hungry."

"Not buying." Jake pulled up the chair in the corner and straddled it. "I just talked to Miss Sweet. She said you didn't eat breakfast either. Said she made pancakes with chokecherry syrup. Your favorite."

Cosmos reached behind him to position one of the three plump, goose down pillows. He pointed to the empty cut glass goblet on the tray. "I ate the pudding."

"You're supposed to eat the meat and potatoes and vegetables first."

Cosmos patted the side of the bed. "Come closer, boy. I've missed you."

"I've missed you too, old man." Jake moved his chair closer to the bed. He took Cosmos's fragile hand for a moment, careful not to grip it too tightly. "Now what's this about your not eating? You'll never get well if you don't put some flesh back on those bones."

"I'm going to be fine. You'll see."

"You want me to have Miss Sweet fix you something else? God knows, we're paying enough—" He cut himself short. "I didn't mean that."

"Nonsense. You spoke the truth. We both know it."

"Look, I've heard about a real sanitarium back East, somewhere in the Adirondacks. The air is supposed to be clean and dry, just what you need."

"Too far."

"We'll take it slow and easy and stop as often as you want."

Cosmos gazed out the window, though darkness obscured the view. "The mountain air back East can't be any cleaner than the air right here."

"You're making this awfully hard on me, you know that."

"You worry too much, son."

"Don't you understand? There's no one out here who can help you."

"But I'm going to be fine. I keep telling you that."

Jake heard the optimism in the old man's voice and cringed inside. If Cosmos didn't see the truth pretty soon, it would be too late. He'd already lost sixty or seventy pounds, shrinking his once robust frame to little more than a sack of bones and sagging flesh. He had night sweats and a chest-shaking cough that drained him of every ounce of energy. He wasn't going to be fine. Jake looked straight into the eyes of the man he thought of as his father. "We've got to go back East."

"To a real doctor? Change your mind about them, did you?"

"You know better than that. I'm just saying we should go back East. If there *are* any decent doctors in the world, they're in the Adirondacks."

"We can't afford—"

"Yes, we can." Jake squeezed the back of the chair to help him stay calm. "Business has been good." He took a wad of bills from his pocket. "See?"

"How many Ben Franklins do you have in that roll?"

"All right, so I don't have anything higher than a ten. But the tens add up, and there're more coming."

"Business stinks. I hear what the others in this place are saying." He gazed again at the blackness beyond the window. "Besides, I just don't feel up to traveling."

"Maybe not this week, but in two weeks, three at the most, you'll be itching to get back on the road. That's where we belong."

"No, I don't think so." He turned back to Jake and spoke with conviction. "I'm supposed to stay right here."

"Supposed to? What the hell does that mean?"

Cosmos smiled, for the first time in months. Since that day back in Idaho when denial of Cosmos's condition became impossible, Jake had watched the enthusiasm in the old man's eyes gradually fade, to be replaced first by worry, then by despair. Until coming to Coventry.

"Oh, no," Jake said, "don't tell me. You've had another one of those dreams."

"Not yet. But I expect to. I also expect to get well. But only if I stay here."

"In Coventry, Montana? Why?"

Sparkles so bright they could have been tears, gathered in Cosmos's eyes. His voice just above a whisper, he said, "Because the magic is here, Jake. I feel it."

Jake knew the kind of foolish magic Cosmos was talking about, but he wasn't one to take away a man's hope. His business was instilling it. So he glanced around the room at the mounted heads of two deer on facing walls and the stuffed owl perched on the dresser and said, "The magic. Sure. But until it finds its way to your room, how 'bout you eat your dinner?"

"No, you eat it. I'll eat breakfast. Every bite. I promise."

Jake eyed the dark brown pot roast, creamy mashed potatoes, and bright orange carrots. "All right." He removed the crystal bud vase with its single stemmed, crocheted rose from the tray and set it aside. "No sense in having all this good food go to waste."

Jake all but inhaled the meal, wondering as he did what he was going to do about Cosmos. After using the last of the buttery biscuits to sop up the gravy, he heard a light, quick knock at the bedroom door and the singsong voice of the proprietress.

"Yoo-hoo, gentlemen. It is I, Miss Sweet."

Jake swallowed quickly and folded his pink napkin. "Come in."

For the second time that evening, Cosmos's eyes lit up. Miss Amabelle Sweet hurried to his bedside with a purposeful attitude and a smile.

"And how are we this evening, Mr. Belinus?" she said as she glanced with approval at the empty tray. "We certainly enjoyed our meal, didn't we?"

"We certainly did," Cosmos said.

Amabelle gave Cosmos an even bigger smile, then

turned to Jake. "I believe you mentioned he was partial to pot roast."

"That I did," Jake said, feeling sure that Miss Sweet wanted him to know he was getting his money's worth. But pot roast or no pot roast, Cosmos wasn't putting on any weight. On that point neither man could deny the obvious. All the symptoms pointed to consumption. The disease was fatal for most people, especially children and the elderly. The only ones who survived were those who ate the best food, breathed the freshest air, got plenty of exercise, and stayed away from anything mentally taxing. Even then, only a fraction of those made it. But Cosmos would make it. He had to.

Amabelle gathered the items on the tray, lifted it, and headed for the door. "I'll bid you both a good-evening now," she said, then with a focused glance and a nod of her head, she indicated she would like to see Jake for a moment. "Before you leave."

"Sure," Jake said, knowing she wanted the next month's fee.

When the two men were alone again, Cosmos said, "How much have we got?"

"At this very minute, enough to either pay the rent or buy more supplies. But don't worry. I'll give her the next month's rent before I leave tonight. Before the week's out, I'll have plenty of money. We've got enough supplies to last till then."

"I don't know how. There's not a doctor for a hundred miles."

"I heard there used to be one here, but he left when the mining business fell off. The druggist stayed. She prescribes as well as fills."

"Laws are different in remote places like this. I'm sure folks know they're lucky to have him."

"Her. The druggist is a woman."

"A woman? Now there's an oddity for you."

"She was at the show tonight. So was Miss Sweet—"

Cosmos sat up quickly. "She didn't say anything, did she?"

"Relax. She didn't say a word."

His breathing labored, Cosmos sank back against the pillows, a look of concern narrowing his eyes. "You're sure she didn't give anything away?"

"She's too smart a business woman to do that."

Cosmos looked relieved. "You're right. She is a smart woman. Pretty too, don't you think? She always smells like roses."

If Jake hadn't been paying attention, he might have missed it—that fleeting, tender look. "You sweet on her, old man?"

"No, no, no. I'm just saying she's pretty, that's all. And she smells good."

"'Cause if you were, that'd be fine with me. You know that, don't you?"

Shaking his head, Cosmos said, "What do I have to offer a pretty young woman like that?" He cast a disapproving glance over his body.

"You get better and you'll have a lot to offer her."

"We'll see. So tell me about the druggist. A woman, you said? You talked to her?"

"I tried to, but she's a real skeptic. Challenged everything I said."

"Was she sincere or just full of bluster?"

"Can't say yet."

"Think she'll make the deal?"

"I can't imagine why she wouldn't. It's money in her pocket. I plan to go see her first thing Monday morning."

"Good, because I have to stay here in Coventry. I have to. You understand that, don't you, son?"

"Sure, I do."

"Good." A corner of the ceiling seemed to beckon to Cosmos.

Jake could always tell when Cosmos had slipped into one of his little daydreams. Jake indulged in a bit of reverie now and then, too. But unlike Cosmos, Jake always came back feeling frustrated.

"So," Cosmos said a moment later, "how many lot lice did you have hanging around the show this evening?"

"Too many. But I'll have their greenbacks before next week is over. You'll see. Besides, all those tight-wad customers make for good referrals. I've been doing a little figuring so I'll know what kind of an offer to make to our lady druggist."

Cosmos made a weak fist. "That's my boy."

"Don't you worry about a thing. I've got this under control. By the end of the week, our money problems will be over. In the meantime, you've got to eat."

Clearly exhausted, Cosmos said, "Just don't get on her bad side. We may be here awhile."

"What's that supposed to mean?"

"You know what I'm saying. She's a woman. Don't bore her with all that baseball talk."

"You don't think she'll care about all the hubbub over the Reserve Rule and the new Players' League?"

"Not at all."

"Hard to believe." Jake winked.

"Trust me on this one, all right? And don't try to sell any chopped grass or flea powder at the show. You leave those to the druggist. Most of them grow their own so it's pure profit. She'll appreciate that."

"Well that'll be easy enough. I'm fresh out of herbs, fresh or dry."

Jake was about to say that he was going to have to go

to Whitefish for more supplies because the general store in Coventry was nothing to brag about, but he noticed that Cosmos had closed his eyes. He shouldn't have stayed this long tonight. And he shouldn't have burdened Cosmos with their financial difficulties. They were only temporary.

His confidence renewed, he went to pay Miss Amabelle Sweet the money he owed her. He gave her half and promised the rest by the end of next week. Tomorrow was Sunday. Stores would all be open, catering to the occasional cattleman who came through. Farmers complained, but Jake understood. Make money when you can. He'd make some repairs to the wagon, get things ready for another show. But on Monday he would strike a deal with the lovely Miss McAuley and all his problems would be solved.

Brenna slept. This time there was no contorted smile to haunt her dreams, just a faceless man standing in the shadows. He held out his hand, offering her an old brass key. When she refused it, he shoved it at her. She wouldn't touch it. With a bridal veil draped across his arms, he reached for her, telling her without words that he had come to resurrect the secret she had buried so carefully, so deeply. She tried to run, but couldn't move.

A fissure of light illuminated the phantom's red vest. He limped forward.

No! Not him!

2

As she had done every morning since that first empty day after her mother died, Brenna placed a white candle in the small earthenware bowl, cupped it in the palm of her hand, and prayed to God. Countless times she thought to do away with the practice. After all, both the prayer and the flame were to summon the Old Magic, but Brenna's hands, unlike her mother's, did not possess the healing art. Vivid memories reminded her. For Brenna, lighting the candle was useless, yet she couldn't bring herself to stop.

Taking a twig from the bucket by the fire, she prodded the gray, powdery coals to find the embers. She drew a light, cradled it with her hand, and touched the wick, summoning the yellow flame with its flickering red thread throbbing at the heart.

Burning a candle in the light of day was an extravagance, but as far back as Brenna could remember, a white candle burned in the green bowl that sat on a small table beside her mother's bed, as it did now next to hers. The bowl had been in her family for seven generations, always owned by a woman.

When Brenna was five years old, her mother showed her how to light the candle. When she was ten, her mother explained that to light the candle was to keep the ritual that the women of her family had begun long before recorded time. That was also the year Brenna learned about herbs and the cycles of the moon. When she was eleven she learned the duties of a midwife and accompanied her mother on her first delivery. She learned how to measure whether evil was growing or receding. She knew there was much more to learn and that the knowledge would not be hers until the twilight of her mother's years. But on her twelfth birthday, a day when Brenna's mother took to her bed with gripping pains in her chest, Brenna took the oath of secrecy and listened as her mother told her where to find her book of chants, knowing that after that day there would be no more wisdom.

The moon would grow to its fullest tonight, marking the end of the time to heal. Over the next two weeks, the healing power that had grown with the waxing moon would dwindle along with the moon itself. Each would become nothing but a sliver, then disappear, only to be reborn again.

Mesmerized by the flame, Brenna started as a sudden noise drew her attention. Someone was knocking at the door.

"Hello?" a man's voice called. "Are you open yet?"

Even if she hadn't recognized the voice, she would have recognized the sound of urgency, no matter how politely disguised. But she did recognize the voice, as surely as she recognized the rapid drumming of her heart.

She glanced back toward the flame and the white

light that surrounded it. She prayed for protection, then left her room to answer the door.

"Good morning, Miss McAuley. Looks like I'm your first customer."

Overwhelmed by the man's nearness, a feeling as pleasurable as it was foreboding, Brenna scanned his dark hair, dark eyes, and captivating smile. "Yes, good morning, Mr. Darrow."

"You remembered my name. I'm flattered. But please, it's Jake."

Though she hadn't stoked the wood stove yet, the room felt unusually warm, uncomfortably close. The tiny dust motes that always danced so gently in the beams of morning sunlight now ran riot, as did her thoughts. Needing something to focus on, she studied his face. The firm chin gave him a determined look, softened slightly by his lips. The fine lines around his eyes said he laughed a lot. He was every bit as handsome in the morning as he was at night.

"I thought you would have moved on by now," she said.

"Not yet." Jake unbuttoned his black frock coat. That's when she saw the red brocade vest, far more beautiful in the light of day. "I know I didn't make a very good impression on you Saturday night." He brushed back a lock of dark hair, but it fell across his forehead again in a touchable, innocent kind of way. He raised his hand to comb it back, exposing more of his vest.

The brocade gave it its rich texture, but it was the vivid color that kept her attention. The few men she'd seen growing up had worn faded gray uniforms of the Confederacy. Those she saw while attending school wore black wool frock coats, sometimes exchanging them for long, snowy white laboratory smocks. Most of the men in Coventry wore either brown suits or faded blue denim overalls. Elton Fontaine wore a green plaid bow tie, Austin solid gray or gray pinstripes. No man in Coventry wore a red brocade vest. She knew the color to conjure both warmth and excitement, yet staring at it now, she felt only an eerie summons to some cold, dark place inside her heart.

He smiled. "So I came to apologize."

If only she could believe that. But as she looked in his eyes, fragments of her dream suddenly took hold of her thoughts. Her vision blurred. The air around him quivered like waves of heat shimmering above the ground on a hot summer day. The more she tried to clear her mind, the faster the image faded, but not before she envisioned the veil she had seen in her dreams. Only one, seven generations old, had those same delicate flowers of white silk floating on a bed of white lace.

Brenna turned cold. The veil was safely locked away. She hadn't even looked at it in years.

"Miss McAuley, are you all right?"

"Why are you here, Mr. Darrow? The real reason."

"As I said, to apologize. I should have introduced myself to you as soon as I arrived in town. I could have put all your concerns to rest right then and there."

"Somehow I doubt that."

He looked taken-aback. "Ma'am, you don't even know me."

"I know enough."

He seemed to ignore her remark, and instead, glanced around the room. "You have quite an operation here," he said.

Brenna knew her furnishings were far from elaborate. The six-foot high pharmacy case was little more than a large desk on a raised platform. A narrow walkway divided the space between the working area at the back of the case and a second-hand unit of shelves and drawers next to a second-hand herb case. She couldn't afford the metal linings for the forty-eight small drawers, so mice were always a problem. She couldn't afford a lot of things, but what she did have, she owned outright. "It represents years of hard, honest work," she said. "And it allows me to meet the needs of my customers."

"Well, I'm going to help you do that to an even greater extent, and save you precious time too."

"I doubt that," she said, feeling the need to protect herself. "I grow my own herbs. I order my chemicals and patent medicines from reputable wholesalers back East. Whatever it is you're peddling, I don't need it."

"I'm not peddling a single thing." He slipped his hand into his pocket and pulled out a wad of bills, all folded in half and held with a gold money clip. "As you can see, I enjoy the fruits of a successful business." He slipped the money back in his pocket. "And in my years of experience, I've learned that one of the worst mistakes a businessman can make is to be greedy. That's why I'm here. Not to sell you something, but to share my customers with you." He looked at the rocking chair by the wood stove in the corner and the three chairs lined up against the wall. "Do you mind if we sit down?"

"Go right ahead," she said, and watched as he walked slowly across the room. He stood by one of the chairs and held it for her.

"Is your leg bothering you, Mr. Darrow?"

"Oh no," he said, much too quickly to be believed. "An old injury. It's nothing."

"I see." She dealt with pain all the time. She knew the shape it gave to the face, the movement it demanded of the body. Mr. Darrow lied.

She walked over and sat down, her spine rigid against the chair. He angled his chair to face her, sat down, and leaned forward. She watched while he braced his arms casually against his thighs, leaving the ends of the black string tie that circled the collar of his white shirt to dangle in the air. The pose drew the vest tight across his chest. The enticing look in his eyes caught her off-guard.

Lacing his fingers, he said, "I can't possibly treat every customer who comes to me. What I'm proposing is that I make an initial examination, then send them to you for further diagnosis and treatment. You bill them. We split the fee."

"I'm not interested." His alluring smile made her uncomfortable and far too aware of his handsome features.

"Don't be in such a hurry to turn me down. Who knows? I could be just the man you've been waiting for."

"No." She stood so quickly she nearly toppled the chair. How she longed for the quiet of the night and the stillness of her room, and the safety of being alone. Instead, her heart pounded louder and louder like a drum whose cadence summoned a terror she'd struggled so long to avoid. Only by the strength of her will could she look him in the eyes and appear calm. "Mr. Darrow, I've practiced in this town for three years. The people here know me. They trust me. The nearest doctor is a hundred miles south in Missoula, so I'm often called upon to treat everything from minor ailments to serious illnesses."

He stood and walked behind the chair. His hands rested comfortably on the back rail. Only the barely perceptible way he adjusted his weight alerted Brenna to his uneasiness. "I've been in the business for more than twenty years. Don't tell me you can't use some extra cash. I didn't see the new *Remington's* among your reference books. That USP is so old it doesn't use the metric system."

"I learned the system in college."

"You still need a new edition."

She didn't need him telling her what she needed. The *United States Pharmacopoeia* and the *Remington's Practice of Pharmacy* were important. She planned to order updated versions as soon as she could.

"In time—"

"How about an analytical balance." He glanced around. "Or a typing machine. I'll bet you're still writing out all your labels and instructions by hand."

"For now, yes."

"What about professional journals? You can't afford to subscribe to any of those yet either, can you?"

"Your point, Mr. Darrow?"

"I can help you."

"Forgive my frankness, but I simply don't believe the citizens of Coventry would seek medical advice from you in the first place. Your operation is just for show."

He laughed, but Brenna heard the hollow echo.

"I'm not talking about people who have serious medical problems," he said.

"What are you talking about?"

"Your time is valuable, Miss McAuley. So is mine. So I'll get right to the point. I've been traveling with the one and only Cosmos Clarion for over twenty years. I've forgotten more towns like this than you'll ever see in your lifetime. They don't all have doctors or druggists, of course, but most have someone who has at least a little more knowledge or experience than his neighbors. He's the one they all go to with their aches and pains."

"I'm well aware of that."

"And I'm sure you're aware of just how hard it is to make a living in this country. People pay you in chickens—if they pay you at all. So when I see a man who has no intention of making a purchase from me, I do what I can to steer him to the local professional. Then, as I mentioned earlier, the doctor and I split the fee."

"But if the patient has no illness, no complaint—"

He tugged on his vest. "I can convince any man, woman, or child that he needs to consult his local professional."

Brenna stared in disbelief. "You would intentionally inflict anxiety on someone and cause him to obtain unnecessary treatment just so you could make money?"

"Don't look so shocked. It's a well known game. Besides, these people are already anxious or they wouldn't be coming to hear me."

"It's scandalous."

"It's reality. Where have you been?"

"In the Louisville School of Pharmacy for Women. Studying analytical and pharmaceutical chemistry, material medica, microscopy, botany—and ethics."

"Look, I never expected to be the one to initiate you into the world of business. If I've spoiled your fantasy, I'm sorry. Nearly every doctor I've met has been a drunk or a doper. I offer them a few bottles of my extra-strength elixir to seal the deal and they're happy. I'm happy. Customers think the local doc is a hero, saving them from some dreadful malady."

"Nearly every doctor I've met has been a dedicated professional with the welfare of his patients his sole concern."

With hardened eyes, he said, "I envy your experience."

This time her heart pounded so loud she could scarcely hear her own words. "You're a charlatan."

"Come on now. That's a little harsh, don't you think?"

"Montana achieved statehood only late last year, but we do have a judiciary committee. Not four months ago it passed legislation proposed by our own Medical Association to rid our state of quackery."

"Quackery? Please. I'm just a businessman, trying to make a living, same as you."

"You prey on the suffering of ignorant people, encouraging them to believe in any lie that holds the promise of relief."

"I encourage them to have hope."

"Mr. Darrow, you are insufferable. Your words may be as smooth as butter and your smile disarming—"

"Why, thank you." He bowed slightly, giving her the feeling she was being mocked.

"You strut around town in that garish red vest—" No sooner were the words out of her mouth than she regretted them, for it was one thing to attack a man's profession, another to attack his person. Jake barely flinched, but her words had found their mark. She knew by the sudden stillness of his body and the slight narrowing of his eyes.

She crossed her arms protectively across her chest. "I'm sorry. That was rude of me."

"Don't apologize for speaking your mind," he said with a deliberate tug on the points of his vest. "That way I know exactly where you stand."

A guilt-laden silence filled the room. "I don't believe we have anything else to talk about, Mr. Darrow. I think it best that you leave now."

"Whatever you say." He walked to the door, paused, and turned around. "We didn't get off on the best foot here and I regret that. All I ask is that you think about what I've said. When you see the wisdom in my offer—and I believe you will—come and see me."

"You won't be in town long enough for that to happen."

"Oh, I'll be around for a while."

"You can't mean that." She followed him to the door, opened it, and braced one arm on the latch, anxious to fasten it tight.

"Sure I do. I just might learn to like it here."

"But why? There's nothing in this town for you."

"Now that's where you're wrong. I haven't yet met the town I couldn't sell."

"The people of Coventry may not be sophisticated, but they aren't stupid either. They'll see through your disguise."

He stared just long enough to double her discomfort. "If I didn't know better, I'd say you want to sweep me out like some kind of vermin. Is that right?"

"I want you to drive your painted wagon out of town and never come back."

He laughed as he stepped onto the wooden sidewalk. "Sorry to have to disappoint you." With that, he walked away.

Still shaking from her confrontation with Jake Darrow, Brenna poured her energy into her work. With several prescriptions to compound before the day was over, she had a busy day ahead of her. Perhaps someday when the railroad reached this far north, she would operate as she had when she first came to Coventry. A doctor would prescribe medication; she would dispense it. But Dr. Delaney had moved south when the Last Chance Mine collapsed and the first signs of a ghost town broke out. In the meantime, she would continue to make a gargle of carbolic acid for laryngitis, a solution of boric acid and morphine for a mild case of ophthalmia, and in general, do what she could to help her neighbors and the consumptives up at Amabelle's.

The door burst open, stirring the brittle brown stems of lavender hanging in bundles from the rafters. Even as Brenna looked up from behind the prescription case, she inhaled the fragrance and relished the instant calm it always brought, a decided difference from the sharp scent of carbolic acid that lingered in the air. She set aside her mortar and pestle, stepped down from the platform, and hurried over to the child who had just rushed in and now stood on the same spot she stood every day, her arms rigid at her sides.

"Why, Phoebe, how pretty you look. Is that a new dress?"

"I have a new hat. See?" Six years old, Phoebe flattened her small, stubby hand against the top of her head, crushing the white straw bonnet onto a skimpy mop of mousy brown hair.

Brenna closed the door to keep out the lingering morning chill, then knelt down and fussed with the bow of pink grosgrain ribbon that held the hat beneath the flat, broad face of Phoebe Halliwell.

"I see your trip to Whitefish was a success. Who took you shopping? Your father or Mrs. Dinwittie?"

"He got me a hat. See?"

"Yes, I do. And it's very pretty."

Phoebe nodded, but her smile dimmed in an instant and the sparkle left her small, wide-spaced, slightly slanted eyes. "I forgot my coat."

"Well, you come sit here by the wood stove and warm up. I'm expecting a few customers later this morning, but after I've taken care of them, we can go to the hotel together and get your coat. On the way you can wear my shawl."

"The pretty one?"

"Of course."

Phoebe looked down at her polished black shoes. "Mrs. Din will be mad."

"Mrs. Dinwittie just doesn't want you to catch cold."

In one motion, Phoebe's shoulders slumped and her mouth drooped.

"Honey, what's wrong?" When Phoebe didn't answer, Brenna said, "It's all right. You can tell me."

Phoebe mumbled as though she were mimicking someone else. "Stupid girl. Stupid girl."

Brenna not only heard but felt the child's pain. Phoebe and her father had come to town six months ago. While Brenna admired Austin's desire to have his daughter lead a normal life, all the money in the world couldn't prevent people from pointing and snickering, and worse still, from urging him to commit her to an asylum, well out of the sight of decent people.

Using her handkerchief, Brenna wiped away the huge tears that welled in Phoebe's eyes. "Remember what I told you?" Brenna said.

Muttering so low Brenna could barely hear her, Phoebe answered, "I'm precious."

"That's right. You're precious."

Phoebe's little pink lips trembled. "And you love me."

Brenna opened her arms and gathered the child to her heart. "Indeed I do."

"All the way to China?"

Brenna felt the vibration of Phoebe's words, whispered like secrets against her neck. She whispered in return, "All the way to China."

When Phoebe finally eased back, Brenna took her

hand and led her to the rocking chair. She held it still while Phoebe climbed up. Then she stoked the embers in the wood stove and added a small log. June in Montana wasn't nearly as warm as it had been in Virginia where she had grown up, but she wasn't complaining. She liked it here. Especially since Phoebe had come to town. The only threat to Brenna's perfect life was Jake Darrow.

The door opened again. A short, slender man stepped inside. With one hand he pressed a green plaid muffler to his throat; with the other he pointed to his mouth.

"Oh dear," Brenna said as she walked over and closed the door behind Coventry's Mayor, Elton Fontaine. "Your throat hurts that bad?"

"Pity me," he struggled to say, "My mission—"

"To talk with every family in the valley," she finished for him. She noticed how quickly Phoebe slipped from the chair and ran to Brenna's living quarters in the back. Brenna wanted to help the little girl see just how worthy of love she was, but in Phoebe's short six years, half her expected life span, there were so many others who told her with a meanness in their voices or plague-like avoidance in their eyes that she was an idiot.

Mayor Fontaine watched Phoebe leave, then whispered, "Coventry must be selected—"

"For Lord Austin's cattle syndicate. Yes, I know. We all know. And we all appreciate what a fine job you're doing to promote our town." She gestured toward the chair, still rocking from Phoebe's quick exit. "Why don't you sit down. You look exhausted. I was just about to mix your gargle, but it will take a few minutes. Can you wait?"

Mayor Fontaine sat in the rocker and leaned back, the tips of his boots barely touching the floor. As he rocked, he massaged his throat with his gloved hand. Then he suddenly leaned forward, stared at Brenna, and mouthed the words, "Oasis of culture and refinement."

"Yes," Brenna said, reading his lips. "And that's exactly what we have here in Coventry, or will have soon. In the meantime, your throat needs absolute rest. So make yourself comfortable while I mix this gargle." She weighed the salicylate of soda, powdered Borax, and glycerin, and put them in a vial. She added a measured amount of carbolic acid and enough water to equal four ounces. She mixed it, poured it into a bottle, and brushed glue on the back of the label she had handwritten earlier. As soon as she could afford it, she was going to buy gummed labels and one of those new typewriting machines. "Here," she said, handing the bottle to him. "You gargle with this every two hours. In two or three days you should see a marked improvement. You should also wear a hat."

He groaned. "Money-back guarantee?"

"I beg your pardon."

"That's what he's offering."

"He?"

The mayor inclined his bald head toward the window. "Amazing Amazon—"

"You were there Saturday night?"

"And you were brilliant!"

She hadn't been brilliant. She had been scared. "Mayor, please. You must rest your vocal chords. I insist."

"Cheap performer . . . for God's sake, the man doesn't even keep his hair oiled!" He clutched his throat and moaned, then shook his finger at Brenna. His voice fading, he said, "He's out to make us look like fools and crackpots. I fear our Coventry is doomed."

"We're far from doomed."

The mayor's eyes brightened. "Oh, but he can't best you, that's for sure!" With a glance toward the back room, he croaked, "It's a fortunate turn of events for all of us that you and Lord Austin are keeping company."

"Mayor, please—"

"The whole town is counting on you. You know that."

"Lord Austin is a businessman. He'll make his decision based on facts." Brenna knew the town considered her their ace in the hole when it came to Austin's choice between Coventry and Whitefish. While she didn't like the position that placed her in, she did appreciate the fact that Austin let Phoebe stay with her while he was away, sometimes overnight. But a vote of confidence in Brenna was not the same as a vote of confidence in the town. She knew that. The sooner Mr. Darrow left, the sooner her own confidence and peace of mind would return.

The mayor leaned forward and mouthed, "If he finds Whitefish more to his liking, then our fair town is doomed to obscurity. Doomed!"

"Where is your sense of optimism? Don't you think Lord Austin will appreciate the fact that we have a fine new library as well as a schoolhouse and a church?"

"We don't have a preacher."

"No, but Ralph is doing a fine job with those sermons of his. And as for culture, why Lester Bodyk has not only ridden on a bicycle, he has both talked and listened on a telephone. He presents a fine lecture on the experience. And don't forget Miss Bonnie June Walton. She will write a letter on her new type-writing machine for anyone at a cost of only thirty-five cents. How many towns in a hundred-mile radius can boast that service? More importantly, this town is populated by honest, hard-working people, the kind Lord Austin would want to hire. I'm sure he's thought of that."

The mayor nodded and gave Brenna a conceding look.

She continued, "When I said you didn't have to worry, I only meant that with any luck Mr. Darrow won't stay long. His kind rarely do. A few days, a week at the most."

Looking somewhat relieved by her words, the mayor rose from the rocker and tightened his muffler. Again, his voice faded in and out as he said, "We can't have Lord Austin think for one minute that we would support such a cheap display—"

"Or he'll choose Whitefish."

"Next thing you know, he'll be playing the banjo and doing a vaudeville routine."

"Lord Austin?"

"Of course not. That . . . that . . . Jake whatever his name is. Why the barbarian struts around half the time without a frock coat and yet claims to be a *professional.*" Clutching his neck, he walked toward the door.

"His name is Darrow," Brenna said. How quickly, how clearly, just the mention of his name summoned his image: white shirt and long muscular arms, red brocade vest and broad chest, piercing eyes, a dangerous smile. The brass key and the bridal veil.

"Darrow, is it?"

"I believe so." Brenna glanced around, feeling the need to be busy. "Do you have any questions about the gargle?"

"That Clarion elixir of his . . . He says it will cure baldness. What do you think?"

"He is, as you yourself said, a showman."

"Well, at least he has a money-back guarantee. I suppose I should be grateful for that."

"You didn't purchase—"

"One bottle. That's all."

Jake stopped pacing and stared at Cosmos. "How can you lie there and tell me to go back to that woman? Didn't you hear a word I said?"

"I didn't hear anything that explains why you're so upset."

"She said my offer was scandalous." He could feel the chords of his throat tighten as he all but spit out the words. "She called me a charlatan!"

Cosmos shrugged his shoulders and sank deeper into the thick pillows behind him. "You've been called a lot worse. So have I."

Straddling the chair by the bed, Jake felt the power of pure frustration clamp his jaws as he said, "She's different."

"Because she's a woman?"

"No. Because she's . . . she's . . ." He pounded his fist against his thigh. "Oh hell, I don't know. Maybe it is because she's a woman." Jake stood and walked to the far side of the room. He turned up the kerosene lamp on the dresser, then did the same to the one on the table next to Cosmos. "It's dark in here."

"Darkness brings its own brand of comfort."

"Well, I want to be able to see you, all right?"

Cosmos squinted. "Pretty, is she?"

"I wasn't trying to make a play for her, for God's sake. I was trying to strike a deal."

"Of course you were, son. I know that." Cosmos lunged forward as a powerful cough racked his frail body.

Jake jumped from the chair and grabbed the glass of water from the stand by the bed. With one arm he braced Cosmos's back; with the other he held the glass to his lips. Cosmos sipped and the trembling eased. "You all right?" Jake asked, wiping the trickle of water from his chin.

It seemed to take forever for Cosmos to speak. "I will be. Soon. You'll see. If I could just get rid of this cough." He relaxed against the pillows as Jake moved his arm. "Now, back to this woman. Help me, son. I wasn't there. I'm trying to picture it. What does she look like? Start with her eyes. What color are they?"

"Her eyes?" Compared to the battle Cosmos waged, Jake's problems weren't worth a dime. Jake couldn't remember the old man ever asking for anything, except that as a young boy Jake always come home on time, and as a young man that he always introduce his lady friends to Cosmos. And now, that they stay in Coventry. "They're green," Jake said calmly, "and they're big. She has black hair, real shiny."

"Ah, green."

The way he smiled Jake guessed he was thinking of his late wife, Livia. Jake knew she had green eyes, too, though he had never met her. She had died in childbirth. So had their son, Penrod. Right after that, Cosmos took to the road. He was near fifty when he took Jake from the orphan train, society's solution to the problem of homeless children and the growing need for labor to settle the West. Several times during those first few months Cosmos had called him Penrod. At the time, Jake thought he was crazy, but he never said anything. Unlike many of the others placed-out by the Boston's Children's Mission, he had found a home, even if it was a wagon painted with stars. He wouldn't risk losing it. As a man, Jake realized that Cosmos had his share of fears, just like everyone else. For Cosmos, the biggest was being left alone, though he never said it in so many words. But that would never happen. Jake swore to it.

"Go on," Cosmos said. "What else?"

"Let's see . . . she's not too tall. Comes up to about here on me." Jake placed his hand on his collarbone.

"Nice figure?"

Jake recalled the assemblage of curves. "Very nice."

"Tell me about her eyes again. Deep green, are they?"

The memory of how she glared at him grew clearer and slowed his words. "No. They're pale green."

"Pale? Are you sure?"

"Oh, I'm sure." They were pale all right, as though they mirrored nothing, or hid whatever was there too deeply to be seen. In either case, she had used them to look not at him, but through him, an unnerving sensation he wasn't likely to ever forget.

Cosmos gave a shaky smile. "The eyes of an enchantress."

"I don't know about that. I just know I can't work with her. I don't want to be anywhere near the woman."

"But Jake—"

"Don't worry. I'll find another way to make the sales we need."

Cosmos closed his eyes and gently nodded, a signal that always preceded a decision that allowed no room for change, as though he'd come to the conclusion with the aid of something divine.

When Cosmos opened his eyes he said, "You have to go back to her."

"Like hell—"

"Hear me out." As Cosmos struggled to sit upright, Jake piled the pillows for support.

"I'm sure you used your best manners when you introduced yourself," Cosmos said. "But did you tell her right away that you realized time had to be a prized commodity to her and that you could save her some if she'd just listen to you?"

"I gave her the same speech I give every doctor and druggist we've worked with over the last twenty years. What are you getting at?"

"Did you talk money?"

"Of course I talked money. I showed her the wad I've got in my pocket. I said there was plenty more where that came from and she could have half." Jake relived the scene in his mind, including her blatant disgust.

Cosmos studied Jake a moment. "What's really bothering you, son?"

"I don't know." Jake shrugged, then moved his chair close to the bed. He opened his mouth to speak, changed his mind, then blurted out, "She can't stomach the idea of having me around. You'd have thought I hadn't bathed in a year."

"I see."

"It's not that she called me a charlatan. You were right. I've been called a lot worse. And it's not that she all but threw me out of her place. That wasn't a first either. But when she looks at me, I feel like . . . like a piece of trash."

"Hurts, doesn't it?"

"Hurt? No, it doesn't hurt. It makes me angry!"

Cosmos gave him an understanding nod. "So it's not that she's important to you in a romantic kind of way."

"Where'd you get a crazy idea like that?"

Jake felt the scant weight of Cosmos's hand gently

patting his arm. "I just figured one day you'd come to me and say you'd met someone special and—"

"Well, trust me, it wasn't today." He stood. "She's not important to me in the least. She's a means to an end. That's all. If you want me to go back and try again, I will. I'll just use a different tactic."

"That's my boy."

Jake suddenly felt the need for fresh air. "In fact, I'm going back to the wagon now to plan my strategy. It's late. You get some rest."

Cosmos raised a finger. "A favor, son. It's important."

Jake turned town the lamps, then paused at the door. "You name it."

"When you go to her shop, look around. See if she keeps a moon chart."

3

No longer called the Coventry Hotel, Her Majesty's Manor still had only three floors, a small check-in desk, a café with only eight tables, and Boldizsar Jones—a hefty cook who complained to anyone who would listen that he made biscuits, not scones, and that he'd put a goldfish in that tall glass bowl before he'd spend another day trying to layer a mess of pudding and fruit inside a fence of fancy cookies.

"Good afternoon, Mr. Jones," Brenna said as she entered the dining room. Still disconcerted over her meeting with Jake Darrow yesterday and another sleepless night, she'd come to meet Austin for an early dinner. She wanted to talk to him about Miss Bonnie June Walton's stenographic abilities and Lester Bodyk's offer to discuss his experience of talking on the telephone. Austin had offered to escort her to the hotel, but knowing how busy he was, she had insisted on walking over herself. The hotel was, after all, only a block from her pharmacy.

"Ma'am," Boldizsar said without looking up, his fingers fumbling as he tried to fold a white linen napkin. "There," he said, taking a step back from the table. "Does that look like a bird to you?"

"Well, it—"

"I knew it," he said and grabbed the pretzeled linen in his beefy hand.

"It wasn't all that bad," Brenna said. "A trifle too intricate, perhaps."

"'A trifle too intricate'? Now you're sounding like him. This whole town is starting to sound like him!"

Brenna knew exactly what he meant. Just this afternoon, Mrs. Harmony, the church organist, had bid Brenna a bright "Cheerio!" upon leaving the pharmacy. Boldizsar was right. Everyone had picked up at least one or two British words. Lord Austin Halliwell had to be pleased.

She turned at the cheerful sound of Austin's voice and found that for the first time in the six months she'd known him she had to force a smile for the tall, lanky man.

"Miss Brenna, you look absolutely divine!" He gazed in admiration.

"Thank you, Austin." Other than her clothes for work, she could afford only two dresses and he'd seen each a dozen times. Still, whether she wore the pale blue or peacock green, he complimented her with enthusiasm. There was no reason for his "absolutely divine" to sound hollow tonight, but it did.

His own wardrobe was a variation on a gray theme. Tonight he wore a light gray summer coat, a subdued gray vest, gray striped trousers, a white shirt with black pearl studs, and a navy paisley ascot fastened with a silver scarf pin. As always, he offered her his arm and led her to "their" table.

"Austin, has anyone mentioned to you that we—the town, that is—have the services of an efficient stenographer, Miss Bonnie June Walton? She even has her own typewriting machine."

"Yes, I believe I did hear something about that. I'm impressed." He waived his hand to summon Boldizsar. "I hear you have a mountebank too, though I don't know that his arrival warrants fanfare."

"You mean Mr. Darrow?"

"You've met him, I understand."

"Yes, at his show last Saturday night."

"So I heard. And has this Mr. Darrow stopped by to pay his respects?"

"In his case, respect is not the most appropriate word." Brenna told him about Jake's scandalous offer.

Austin waved to Boldizsar again, then said to Brenna, "Well, I'm pleased to know you saw through his sordid tactics."

When Boldizsar approached them, Austin scanned the newly typed menu and without looking up, said, "The lady will have roast mutton with mint jelly." He gave Brenna a questioning arch of his brow and when she nodded, he continued. "And a thick cut of your roast beef with Yorkshire pudding for me." He set the menu to the side. "But first a bottle of your finest burgundy."

"A bottle of red."

Austin laughed and said to Brenna, "How I love the American humor! It puts me in mind of my days as a youth at Eaton. Have I told you the story of . . . "

Brenna set aside her planned litany of Lester Bodyk's accomplishments and listened as Austin told her of the responsibilities that burdened his privileged childhood and made it necessary for him, the youngest of four boys, to seek his fortune abroad. By the time they'd finished eating, her head throbbed from the repeated images of the perfectly manicured lawns and the neatly trimmed hedges that surrounded the gray granite estate he called home. Nothing at all like a medicine wagon.

She wondered what kind of legacy Jake Darrow had been given. What kind of man would willingly bring on anxiety in another? She hadn't seen him at all today and still he invaded her thoughts.

"But as luck would have it," Austin said, as he always did, "there were the four of us and only one Halliwell Hall. I had no choice but to come to America." He slipped his hand into the breast pocket of his jacket and removed a small box. Offering it to her, he said, "That's why I want you to have this."

When she hesitated, he said, "Please. It is but a small token of both my gratitude for your interest in Phoebe and my sincere affection."

Brenna took the small, black velvet box and raised the lid. Inside was a gold friendship circle with three small diamonds clustered to one side.

"Do you like it?"

"It's beautiful. But Austin, you don't have to give me a gift for taking an interest in Phoebe. She is gift enough herself."

Though she would never describe his features as soft—his blond receding hair and his hazel eyes were somewhat attractive—the mention of his daughter brought a soulful look to his face. "She is my temporary treasure," he said, "on loan from God. I know what people say, but she is not a freak. And I refuse to bury her alive in some lonely, filthy asylum. She's just a child. You understand, don't you?" Austin reached across the table for her hand.

"Of course I do." Brenna took his hand in hers, knowing that if Phoebe were her own daughter, she would want her to enjoy life as much as possible. Unlike Austin, however, she would do her best to shield Phoebe from the pointed fingers, ugly taunts, and gasps of horror that the child had come to know all too well.

In the brief silence that followed, Brenna wondered how Phoebe's remaining years would be spent. Though she knew Austin loved his daughter dearly, he was often away on business. Mrs. Dinwittie took proper care of her, seeing to it that her clothes were clean, her shoes polished, her meals ample. But there was more to caring for a child than that, especially a child like Phoebe.

Brenna remembered the first time she saw Phoebe, standing next to her father, her head bent down, her hair falling in her face. Loving Phoebe hadn't been a gradual thing on Brenna's part. It had happened in an instant.

"You will accept the pin, will you not?" Austin's face looked strained and Brenna wondered if he, too, had been wondering what kind of future his little girl would have.

"I'll wear it with pride."

Visibly relieved, he raised his glass. "You've become quite important to both me and Phoebe, but surely you know that."

Brenna was so certain he would say "To Phoebe" that she raised her glass without listening. The instant their crystal touched, she heard the echo of his words.

"To family."

Since the change was made back in 1884, a pitcher didn't have to use a straight-elbow delivery to pitch the ball. He could use as many in-curves and out-shoots as he could devise. The idea was to deceive the bat man with a curve. That way there wouldn't be much hitting in the game, and all the experts said a small score was proof of a well-played game. And by now, the experts also agreed that the curve ball was neither contrary to the laws of motion nor merely the hallucination of a willing imagination. What the experts didn't know was that all a good pitcher had to do was use his middle finger to give the ball a sharp twist.

Yes indeed, Jake thought as he sat in the narrow doorway of his wagon, his legs braced on the portable steps below. A man certainly could throw a ball in something other than a straight line. He studied the small ball in his right hand and maneuvered it until the seams lined up just where he wanted them. Then he slammed it into the battered brown leather glove that covered his left hand. Using a glove wasn't sissified at all. Unlike so many critics, he had felt the sting of a ball slamming into his bare palm often enough to know.

He drilled the ball again. And again. He wasn't at all like the inexperienced fan who stood at the edge of the field, watched, and scoffed, "I could do that." Jake knew better. He had played in enough games to know. Well, he hadn't actually played all that much, just a few back alley and cornfield games with local men, none of whom knew as much about the game as he did. As soon as his leg interfered, and it always did, he'd be told to quit. But he had watched the game many times. And he had practiced even more. He had a passable spit-ball, a much better fade-away, and a damned near perfect curve ball. What he didn't have were two good legs.

A small kerosene lamp inside the wagon gave just enough light to draw a few bugs, but hardly enough to illuminate the field of weeds in front of him. The full moon took care of that just fine.

He stood, walked down the stairs, and stretched.

The pitcher was the most important man in the game. Because of the strain on a pitcher's arm and wrist, most teams had several twirlers, some half a dozen. Baseball was no longer a game for amateurs. Managers hired only the best players, men who could draw a paying crowd. Newspaper clippings about the war going on right now between players and owners filled a box inside the wagon, but all Jake was really interested in was playing ball. If he were on a team, he'd draw the people in. He knew he could.

The shouts and whistles of an imaginary crowd greeted him as he walked away from the wagon and onto the moonlit field, where he tucked his only ball into his pocket where it would be safe. He picked up a clod of dirt he'd loosened with his heel. He had been working on a wind-up that didn't require him to draw his left knee up as high as most pitchers did. He knew he was sacrificing precision because of it, but he just couldn't get that knee up any higher. His right leg was strong enough for two. So was his right arm. As long as he kept practicing, he'd have himself a pitch that would turn the ball into a locomotive and strike out every batter who faced him. He executed the movements. Almost perfect.

As always, the exhilarating feel of form and motion gave him confidence. Though he knew no one would be about this time of night, he still looked around to be sure. A pitcher had to take his turn at bat. If he got a hit, he had to run.

Jake set his sites on a spot in the distance and thought about nothing but his leg as he tried to draw up his left knee. He broke out in a sweat, then tried again. And again. This time he thought about the holier-than-thou Brenna McAuley. She was so sure he was a loser. This time the imagined roar of the crowd came close to drowning his very real groan. With that, he set out running.

What he wanted to be a mile was only a few yards, but it was something. Panting with every step back to the wagon, he reached the door and looked up at the starry sky. His leg ached so badly he knew sleep would be impossible. But someday, someday when he left the medicine show, he was going to be a pitcher in the game of baseball. And he would be great.

Another morning. Another candle. Brenna gazed at the flickering flame and searched her soul. The years had robbed her memory of the sound of her mother's voice, but not in a lifetime would she forget her mother's words. *Your dreams will show you what you are not yet willing to see.*

What? A bridal veil that had brought her only heartache? A key to remind her to keep the veil locked away? What else was there to see?

There was Jake Darrow. He was little more than a carnival pitchman who belittled her efforts and laughed at her principles. He was a schemer who didn't deserve the time her thoughts insisted on giving him. Why should he be the man to haunt her dreams? Was she to imitate him and stand before a crowd? Admit her guilt? Or worse yet, be pressured into trying—and failing— once again? And kill someone else?

Memories preyed on her as she stepped into the shop and slipped on her apron.

Hours later, Jake Darrow continued to occupy her thoughts. Though his wagon remained parked at the end of Main Street and his horse at the livery, she hadn't seen the man himself in nearly two days, yet without closing her eyes she could see his dark eyes and

his engaging smile. Amabelle was right. Jake Darrow
was a most handsome man. Boastful and manipulative,
yes, but he was also a man in pain.

Brenna finally blinked and released her grip on the
mortar and pestle. She didn't know how long she'd
stood behind the counter, slowly grinding the dried
orange peel into a fine powder, all the while staring at
the label on the bottle in front of her and an artist's rendition of Cosmos Clarion. He appeared to be of
medium height, not as tall as Mr. Darrow, nor as handsome. Mr. Clarion was a heavier man, too. Thick hair,
white as snow, surrounded his round head like a halo,
sticking out here and there like bolts of lightning, not at
all touchable. In one area, however, he and Mr. Darrow
were one of a kind. Each looked every bit the showman.

The drawing on the label showed Cosmos Clarion
standing next to a desk, his hand on the top of a world
globe. Behind him was a poster of the solar system. She
could hardly label his suit conservative, not with the
lightning bolts on the lapels. His vest, with its embroidered stars and shooting comets, marked him a man of
magic, or at least one who wanted people to think him
such.

If so, it also marked him a fool. For though good,
upstanding citizens no longer burned witches at the
stake, those same upstanding citizens could turn on
anyone, man or woman, who appeared to have knowledge or ability out of the ordinary. They would blame
him for every failure, isolate him from the community,
leave him to die alone and lonely, or to travel the world
in search of obscurity. No, a man of magic would never
openly admit to having such knowledge, unless he were
absolutely sure of his abilities. All that could be hidden
would be hidden well. All that must remain in the open
would be disguised. But perhaps the costume was sim-

ply part of the show for Mr. Clarion. Perhaps he had no interest in magic at all.

She turned her attention back to the making of a confection in the mortar. Phoebe liked the taste of oranges and ginger. If Brenna could get her to eat carrots by masking the flavor with something the child liked, then so be it.

Brenna looked up to find Mrs. Dinwittie stepping smartly through the door, here to pick up her medication. She was a widow of advanced years, tall and slender, always dressed in brown. In tow was Phoebe, wearing a dark gray coat buttoned up to her neck, her eyes downcast.

"Good morning, Mrs. Dinwittie. Phoebe." Brenna left her counter and hurried over to give Phoebe a kiss on the cheek. Instantly, Phoebe nuzzled against Brenna's neck. "Have you come to stay with me today?" Brenna said.

Her eyes imploring, Phoebe looked up at Mrs. Dinwittie, who answered, "Begging is for dogs, not children."

"I'd love for her to stay," Brenna said, slipping her arm around Phoebe's shoulders. "She can keep me company and help me around the shop."

"Help you? Come, come, Miss McAuley. What can she do?"

"I can fold towels!" Phoebe shouted.

"That's right," Brenna said. "And you do a fine job."

The natural arch of Mrs. Dinwittie's gray eyebrows gave her face a perpetually skeptical look, an impression reinforced by her words to Phoebe. "Am I to assume then, little Miss Halliwell, that you are no longer afflicted with a mulligrub?"

"You have a stomach ache?" Brenna asked Phoebe, having heard Austin use the word.

"Nothing ails that child except low spirits. Nothing but the obvious, that is. If she were my child, I would be far too ashamed—"

"I'll bring her back to you by four o'clock. How would that be?"

"You'll see to it she doesn't nasty her clothes."

Phoebe spoke up. "I have my own apron!"

"You will speak when you're spoken to, Miss Halliwell!"

Brenna ached to see Phoebe stiffen. "Phoebe, why don't you go in the back room and wait for me?"

Phoebe ran.

Once the child was out of earshot, Brenna said, "Must you be so hard on her?"

"You are finding fault with the way I am raising that child? You who have never been a mother?"

"A child needs to be encouraged, not criticized. Especially a child like Phoebe. I don't have to be a mother to know that."

Mrs. Dinwittie glared at Brenna, who glared right back.

"I'll have my medicine now," Mrs. Dinwittie said. "If it's ready."

"I have your laxative right here." Brenna walked back to the counter and took the labeled bottle from those lined up in a square wicker basket on the shelf.

Mrs. Dinwittie tucked the bottle into the drawstring fishnet bag she carried by her wrist. "I should think Whitefish will attract an apothecary of their own soon."

"Or Coventry a doctor."

Mrs. Dinwittie pressed her thin lips together in a smile. "Not one minute after four o'clock," she said, then turned and marched out the door.

Brenna gave herself a moment to calm down before heading to the back room.

Brenna's living quarters consisted of two rooms: an L-shaped kitchen and parlor, and a small bedroom, both sparse in furnishings but made warm by a collection of white-painted baskets filled with dried wildflowers in dusty shades of pink and purple, blue braided rugs on the floor, and panels of snowy white lace at the windows. Stiff as a board, Phoebe sat on one of the two kitchen chairs, her hands folded in her lap.

"Do you want to remove your coat?" Brenna said, then glanced toward the window. "The sun is out. Looks to be a beautiful day."

"All right," Phoebe said as she climbed down from the chair. She stood still. Waiting.

"Go ahead," Brenna said. "You can do it."

Phoebe stared down at the buttons, then traced the center one with her finger. Without another moment's hesitation, she grasped the round flat disk. When it didn't release immediately, she yanked. The button sailed across the room. Her eyes filled with tears. "I messed up."

"It's all right," Brenna said. "Here, let me show you again." When she'd gotten Phoebe's coat off, Brenna said, "Go find the button and I'll sew it on."

Phoebe was at one end of the room, crawling over the rugs and the wide-planked wooden floor. Brenna was at the opposite end of the room, removing a basket of sewing supplies from the shelf of an old curio cabinet in the corner. She felt Phoebe tug on her skirt.

Pointing to the closed compartment at the bottom of the cabinet, Phoebe said, "What's in there?"

"Nothing that would interest you, honey."

"But what is it?"

"Just something that belonged to my mother."

"A treasure?"

More like a curse. "In a way."

"Can I see?"

Brenna hadn't opened that door in years, not caring that it had warped. "Why don't we go outside in the garden. I'll show you all the new plants that are coming up."

"My mother is dead," Phoebe said matter-of-factly as she knelt down. She traced a circle around the latch on the lower door. "She didn't leave me any treasures."

Brenna knelt down beside her. "Then I'll show you my treasure."

Phoebe grinned.

With her hand trembling and her heart beating like a wild animal suddenly caged, Brenna tugged on the door until it opened.

Phoebe peered into the dark shadows of the cabinet and gasped in awe. "What's that?"

A short time later, Jake stepped into the pharmacy.

"Well, hello there, young lady." He smiled at the girl in the pink calico apron who was sitting on a stool at Brenna's counter, meticulously folding small, bleached-white towels.

"I don't know you," the girl answered in a tone that allowed no argument.

"True enough," he said, noticing the absence of fear in her small blue eyes. "My name is Jake Darrow. I see you're helping Miss McAuley."

"I'm folding towels."

"Doing a good job too."

Her eyes seemed to double in size as a smile brightened her face. "I'm Phoebe."

"A pleasure to meet you, Miss Phoebe," Jake said and bowed from the waist. Without thinking, his hands moved to grip the points of his vest, but came up empty. He hadn't worn it. She'd thought it garish.

The sound of a door closing drew his attention to the back of the pharmacy. In an instant, Brenna appeared, a wide basket of laundry in her arms. She set it on the floor and walked toward him, a challenging look in her eyes.

"What are you doing here?" She glanced at Phoebe, who had stopped folding towels and sat gazing at Jake.

"I came to apologize," he said.

"Again?"

She didn't seem to be at all receptive. "Looks that way. I made some assumptions. I was wrong. I'd like to think we could start over."

"Start what over?"

"Our professional dealings." He paused, hoping she would acknowledge at least the possibility of their having professional dealings, but she said nothing.

"Look, Miss McAuley. I don't like it any more than you do, but I can't leave Coventry for a while. I've got business to settle first. While I'm here, I have to make a living. I do that by selling the Clarion elixir."

With a shrug of her shoulders she said, "So what do you want from me?"

"Only what's fair—your admission as a professional that my elixir has nothing in it but vegetable compounds."

"Is that the truth, Mr. Darrow?"

"Absolutely."

"And you expect me to simply take your word."

"You could," he said, though he doubted she'd believe anything he said, even if he told her she was beautiful and that Cosmos was right. She had the eyes of an enchantress.

She glanced toward the back of the counter where

the bottle of Clarion Compound sat. "I'll have to wait until I do my own analysis. I'm sure you understand."

"Of course. When do you think—"

"I don't know. Later this week. Perhaps not till next. It's difficult to say. I've been very busy."

"I see."

"You might consider peddling your wares in Whitefish."

"No, I think I'll stay right here." The idea that his livelihood depended on this woman's nod of approval grated like nothing before ever had. He had to be patient. Given time, he'd persuade her to his side. Persuasion was, after all, his business.

Flashing a broad grin, Phoebe looked up at Brenna and shouted, "He's pretty!"

Jake chuckled. "Why thank you, Miss Phoebe. I think you're pretty, too."

Phoebe bounced on the stool. "He thinks I'm pretty, too!"

"And you are," Brenna mumbled as she fussed with the stack of towels on the counter.

Seeing Brenna turn crimson was worth all the money he had, though admittedly that wasn't much. But trying to take advantage of her discomfort wasn't a good idea. Not that he wasn't above trying. He just didn't think it would work. "I'll stop back in a few days," he said and headed toward the door. "It was a pleasure to meet you, Miss Phoebe."

Phoebe giggled and looked up at Brenna. "Can we show him your secret?"

"No!"

Phoebe's lower lip trembled as her eyes filled with tears. In an instant, she had buried her head against Brenna's heart, an action too quick, too comfortable, for it to have been the first time.

"It's all right," Brenna murmured as she stroked Phoebe's hair. "It's all right."

Jake watched it all, surprised at how relieved he was to see that Phoebe had someone to care for her, even more surprised at the show of tenderness from the righteous Brenna McAuley.

Easing from Phoebe's embrace, Brenna turned to Jake. The no-nonsense tone of her voice returned. "I believe you were leaving."

Jake nodded, stepped outside, and pulled the door behind him. So Miss McAuley had a heart after all. Good. That would make his job a lot easier. She also had a secret. He wondered what it could be. A double set of books? Wouldn't that be a surprise.

As he headed back to his wagon, he thought about Phoebe again. He'd seen children like her before, in the asylum where his mother had been locked away. Barefoot, eyes vacant, wearing sacks, walking in circles, or lying like lumps on orderly rows of cots. No, those children couldn't have been like Phoebe.

He never did get to see his mother. Oh he tried, but the Boston's Children's Mission and good old Dr. Powers whisked him away, put him on an orphan train headed west, and that was that.

He shook the painful memory from his mind. Only then did he remember he was supposed to see if Brenna had a moon chart. Well he wasn't going back in there now. He'd try again in a few days. Give her a chance to reflect on his apology, or reconsider his offer. Besides, he had a lot to do before Saturday night's show.

Hours earlier he had nailed empty tomato cans to the ends of four broom handles and planted the poles at the four corners of his stage. Into each can he had stuffed cotton. Now he drenched the wads with alcohol, then held a long wooden match to each can. In an instant he had four flaming torches, lighting the way for the gathering crowd.

He didn't use ventriloquism or prestidigitation. He didn't tell jokes or play a banjo. He and Cosmos had teamed up with a busker once. The man sang everything from rowdy drinking songs to heart-wrenching ballads. But the busker was smitten by a pretty girl's smile and left the show after only a week.

Cosmos had taught Jake the finer points of selling. "A man'll think with his heart every time," Cosmos always said. "It's your job to make him think he's using his head. When he comes to the conclusion that what he needs is a bottle of the Clarion Compound, he'll have no one to argue with but himself. And he won't do that. Not in front of his neighbors."

Jake spread a white cloth over the table he'd placed center stage. Tonight, instead of the picture of the once-beautiful woman rendered unattractive by fits, he would use the tapeworms. He'd gotten them from the stockyard in Missoula. Like eight-inch snakes, but flat and transparent, they tangled in a jar of formaldehyde. When the moment was right, he would lift the jar from under the table, setting the menace in floating motion. The women in the audience would wince and glance protectively at their children. Then they would either buy the elixir outright, or nudge their husbands to make the purchase.

Jake didn't really like to use the tapeworm jar. The smell of formaldehyde reminded him too much of hospitals. But few of his props were as effective.

"Step right up!" He waved to a man in a brown threadbare suit and a woman with one babe in her arms and another clinging to her wrinkled skirts.

In a matter of minutes there were dozens of similarly dressed men and women gathered around the stage, none of them paying any attention to him. That was fine. They needed time to socialize with their neighbors, to find out whose cow had calved, whose machinery needed repair, who planned to buy what piece of land. The gang of urchins they brought with them screamed with delight as they ran around the open field.

Jake pretended to add finishing details to the items on his table as he listened to the neighbors talk. The man who kept looking at his pocket watch and commenting that he didn't have time to stand around and wait would be Jake's first conquest. Then he'd go for the man with his wife, whose five small children, clothes clean and hair combed, stood at attention like little soldiers. Both of these men displayed a kind of control that earned the respect of others. Once these two men made the intelligent decision to buy, the others would follow suit.

In early June, shadow-filled twilight still ruled the evening sky. There would still be enough of a moon to be useful, too. Jake noticed more and more wagons driving up to the empty field. The first show usually drew a fair crowd; the second often doubled, though his shows were usually on consecutive nights, not a week apart. Still, he recognized a velvet night when he saw one. With all these people, tonight promised to be one of the smoothest.

He stood at the edge of the stage, his legs spread apart, his arms beckoning. "Ladies! Gentlemen! Come closer. Don't be afraid."

The man with the watch headed right for the stage. The general issued a silent command and his wife and troops marched up front too. Others followed, stirring the air with fragments of conversation and the odors of cooked cabbage that clung to their skin, and manure that clung to their boots.

"Tonight, ladies and gentlemen, I'm going to share with you the advances made in the field of medicine, for as you know, we live in a modern age. Back East there are five-story buildings that scrape the sky, inventions that make it possible for a husband to talk to his wife though they be on opposite sides of the city." He walked back to the table and retrieved one of four dozen gleaming bottles of elixir. "You will tell your grandchildren of this night. I promise you that. For tonight, those of you with the intelligence to see the unparalleled value in this bottle"—he held it up high— "of Cosmos Clarion's Curative Compound will have the opportunity to obtain it for yourselves and for your families."

He made eye contact with as many people as possible, but always returned to the man with the watch. "The pressures men face today are unequaled. To run a business or a farm, to support a wife and children, to contribute to the good of society—why I've known many men, industrious men, who have collapsed under the strain. I've also seen that rare breed of man who is capable of shouldering such a load and shouldering it well. In researching the phenomenon, I came to the conclusion that the successful man is the one who takes care of himself. He exercises regularly. Eats balanced meals. And he takes one of several—for I'll admit there are more than one—of the highly rated health tonics on the market today, the Clarion Compound being number one."

The man with the watch nodded.

"And how many of you face that never-ending struggle to maintain the order and cleanliness that marks a well-run home? Every one of you, I'll wager.

That kind of work takes energy. Lots of energy. And that's just what the Clarion Compound provides—and in abundance."

He paused, just long enough to let folks say a word or two to each other, then added, "The price is so small I almost forgot to mention it. Two dollars a bottle. Hard to believe, isn't it? All this for only two dollars?" As soon as he said the words, he shook his head vigorously. "No, I can't charge you the full price. Not on my first night. What kind of reputation would I get if I didn't offer you a special discount on the first evening show I've ever held in your fair town? One dollar." He picked up another bottle of elixir. "And not just for one bottle, but for two! You heard right, folks. Tonight and tonight only, you can buy two bottles of the number one rated health tonic in the country for a quarter of the regular price."

The two men up front held up dollar bills. "Thank you, sir," Jake said to each of them as he exchanged their money for the elixir. Just as he knew it would, a sea of dollar bills suddenly waved in the air like wheat in a breeze. "Step right up, folks. I've got plenty." Did it get any easier than this? He wouldn't even have to use the tapeworms. Ignoring the pain in his leg, he bent down to exchange bottle after bottle for dollar after dollar till his pockets bulged.

"Mr. Darrow, my research doesn't support your claims."

Jake turned to the sound of the voice, though he didn't have to see her to know it was the lovely Miss McAuley who had issued yet another challenge.

4

"*What can I do for you* this beautiful evening, Miss McAuley?"

From where she stood, six rows back, she raised her voice. "Short of leaving Coventry?"

Jake laughed as he tugged on the points of his red vest. "You're not afraid of a little friendly competition now, are you?"

She made her way to the front of the crowd. Once at the foot of the stage, she looked around for stairs, but there were none, at least not in the front where a person with an ax to grind might have access.

"Care to join me?" Jake said, bending forward.

"Indeed I would." She rested her basket on the stage. Grateful for the barrier her gloves provided, she clasped his outstretched hand. Bracing one foot in the framework below the stage, she boosted herself up as he pulled. His grip was strong. Standing beside him, she reached into the basket and withdrew the bottle of elixir she had purchased one week ago tonight. She raised the bottle high for emphasis, clutching it as tightly as she had only moments ago clutched his hand. Turning to Jake, she said, "Since my pharmacy is not equipped for a complete chemical analysis, I'm at a loss as to identify whatever it is you call your secret ingredient. But I did boil down your elixir, and in doing so smelled the alcohol—"

"Now just a minute!"

"I tasted the ash as well, Mr. Darrow. Alcohol."

"A little, yes. But just enough to keep the mixture stable, to preserve it."

"Come now. When are you going to tell us the truth?"

He scanned the crowd, his eyes pleading understanding. "I am telling you the truth. There isn't enough alcohol in that bottle to do any harm."

"Not to an adult perhaps. But what about to a child? Nowhere on your label do you include instructions for dosage. What if a child should ingest this entire bottle?"

"I don't sell the elixir to small children."

"But many of the trusting people who buy it have small children." She had treated several patients whose well-meaning parents wanted only to soothe sore gums or an aching stomach.

"Ladies, gentlemen. Miss McAuley here is absolutely right. The label does not include instructions as to proper dosage. An oversight on the part of the printer, I'm sure. I'll see to it myself that the new labels include complete instructions."

"And in the meantime?" she asked.

"In the meantime, I would recommend no more than two teaspoons."

"How often? Every four hours? Every six? Eight? As needed?"

"Hmm," Jake said, arching his brow. "Sounds to me like you don't have much faith in your neighbors. I'm sure they know enough to give my medicine, or yours, or anyone else's for that matter, time to work. They aren't going to overdo it. Why I'll bet each and every one of these women here—and maybe a few of the men—have roasted garlic for easing asthma, brewed a little catnip for colicky babies, taken a bit of beet root for a sluggish liver."

Brenna noticed the nods in the audience and the mumbled testimonials to their own home remedies. "What about purity, Mr. Darrow? How carefully do you select your ingredients? Can you warrant them to be of prime quality?"

Jake took a bottle from the table behind him and held it to his heart, label facing front. "If I were not so devoted a follower of the great Cosmos Clarion himself, I would be honored to have my own name and likeness labeling this product. That's how strongly I believe in its healing properties."

Why couldn't he be as honest as he was handsome? Brenna pointed to the name emblazoned in red letters six inches high across the side of the medicine wagon. "And just where is the world renown Cosmos Clarion? Or is he a figment of your imagination?"

"Oh, he's real, all right. I'll swear to that. He'd be here with me if he could, but decided it best to remain back in Missoula where he could carefully monitor the progress of a new elixir. He'll join me at some point in the future."

She glared at him. "So you'll be moving on?"

He glared right back. "No, no, no. I'll be staying right here. Mr. Clarion and I determined before I left Missoula that we would rendezvous in Coventry. So until he is able—I mean until he arrives—I intend to stay right here."

Brenna caught the slip and the slightest flicker of

discomfort in Jake Darrow's brown eyes. Perhaps his story about Mr. Clarion was not entirely truthful either.

"So tell us, what else do you plan to sell while you wait for your new batch of elixir? Powerful red-devil salve? Mysterious Indian blood tonic? Magic soap?"

He smiled, then turned to the audience. "Ladies and gentlemen, if I could offer you a cake of the very same soap used by this beautiful woman standing here next to me, you'd buy it, wouldn't you? You'd jump at the chance. Just look at that creamy skin."

The audience clapped. A few men whistled. Brenna felt the heat rise to her cheeks. Low enough for only him to hear, she said, "How dare you."

Loud enough for everyone to hear, he answered, "What do you think, folks? Should we make her share her secret with us? You do have a secret, don't you, Miss McAuley?"

"You win, Mr. Darrow. For now." She turned abruptly, crouched down at the edge of the stage and jumped off. She couldn't get through the crowd fast enough, though at every turn someone said, "He's just having a little fun, ma'am."

A little fun? A little fun? She marched down the street to her shop, shoved the door open, and stepped into the darkness.

She yanked off her gloves and lit one of the lamps. Was nothing sacred to that man?

In the midst of her ruminating, she noticed that the door to her living quarters was open wide. She was sure she had closed it before going out.

Her lamp held high, she walked across the room, into the kitchen, around the corner to the parlor and adjacent bedroom. Slowly. Silently.

Phoebe? There she was, asleep on bed, curled up in a ball.

Brenna set the lamp on the table and bent down. She placed her arm on the child's shoulder. Phoebe stirred and opened her eyes, which were still heavy with sleep.

The little girl's skimpy hair slipped through Brenna's fingers as she brushed it aside. "What are you doing here?" Brenna asked. "Are you all right? Where is Mrs. Dinwittie?"

Phoebe sat up and wiped her mouth on the back of her sleeve. Shoulders slumped and eyes downcast, she said, "She's gonna be mad."

"But where is she?" Brenna knew Austin had gone to Whitefish for a few days. Though Mrs. Dinwittie wasn't known for her tender heart, it wasn't like her to be neglectful of her duties, especially with Austin out of town.

Each word softer than the one before, Phoebe said, "She's getting ready for the play."

"The Shakespearean Club, of course." Brenna looked around for Phoebe's coat and saw it folded in half on the chair. "I think we'd better go over to the church and let her know you're all right."

"Okay. But first I have a surprise. Okay?"

Brenna had never seen Phoebe look so mischievous, so like a normal child. "What's the surprise?"

Phoebe pressed both hands on the lump beneath the quilt. "Close your eyes."

Brenna covered her face with her hands.

"You can open now."

Brenna lowered her hands, not knowing what to expect, never dreaming she'd see what she did: Phoebe sitting in the middle of the bed, Brenna's bridal veil covering her head.

"My veil!"

Phoebe pulled the lace from her head, instant tears halting her words. "I'm sorry."

Brenna gathered Phoebe in her arms, no longer surprised by the intensity of the child's desperate embrace. "Don't cry," she murmured as she stroked Phoebe's back. "Everything's all right. I was just surprised. That's all."

She should never have shown Phoebe the veil that day. She should have kept it, and the memories it evoked, in the cabinet where it belonged. But it was too late now.

Considering the last time she had seen the veil wrapped around a child, her hand held surprisingly steady as she lifted the delicate white lace from the corner of the bed where Phoebe had tossed it. She remembered as though it were yesterday.

She had never seen convulsions so severe. Never seen them in a child so young, a boy barely two months old, first blue, then black as coal, gasping from the lack of air. She had, however, seen the anguish in the young mother's red-rimmed eyes. If it had been Brenna's mother who had wrapped the naked infant in the bridal veil and with capable, trusting hands had gently lowered the child into the basin of warm water, the little one would have recovered. The young mother's tears would have been for joy.

But it was Brenna, not her mother, who had been roused from her sleep that thick-aired summer night. It was Brenna's faltering inner strength from which the young mother was to have drawn hope. It was Brenna whose small, trembling hands had fumbled every step of the way, Brenna's childlike voice that chanted again and again until she herself had fallen into the trancelike state, "A thousand shall fall . . . but death shall not come nigh thee .. . . A thousand shall fall . . . "

Hours later she had stood alone in the dim light of the Tidewater shanty, the lifeless infant still in her arms, water soaking her nightgown, dripping through the cracks in the wide-planked floor.

Phoebe tugged her sleeve. "I'm sorry I took your secret treasure."

"It's all right," Brenna murmured, reliving the sorrow she had buried so long ago.

"I wanted to play bride," Phoebe said, pulling from Brenna's embrace. She reached up and touched Brenna's cheek. "Why are you crying?"

Brenna gathered her thoughts and stood up, pulling Phoebe with her. "I was thinking about something sad," she said. "But I'm better now and I think we should go find Mrs. Dinwittie. She's probably worried sick about you."

"What will you do if the sad thing comes back?"

"It won't. I won't let it." Brenna stared at the veil, draped across her pillow. She would never try to practice the Old Magic again. Never.

"There now," she said. "Let's get your coat."

"Want me to button it by myself? I can." Phoebe ran to the chair and grabbed her coat. "Watch me."

Mrs. Dinwittie stood in the center of the small group of men and women at the front of the church, her back ramrod straight, both arms outstretched, both hands fisted. With her thick eyebrows drawn in an angry vee, her eyes full of fury, she raised her right arm and suddenly drove it down with the force of Hercules. "The Fatal Blow!" she cried, then turned her head in dramatic fashion from the sight of the imagined wounding.

Everyone clapped.

Brenna had never seen Mrs. Dinwittie smile before and now the woman absolutely beamed. She and

Phoebe stepped in and quietly pulled the door behind them.

Amabelle Sweet continued to applaud as she bubbled with praise. "An encore, Mrs. Dinwittie, please."

Phoebe pulled on Brenna's hand. Her little blue eyes wide with wonder, she said, "Is Mrs. Din happy now?"

Though she found it hard to believe herself, Brenna said, "Yes, I think she is."

"Hooray!" Phoebe shouted and clapped with all her might.

The sound drew the others' attention. Mrs. Dinwittie blanched and covered her gaping mouth with her hands. "Oh dear," she cried, transforming from the beloved star to strict disciplinarian as she first ran, then slowed, then marched, to the back of the church.

Phoebe hid her head in Brenna's skirts.

Face-to-face with Brenna, Mrs. Dinwittie snapped, "There's no need for you to cast such an optic at me, Miss McAuley. I acknowledge fully my lapse in duties."

"It's dark outside, Mrs. Dinwittie. This child could have come to all sorts of harm. Yet you have the nerve to stand there and simply acknowledge your neglect?"

Mrs. Dinwittie pressed her lips in a tight straight line as she locked her hands together and pulled them to her waist. "I assume the girl came to no harm."

"No thanks to you."

Mrs. Dinwittie seemed to consider the situation. "I believe it's time I took the child home." She retrieved her shawl from the row of pegs across the back wall. After flinging the heavily fringed black wrap over her shoulder, she stretched out her left arm to Phoebe. "Come." Taking Phoebe's hand, she nodded goodnight to her fellow thespians and left.

Brenna stayed awhile to visit with Amabelle. She

asked how things were at the house of recovery. Amabelle, who loved to chit-chat, answered, "Busy."

Brenna went home with the vague feeling that Amabelle was worried about something, though the older woman denied it quickly. Too quickly.

Brenna knew from conversations with Austin that Mrs. Dinwittie wasn't a bad woman. She'd been a faithful employee of the Halliwell family for over three decades. She had her first and only child when she was forty-three. Only after her husband and son were killed in a fire did she exhibit the bitterness that seemed so much a part of her now. Austin's mother had suggested he engage Mrs. Dinwittie as a housekeeper. Three months later, she accompanied him to America.

Amabelle was near Mrs. Dinwittie in age, though she had never married. She had a hope chest full of embroidered linens, crocheted doilies, quilts, and neatly hemmed dish towels. She had shown the entire contents to Brenna one dreary winter evening, including the new Bible with half of the family tree penned in Amabelle's gentle black script.

Brenna didn't know if she would ever marry. At twenty-four, she wasn't old, but she was past her prime. When she was younger, she dreamed of getting married and raising a family. She had put all that aside when she set out to pursue her education.

As she reached the door, she turned toward the flickering torches of the medicine show on the edge of town. Jake Darrow. How could that man sleep at night knowing he sold nothing but hope while he profited from other people's desperation?

Brenna opened the door and stepped inside, embraced by the world of science she loved. With pure ingredients, proven formulas, and measured doses, she could heal with little chance of doing harm. The words of a chant didn't matter. Nor did the fullness of the moon, or the love that was said to empower a simple length of lace.

A short while later, Brenna turned down the lamp and dressed for bed. The bridal veil was tucked away in the cabinet. She prepared to close the window, but carried on the cool night air was the clear, resonant sound of Jake Darrow's voice and the applause of those whom he held spellbound.

She rested her head against the window frame, closed her eyes, and listened. Was this what it was like to communicate on the telephone? To recognize another's voice from a distance, to hear his every word clearly and know they were meant for her?

She could hear him talking to the crowd, enticing them to come closer. He could have been standing right beside her, so clear was his voice.

"I may not know exactly what you want," he said. "But I do know what you need. That's why I'm here."

One of the many things Jake liked about baseball was that a man of low birth and poor breeding could become the idol of the rich and cultured. He may have been born poor, but his mother had taught him the meaning of loyalty, the honor in a promise made, and the value of hard work. He had learned on his own all about betrayal. And even more about the humiliation of being tagged and passed from couple to couple, only to see the well-dressed husband or wife point to his leg and shoo him along.

Leaning against the open door of his wagon, he gazed into the night. The crowds had all gone home, children to their beds, husbands and wives to each other's arms. He couldn't remember how many farms or factories he'd been sent to on a ninety-day trial, or how many times he'd been loaded back on the next westbound train with dozens of other unwashed, hungry kids naive enough to keep singing the hymn, "Oh, think of a home over there." He never joined in.

But none of that mattered when it came to baseball. Baseball was a game for men of character.

He closed the door on his vision of being one of baseball's finest and turned to the only other world he knew. He eased his way down the narrow center path to face one of the many wooden compartments built into the sides of the wagon, to the one with his first name carved into the face. He opened the door and retrieved an old cigar box. The scent of tobacco had long since dissipated, as had the heartache he used to feel on those few occasions when he allowed himself to look at his past.

Carefully, he sorted through the newspaper articles about the Boston Beaneaters, the knife that had belonged to the father he had never known, thanks to the battle of Gettysburg, and the one tintype he had of his mother. It had been taken in 1867, the year before she was sent away. The picture had captured in sepia tones what Jake remembered as her simple gray dress and dainty, blue-ribboned cap—the one she always wore to church. He was in the picture too, four years old, wearing the little red jacket she had made for him. Tintypes didn't come cheap. How many times over the years had he looked at that picture and criticized her memory for spending the money they could have had for food or rent? How many more times had he whispered his gratitude to the image of the woman who had so little reason to smile?

He slipped the picture back in the protective leather sleeve he had made for it and returned it to the cigar box.

He rummaged through the loose change at the bottom of the box and picked out the shiniest silver dollar of the lot and rubbed it on his sleeve. Women liked money. At least the women he'd known had. To prove his point he had only to recall the talk he'd heard about the high-principled Brenna McAuley and the stuffy Englishman Halliwell. The man had enough money to buy Coventry outright if he wanted to. Maybe he was the one Jake should be talking to. He sure wasn't getting anywhere with Miss McAuley. Not that he cared. Her lack of cooperation just made things more difficult for him. But not impossible. Oh, no. Never impossible.

For the third time in as many minutes, Brenna rearranged the small ointment jars on the shelf. She had inventoried her toothbrushes, twice. The same with the small tins of menthol plasters. She didn't have that much in the way of inventory, so counting it all wasn't a difficult job. Still, she felt frustrated.

She looked at the front window, empty except for the plain white letters that told viewers they were looking at the Coventry Pharmacy. She needed a show globe, the two-gallon size cut with diamonds and stars, guaranteed, according to the Schieffelin catalog, to reflect a brilliant light. Schieffelin also offered a twenty-three-inch high imitation malachite pedestal on which to place the globe. But four dollars for the globe and two dollars and fifty cents for the pedestal would strain her budget.

She also wanted a new tablet triturate mold, the one with interchangeable plates. With her simple little four-inch mold, all the tablets she made were the same size. Like the show globe, however, any new equipment was out of the question, including a soda fountain, though by now every self-respecting pharmacy back East had a soda fountain.

She looked at the show globes one more time before shoving the dog-eared catalogue in a drawer. Then she plunked a sheet of paper and a pencil on the top of the glass counter. If anyone wanted to buy something while she was out, he could write down what he took and leave the money. She just had to get out.

Walking briskly along the wooden sidewalk, Brenna nodded good-day to those she passed, but didn't stop to chat. She hurried past the blasts of hardwood heat from the blacksmith shop and the musky odor of the stables. She would walk to the bank of the river, turn around and walk back. Yes, that's exactly what she would do. The exercise would clear her mind.

Instead, she headed for the bright blue wagon with its yellow moons and stars.

At the end of the street, the sounds and smells of commerce gave way to the shouts and whistles of boys playing what she recognized from her days in Louisville as the game called baseball. She couldn't believe it had found its way to a place as remote as Coventry. Off to the side she saw Jake Darrow's wagon, the door closed, the stage empty. No sooner had Brenna admitted the man into her thoughts, than she saw his broad back, his white shirt rolled to the elbows, and heard his powerful voice.

She had made it perfectly clear she wanted nothing to do with a man who would intentionally deceive others, especially when the deception gave trusting people false hope. She knew he was angry because she wouldn't endorse his worthless product, angry because she hadn't been fooled by his disguise as a man of medicine. And yet he continued to seek her out, both in her shop and on his stage, persisting in his efforts to somehow link his interests with hers. Why?

She wandered closer.

"Atta boy, Albie! You're getting it! Now this time when Raymond pitches the ball and Dickie swings, you keep your eyes open so if Dickie misses it again you can catch it. Got that?"

From a squatting position, Albie Foster, ten years old, the eighth of the butcher's black-haired children, nodded. "That's better," Jake said as he picked up the ball and tossed it back to the pitcher. "And Dickie, you keep your eye on the ball. Remember what I told you about the strike zone?"

"I think so." The eleven-year-old Foster boy squinted as he seemed to study the empty space next to him. Then he raised the splintered plank, gripped the narrow end, and swung at an imaginary ball.

"Good," Jake said. "Remember to follow through on your swing. You want to give it all you've got, every single time. Most of all, don't be afraid. Sometimes a pitcher will deliberately throw the ball close to the batter, make the batter think the ball is going to hit him."

"Raymond better not hit me!"

Jake put his hand on the boy's shoulder. "The pitcher needs to find out if you're afraid. He wants you to be afraid. That's why you've got to step up to the plate and stare the pitcher right in the eye, let him know that no matter what he throws, you're ready. Think about Charlie Riley of the Columbus Babies. He hit two home runs in his major league debut."

Dickie squinted and swung again as Jake waved for the others to come closer. From their positions fanned across the open field, they ran to Jake, some in blue overalls, some in dark knickers, all grinning. When they gathered around, Jake said, "You're doing a good job out there. But I want to hear a little more chatter, and as soon as we get a hit, I want to see a lot of hustle."

Brenna hadn't seen some of the boys since last fall. How could they have heard about this get-together? She noticed several horses tied behind Jake's wagon. How did the boys manage to get time away from the farm?

Stepping closer, she could see Albie Foster let a black leather work glove, ten times too big for his hand, slip to the ground. Apparently, Jake saw it too.

"Now listen up, boys, and listen good," he said. "I don't want to hear even one more wisecrack about Albie being a sissy because he's using a glove to catch the ball."

Elliott Weems, the wheelwright's son, made a face. So did Lars and Leif Odell. Jake cast a harsh glance their way. "Don't you boys read the newspaper? Before long, every single one of you boys will be wearing a glove. And I'm talking about official baseball gloves. A good glove doesn't just protect your hand. It makes you play better." He looked straight at Raymond. "Tell them yourself. Do you pitch better with the glove or without it?"

The sixteen-year-old Foster drilled Jake's one ball into Jake's one glove. "Pa says every job needs the right tool. And I say a pitcher should wear a glove."

Dickie kicked up a shower of dirt with his bare toe. "How come he always gets to be the pitcher?"

Albie nudged the dirt in the same manner. "Yeah, how come?"

Jake tousled the smaller boy's hair. "This is just our first day. You'll all get your turn to pitch. Every one of you. You'll all get to bat, to play each base, to play the outfield, and to catch. Fair enough?"

The boys looked at each other then back at Jake. "Fair enough," they said.

"All right, that's it for today. I'll see you back here in one week. Same time. We'll talk about bunting and stealing bases. And I'll show you how to protect your fingers from getting broken if you're sliding in head first."

Raymond Foster took off Jake's glove and handed it to him, along with the ball. "Thanks," he said. "I really meant what I said about pitching better with a glove."

Brenna caught the eye of Dickie and Albie Foster. They giggled, then said something to Jake.

He turned toward her, hesitated, then smiled.

"See you next week, Coach!"

There was no mistaking the enthusiasm on Jake's face as he waved to Raymond Foster. "Work that arm, you hear me?"

"Yes, sir!"

Raymond performed some sort of arm-winding exercise while he waited for his younger brothers to retrieve their things from the pile of jackets, caps, straw hats, and bowlers at the edge of the field. Then they, like the others who had gathered around Jake, shouted greetings to one another and scattered in all directions. Brenna had never seen the Foster boys look so happy.

Nor had she ever seen a man look so handsome.

Jake didn't stop to lower his shirtsleeves before coming toward her. She caught herself staring at his muscled arms, broad shoulders, and the open neck of his shirt.

"I didn't know you were a fan," he said as he came closer.

Her voice caught slightly before she said, "I'm not."

"Just curious?" He tucked an oddly designed leather glove under one arm.

"I was out for a walk, that's all."

He nodded, the suspicious look in his eye softened by his smile. "So you haven't been following King Kelly?"

"Who?"

"Catcher for Boston."

"No, Mr. Darrow. I have not."

"Three years ago that man got the richest contract in baseball history: two thousand dollars for playing and another three thousand for the use of his picture."

Brenna gasped. "For playing a game?"

"For drawing a crowd, for making the team's owner a lot of money. They say Kelly's the trickiest player in the game, every bit the showman."

"A showman? It appears you know a lot about that yourself." Recalling their very public, very heated, verbal spar, she looked straight into his eyes, ready for another round.

He didn't flinch. "You're not still upset about last night, are you?"

"About the fact that your elixir contains alcohol when you swore otherwise? Yes, I am."

"I need it to preserve the other ingredients. You understand that, I know you do. Even the great Lydia Pinkham's vegetable compound contains alcohol. She says so right on the label."

"But you don't."

"I see. So if I have new labels printed, ones that state clearly that the Clarion Compound contains no more than ten percent alcohol—and that's the truth—you'll endorse the product?"

"No."

"But you just said—"

"Alcohol or not, I don't believe in encouraging people to think they can buy a miracle. With your outrageous cure-all claims, that is what you're selling."

He looked puzzled. "You don't believe in miracles, Miss McAuley?"

"What I believe in is not the issue."

"Oh, but I think it is."

His intense gaze made him look like a hypnotist, and made her feel uncomfortable.

"I think you're denying the power of the mind. If a man believes my elixir will ease the ache in his head—if he truly believes—then the elixir will ease the ache in his head. Don't you agree?"

"I didn't come here to discuss my philosophy or to argue with you again."

"I'm glad to hear that, though I can't say I've ever faced a prettier skeptic."

She glanced away, her discomfort outweighed by the pleasure of knowing he found her attractive.

"So, why did you come?" he asked.

Combined with the return of the devilish grin that instantly softened the angles of his face, even a simple question became complicated. "I just wanted to take a walk along the river. Get some fresh air," she said. "That's all."

He smiled. "The river is in the other direction."

Despite her misgivings about his business, despite the inner voice that even now told her to heed the warning of her dream, she smiled back. For not once had he mentioned the ancient healing arts, or even hinted that he knew of her past. His reference to the power of the mind was merely his stock in trade. Perhaps she had misinterpreted the message of her dreams and Jake Darrow posed no threat to her at all. The possibility relieved her.

"So, did you see the boys play?" he asked. "What they lack in experience, they sure make up in heart."

"They were having a lot of fun. That was obvious. How did you manage to get them all together?"

"They did that by themselves. I saw a few of them out here yesterday. Not one knew enough about the game to take charge, so all they did was argue."

"That's when you stepped in?"

"I taught them the basics. Told them if they came back today, I'd give them a few pointers."

"You seem to know a lot about the game."

"I follow it." He brushed the hair from his forehead, a gesture that enhanced the easygoing look created by his rolled sleeves and unbuttoned collar. "Ever heard of A. G. Spalding?"

"No."

"Spalding pitched for the Boston Red Stockings— they're the Boston Beaneaters now. Took them to four consecutive championships. Then Chicago offered him a five-hundred-dollar raise and a quarter of the gate, so he left. Boston was in mourning. The next year he took Chicago to the championship. The year after that he stopped pitching altogether and opened a sporting goods store."

He slipped the glove from under his arm and offered it to her. "This is a pitcher's glove."

She took the glove. The leather was still warm, still conformed to his hand. The shape of dreams.

He took out the dirt- and grass-stained ball from his pocket and turned it so the script "Spalding" was visible. "Spalding makes these balls. He paid the National League a dollar for every dozen balls their teams used. That makes these balls the 'official' league ball. Now he manufacturers gloves, bats, uniforms, everything."

She really didn't care about Mr. Spalding or his sports enterprises, but she was enjoying the conversation, perhaps because the subject was neither his elixir nor his business practices. And perhaps because the sight of Jake Darrow showing those boys how to play baseball cast Jake himself in a different light, a pleasant light. "So you think this game will catch on?" she asked.

"Catch on? It caught on before the Civil War. Why I've heard tales that during the war itself, ball playing became a mania in the camps, North and South. On a baseball field you forget who's the officer and who's the recruit. You just play!" For a mere second he seemed lost in some memory of his own, then said, "Some say baseball is already the symbol of America."

"An offshoot of cricket? The symbol of America?"

His eyes bright, his voice resonating from some deep vein of emotion, he said, "Baseball has no overseas ancestors. None. Baseball is all American. It's a game that affords a man from even the most humble of beginnings—" He paused. "I'm boring you," he said. "I get carried away sometimes. Sorry."

"I wasn't bored." So this was how it felt to be swept on the sudden tide of this man's impassioned words. She stroked the glove one more time, noticing how the spread of the palm and the slight bend of the fingers conformed so intimately to Mr. Darrow's hand. She returned his glove and observed every movement as he tucked it between his muscular thighs. Suddenly aware that he had been watching her watch him, she felt the heat of her betraying blush and pressed her hands to her cheeks.

In that one awkward moment, nothing felt more natural than to be standing so near to this man that she could see his eyes darken. He tossed his glove aside and took one small but significant step closer. Tentatively, he touched her cheek. Craving more, she tilted her head. The movement of his mouth to hers was slow, their shared breath delicate. His gentle kiss silenced the sounds around them, causing all thoughts of danger and dreams to vanish.

Second thoughts quickly shielded her heart.

She glanced away, toward the empty field that had only moments earlier come alive with the innocent energy of youth.

"I've been away from my shop longer than I had planned," she said. "I must be getting back."

"I'll walk you."

"No," she said quickly. "I mean, that's not necessary."

"Don't want to be seen with me, is that it?"

"It's not that. It's just . . . well, it could create the wrong impression, that's all."

A steel shade dropped behind his eyes. "And what impression might that be, Miss McAuley? That you've lowered your standards?"

Taken aback by his defensive attitude and feeling the need to protect herself, she met his stare. "That I was in some way supporting your miracle-cure claims."

"Ah, yes, and you don't believe in miracles."

"I don't believe they can be bought and sold."

She could feel what little gains they'd made crumble, one word at a time. In that very instant she rationalized that it didn't matter at all how they felt about each other. Just as quickly, she admitted that it did matter. At least a little. At least to her.

"Good day, Mr. Darrow." She lingered a fraction of a second, hoping he would say something to indicate he understood her reasons for not wanting him to accompany her in public. Instead, he rolled his sleeves down, and with the kind of silent force that hid deep anger, he punished the dusty creases in the starched white cotton, one stroke at a time.

5

His legs too weak to hold him, Cosmos gripped his cane and took another agonizingly slow, painful step toward the window. As with all invalids, it was his moral duty to do everything he could to improve his health. Exercise was critical. Not that he had a wife and child dependent on him anymore. Livia was gone. So was little Penrod. How long had it been now? Thirty years? Forty? He longed to close his eyes and rest, but feared he would lose his balance. Where had the time gone?

He braced himself to cough, and as he did, heard the hollow sound of his lungs. Ah, but he still had Jake, though it wasn't Jake who needed him anymore. No, it was the other way around. Had been for years. Cosmos glanced toward his rumpled bed and one of Jake's dog-eared Horatio Alger books. What had he ever done to deserve such devotion from that boy?

Pain shot through every joint as his bare, bony feet shuffled to make one more step across the braided rainbow rug. He had cut such a fine figure in his youth. Twenty years old and foreman of one of the finest textile mills in Lowell, Massachusetts, he had met Livia. She had been examining a bolt of beige cotton at the counter in Lawrence LeDuc's Dry Goods. He convinced her to buy the deep green silk. Said it matched her lovely eyes.

She was a beautiful bride, and an even more beautiful mother. In less than a month, fever had claimed her and their son, leaving Cosmos with an empty ivy-covered cottage, an empty white wicker cradle, and an empty four-poster bed.

With nothing left, he thought it would be easy to walk away. Leaving, however, had been the hardest thing he had ever done.

He had tried to find a healer when he realized how sick Livia was. His mother had been a healer, his grandmother too, devout women, wise and kind. But they were dead. Without a daughter to carry on the secret rituals, the Old Magic had died.

He remembered being a small boy, sitting on the floor, hiding in the folds of his mother's skirt, listening just as she listened, to another tear-choked plea for help brought by another desperate soul. She had always said she would do whatever God permitted. After that, she would leave the room to chart the moon.

Nothing could be done during the waning period when the moon, not the healer, held the power. To even try to heal then risked death for patient and healer alike. Cosmos recalled the times his mother had been forced to wait before beginning a series of rituals. Sometimes it was too late.

Beads of sweat along his brow, Cosmos gripped the edge of the windowsill and lowered himself to the chair and its floral cushion. He closed his eyes for a few moments, waiting for his breathing to quiet down. He had been led here. Oh yes, just as surely as Moses had been led to the Promised Land, Cosmos Clarion had been led to Coventry.

He opened his eyes, thirsty for the vision of the mountains that had called to him all those months ago. To simply gaze at them made his legs feel stronger, for the day would come when he would climb those rugged slopes. Someday. To look at the four cords of unsplit wood next to the back porch made him want to get out in the fresh air, to grip a heavy ax and raise it over his head, to swing, to hear the splintering of hard wood and feel the power vibrate through his arms. He would do that, too. Someday.

Last night he finally had the dream he had been waiting for. He saw himself as a younger man, his shoulders broad, his arms sculpted with muscle, his chest and belly hard as a rock. Floating toward him was a young woman, her arms outstretched, a candle in one hand, a key in the other, her face hidden by a white veil. She never said a word, but whoever she was, she knew the Old Magic and she was here in Coventry.

Just to think of the dream encouraged him. For even now, on this very same summer evening as he sat and monitored the heavens, he knew that she, too, was out there watching, waiting for the power of the new moon.

Cosmos closed his eyes again, hovering restlessly around the deep sleep that had eluded him for months. Hours later, he was startled by a feather-light rap at the door.

"Yoo-hoo! It is I, Miss Sweet."

He scrambled for his cane, but it had fallen too far from the chair for him to retrieve. Hastily, he straightened the front of his flannel pajamas and combed his hair with his fingers. "Come in," he said and prayed he wouldn't fall into a coughing fit. In the scant week he had been living in the home of Miss Amabelle Sweet, he had come to welcome her presence and enjoy her conversation. He hated to think she would find it painful to be in his company.

Amabelle entered in a cloud of delectable aromas, a dinner tray balanced on one hand. "Why Mr. Clarion—I mean Mr. Belinus—how can you possibly see in here without a light?" She set the tray on the small table beside the bed, lit the lamp, and looked around. Without waiting for his answer, she picked up the table and tray and carried them across the room. "There now. You can eat your dinner right in front of the window, though there's not much to see out there this time of night."

Cosmos watched as she fussed with the items on the tray, moving the bud vase of daisies to one side, the clear crystal salt and pepper shakers to the other. "Smells good," he said.

"Pork roast smothered in fresh rosemary, buttermilk gravy, homemade apple-nut chutney, candied sweet potatoes, fresh asparagus, honey-wheat rolls right from the oven, and chocolate pudding with whipped cream." She flicked the lace-edged pink napkin in the air and handed it to him. "I am determined to fatten you up."

She was such a handsome woman, her hips round, her bosom nice and full, her plump cheeks pink from good health, not the flush of fever. Cosmos spread the napkin on his lap, painfully aware of how unattractive he must look to her by comparison.

Amabelle tilted her head to one side, making her look for all the world like a young girl, totally unaware of her beauty. "Can I get you anything else?" she asked.

"Did I ever tell you," Cosmos said, breaking a roll in half, "that I was once the foreman of the largest textile mill in Lowell, Massachusetts? I was only twenty years old, just barely."

"And you were the foreman?" She retrieved his cane and propped it next to him, then sat down on the window seat. She smoothed her white ruffled apron across her lap, then primly folded her hands. "Well, I'm not surprised. From the day you and young Mr. Jake arrived at my door, I recognized you as a masterful man."

She had a beautiful smile, a voice like music, and eyes that sparkled with life.

He sat as straight as he could. "I remember times when I worked fourteen, sixteen, hours a day, running up and down those steel stairs, two at a time. 'Course I was a young man then." He cut into the thick slice of pork and noticed how little flesh was left on his hands.

"I'll bet you were the best foreman that mill ever had."

"The best? I don't know about that—"

"Oh, but I can just picture you, Mr. Clarion—I mean Belinus."

Cosmos set his fork down and looked into her trusting, chocolate brown eyes. "I hate having to put you in this awkward position. I hope you know how much I mean that."

"It's all right."

"No, it's not. Jeopardizing your reputation to protect me . . . But you see, if folks knew that the creator of the Cosmos Clarion Compound himself was spending his days lying in a bed, wasting away by the hour . . . "

"You don't have to explain. I understand. Truly."

She turned her head a moment and when she looked back, her eyes were bright with tears. Blinking them away, she stood and headed for the door.

"Miss Sweet, what's the matter? What have I said?"

"It's nothing."

"But you're crying. Please. If I've offended you—"

"You haven't."

"Then what is it?" He gripped the sides of the chair, thinking he could go to her, comfort her, then realized how foolish the idea was.

She slipped a lace-edged handkerchief from her pocket and dabbed her eyes. "I know you aren't well. If you were, you would never have come to me. I mean here—you would never have come here. But . . . well, it pains me more than I can say to think of your not recovering."

"It does?" He remembered looking at his sweet Livia that same mournful way the night she came down with the fever. He remembered thinking that if she died, his happiness would die with her. It had. He and Miss Sweet barely knew each other and it was unthinkable that she could care for him in any way beyond what she was being paid to do, and yet . . . He looked at her glistening eyes and felt a surge of determination. "Oh, but I will recover, my dear. I will. I've never been more certain of anything in my life."

She blushed the softest shade of pink. How had such a desirable woman remained single? It was the height of arrogance to think she could ever be interested in him, a man more than twenty years her senior, and certainly not while he was sick. But as soon as he found the magic . . .

Amabelle folded her hands in prayer and drew them to her heart. "You must concentrate on getting well, Mr.—"

"It's Cosmos. My mother named me after the patron saint of physicians." He captured every nuance of emotion on her face, hoping he would see nothing to dissuade him from plunging forward. "Would it be too bold for me to ask that you call me by my given name?"

For several agonizing seconds, she said nothing, then tentatively asked, "Would you like to call me Amabelle?"

"Indeed I would . . . Amabelle." He could no more control his smile than he could the weather. "There is no use in denying the obvious," he said as he looked down at his emaciated form. "But, rest assured, I will not remain an invalid forever." He picked up his knife and fork. "How can I not get well when I am given such fine nourishment?"

As she fumbled with her handkerchief, her blush deepened. "I'll return later for the tray," she said, placing her hand on the cut glass knob. "Perhaps tomorrow afternoon, if you're not too tired, I might persuade you to tell me how you came to own a traveling medicine show. I'm certain it's an interesting tale."

"Tomorrow. Yes, indeed. Tomorrow would be fine. I'll look forward to it."

Long after she left, Cosmos sat by the window savoring the pleasure of having enjoyed the company of such a beautiful woman and thinking about how delightful tomorrow afternoon would be. Try as he might, however, sores in his mouth kept him from eating even half of his dinner.

The white ruffled curtains breathed easily in and out of the open bedroom windows. His feet propped on the wooden bedrail, Jake rocked back and forth in the straight-legged chair, daring it to give way, waiting for Cosmos to wake up. Even after a rousing, late-night performance, Cosmos always rose with the sun. Not today. At least he wasn't coughing—hadn't once in the entire hour Jake had been sitting there.

Jake had already spoken to Miss Sweet that morning.

She said she had looked in on Cosmos earlier, and finding him sleeping so peacefully, decided to wait until he woke to prepare his breakfast. Though she wore the same high-necked white ruffles she always wore, and the same pink porcelain rose at her throat, she looked different. Maybe she just sounded more cheerful than usual. More importantly, and much to Jake's relief, she hadn't mentioned the balance he owed her on the rent.

Before he could pay the rent, he had to whip up another batch of elixir. That meant a shopping trip to Whitefish, but he needed to talk to Cosmos first. They had to come up with a new formula, something with all the flavor of the Clarion Compound, but without the alcohol. Something that would satisfy the influential Brenna McAuley. Either that, or once and for all, he had to convince Cosmos to leave Coventry.

Bolstered by three plump pillows to keep him from choking on the mucous that filled his lungs, Cosmos lay slanted like a pitchfork against a mound of hay. Jake had given up trying to figure out if it was the waking that brought on the cough, or the need to cough that woke Cosmos up.

Cosmos slowly turned his head, squinting at the bright light that filled the room, his body suddenly racked with hacking spasms. Jake jumped up, toppling the chair behind him. He slipped one arm behind Cosmos to brace him from the back, and pressed his other hand to the old man's chest to keep him from falling forward. This fit lasted longer than any thus far. With each visit, Jake's apprehension grew.

He lingered over Cosmos, brushing a limp tendril of white hair from his fevered brow. He wished there was a way for Cosmos to absorb some of his strength, his health. For unless Cosmos improved, any day now the hemorrhages would start. Then the death rattle. That, God help them both, would be the end.

Damn it! Cosmos was going back East, like it or not.

For the next few minutes, Cosmos lay against the pillows, struggling for each short breath. A few more minutes and his breathing returned to the steady but shallow intake Jake had come to accept as normal. Jake heard the pounding of his own heart loud and clear, remembering the feel of Cosmos's spindly ribs crashing against his palm.

"Hey, you old hound dog," he said, steadying his chair and then his voice. "About time you woke up and joined the living."

"My idea exactly." Cosmos took note of the light at the window. "What time is it?"

"Ten o'clock."

"Ten? Oh no." As though the white cotton sheet was made of lead, Cosmos struggled to move it aside.

"Getting up?" Jake said, ready to help Cosmos with his usual morning ablutions.

Cosmos draped his arm across Jake's shoulder, eased off the bed, and steadied himself with his cane. Together, they walked a few steps past the white bowl and pitcher on the washstand, toward the privy chair behind the rose painted screen in the corner. "I have to bathe this morning, too. And shave."

"You bathed yesterday. Remember?"

"I'm bathing again today."

"Whatever you say."

A short while later, Cosmos stood by the washstand, the hems on the sleeves of his red flannel pajamas wet, his skimpy white whiskers full of creamy lather. He clutched a fresh cake of Sweetheart Soap, watching the opalescent bubbles dance. "I need some help," he said, turning to Jake, who stood right beside him. "I've dropped this soap three times. I don't think I'd be doing myself any favors by trying to use a razor."

Jake unhinged the pearl-handled razor Cosmos had used for the last ten years. One long, slow stroke at a time, he scraped the lather and whiskers from Cosmos's face, revealing as he did soft wrinkled skin and a smile.

"What's with the fuss?" Jake asked as he wiped away the last traces of lather. "Thinking about hitting the road?"

"Just as soon as we can." Cosmos's hand shook as he ran a brush through his hair and leaned closer to the oval mirror, checking his reflection from left to right. "In the meantime, I'm stepping out."

"Today?"

"You heard me." Using his cane, Cosmos pointed to the tole-painted chiffarobe that dominated the far corner. "Get me my good shirt. The one with the pleats."

"Pleats?"

"I can't very well socialize with a lady while I'm in my pajamas." He turned back to the mirror and straightened his shoulders. "I need a pair of pants I won't swim in, too. All mine are too big." He eyed Jake's slim, faded denims. "I bet they'd fit me."

"Oh, no."

"Son," he pleaded.

"What am I supposed to wear?"

"You can take a pair of my pants and hold them up with suspenders. Just till you get back to the wagon."

"Why don't I run back to the wagon right now and get you a pair of my pants. I think that's a much better idea."

"No! There's no time! She'll be here soon."

"All right, all right." Jake closed the door, then sat on the straight-backed chair and tugged off his boots. Despite all the darning on the heels and toes, his socks still slipped on the highly polished floor as he walked over to the chiffarobe. He pulled out a pair of gray plaid suit pants, the most conservative thing Cosmos owned. "So who is this lucky woman?"

"None other than the lovely Miss Amabelle Sweet herself. And I want you to know it was she who asked me."

"Hmm," Jake said. "Now this could be interesting."

It took every minute of an hour for Jake to get Cosmos dressed. While unbuttoning and buttoning, pulling and tugging, they talked about the need for a new elixir and considered a number of ingredients known for flavor and color and general appeal. Jake didn't mention his theory that if Amabelle had taken a fancy to Cosmos, she might give them a break on the rent. The idea was too obvious not to have occurred to Cosmos, though he hadn't mentioned it either. Maybe Cosmos wasn't thinking of business when it came to Miss Sweet.

Clearly exhausted, Cosmos sat in the chair by the window. The white pleated shirt, crisp white collar, and gold coin cufflinks made him look as sophisticated as ever. It was surprising how rugged and how healthy Cosmos looked wearing Jake's blue denims.

Jake snapped a pair of red suspenders against his shirt and bunched up a good twelve inches of gray plaid fabric floating around his waist. "I'm getting back to the wagon now," he said. "Before anyone sees me. Then I'm going straight to Whitefish. I'll report back in a few days. And then you can tell me all about your engagement with Miss Sweet."

Cosmos coughed a little, but recovered quickly. "I owe you, son. And I'll pay you back. You'll see."

"Damn right, you will." Jake headed for the door. "Hey, you didn't get your breakfast. I was supposed to let Miss Sweet know when you woke up. I'll go get her now."

"No, no, no. Don't do that. She'll be bringing lunch pretty soon."

"But aren't you hungry?"

"No. Besides, I'd rather wait and eat with Amabelle. Like a picnic. That's how we planned it. You understand."

"Amabelle? A picnic?"

"You heard right."

"You old rascal."

Cosmos coughed again, only this time he couldn't stop. The force had him gripping the arms of the chair.

Rushing to his side, Jake braced him, his own fears mounting with each spasm. "Take it easy now," he said, gently patting Cosmos on the back, and rubbing little circles meant to say everything would be all right.

Cosmos leaned back. The sudden appearance of blood on his white pleated shirt, nose, and mouth, told both men otherwise.

Jake ran for the towel, wet it, and wiped away the evidence. Only the wet, brown-ringed stains made denial impossible. He felt his throat close up, too tight to say a word.

Cosmos patted him on the arm. "I'm going to be all right. You'll see. If I could just get rid of this cough."

"Yeah."

They stayed like that for a moment or two, old memories and new hopes making it impossible for them to look at each other. Until Cosmos took as deep a breath as he could and took Jake's hand.

"Son, I don't know how much longer I can hold on. I've got to know if she charts the moon."

"I understand."

Whitefish would have to wait.

6

"I'll be with you in a moment, Mr. Darrow."

"No rush." Wearing a black suit, white shirt, and his red brocade vest, Jake had been sitting on one of the chairs by the window for at least ten minutes, the black-booted ankle of one long leg propped on the knee of the other. The first time she looked over at him, he was sitting still, the reflective look in his dark eyes making him appear quietly content. These last few minutes, however, as Brenna affixed a label to her third prescription that morning, she noticed how restless he had become, looking around as though taking in the sights for the first time.

What was he peddling now? Baseballs? Genuine Spaldings, guaranteed to make any pitcher a star?

Brenna flipped to the page marked Tuesday, June 10, in her day-book and read the notation: Sarah Zimmerman, thirty sulfate of iron pills, two dollars.

"Here you are, Sarah," Brenna said, stepping down from the raised platform behind the tall, black walnut prescription case. She handed the small bottle to the town's librarian. "Take one a day for thirty days. I'm certain you'll witness a marked improvement in your vitality."

"I do hope so. I do indeed." Sarah looked at Jake, who nodded and smiled. "Why, with the collected works of Lord Byron, Shelley, and Keats—the great English poets—having all arrived within the week, I've shelved more books this past month than in the past year. Not that I'm complaining. Oh no. No, indeed."

Turning back to Brenna, Sarah raised the corner of the red-checked napkin that protected the contents of her shopping basket and wedged the bottle of pills between two long loaves of bread. She lifted the drawstring calico sack that distinguished all purchases made from Sweet Dreams, Miss Clementina Talbot's House of Candy and Confection. Coventry's latest storefront operation was actually nothing more than the front window of Clementina's parents' home.

"Care to try an English toffee?" Sarah said to Brenna, skillfully opening the sack with her fingers. "I find it a sophisticated and delightfully refreshing change from drab taffy. Lord Austin recommended it."

"I'll be closing for lunch shortly. Thank you just the same."

"As you wish." Sarah drew the strings of the little bag and tucked it deeper into her basket. As she rearranged the checkered napkin to cover her purchases, she took a peek over her shoulder. Brenna followed the direction of Sarah's attention and noticed that Jake had shifted his position. She wondered if his leg bothered him.

Angling herself so Jake could see only her back,

Sarah leaned forward and slowly mouthed the words, "Bank robber."

"What?"

Sarah pressed her sausage-soft midriff into the counter and craned her neck toward Brenna. Using the palm of her hand like a fan, she shielded the side of her face and whispered, "His leg. Haven't you noticed? I'll bet he was wounded robbing a bank."

Instantly wide-eyed, Brenna glanced at Jake. As though he had been expecting her to look his way, he smiled.

Shielding her mouth again, Sarah continued. "My guess is he's been on a spree of ruthless violence. Probably robbed and murdered the man Clarion, then stole his wagon."

"Sarah!" Realizing she had raised her voice and that now Jake was staring at her, Brenna fussed with the pad of paper and pencil on the counter.

Sarah lowered her eyes and barely moved her lips. "Who knows what wanton behavior he might engage in should a beautiful, helpless woman stumble across his path." Repeatedly, she cupped her black crocheted snood, drawing attention to the bundle of unruly, bright red curls she complained of so often.

Jake Darrow a criminal? Brenna had never heard of anything so outrageous in her life. An unscrupulous showman, yes. But a robber? A murderer? Impossible. "I don't know where your information came from," Brenna said quietly, "but I wouldn't repeat your theory without proof."

"Oh, it's no theory. I have my sources. I am, after all, a librarian." Sarah fussed with one of the loaves of bread protruding from her basket and continued to whisper. "Of course, I'm not afraid of him myself. But you, you be careful. That man is dangerous. Very, very, dangerous."

Cupping her curls one more time, Sarah turned to go and loudly cleared her throat. "Toffee, Mr. Darrow?"

"No, thank you," he said as he stood and headed toward her. He had barely opened the door when Sarah flew out of the shop.

Shaking his head, Jake walked over to the counter and braced his arms on the very same spot where Sarah had just expressed her fears.

Brenna stepped back up on the platform, disturbed to find herself eye-level with him. Jumbled images rushed through her mind: Jake with a gun—though only for self-defense, of course; Jake being chased by a posse—unjustly accused; Jake and a woman in a torrid embrace, her lips swollen from the pressure of his endless kiss.

"What spooked her?" he asked.

"What makes you think she was frightened?" Brenna squirmed under his sudden scrutiny.

"Oh, I'm pretty good at reading people's faces."

Brenna closed her day-book and pushed it aside. "What can I do for you, Mr. Darrow?"

He gave that oh-so-common nonchalant shrug of the shoulders that alerted her to thoughts of something important.

"I have this friend back in Boston," he said. "He's an invalid. Looks like consumption, late stages."

"I'm sorry to hear that. How old is your friend?"

"Oh, he's not old. Not at all. In fact, he's young. Younger than I am. Has a wife and a small child. He was supposed to go back to college, but . . . "

Brenna nodded. She knew the scenario all too well. Anything mentally stimulating would quickly rob the invalid of what little strength he had left. School or business, even social obligations, all were out of the question for any invalid, especially a consumptive.

"Well, you see," Jake continued, "I got a letter from him a few months ago. His doctors are telling him to come out West."

"Many male consumptives are doing just that, while female victims are encouraged to remain at home. Continued exposure to clean, fresh air, whether at home or abroad, is critical to recovery, as is diet and exercise. Proper care may force the disease into remission, and may arrest it altogether."

"Yeah, well, he's convinced that if he just jumps into a deerskin suit and trots off into the mountains, he'll be cured."

"I take it you don't agree."

"He can hardly walk."

Brenna noticed the concern that creased his brow. She knew how horrible it felt to stand helpless in the face of a loved one's futile struggle for life. "Twenty years ago consumption took the lives of one in five Americans," she said, hoping Jake would take heart. "Today, thanks to medical science, those numbers are greatly reduced. Your friend is young. Perhaps he will live long enough for science to find both cause and cure—"

"He's dying now!"

Jake took a slow, deep breath as he raked his fingers through his hair. In the scant seconds before he spoke, she saw both desperation and devotion in his eyes. He couldn't be a criminal.

"I guess that's what happens to all consumptives," he said at last. "It's just a matter of time. Right?"

"Maybe not. I have heard of some who have fought the disease and won. A few anyway."

"Miracles?"

She gave him a soft smile. "I suppose there have been a few."

Resignation hung in the air and forced a lull in the

conversation, until Jake said, "If a man who had consumption came to you for help, what would you do for him?"

Brenna glanced at the nine-foot-high arrangement of shelves and drawers, and next to it the smaller herb case with its forty-eight drawers and forty-eight round porcelain knobs. "Medicine has come such a long way," she said, "and yet when dealing with consumption, there is little I could do for your friend short of suggesting the standards of healthy diet, fresh air, and exercise. His doctor has prescribed such a constitutional treatment, hasn't he?"

"His doctor? Oh, of course."

Jake studied the bottles on every shelf and the labels on every drawer with such intensity Brenna wondered if he thought she had lied to him. "Were you looking for something in particular?" she asked, positioning herself in front of the herb case and a slightly discolored white drawer knob around which she had just that morning tied a slender white ribbon.

"The *Farmer's Almanac*. Do you have a copy?"

"I had only a few to begin with. They sold quickly."

"Oh."

"No need to look so disappointed, Mr. Darrow. I'm certain Sarah Zimmerman has a copy at the library."

"But you don't have one here."

"No, I don't."

With a contemplative look on his face, he walked over to the side wall and spent a moment studying the shelves of soaps, sponges, paint and varnishes, stationery and inks, and sickroom supplies. "So, if a farmer needed to figure just how many days until the next new moon or full moon or whatever so he could plant his crops, you couldn't help him." He turned around to face Brenna. "Or could you?"

Caution slowed Brenna's words. "What do you mean?"

"Now you're the one looking strange," he said. "I just wondered if you had some other book, or chart . . . or something else that a person might use to, you know, keep track of . . . of the moon."

"I operate a pharmacy. I study medicine, not astronomy."

He ran his hand through his hair and she noticed a fine sweat along his brow. Or had she only imagined his discomfort because she felt those very same beads of agony on her own skin?

"But aren't there some kinds of healing arts that require such knowledge?" Jake said.

"None that I practice."

"But maybe you've heard of them. When we were traveling across South Dakota, I heard about some German women, devout women, highly respected, who could heal people by using chants and rituals. Something called 'brack' or maybe it was 'brock.' I know some people called it the Old Magic."

Brenna drew a curtain of steel between her heart and her eyes. "I don't have what you're looking for."

He didn't move. His eyes didn't glare with accusation or blaze with challenge. They simply held steady.

She waited until she was sure she could speak with as steady a voice. "This information you seek, is it for your friend?"

"Yeah."

"I've told you the treatment that science recommends. If you insist on pursuing something else, I suggest you go back to South Dakota and look for a *brauchere* who can help you."

"*Brauche!* That's it. So you have heard of it."

Brenna locked all expression as frightening memories filled the silence. Only her heart refused to be controlled, and it fluttered like a butterfly caught in a net.

The sudden presence and high-pitched chatter of Mayor Elton Fontaine broke the painful spell, though one more look at Jake Darrow's determined face and Brenna knew the torture that waited for her in her dreams.

"Miss McAuley! Listen to me! My voice has returned to full force and vigor, thanks to you."

"I'm glad to hear that," Brenna said. She reached for her day-book, but it slipped through her fingers and fell on the floor, the heavy thud sounding like thunder. Quickly, she retrieved it and set it on the counter. With her fingers clutching the heavy green binding, she said, "Mr. Darrow, was there something else?"

"It can wait. You go ahead." He sat back down.

If she could out-race her fears, she would run. But if she'd learned anything in school, it was to not be reckless, but to proceed with caution.

Elton Fontaine tightened the knot on his green plaid bow tie. "I say there, Darrow, old chap, I'm surprised to see you're still hanging around. I thought you'd have departed for Great Falls by now. You did say you were headed east, didn't you?"

"I've changed my mind. In fact, I might just settle down here."

Brenna's heart all but stopped.

"Oh dear," Elton said. "I mean, whatever for? Surely you've exhausted your opportunities in our little town. I mean to say, we've hardly the population to warrant your time and effort, your very valuable time and effort."

"Now, Mayor, you're just too modest. I've seen what's happening in your little town: a new candy store, a busy bakery, your own library. Why, I was at the barber shop just yesterday and Mr. Newton made a point of telling me, not once but three times, that his new barber pole twirling just outside the door is the tallest in the state of Montana."

"Oh, you can't believe anything Ralph Newton says."

Jake raised a questioning eyebrow. "He's talking about buying a second chair."

"That foolish Newton. I'll have to speak with him straightaway. Living in the protective shadow of these magnificent mountains, it's easy for one to turn a blind eye to the serious problems, the very serious problems, that plague this new state of ours."

Elton fiddled with his tie again. "You're a businessman," he said, "well traveled. I know I don't have to tell you that the price of silver has fallen to half its value. Nationwide, businesses are closing. Banks as well."

Nodding, Jake said, "Even so, there's a handbill tacked to every storefront on this street inviting residents to get involved in your new theater group. And a man around here would have to be stone deaf not to have heard about the competition that Englishman Honeywell has going between your town and Whitefish."

"Not Honeywell. Halliwell. Lord Austin Halliwell. A smart businessman, oh yes, indeed. With the ruination of so many ranches, he recognizes this as an opportune time to buy. Oh he's a fine chap, a fine chap indeed." Bobbing his head, the mayor turned to Brenna. "Don't you agree?"

"Lord Austin is a highly respected and wealthy man. Should he decide to settle in Coventry, the entire town would benefit."

"Especially you," Jake said to Brenna, "if I heard right."

Slowly, resolutely, Brenna crossed her arms. "I don't know what you've heard."

"Come, come now," the mayor said. "The truth is something to be proud of. Lord Austin Halliwell has taken quite a fancy to our Miss McAuley, giving us a decided advantage over Whitefish—though that doesn't assure us a victory, you understand." He ran his finger between his neck and the board-stiff collar of his shirt and grimaced. "We may well go the way of so many other towns, inhabited now only by ghosts."

"Appears to me," Jake said, rising from the chair, "that your fair town is determined to thrive where the rest of the state is dying. I also get the feeling every man in this town is turning into an English dandy."

"Now, now, we're merely trying to make Lord Austin feel at home. Isn't that right, Miss McAuley?"

"We do what we must in order to survive," she said.

"And on that," Jake said, "we all agree."

"Well," Elton said to Brenna, "I must be going. I merely wanted to demonstrate the results of your fine education and extend my gratitude."

Brenna prayed that Jake would follow the mayor out the door. Instead, he remained behind.

"The library is open now," she said. "Didn't you say you wanted to read the *Farmer's Almanac*?"

He glanced at the glass cabinet of toiletries on one side of the room and at the shelves of household supplies on the other. "What I want is a means to chart the moon." He stopped suddenly and raised his hand. "No. What I want is to know how *you* chart the moon."

"What makes you think I do?"

He walked toward the pharmacy case at the back of the room, where Brenna stood, finding it harder and harder to breathe.

"Are you saying you don't?"

"I'm saying you're wasting your time."

"But you know about *brauche*."

"I learned of various healing methods in school."

"I see."

He studied her for a long, agonizing moment, and when he spoke, it wasn't just his words, but his deep, spellbinding tone that threatened to shatter what little composure she had left. "People used to believe that a woman could unleash a thunderstorm simply by letting down her hair. Did you know that?"

"People are always looking for someone they can blame when things go wrong."

"Has that ever happened to you, Miss McAuley? Have you ever been blamed for something that went wrong?"

"Let's understand one another, Mr. Darrow. I have no interest in your past. I see no reason for you to be interested in mine."

He didn't budge. "I was born in Boston, 1863. My father died at Gettysburg. My mother used to say I looked like him. Who knows? She died in an asylum."

The need to protect herself outweighed the rush of compassion she felt for the little boy inside the man, for the man was more than capable of taking care of himself. "Why are you telling me all this?"

"Because I need to know about your past."

"But, why?"

He looked around the room again, just as he'd done a dozen times since he walked in the door. He rested his arms on the counter and leaned closer. "Don't you see? I have to find someone who knows the Old Magic."

"Have you talked to Sarah Zimmerman? She's our librarian. Better yet, you could go on to Great Falls and talk to the doctors there."

He scoffed. "Yeah, well I would, but you see, my friend had this dream—"

"A dream?" Brenna struggled to remain calm as she felt the net closing over her again.

"Yeah," Jake said, looking her straight in the eye. "He's convinced that the magic he needs is here in Coventry. And that all I have to do is find the person who has it. . . . He's also convinced that person is a woman."

She cursed her nervous laughter. "I'm not the only woman in Coventry."

"He told me to look for a woman with pale green eyes."

Brenna turned away, fussing with the items on the counter. But her hands shook. Her heart raced. And her eyes saw nothing but what was supposed to be a near invisible, slender white ribbon knotted around the seventeenth white knob on her herb chest. "So you're seeking this information for your friend."

"He's more than a friend. He's like family."

His friend was back in Boston, a progressive city with hundreds of good doctors. She turned to face him. "I'm sorry, Mr. Darrow. I can't help you."

"You can't? Or you won't?"

"I can't."

He hesitated and she thought he was going to barrage her again. Instead, he shook his head sadly and went to the door. "Sorry to have bothered you." Before she could reply, he had gone.

"'The course of true love never did run smooth.'" Amabelle filled Brenna's glass with apple cider and set the pitcher on the small wooden table between them.

"Who said anything about love?" Brenna leaned back in one of a dozen heavy wooden rockers lining the spacious front porch. As she sipped the cold cider, she gazed beyond the roughly hewn cedar columns supporting the wide overhang to a view of the meandering Flathead River. "I just said he had a tragic childhood."

"Never mind me, dear. I was simply quoting Mr. Shakespeare. Amabelle braced the toe of her boot on the floor and set her rocker in motion. "But you did say Mr. Darrow was handsome."

"Everybody says he's handsome."

"You also said he devotes a lot of his time teaching the boys how to play ball."

"Well, he has to have something to do. He can't be on stage every hour of the day."

"Oh yes, those shows of his. So entertaining. What was it you said about his voice? That it was powerful. That it mesmerized."

"Not me. His voice doesn't mesmerize me. I only meant to say that he has a distinctive voice and that some people might be swayed by it."

"Cookie?" Amabelle passed a plate of heart-shaped sugar cookies.

"Thank you." Brenna took one and bit off the tip. She had come to learn what, if anything, Amabelle had heard about Jake Darrow. She didn't believe for a minute that he was a bank robber, but she didn't trust him, either. Especially not after today. "I'm glad you had a little time to visit this evening. I know how busy you've been."

"Oh my, yes. But I'm going to have to hire a live-in girl."

"I knew you had been thinking about it."

"I plan to advertise in all the big papers back East. I want someone who has not only compassion for people but who has experience in caring for invalids. With so many of them—invalids, that is—coming out West, I need help now more than ever. My two day-girls take care of the laundry and cleaning and serving the meals. But I'm cooking and caring for eight men, and every day the mail brings another inquiry."

"You provide an important service, Amabelle. I know the only reason I stay in business is because of your patients."

Amabelle brushed a scattering of crumbs from her lap. "If all goes well, our Coventry could become quite the health resort someday for women as well as men." She reached for another cookie. "Is Lord Austin any closer to a decision?"

"I don't know. He's been in Whitefish for the past few days."

"When will he be back?"

"A week. Ten days. I'm not sure."

"So, he hasn't said anything to you?"

"No. Why would he? We're not engaged for goodness sake!" Brenna sighed in disgust. "I'm sorry. I've been busy myself. And obviously not handling it all that well."

"Put it behind you. One of the benefits of friendship is the freedom to speak your mind."

"Thank you." Brenna focused on the seamless blue sky. "The fact that you plan to hire a live-in is a sign of growth. I'm happy for you."

Amabelle nibbled a cookie. "Just knowing relief is in sight lessens my guilt about pursuing certain . . . personal interests."

"The thespian group?"

"Oh yes, that too. But I was referring to something more, well, more personal."

Amabelle's efforts to hold back a smile made Brenna all the more interested. "A gentleman?"

Amabelle blushed two shades pinker than her dress. "It's silly, isn't it? A woman my age?"

"No, it isn't silly. It's beautiful. Now, tell me everything. Who is he? Where did you meet him?"

Before Amabelle could answer, two parchment-faced men, their chicken-skin necks wrapped in shawls, walked feebly out on the porch. A younger man, his eyes empty of hope, walked behind them. All three nodded their greetings and took the rockers at the far end of the porch. Brenna knew each one. Sixty-two-year-old Webley Heller, ophthalmic ointment. Fifty-year-old Oscar Gage, iron tonic. And poor Valerian Boyd, barely thirty, mercurial ointment for syphilis.

Suddenly Amabelle seemed distant. Brenna lowered her voice. "You haven't told me about your special friend."

"He's . . . he's one of my patients. A new one. You haven't met him."

"A patient? What's his name?"

"Belinus. Mr. Belinus. He's not doing all that well right now, but he's going to get well soon. I'm certain of that." Amabelle paused. "Oh, Brenna dear, he's so intelligent, so thoughtful. And he's well traveled. Why, he's been all over Europe. We were supposed to have a little picnic in his room, just the two of us, but he wasn't feeling up to it." She picked up one of the heart-shaped cookies and eyed it wistfully. "That's why I'm so glad you stopped by." She sighed. "He's such a handsome man. And he . . . he thinks I'm beautiful. Isn't that silly?"

"It's sensible. You always said you were waiting for the right man. Now you've found him."

"Yes," Amabelle said softly. "I believe I have."

"So tell me, what brought him to you?"

Amabelle's eyes watered instantly. "The same thing that brings all these other men to me. Consumption."

7

Brenna hadn't touched the small, leather-bound book since she came to Coventry. Until today. Now, she sat on the stone wall that bordered the back of her garden, carefully turning the delicate pages. The walls on the other three sides of the garden were only half as high, but it was enough to give the enclosure the sense of privacy she sought, for just to look at these chants and rituals breathed life into a legacy long dead. Barely past dawn, the sun had hours to go before it would reach its full power. Pressing her palms against the cool, moist rocks, Brenna closed her eyes to the painful memories, but they were always right there, just beneath the surface, like so many small seeds waiting for the sun and rain that would enable them to grow.

Just yesterday Brenna was given knowledge of two people afflicted with the disease of wasting away. Not any two people either. One a mile away, the once-in-a-lifetime romantic interest of her best friend. The other half a continent away, a friend of a man she had every reason to avoid.

She gazed at the lavender with its silver leaves and delicate purple spires, the small rosemary shrubs, their pungent, deep green nettles gently sweeping the stones, and the trailing pinks that cascaded the walls. In each corner stood dark and light blue spires of delphinium and foxglove for the heart. Radiating from the sundial in the center were the beds of parsley, mint, and thyme, purple and blue columbine for all-purpose healing, clove-scented pink carnations and gillyflowers for epilepsy and plague, and marigolds to dispel malignancies.

If she had her mother's power, she would do all she could to help Amabelle's friend, provided he believed in the Old Magic. For it wasn't enough for the healer to have faith and strength. The invalid's belief had to be just as strong. It was the invalid's own strength and hope that would have to support the body in its struggle against the disease. She would help Jake Darrow's friend, too, for he truly believed. But he was 2,000 miles away. Besides, Brenna didn't have the power.

But if she did . . . oh, if she did, and if Amabelle's friend believed, she could do as her mother had done, and with God's help, restore the poor man's health. She clutched the book to her heart and savored the joy of what might have been. Of course, there were rituals to be followed. To deviate in the slightest risked great danger to both the sick one and the *brauchere*, for the sickness could strike back at the *brauchere* with a vengeance. Aah, but the risk was worth it to help someone.

Her foolish notions aside, maybe there was something she could do for Amabelle's friend. A tincture of opium would relieve the inevitable cough. She wondered why Amabelle hadn't asked her to look in on him yet. Resolved to do what she could, Brenna stood and left the garden, half of her legacy flourishing in the soil, the other half struggling to survive in her soul.

Struggle still marked her dreams, too. Though her dreams last night contained none of the anguish she expected, they were painful just the same. Jake still held the bridal veil and the key, but he made no effort to reach for her, the seductive look gone from his eyes, replaced with one of enormous sadness. As his image receded into the shadows, she saw herself standing precariously on the edge of Amabelle's wide porch, her outstretched arms aching with emptiness, while two wild animals scrambled to dig away the foundation. The thread of her mother's voice spun around her like a silver web.

As you believe, so it will come to pass.

Several hours later, Brenna unlocked the front door of her pharmacy and opened it wide. A few flies were a small price to pay for the warm bath of sunlight. That's when she noticed the back of Jake Darrow's medicine wagon negotiating Main Street's web of ruts, heading out of town, toward Whitefish. Perhaps he had thought about the mayor's words and had decided not to stay.

She couldn't explain the sudden and overwhelming feeling of loneliness.

Jake would have done anything to spare Cosmos the disappointment of learning that there simply was no moon chart in Brenna's pharmacy. He could still picture the old man as he closed his eyes and nodded his head, silently accepting the truth that without the Old Magic his time had come. But instead of urging Cosmos to go back East, Jake kissed his forehead and promised himself he would find a way to get into Brenna's private rooms. Maybe that's where she kept the magic.

But first, Jake had to go to Whitefish. He had talked it over with Cosmos that morning, too, and both men agreed. Whitefish had more people than Coventry and carried more supplies. Jake would brew and bottle a new batch of elixir, pitch it to the new crowd, and come back to Coventry with the money for several months' rent. The plan was optimistic. Not because Jake doubted his ability to sell all the elixir he made, but because now both he and Cosmos knew that time was short.

Of course, now that Amabelle Sweet had a personal interest in Cosmos, she might be lenient on the rent, though she hadn't mentioned it and Jake hadn't asked. Besides, even if Miss Sweet said Cosmos could stay as long as he wanted for free, Jake still needed to get money and get it fast. He had to buy food and supplies. He had a bill at the livery.

Maybe Brenna was telling the truth and she didn't know anything about the Old Magic. One thing was certain. Her shop needed a lot of repairs, and in all likelihood, she didn't have the money. If that was the case, she might be willing to make up some kind of ceremony for Cosmos—pretend she had the magic—if the price was right. All the more reason for him to accumulate cash.

With a clear vision of Brenna in his mind, Jake headed north. Somewhere along the way, between watching the tranquil circles of a hawk and listening to the steady clomp of his horse's hooves, he thought of all the things he could do to fix up Brenna's shop. Replace the cracked glass in the cabinet that held the shaving gear and toiletries. Reinforce the shelves that held the household supplies. Build her some kind of stand for displaying small items like toothbrushes. He could even replace that cluster of discolored knobs on the herb chest. Then maybe she'd smile at him again the way she did that day at the baseball field. It began with the softening of her lips, the tentative lift at the corners of her mouth, then the full expression of pleasure.

Jake laughed out loud, startling his horse. The most beautiful woman he'd ever seen and he wanted to be her carpenter. Oh, he'd been alone too long. Much too long. Despite the fact that Brenna McAuley couldn't, or wouldn't, help him, the idea of getting into her room held enormous appeal.

". . . Out of the marrow. Out of the bone. . . . Out of the marrow. Out of the bone. . . . "

Brenna drifted back from her reverie, fragments of the chant still echoing in her head, framing her lips to repeat the words yet again—until she realized that Phoebe had been watching her, wide-eyed and silent, from the opposite corner of the garden.

"What's the matter?" Phoebe said.

"Nothing." Brenna pressed her palms on the sun-baked stones of the wall on which she sat, desperate for the anchor. She had engaged in a quiet moment of meditation, that's all. Not stepped on that timeless landscape that has no boundaries, the garden where the magic grew. She had no need to go there. Yet even now, as her senses captured the solid fragments all around her, she could still see the triangles of the carnation's scent, still taste the blue of the columbine.

"What kind of poem were you saying?"

"Oh, just an old one, not for little girls." Brenna stood and held out her hand while Phoebe climbed over the wall. "Did Mrs. Dinwittie walk you over?"

"She said I could go by myself. She watched me from the window."

"I see. Well, let's go inside. We have to get ready to climb the mountain to see Miss Amabelle. She's expecting us for lunch."

"Mrs. Din said the pretty man is gone."

Brenna forced down the lump in her throat. In barely two weeks' time he had unearthed not only her fears, but her legacy, and had dared her to face them both. "Yes. He's gone."

"But I liked him. He said I was pretty."

Brenna sat back down on the wall. Jake was gone. Logic told her she should feel relieved. Instead, she felt abandoned. She pulled Phoebe on her lap and gently brushed the powdery bits of stone and leaves from her hands. "I know what. I'll tell you your favorite story, the one about the goddess named Phoebe."

Phoebe sniffed and gazed at the ground, but said nothing.

"Once upon a time, in the old countries of East Anglia and Saule, the people believed that the sun was ruled by a beautiful goddess named Phoebe. She was a very special goddess because she could look at a person, and no matter how many masks he wore, Phoebe could see the man's true self. And Sunday, which is today, was Phoebe's favorite day."

"Why did the pretty man leave?"

It took a moment for Brenna to answer. "I guess he didn't find what he was looking for."

"What was he looking for?"

"A miracle."

Jake stared at the pint-sized mug filled with liquid the color of burnt copper. Easing the mug back to the bartender, he said, "I ordered a beer."

The bartender wiggled his pencil-thin mustache. "We at The Royal Crown Pub serve only ale. A hearty, flavorful brew. Nice and warm." He directed the mug back through the watery path on the dark counter. "Come, come, old chap. Let's give it a go, shall we?"

"No thanks." Jake rose and grabbed his hat. "I'll head over to the Longhorn. Play a few hands of poker and drink a beer, a *cold* beer, a *real* beer."

"I believe you mean the London."

"The saloon on the corner. Red awning."

"Quite right. The London. Two chess games nightly. Dart tournament every Saturday night. No poker. No beer." He positioned the pint of ale directly in front of Jake.

"The London." Jake let the implications sink in, then slapped two bits on the counter and sat back down. He sipped the ale and winced. "I thought things were bad in Coventry—"

"So you know about the competition for Lord Austin Halliwell's—"

"I know all about it."

"Is it true he fancies their druggist? We've been trying to get him interested in one of our fair damsels, but to no avail."

"Keep trying."

"Oh, we shall." The bartender's eyes sparkled. "We're taking other steps as well. A number of us have formed a lawn tennis club. We get together every morning before breakfast. Does Coventry have a club?"

"Beats me." Jake tried the ale again. "When was the last time this town saw a good medicine show?"

The bartender wiped the counter as he thought for a moment. "Good or bad, we haven't seen any entertainment in over a year, maybe two. Why?"

For the first time since arriving in Whitefish that afternoon, Jake smiled. "Because that, my good friend, is the reason I'm here. And come tomorrow night, I hope to educate and enlighten every man, woman, and child in this town."

"Delightful! What sort of acts do you have?"

"No acts. Nothing but the truth. You see, I plan to offer your neighbors the chance to purchase the original Clarion Compound, the elixir made by the one and only Cosmos Clarion himself."

"An elixir. Hmm. This show of yours, they have them in England, do they?"

"Not like mine."

Shaking his head, the bartender lowered his voice. "You might want to give away some crumpets with your elixir. Maybe a certificate for some fish and chips. We're serving them right here. Every night."

"I don't think so."

"I'd be willing to work with you on it. Split the cost. What do you say?"

"No. See, that just doesn't fit in with my plan."

"Then prepare yourself to face adversity."

"Why's that?"

"Well you see, the town is unlikely to support any endeavor not endorsed by Lord Austin Halliwell. And unless you can bring some English aspect to your performance, well . . ."

"What the hell is going on here?" Jake looked above the bar at the large portrait of Queen Victoria and the Union Jack next to the stars and stripes. "This isn't England. It's Montana, the state of Montana. Where's your state flag?"

"Yes, yes, I know. The flag is on order." The bartender looked around. "Please, sir, keep your voice down."

Jake stood and turned so he could address both the bartender and the crowd. He tugged on the points of his vest. "Monta na hasn't been a state for a whole year yet and you're already willing to sell her down the river for fish and chips and crumpets?" He noticed how many men hung their heads, diverting their eyes. "Where's your poker game, men? Where's your cold beer? Where's your baseball team?"

"Cricket," the bartender said. "You see, Lord Austin has asked that everyone learn to play. . . . " He stopped, nailed to the wall by Jake's stare.

"He's got you playing cricket?"

"Well, we're only just learning, but we do enjoy the game ever so much, don't we, gentlemen?"

Several of the men got up and headed for the door. The others turned away. Jake called out, "Gentlemen, wait. Look, I've traveled all over this great country. I know times are hard. I understand the need to survive. But please, don't sell your souls!" When no one spoke to protest, he added, "Come to my show tomorrow night. We'll talk about King Kelly and the Boston Beaneaters, and the Reserve Rule, and salary caps, and I guarantee you'll walk away feeling like the men you are, the American men you are."

One of the two customers at the door stopped and tipped his hat. "I'll be there."

"Me, too," said the other.

Several of the others nodded to Jake, indicating they'd be there. He could feel the fire build in his belly, but he stopped himself from saying any more, knowing that without a bottle of elixir in his hand to sell, he'd be wasting a good speech. Trouble was, when it came to the subject of baseball and America, Jake was speaking from the heart. A clash with Lord Austin Halliwell looked unavoidable. Good!

*   *   *

Most of the men who came to recuperate at Miss Amabelle Sweet's House of Recovery had come on the orders of their doctors back East. Though Brenna doubted the ability of fresh air to cure an invalid who had advanced to the final stages of consumption, she recognized her own financial stake in the perpetuation of the idea. She could see how physicians eager to establish a practice and land promoters eager to sell their land would also want the West portrayed as a place where the miracle cures were a daily occurrence. And people believed.

Brenna took Phoebe's hand in hers as they climbed the six wide steps of Amabelle's front porch. The first time Brenna had brought Phoebe with her, Phoebe had hidden her face in Brenna's skirt. Now and then one of the newcomers would stare or make some unkind comment to the men around him, as though neither Brenna nor Phoebe could hear, or if they could, it didn't matter. Most of the time the men, particularly the older ones, would simply smile and wave as they did now. Sometimes the younger ones would turn away, though Brenna suspected their reaction was more from their own self-consciousness over their shrunken forms and their spindly legs.

Brenna thought of Jake and his friend. From the day Jake first drove through town, she wanted him to keep moving, to leave and never come back. Now he had gone. She admonished herself for caring. It wasn't as though she had information to impart to him, or had left personal words unspoken. Yet she missed him. How foolish she had become.

The wide, double doors were propped open with black-brown barrels of vibrant red geraniums. Brenna and Phoebe stepped into the center hall, where the aromas of pot roast and buttermilk biscuits competed with that of bleach.

Phoebe giggled the moment she saw Amabelle hurrying toward them, her arms outstretched.

"How's my favorite visitor?" Amabelle said, bending over to enfold Phoebe in her arms.

Brenna had been concerned that her own damp spirits might affect Phoebe, but seeing her snuggle in Amabelle's warm embrace dispelled her worries. If only Brenna's disappointment could be mended as easily.

Amabelle ushered them into the front parlor, where a fleece rug anchored four heavy wooden rocking chairs and two matching sofas. Above a massive stone fireplace hung the mounted heads of bear, moose, buffalo, as well as the portrait of a hunter, his buckskin suit and rifle marking him a man of adventure.

"Tea and cookies?"

"I don't want to spoil her appetite," Brenna said, glancing at Phoebe, who was sitting on the rug, stroking the thick clumps of once-white fleece.

"Of course."

They sat and talked about everything from Amabelle's efforts to hire help, to Brenna's garden, to the upcoming Fourth of July celebration. All the while, Brenna couldn't help but notice the distracted look on her friend's face. "Amabelle, are you well?"

"In comparison to my guests, yes, quite well."

"But?"

The older woman hesitated, her eyes suddenly bright with unshed tears. When she spoke, her voice caught. "He's . . . he's dying." She grabbed a lace-edged handkerchief from her apron pocket and dabbed her eyes. "I've finally met the man of my dreams and he's . . . "

Phoebe looked up and tilted her head in puzzlement. "Who's dying?"

"Oh, dear," Amabelle said to Brenna. "Sometimes I forget that there's absolutely nothing wrong with the child's ears."

"I understand," Brenna said, then turned to Phoebe. "Miss Amabelle has a special friend and he's very sick."

"Why don't you make him get better?"

"I don't think I can."

Amabelle dabbed her eyes. "He coughs and I fear his bones will break." Her voice caught again. "He's so weak."

Amabelle stood, her hands clutched to her heart in a tight knot, the hope that whitened her knuckles not reaching her eyes. "You might be able to make him more comfortable. Yes?"

"I'll do whatever I can." She remembered her mother's words. *When the path of faith is not yet clear, they will take the path of desperation. But they will find you.*

Brenna reached for Phoebe's hand and the two of them followed Amabelle out of the parlor, down the central hall with its red Oriental runners and up the farthest set of stairs.

They followed the hacking sounds of a hollow cough and stopped outside the closed door of the room at the farthest end of the hall. Amabelle took a deep steadying breath, but Brenna saw no lessening of the anguish in her friend's eyes.

"His name is Mr. Belinus."

"And?" Brenna asked, accustomed to hearing at least a short synopsis of each guest's history. When Amabelle didn't answer, she prompted her. "Does he have family? Where's he from? His occupation?"

"Oh, dear." Amabelle glanced at the door with a questioning look. "Must you really know all those details? You see, Mr. Belinus has asked that I preserve his privacy and I would feel traitorous if I—"

"It's all right," Brenna said. "You don't have to say anything more. I'll talk with him and he can tell me as much as he wants to. Besides, I already know he's a fine and decent man. You wouldn't have given your heart to anyone less."

Clearly relieved, Amabelle said, "Remember when you told me that Beltane was a time for mystical unions? You know I can't profess to believe such notions, but it was the first of May when Mr. Belinus was brought to me, the very day. He was weak even then, but . . . well, you'll see for yourself. My only regret is that I didn't call you in sooner."

Belinus was the name of the ancient solar deity for whom Beltane was named. The coincidence made Brenna wary.

Amabelle placed her hand on the doorknob and knocked. "Yoo-hoo."

A man's voice, soft in its volume, shallow in its strength, echoed tenderness with his one-word reply. "Amabelle!"

Brenna followed her friend into the room. Much later she would recall the brilliant sunshine bathing the emaciated form of the man in the red flannel pajamas as he struggled to sit up and the scent of pine drifting through the white ruffled curtains. All she saw now was the distinguished face and the wild white hair of the man whose image identified the bottle of elixir she had held in her hand just that morning.

Cosmos Clarion.

Amabelle hurried to his bedside. "Mr. Belinus, I'd like you to meet my dear friend and Coventry's pharmacist, Miss Brenna McAuley."

"Aah," he said with a relaxing sigh. "My sincere pleasure, Miss McAuley." Slowly, he bowed his head in greeting, though his gaze never broke from hers, not for one second. "My fate has been placed in your hands. At last."

Vaguely aware that Amabelle was looking at her strangely, Brenna keenly felt a chill race down her spine. "Mr. Clarion."

"Oh, heavenly days!" Amabelle pressed her fingertips to her lips, the pink of her cheeks draining in an instant. "How did you know?" She turned to Cosmos. "I kept our secret! Truly!"

Cosmos reached for Amabelle's hand and kissed it, though his gaze still locked with Brenna's. "I know you did, my love."

"You're not angry?"

He drew her hand to his heart and spoke just above a whisper. "For bringing the key to our destiny? How could I be anything but grateful?"

Brenna fought the sensation that threatened to overtake her, that merging of mind and feeling that called her to a place of vastness and profound silence where every word had only a rhythm and even now the cadence of "destiny" vibrated in her bones.

The sudden feel of Phoebe's tug on her skirt broke the spell.

"Is he the one that's dying?" Phoebe asked.

Brenna drew Phoebe closer. "This is Miss Amabelle's friend."

"Her special friend?"

"Yes." Brenna saw the adoration that passed between Amabelle and Cosmos Clarion. So many things made sense now: the reason Jake insisted on staying in town and his anxiety over the health of his friend. The ache in her own heart eased a little as she realized the rest of the truth: Jake would have to come back.

Cosmos raked his fingers through his thin white hair and smiled with genuine warmth. "You'll forgive my appearance, won't you?"

Brenna nodded as she took in the dark circles under his eyes, the gray complexion, and the splatter of dried blood on the front of his pajamas.

Cosmos kissed Amabelle's hand again and said, "Do you mind giving us a few minutes alone, my dear? Your friend has come to perform her magic and I'm eager to begin."

"I'm a druggist," Brenna answered quickly.

Hurt filled Amabelle's eyes. "He only meant—"

"I know," Brenna said. "I'm sorry." Cosmos Clarion couldn't be blamed for believing she could heal him.

She gave Phoebe an added hug and said, "You go with Miss Amabelle now. I'm going to stay here and talk with Mr. . . . Belinus."

"Can I play bride?"

Amabelle bent forward, bringing them eye-to-eye. "Yes you can. And I have just the thing for you."

When they had gone, Brenna sat on the chair next to the bed. She didn't mean to stare, but the man on the bed was a skeleton of the man on the label of the Clarion Compound—sunken face and gaunt limbs instead of the full cheeks and robust countenance, wrinkled red pajamas instead of a dark suit with lapels embroidered with moons and stars. But the twinkle in his eyes was identical. She'd thought it merely an artist's rendition on the label, designed to make the man look trustworthy, a bit mysterious, and very compelling. But the illusion had not been created. It had been captured.

Brenna lowered her gaze to her tightly knotted

hands. "Why don't you tell me about yourself, Mr. Clarion. When did you experience the onset of symptoms?"

"I had the first dream when we were down in Beaverhead County—"

"Approximately how much weight have you lost since the symptoms first manifested?"

"Jake insisted we keep heading east. He wanted me to go to some sanitarium back there. I told him we had to head north."

"I need to know about your cough—its intensity and duration. The frequency of the night sweats. And your daily habits in eating and exercise, before as well as after the symptoms."

Cosmos eased himself on his side, making it difficult for Brenna not to look at him while he talked. "He still wants to bring me back East. But I told him I wouldn't go. Not after that second dream. No, sir."

"Are you able to sleep through the night?"

He thought a moment. "I can't say that I ever heard an actual voice. It was more a feeling. But the message was clear. I was supposed to come to Coventry."

"Mr. Clarion—"

"Coventry, Montana. That's where I would find the magic."

Brenna steepled her fingers in a semblance of prayer and made no attempt to hide her frustration. "I can't help you if you won't listen to me."

"I'm not the one who isn't listening."

She stood and walked to the window, feeling the need to put distance between them. "I am not the one who needs help."

"Forgive me, Miss McAuley, but I think you do. We both do."

She stiffened. She turned and stared at him, upset

by his ability to rattle her, and determined to take control of the situation. "I'm going back to my shop now. I'm going to prepare lozenges of licorice and opium. You can suck on them during the day to quiet the cough. A tincture of opium for nights—I assume that's when the cough is at its worst. I'll be back in a few hours. I'll also bring seltzer water for your stomach; Amabelle said you were having difficulty with digestion. Tomorrow I'll begin a wine of iron to strengthen your blood, though that will take a good ten days to concoct."

He held her gaze. "And the magic?"

"The only magic I deal in is the proven findings of medical science."

He opened his mouth to say something else, but just then Amabelle and Phoebe returned.

Phoebe went straight to the bed, dragging an old white curtain behind her. "Do you know any stories?"

Cosmos smiled. "Indeed, I do. Astounding stories of wild buffalo and giant eagles. Amazing stories of shooting comets and colliding stars. Would you like to hear one?"

Phoebe climbed on the foot of the bed. "Do any of them start with 'Once upon a time'? That's the kind I like."

"That's my favorite, too," he said and coughed a little, then a little more.

Brenna saw the plea for help on Amabelle's face. She came to the bed and held out her hand for Phoebe. "I think you had better let Mr. Belinus rest now."

"No," he said quickly. "I'm fine now. And I would so enjoy the company of a beautiful princess."

Phoebe giggled and bounced on the bed.

Brenna said to Amabelle, "I'm going to go back to the pharmacy for some cough syrup and throat lozenges. Will you keep an eye on Phoebe for me until I return? She's to stay with me for the night."

"Of course, dear. Don't worry about her. And thank you."

"Phoebe, I'll be back in a little while. Stay here with Miss Amabelle."

Her eyes still on Cosmos, Phoebe said, "All right."

Amabelle nodded to Brenna. "You go ahead. I'll stay right here."

"I'll hurry," Brenna said.

Cosmos smiled his thanks, then said to Phoebe, "I'll tell you a story and then you can tell me a story."

"I don't know any stories."

"Then you can sing me a song."

"Okay."

While Cosmos summoned Phoebe closer with "Once upon a time there was a beautiful princess," Brenna hurried out of the room.

The poor man lingered in the encroaching shadow of death. Brenna understood now why Jake had been so upset, so insistent on finding someone or something that would help his friend. The "friend" wasn't a young man back East with family and physicians. He was an old man right here at Brenna's back door, an old man who had no one but Jake.

She rushed into her pharmacy, welcomed by the ever-present clean fragrances of sandalwood and euca-lyptus, camphor and cloves. With equal relish, she inhaled the sharpness of sulfur and vinegar, as well as the ink she used to write instructions—a composite of smells that promised relief, a sacredness that assured her she had taken the right course in life.

Every time Brenna went to Amabelle's place, she saw men who prayed one way or the other that their broken lungs would mend. Jake's feelings of helplessness and rebellion were all too common against a hideous disease that showed no mercy to young or old, rich or poor.

Brenna slipped on her apron. Though her mission of the moment was to bring comfort to Cosmos Clarion, she couldn't deny wanting Jake to know that she was actively engaged in helping his friend. Nor could she deny the happiness she felt at knowing that Jake Darrow would be back.

Three hours later, her basket full of soothing remedies, she returned to Amabelle's House of Recovery, hurried past the parlor and down the hall with its red Oriental runners, up the farthest set of stairs, and along the narrow balcony.

The door to Cosmos's room was open. As Brenna approached, she could see Phoebe, Amabelle's old white curtain draped over her head. She had crawled closer to Cosmos, whose head and shoulders had sunk deep into the pillows piled behind him.

Brenna slowed her steps, not wanting to frighten Phoebe by bursting in on what looked to be a quiet, spellbound scene.

A few feet from the door, she saw Phoebe reach out and stroke Cosmos's hair. She saw Cosmos smile. "Now it's my turn," Phoebe said.

Standing in the doorway, Brenna's heart all but stopped as she heard Phoebe recite slowly and clearly, "Out of the marrow, out of the bone. Out of the marrow, out of the bone."

8

"Phoebe."

As calmly as she could with her heart racing in fear, Brenna walked toward the bed and took Phoebe's arm. "It's time to go now."

"Let me go," Phoebe yelled.

She loosened her hold, not realizing until then how tightly she had gripped Phoebe's arm. But if she had to pick up Phoebe and carry her out, she would. "We have to go now."

When they reached the hallway, Brenna closed the door behind them. She crouched down and took Phoebe's hands. "Now you listen to me carefully. I just spoke to Miss Amabelle. She's in the kitchen. You go there and you stay till I come for you. Do you understand?"

"But I want to play with Mr. Belinus and—"

"Not now. You go to the kitchen and stay with Miss Amabelle."

"But why?"

"Because I have to talk to Mr. Belinus alone."

Brenna gave Phoebe's hands a gentle squeeze as she told herself to calm down. "But first, I need to know something. Where did you hear those words?"

"What words?"

"The words . . . the words to the poem you were just reciting."

"You said them."

"No, no, no. Someone else must have said them. Think carefully. Who was it?"

"It was you. In your garden. I saw you. You had a little book in your hands and you said the words."

Brenna remembered. "The poem is supposed to be a secret. I should never have said it out loud myself."

"Who told it to you?"

"My mother. That's why it's so special to me. Do you understand?"

Phoebe nodded, her blue eyes wide with awe. She leaned close to Brenna's cheek and whispered, "Want me to blow it away?"

Brenna sighed with relief. "Oh yes, that's perfect. You can blow it away."

With a mischievous grin, Phoebe hunched her shoulders and drew her chin down to her chest. Cupping her small hands to her mouth, she whispered, "Out of the marrow, out of the bone. Out of the marrow, out of the bone." Then she snapped her hands together and brought them to her lips. She filled her cheeks with air. She blew on her hands—Poof!—opened them, and looked up at the ceiling. "All gone," she said with a big smile, then showed Brenna her palms as proof.

"Thank you, Phoebe. I feel better now. I want you to go down to the kitchen and stay with Miss Amabelle. I have to talk with Mr. Belinus."

Phoebe hesitated, then flung herself in Brenna's arms. "Do you still love me?"

"Of course, I still love you. I'll always love you." She relished the cuddly feel of Phoebe's small arms around her neck and the tight squeeze that said the child enjoyed the closeness too.

"All the way to China?" Phoebe whispered in Brenna's ear.

"All the way to China."

Phoebe pulled back. "I'm gonna go see Miss Amabelle now." And with that, she skipped down the hall.

Brenna stood and smoothed her skirt, trying to put her thoughts in order. She would rather face a grizzly bear than go back in that room. But if she didn't, if she pretended that nothing had happened, then she would have no one but herself to blame when Cosmos told Amabelle that her best friend could help him, but wouldn't. Because if what Jake said was true, that Cosmos knew about *brauche,* then he knew the significance of the words Phoebe had said.

Brenna knocked, waited for Cosmos to answer, then opened the door.

He didn't appear to have moved. He still sat upright in the bed, bolstered by mountains of white, downy pillows. His hair still looked as thin as straw and as wild as weeds. But his eyes sparkled, and his lips formed a shaky smile.

She picked up her basket from where she had left it by the door. "Look," she said as she came toward him, lifting one item at a time. "I've brought lozenges to ease your cough and seltzer for your stomach."

She placed the basket on the side of the bed and retrieved a small bottle. She unscrewed the mushroom cap and shook an opium and licorice lozenge into her palm. "Here," she said, handing it to him. "It will suppress your cough and allow you to rest."

He took the disc and placed it on his tongue. The

expectant smile never left his face. "That little girl, Phoebe. She's a delight."

Brenna never knew what to expect whenever someone talked about Phoebe. She felt her guard go up. "Yes, she is."

"Jake said he'd never seen one of her kind so talkative, so full of energy. He told me all about her."

"And since 'her kind' are always shuffled away to some asylum, how many children like Phoebe do you suppose Jake has ever seen?"

"Now, now, dear. Don't pull away like that. I know how much you love the child. Even if I hadn't seen it for myself, Jake told me."

"He did?"

"He told me how you let her help you in the shop, how you take her for walks in broad daylight, how you encourage her to do her best, how you hold her when she cries. He told me all about it."

Brenna had no idea Jake had noticed all that.

"Jake recognizes love for a child when he sees it," Cosmos added. "He spent a fair amount of his young life on an orphan train. He knows a lot about kids who aren't wanted for one reason or another."

"I didn't know."

"No reason you should. I'm just telling you now so maybe you'll understand him a little better."

Brenna sat on the chair next to the bed. "He told me his father had been killed at Gettysburg and that his mother had been committed to an asylum."

"He told you about his mother? I'm surprised. I thought I was the only person in the world who knew about her."

Brenna felt strangely privileged to know Jake had shared such private information with her. "He said he was five years old when she was committed. He didn't say anything about being put on an orphan train. I just assumed he was raised by relatives."

"No, nothing that homey."

"If you don't mind my asking, how did the two of you wind up together? I suppose Jake had his own show and the two of you joined forces."

Cosmos gazed into space for a moment. "We joined forces in Kansas City. I wasn't really looking to take on a partner, but I remember seeing a group of those kids all lined up at the train station. Each one carried a handbill that glorified all the education and training they had received. Some of those kids were only two years old." He shook his head sadly. "When I reached Jake, he stepped out of line, right in my path, and shoved that handbill in my face. I read it. I told him I couldn't afford him. He stuck his chin in the air and said he knew how to work in a mill or on a farm. When I said I traveled around a lot, he said he could collect rags or sell newspapers, but he didn't like to beg and he refused to steal. And then he added that he didn't eat much. He was barely eight years old."

Cosmos paused, his eyelids heavy. "I didn't mean to go on and on like that, but Jake . . . Jake is a good boy."

"When do you expect him back?"

"Oh, I'd guess a week or so."

Brenna stood and took each item from her basket and arranged it on the table next to the bed. "It's getting late. I need to get Phoebe and head back now. The medicine should allow you a good night's rest."

He looked up from his pillows and smiled. Now she knew where Jake had learned his charm. "Come early. That'll give us time to talk about the magic."

Brenna stiffened.

"I'm a druggist," she said.

"And a *brauchere*."

"No, I'm not."

He looked puzzled. "Out of the marrow. Out of the bone."

"I'm not a *brauchere*!"

"My own mother practiced the Old Magic. I've heard those words. I know—"

"I heal by following the proven findings of medical science."

He strained as he sat up in bed. "You are a *brauchere*. I know you are."

Memories made it difficult for Brenna to speak. So she stood there a moment, then finally said, "You're wrong."

Cosmos looked down at this chest, where the blood from an earlier coughing spell had dried. His labored breathing bore the strain of his words. "When Jake told me about you—a woman with pale green eyes . . . and then when he said you were a druggist . . . and then I had the dream. I thought for sure . . . "

"You made a mistake."

Slowly, he leaned back against the pillows. "Don't you believe in the Old Magic?"

"You don't understand. It's not that simple."

"The magic does run in your family, doesn't it?"

"Yes, but—"

He tried again to sit up, but collapsed. "Then help me understand! Why have you denied your legacy and with it my chance to live?"

"I'm doing the best I can!"

"Is it because I'm in love with Miss Amabelle? I am, you know. She's the finest woman I've ever met."

"No!" Remorse slowed her words. "Amabelle is my best friend. I want her to be happy. And I know . . . I know she loves you too."

"Then why won't you help me? Why won't you help us?"

Brenna sat back down. She stared at her hands, unable to keep them from trembling. "Yes, my mother had the gift in her hands. And her mother before her. But as happens from time to time, a weak link in the chain causes all to be lost." She blinked back the tears that filled her eyes. "In the eyes of my maternal ancestors, I am that weak link." She looked up at Cosmos. "If you do indeed know about the Old Magic, you know what that means."

The luster in his eyes dimmed as reality weighted his words. "The *brauchere* herself must believe she has the power. Or all is lost."

The sobering truth gave Brenna no pleasure. She reached for the bottle of lozenges on the dresser. "That's why I've turned to medical science. The ingredients are pure, the dosages measured."

"Playing it safe," he said.

They sat there for a few quiet moments. Finally, Cosmos spoke. "How old were you when you received the instruction?"

"Twelve."

"Hmm."

A few more quiet minutes passed, time for Brenna to remember in detail best forgotten her mother's death and burial, the baby's death and burial, and her own desperate need to run away. She had more time than she wanted to remember the loneliness that always followed her, and the fear that the pain itself was strong enough to kill her.

Cosmos held out his hand. She clasped it, clung to it as though it were a life preserver and she about to drown.

"Talk to me about it, Brenna dear," he said softly. "It might help."

She shook her head. "The past can't be changed."

"What about the future?"

"There have been many times I've wished for the healing power, never more so than now. Please know in your heart that if I had truly inherited my mother's legacy, I would perform the rituals for you." She slipped her hand from his and stood. The weight of her past pressed down on her shoulders. "But I did not inherit the legacy. Pretending won't make it so."

"Are you going to tell everyone about me now? That the robust Cosmos Clarion is nothing but a sick old man?"

"I don't see what purpose that would serve."

"Thank you, Brenna." His eyelids heavy, Cosmos leaned back and closed his eyes.

"I cure fits."

Jake gave the Whitefish crowd everything he had: the sketch of the beautiful young woman in her last days, the glowing endorsements—embellished considerably for this audience—even the jar of tapeworms. Under ordinary circumstances, he wouldn't have held his first show in a new town on Friday the thirteenth, but he wasn't operating under ordinary circumstances. Fortunately, everything had gone well. By the time he was ready to pack up for the evening, he had made enough money to pay Miss Sweet the next two months' rent, buy supplies, and splurge on a steak dinner for himself.

He had just locked the door to his wagon, when Sheriff Wagner, a man around Jake's age, and a lanky man in a fashionable gray suit and bowler hat stepped up to him.

"Evening, Sheriff," Jake said and nodded politely to the other man.

"Evening, Darrow."

"What can I do for you gentlemen?" He noticed that neither man smiled and that the sheriff looked more than a little uncomfortable. "I know, Sheriff. How about a free bottle of the Clarion Compound to go with the one you bought this evening? I know once you try it, you're going to wish you had more."

The tall man nudged the sheriff. "Go on, see to it."

Wagner cleared his throat. "Well, Mr. Darrow, the thing of it is, I need to see your permit."

"My permit for what?"

"For open-air peddling."

"I don't understand. I came through your town early last month and checked your local ordinances. You didn't require any kind of permit then."

The tall man spoke up. "We do now, my good man. This is a civilized community."

Jake studied the arched brows and pinched lips. "You must be Halliwell."

"I see you've heard of me."

"Ale, darts, the Union Jack, cricket? Yeah, I've heard of you."

"Shall I conclude from the curtness of your words that you disapprove of the improvements I've brought to this fair city?"

"I wouldn't call them improvements, not when you kill the character of the town in the process."

"Why, if I weren't a gentleman . . . "

"Go ahead, Halliwell. Spit it out. If you weren't a gentleman, you'd what? Take a crack at me? Or stomp your foot?"

Austin turned to Wagner. "Well?"

"Look, Darrow, I'm sorry. But the deal is you've got to have a permit to be a street vendor. That's the rule now."

"Okay, so I'll get a permit. First thing in the morning."

Austin snickered. "Sorry, my good man, but the

municipal offices aren't open for business on Saturday. You'll have to wait till Monday."

"Now wait a minute! Saturday is my busiest day. You can't do this to me."

Halliwell said to Wagner, "I presume you intend to levy a fine for today's activity, yes?"

"Oh yeah," Wagner said with little enthusiasm. "That'll be fifty dollars."

"Fifty dollars! What the hell's going on here? What is it, Sheriff? You like riding in that dandy's hip pocket?"

"I'm just trying to do my job."

"What's the fuss?" Austin said. "Surely a man as successful in business as you must have a superfluous fifty dollars floating around."

"I work hard for my money. I don't consider as much as one penny superfluous. But then I don't imagine you understand work." Jake turned to Wagner. "Can't we come to some kind of agreement here?"

"Sorry. It's pay the fifty dollars or spend the night in jail."

Jake threw up his arms. "Then lead me to the lock-up."

"Now, now," Austin said, picking an imaginary piece of lint from his sleeve, "I've no desire to be the cause of anyone being incarcerated and certainly not for the lack of a selling permit. I'm simply doing my part to bring civility to this frontier wayside."

"That's bloody generous of you, but I don't need your favors."

Austin glared at Jake, then said to Wagner, "My fiancée, Miss Brenna McAuley of Coventry, has had professional dealings with this man. She had nothing good to say about him."

Jake glowered. "Your fiancée? Since when?"

"My personal affairs are none of your concern, Darrow. Good evening, Sheriff. I believe I'm expected at The Royal Crown about now. Chess, you know."

"That woman's too smart to marry you."

"I beg your pardon."

"You heard me."

"And just what do you think she would find objectionable? My vast fortune? My sterling lineage? What, pray tell?"

"Your pompous attitude."

Austin chuckled. "Most of the time I find the brashness you Americans display so freely to be rather refreshing. But you, sir, are simply impertinent." He nodded to Wagner. "As I said, I've no wish to have the man jailed. Simply regulated."

Wagner looked pained. "Yeah, but we've got this law on the books now and it's my duty to uphold it." He gestured for Jake to proceed him. "After you."

"Let's not be hasty," Austin said, reaching into his pocket. He pulled out a jeweled money clip and from it slipped several bills and handed them to the sheriff. "There. Now no law has been broken."

"Now wait just a minute," Jake called out to Austin, who was walking away. "I don't want you paying my fine!"

Austin turned around and arched his brow. "I rather like the idea of having you indebted to me."

"I'm not indebted to you. Do you hear me?"

Austin kept on walking. Jake turned to the sheriff. "Give him his money back. I want to spend the night in jail."

"Sorry. Fine's been paid. You're free to go."

Jake knew what he ought to do. Swallow his pride and thank Lord Austin Halliwell for his generosity. But he couldn't bring himself to do it.

The following morning, Jake was all ready to leave town when he saw the bartender from The Royal Crown Pub scurrying along the street. The man had pulled his socks up over his pants, giving them the look of knickers. He wore a small plaid cap and carried a wide, long-handled paddle. "Hey!" Jake called to the man. "Where are you headed?"

"Cricket! Care to join me? All the regular blokes will be there. You'll have a jolly time."

"Will Halliwell be there?"

"Absolutely!"

Jake considered his options. Leave with his money in his pocket but his tail between his legs, forever in Halliwell's debt. Or have one more go at the insufferable bastard—just for the hell of it. Jake had no personal loyalty to either Whitefish or Coventry. He just couldn't stomach the way Halliwell pushed people around. What on earth did Brenna McAuley see in that man?

"Wait up," Jake called to the bartender. "By the way, what's your name?"

"Ted."

A few minutes later, Jake and Ted arrived at an open field behind the school. The men, all with their socks pulled up over their pants, were gathered around Austin.

"The point of the game," Austin said, "is to make the most runs. The party which makes the most runs wins the day. Now, to accomplish that end, you are to deflect all balls bowled toward your wicket and, most importantly, do so gracefully and in good form."

Jake noticed that one of the men raised his paddle the way a baseball player would hold a bat. "No, no, no," Austin said, clearly annoyed. "Hold it down. Cricket is not a game of wild slugging."

Austin pointed to a nearby chair. "The umpire will sit over here and maintain total tranquillity of mind as he observes the proceedings. If he determines your hit to be worthy, he may accord you not one but several runs, though you don't actually have to leave your post. You simply stay where you are and maintain good form."

Jake let out an admiring whistle as he approached.

Austin stiffened, then turned around. "Well, well," he said, "Does your presence indicate a decision to stay in this fair town?"

"No, I'm leaving. But I heard about what you'd done to these fine men—these fine *American* men, and I had to see it for myself." Jake noticed several men lower their gaze. "What's the matter, fellas, your bloomers pinch?"

Austin marched over to Jake. "I take it you do not approve of the sport of cricket."

"What I don't approve of is your forcing these men to play."

"Force?" Austin laughed. "These are grown men with minds of their own. I'm flattered to be credited with such influence, but please, Mr. Darrow, your assessment does not match the reality." He gestured to the men around him. "Go ahead, gentlemen, tell Mr. Darrow here why you've elected to learn the game of cricket."

Ted waved his hand. "To give us culture."

"And there you have it," Austin said.

"Now tell the truth, Ted. Why is it you have to have this particular kind of culture? This English kind of culture?"

"So Lord Austin will pick Whitefish as the site of his syndicate."

"And if Halliwell had never come to Whitefish . . .

what would you men be doing out here on this field on a beautiful day like this?"

"Why, we'd be playing baseball."

"Theodore!" Austin blanched.

"Well, it's the truth," Ted said, looking around for a show of support. "Everybody knows that."

"I rest my case," Jake said.

"Well, I must say, this revelation has caught me quite by surprise." Austin turned to the men around him. "And here all this time I assumed your collective interest was sincere."

"But it is," Ted said. "We really do want you to pick Whitefish."

"I simply don't know how I can, now that I know your pursuit of culture is nothing but a sham."

Ted gasped. "Does that mean you're picking Coventry?"

"I intend to take another look at their efforts to instill culture and refinement in their fair town."

Jake made no attempt to hide his grin. "Don't count on getting up a game of cricket over there. I've put together a pretty good baseball team."

"You? Forgive my bluntness, but you're a cripple."

"That's right," Jake said, forcing down the sudden bitterness Austin's words evoked. "I even manage to play now and then."

"I meant no offense," Austin said. "In the game of cricket your handicap would pose little or no problem, but it was my understanding that to play the game of baseball, one had to run."

Shut up and walk away. Jake knew that's what he should do. Just shut up and walk away. Instead, he stood there, letting the sting of Austin's words fan the anger that had been smoldering inside for years. "Your understanding of the game is correct." He looked at the men standing around. "Why don't you have Ted and the boys here show you how to play baseball and we'll have us a game. Coventry against Whitefish."

"Are you saying you'll actually play?"

"I will, if you will. We can play for that fifty dollars you put up last night."

Austin was silent.

"Give it a go, sir," Ted said.

"Yeah," one of the other men said. "We can take Coventry blindfolded."

"What's the matter?" Jake said. "Afraid of a cripple?"

"Heavens no. I'm merely contemplating how we might make this little challenge more interesting. A more substantial wager perhaps?"

Jake slipped his hand in his pocket, assuring himself that the money—one hundred and twenty dollars—was still there.

"Yes," Austin added. "I think a substantial wager might add just the desired element of risk. What do you say, Darrow? Two hundred dollars? Or is that too rich for your blood?"

Two hundred dollars? There was no way Jake would let Halliwell see the anxiety he felt. Two hundred dollars? That was four months' care for Cosmos. It was two hundred bottles of elixir. "Two hundred it is," Jake said. "We'll play in Coventry. The last Saturday in August. That'll give you two and a half months to practice."

"Fair enough."

Jake extended his hand. Austin accepted, surprising Jake by the firmness of his grip.

9

Jake parked his wagon at the end of Main Street and walked up the foothills to Miss Amabelle's place. Aromas of roast chicken and rosemary wafted from the open doors as he climbed the wide front steps.

One of several pitifully thin men, all wrapped up in heavy wool shawls, a lap blanket across his knees, called from his rocker. "Just in time for supper, Darrow. As usual. Come on over. We're playing a new tune on the music box." He spit into one of several brass spittoons lined along the porch. The man next to him immediately spit into the same receptacle. "Did you recognize it? That was 'Nearer My God To Thee.'"

"No. Can't say as I did. But I'm glad to see you gentlemen in such fine form this evening."

"They hauled Webley Heller away in a pine box a few hours ago. He won't be needing any more of your miracle cure."

"I see." Jake knew the man meant no offense. Humor was his way of coping with the curse of being forced to plan as though he had a future when he knew he, or either of the men sitting next to him, could die at any time.

"Yep," another man said. "But now we've got us an extry rocker. Think you could get your friend Belinus to join us? I hear he's quite the storyteller."

"That he is. I'll pass along the invitation. I'm sure if he's up to it, he'd love to join you." Jake couldn't wait to see Cosmos. He left the men on the porch, hurried down the hall and took the stairs two at a time, relieved that it hadn't been Cosmos who had died that afternoon.

Amabelle Sweet was pulling the door to Cosmos's room shut just as Jake approached.

"Oh, Jake," she said, folding her hands together and drawing them to her heart. "I'm so glad you're here."

"What is it? Has something happened? Is he all right?"

"For the moment, yes. But—"

"What is it?"

Her voice quivered. "He has lost all hope."

Jake reached for the doorknob. "You go on. I'll take care of him."

"I'm afraid to leave him alone, but I have other patients to care for and—"

"You don't have to explain. I understand. I'll stay with him tonight. I'll bunk right on the floor."

Amabelle looked relieved. "I'll bring you several quilts and a pillow. And what about supper? Have you eaten? I have plenty."

"Ma'am, I'd never turn down your cooking."

Amabelle grinned, even as sadness filled her eyes. "I'll be back," she said, patting him on the arm.

Jake composed himself as he watched her scurry down the hall, to all the other men who were watching each other and waiting to see who would be carried out next.

The door creaked as he opened it.

Amabelle had turned the lamp down low. Ghostly shadows played down the walls and across the floor, drawing Jake's attention to the bed. Cosmos turned toward him. What little vigor he had managed to hold on to was now gone.

Jake took his time walking across the room, not because he wasn't eager to see the man he thought of as his father, but because he didn't know what to say.

"Come closer, son. I've missed you."

Jake rushed over. "I've missed you too, old man." He grabbed the chair and pulled it as close to the bed as he could, then sat down and reached for Cosmos's hand. It felt as limp as a rag.

"Whitefish was a success. I made enough to settle up with Miss Sweet, and then some. Here, look." He reached into his pocket, pulled out the wad of bills, then shoved it back when Cosmos didn't react. "I also got an idea for a new elixir. We'll use tea as a base and flavor it with raspberry or peach or any number of other fruits. I think people will go for it. Oh, and I've got to tell you about Halliwell and about the baseball game—" He caught himself and faced the fear that had gripped him since he walked up the front steps. "Hey, what's this? You getting allergies or something?" He grabbed a handkerchief from his hip pocket and dabbed Cosmos's cheek, blotting the first of several tears. "Hey, come on now . . . "

Jake looked around for something, anything, that would bring relief to Cosmos's failing body as well as to Jake's aching heart. He reached for the edge of the quilt and pulled it up, tucking the edges around Cosmos's shoulders. "There," he said, smoothing the hem again and again. "You warmer now? It gets so damn cold at night."

"Son . . . son, there's no magic here. I was wrong."

"Now, wait a minute," Jake said, raking his fingers through his hair, trying to sort his thoughts. He was about to say how happy he was to have Cosmos come to his senses, but he couldn't. Seeing the old man like this made him realize how powerful the mere belief in the magic had been. If Cosmos needed magic, Jake would find it. Hell, if Cosmos had said he needed an elephant to get well, Jake would find one.

"What about Brenna McAuley?" Jake asked. "The whole time I was in Whitefish I was thinking of how to get into that back room of hers—you remember, to find out if she has a moon chart."

Cosmos shook his head. "No use."

"But your dream . . . you were so sure."

"I was wrong."

Jake slapped his palms against his thighs, needing to feel something other than helplessness. "What the hell happened here while I was gone?"

"Look on the table."

Jake glanced at the heavy oak table next to the bed and the bottles of medicine. He picked one up and read the label. "She was here?"

Cosmos nodded and forced a smile. "Recognized me in spite of . . . in spite of everything."

"Oh, no."

"It's all right. She won't say anything."

Jake scoffed. "Somehow I doubt that." He dragged his fingers through his hair again. "So fill in the blanks for me. She came here. She recognized you. She brought you some medicine. And then you decide the whole reason we've stayed in this town is no longer valid. What am I missing?"

"She's not a *brauchere*. We talked about it."

"Just like that?"

"Not exactly, but, well, what difference does it make? She doesn't practice the Old Magic. Her mother did. Her grandmother, too, and on down the line. But she insists the gift stopped with her mother. She can't help me."

Jake stood and paced the floor. "She can't, or she won't? Maybe what she needs is a financial incentive—"

"No. You don't understand. She won't perform the magic because she doesn't believe she can. And if she doesn't believe, well, it's no use."

"So what does that mean? You're just going to give up and die? Just like that?" He stared at Cosmos, knowing there was no justification for his anger, feeling it all the same. "Maybe she never was the one we were looking for. Maybe there's someone else around here—"

"There's no one else."

"Listen to you! Since I was eight years old you've been telling me that a man succeeds by the power of his vision, that whether he's a farmer or a factory worker, it's his bravery . . . it's how he looks at his own future . . . that's what makes him rise to the top."

"I know, son, but—"

"No! I don't want to hear your excuses. I can tell what your vision is. You're seeing yourself being carried out of here in a pine box and leaving me to—" He turned away, the words and the image they evoked choking him.

"Jake, come sit down. Listen to me."

His feet felt like lead as he walked over to the bed and sat down. Calmer now, Jake said, "Sorry."

"I don't like this any more than you do, but I know I don't have much time and there are things I need to do. First, there's that insurance policy. Two thousand dollars. It all goes to you. The paperwork is in the wagon, in the metal box."

Jake nodded.

"Livia's wedding ring is in there too. I'd like you to give it to Amabelle for me. I've grown fond of her. You know that."

Jake nodded again.

"See that meadow out there?" He directed Jake's view to the window and a sea of green-gold grass dotted with white daisies. "I want to be buried out there."

"That's enough," Jake said and stood again. "Why don't I just go into town and have a few coffins brought to your room. You can try them on for size. What do you plan on wearing? Your fancy white shirt with the pleated front?"

"Please, Jake. I know you're angry."

"You don't know shit! I go away for a few days and come back with money in my pockets, a great idea for a new elixir—one that could make us more money than we ever dreamed of. I even challenged Halliwell to a baseball game—and made a two-hundred-dollar wager. Did you hear me? A two-hundred-dollar wager. Because I know I can win. I know it. Of course, you won't be around to see the game. You'll be out there in the meadow, six feet under. 'Cause that's where you *want* to be."

This time Cosmos said nothing.

"I'm going into town for a while," Jake said. "I'll be back later." He slammed the door behind him.

It was the second of the moonless nights.

Cloaked in cold, thin darkness, Brenna knelt amidst the herbs and flowers she had planted last year, some the year before. Each fall the perennials passed through the corridor of death—their leaves turning dry, their branches brittle, color bleeding from their blossoms— only to rest, to gather strength, to be reborn.

Each new plant, daughter of the one before, would have to push against the hardness of the earth, would have to struggle to reach the place of light. But when it did, it would achieve its purpose and thrive.

Brenna inhaled. The earth's aroma, redolent with expectancy, usually soothed her troubled thoughts, but not tonight. She had only a vague awareness of the crisp, thin fragrance of sage stirred by her hand, the dense velvet of deep green moss, and the damp cold seeping through her skirt. Her thoughts were with Cosmos Clarion.

She had gone to see him every one of the last three days. He answered her questions about the weight he had lost, the severity and duration of his cough, the night sweats. He no longer mentioned the Old Magic. He no longer smiled.

She raised her eyes to the ink-black sky and opened her heart to things unseen. During the dark nights of the balsamic phase, the wisdom of the entire lunar cycle gathered together, unified with one focus: to embrace the destruction and death of the old, knowing it signaled the imminent renewal of life. Cosmos was dying.

When she finally stood, her legs were stiff, her skirt damp and stained. Rather than disturbing her, these markings of the passage of time assured her that she could still travel to that place of stillness and contemplation.

She looked up. In the dark of night she would never have known there was a thick bank of clouds moving swiftly across the sky—except for the intermittent twinkling of a star. She whispered her gratitude and went inside, praying that someday she would find the peace that eluded her.

First thing tomorrow, she would write a letter to the

dean of the Louisville School of Pharmacy for Women and ask if there had been any new developments in medicine or treatment for consumption. There had to be something more she could do for Cosmos Clarion, for Amabelle, for Jake.

Jake had to be suffering. The anguish of being unable to help a loved one weighted down the heart with rocks that might become less of a burden to carry in years to come, but would never fall away. Despite his swagger and seductive promises, she felt compassion for him, knowing the loss he faced.

Two hours later, her skin still moist from a hot bath, her hair loose about her shoulders, Brenna gathered her threadbare gown of cotton lawn around herself to keep from tripping and climbed between the cold sheets. The heat of her body spun a warm cocoon. She curled up and closed her eyes.

The pounding woke her up.

"Just a minute," she called out as she threw back the quilt and grabbed her robe. The Pensak baby wasn't due for months. Mr. Dobitsky was recovering nicely from the fever. Maybe it was someone from Amabelle's. Oh God! Maybe it was Cosmos!

Brenna knotted the sash of her robe as she ran barefoot into the pharmacy and yanked open the door. "Jake!"

He stood there with his hair disheveled, unshaven, his eyes red and puffy, looking every bit as lost and lonely as she had imagined he would.

She stepped back, encouraging him to come in. "Is Cosmos all right? Has something happened?"

His voice was strained. "You know, don't you?"

"Yes." That Mr. Belinus is none other than Cosmos Clarion? Yes. That Jake had no one else in the world? Yes.

Brenna turned up the lamp. "I saw him earlier today," she said, suddenly aware that he was looking at her strangely. She pulled the lapels of her robe closer together and held them with her hand. "He was resting comfortably. Has something happened?"

Jake turned his attention to the items on the shelf, leaving Brenna to wonder if he had recognized her discomfort. "He's not dead yet, if that's what you mean." He raked his hand through his hair, paused, and turned to face her. "Look, I'm sorry. I didn't mean to snap like that."

"It's all right. I know this can't be easy for you."

"He's got one foot in the grave and he's acting like he can't wait to jump in."

Brenna watched as he paced, as he looked up at nothing in particular and shook his head. There were no words that would make his ordeal any easier. She knew that. Yet she wanted so much to do something to ease the pain she saw in his eyes.

"Look," he said, as though he had been grappling with a problem and had finally come to a conclusion, "I know all about the conversation you had with him, all about the magic. He says you won't do it."

"He's right." Wanting to offer an alternative, she looked over her shoulder at the shelves of patent medicines and raw ingredients. And away from the herb chest with its small drawers and porcelain knobs, the one slender white ribbon circling the knob that marked the arrival of tomorrow's new moon. "Tomorrow I'm going to write to the school of pharmacy where I graduated. I'm going to ask them to tell me of any new developments in the treatment of consumption. Perhaps there's been some new discovery."

"Look," he said, pulling a handful of dollars from his

pocket. "I made a lot of money in Whitefish—a lot of money. I'll pay you to do those rituals. I'll pay whatever you want." He looked like a boy standing on a street corner hawking newspapers or selling apples, begging someone to take what he had to offer.

"You don't understand," Brenna said, emphasizing her words. "I can't perform the rituals."

"But we came all this way."

"I'm sorry—"

He shoved the money back into his pocket and took several quick steps toward her. "You're the only reason we're in this town. I wanted to take him back East, but he wouldn't go. Now he's too sick."

He stopped abruptly, leaving Brenna with the feeling that if he had come closer, he would have grabbed her shoulders in an effort to shake some sense into her. Despite the intensity of his growing frustration, she didn't feel the least bit afraid, knowing it was love for Cosmos that moved him.

"Don't you think I would help you if I could?" she said. "But what you're asking is impossible."

"No! It's not impossible. I know you don't believe in miracles, but all you have to do is tell him you can work the magic and he'll believe you. And if he believes he'll get better, he will get better. Don't you see?"

His eyes beseeched her for help. "Do you have any idea what kind of a life that old man has had? His wife died in childbirth the year they were married. His son died, too. The loss all but killed him. He sold everything but his memories—he tried to drown those in whiskey. Then he bought that medicine wagon and just headed down the road. He's crisscrossed the country I don't know how many times, giving away half of everything he's made. He's a sucker for a sob story. Always has been."

"But didn't he tell you that I'm not a *brauchere*, that whether or not I want to perform the rituals, I can't?"

"Yeah, he told me. But, you see, he took me in when I was having some hard times. I owe him." He sniffed and wiped his eyes with the back of his hand. "And I love him."

He turned away.

"Don't be embarrassed by your sentiment," Brenna said. "The language of love is one too rarely spoken." She didn't stop to think about where her actions might lead. She simply followed her heart and went to him.

She placed a hand on his shoulder and looked into his eyes. "Love makes the bearer vulnerable." She was not surprised when touching him freed a powerful longing in her soul. "And yet, that's where its greatest power lies." The intensity in his eyes inspired her to raise her hand to his face, to trace the outline of his mouth and linger on his lips. For she'd known all along that, despite her fears and misgivings, her destiny was in some way linked with this man.

She closed her eyes and felt the slight trembling of his hand as it lightly stroked her hair, the gentle pull as he cupped her heavy tresses and let them slip through his fingers. Her own hands descended slowly to his chest, relishing the texture of his shirt and the warmth of his skin.

Smoothing her hair from her face, he said in a thick voice that betrayed the hunger of a healthy man, "Your fiancé wouldn't approve of this."

"Who?"

"Halliwell." Ever so lightly, he touched his lips to her forehead. "I ran into him in Whitefish. He called you his fiancée." Again he kissed her forehead, then her eyelid and cheek.

"Mmm." She savored the feeling. "I don't know why he would say that. We've never discussed marriage."

"You haven't?"

"No."

"Good."

Eyes closed, she felt him smile. She also heard his intake of breath and sensed the air around them change. She tilted her head to welcome his lips.

There was no pressure at first, merely the delicate sensation of soft skin and the faint smell of whiskey and worry. But as his arms enfolded her, drawing her deeper into his embrace, the tenderness of his kiss gave way to the desperation she knew he felt. She responded with equal intensity, parting her lips, inviting him to take whatever comfort the moment could give.

As though in the throes of exquisite torment, he kissed her with a desire that threatened to take her breath away. A rush of intense, luxurious heat warned her that the hunger in this prelude to mating would not be satisfied easily—her hunger as well as his. She pressed her hands to his chest, seeking the space of a second thought. He offered no relief, however, and instead, tightened his embrace and plundered her mouth with his tongue.

He slipped one hand between the crush of their bodies and loosened the knot of her robe. Concern over what she should do and what she wanted to do mounted as he used both hands to ease the cloth from her shoulders, both hands to smooth the paper-thin fabric of her gown across her breasts.

"Jake . . ."

She was surprised by the husky sound of her voice, and the primitive desire that kept her from moving away. She felt the arousal of her nipples first against his palms, then as his fingers emphasized the hardened buds through the gown she wished would disappear, and, finally, as he lowered his head to draw both fabric and flesh to his mouth.

"Jake . . . "

The movement of his tongue and the warmth of his breath moistened the cloth, leaving her vulnerable to the chill in the air and grateful for his heat. She could no more fight the pull of his mouth on her breast than she could the pull of the moon on the tides. Nor did she want to. Instead, she ran her hands along his shoulders and nape, into his hair, and pressed him deeper to her bosom. Then the reality of where such passion could lead hit her.

"Jake, no."

She was disappointed by the sudden cessation of the tempest that still managed to charge the air around them, though she quickly gathered her senses and took a step back.

If his appearance mirrored her own, then she understood the arousal that darkened his eyes. His skin was flushed. His lips lustrous and swollen. His arms were still eager to claim her again.

"I'm not sorry," he said.

She managed a hesitant smile as she rearranged her robe and knotted the sash. "I wasn't asking you to apologize."

"No?"

"No. Just to give me time."

He took her hands and drew them to his lips. He kissed them with the tender kind of pressure that speaks of gratitude and asks for understanding. Giving them one last gentle squeeze, he let them go. "I know I shouldn't have come here tonight, but I couldn't stay away."

She could hear the strings of his heart pull taut

again, holding emotions at bay. "You don't have to
explain."

"Yeah, well, I'd better go. Not that I want to."

"Yes," she said, already feeling the emptiness. "Not
that I want you to."

He smiled. "A few weeks ago I would never have
thought this was possible."

"This?"

A seductive gaze darkened his eyes as he laid his finger against her lower lip. "This."

The invitation floated on the gentle breeze of his
warm breath. Eager to accept, she returned to his arms.
She had thought the springs of life had passed her by,
to be enjoyed only by those whose souls were not
encumbered by the heaviest debt of guilt. Yet here she
was, her heart awakening to the kiss of a man she had
met in her dreams.

Even as he cradled her in a soft, loving embrace,
she knew all was not as it should be. There were
issues of Jake's elixir and her treatment of Cosmos to
be discussed. But the transformation between a man
and a woman, those changes that implied a willing-
ness to explore the next step, those changes had to
start somewhere, didn't they? And if both the man
and the woman wanted to see the feelings they shared
flower, then each would bring trust to their embrace.
Brenna didn't know if such feelings mattered to Jake,
but she recognized the knot of anxiety as she admitted
just how much they mattered to her.

Brenna felt unsure of her world as he stepped back.

"I had really better go now," he said. "I was knocking loud enough to wake the dead, or at least your
neighbors. It wouldn't look good . . . well, you know."

"Of course." With the windows closed against the
cool night air and space enough for a small garden

between each building, it was doubtful her neighbors to the left or right could have heard Jake's knock. She didn't know if Jake realized that, but she appreciated his concern. She walked with him to the door.

He lingered. "Hey, I'll fix that glass cabinet for you, if you want. I'm pretty handy."

"The cabinet?"

"The glass. It's cracked. I noticed it the other day."

"You did?" Brenna didn't want to be suspicious, but she couldn't help but wonder what else he had noticed.

"Yeah. How 'bout it?"

"Thank you, but I can't afford—"

"I'm offering to do it for free, except for the materials. It's usually the labor that's expensive."

Brenna couldn't help but think how nice it would be to get a few repairs made. Jake was right. The expense was in the labor, not the materials. She could afford a pane of glass.

"I've got time on my hands right now," he said. "I like to keep busy. I can't put on a show every night of the week. Folks will get bored."

She couldn't imagine anyone getting bored with him.

"You need to have the work done," he continued as he glanced around. "I could reinforce those shelves too." He shrugged his shoulders. "So, what do you say?"

She tucked one hand tight to her waist and with the other clasped the lapels of her robe. So much felt at stake. "I could fix dinner for you."

He grinned. "Are you as good a cook as Amabelle Sweet?"

"No."

"Doesn't matter. I'll be here with my tool box first thing in the morning."

"In the morning? I don't mean to sound ungrateful, but with customers around, the interruption . . . "

"You're right. I hadn't thought of that. How about tomorrow afternoon instead? Late. You can feed me some supper and then I'll get to work. What do you think?"

Brenna envisioned her white damask tablecloth, a vase of daisies, lamb chops, asparagus, and new potatoes. And Jake Darrow sitting across the table from her. "That would be fine."

"In the meantime," he said casually, but with eyes filled with concern, "if you think of anything else that might help Cosmos—"

She placed a reassuring touch on his arm. "I'll do everything I can."

He nodded, then stepped outside, pulling the door closed behind him.

Brenna turned down the lamp and headed toward her room. She had been kissed before, but not like that. Much as she longed for the experience again, she knew it came with a price. Someday soon, Jake would leave Coventry, with or without Cosmos. His talk of staying was merely a cover.

She stopped at the herb chest and let the slender satin ribbon slip through her fingers. How could she explain to Jake what she couldn't explain to herself— that she couldn't simply give up what she now called a meaningless habit, this charting of the moon, what she had told herself in school was nothing but an old custom, but what she remembered all too vividly as part of a serious ritual?

10

Jake still filled Brenna's dreams. He still moved in dark shadows, slowly, the intricately flowered bridal veil draped across one arm. The determined look in his eyes still made her feel wary, but this time his expression was softened by the hint of a smile. He still held the pitted brass key in the palm of his outstretched hand. But this time, rather than recoiling in fear, Brenna stood her ground, examining the key from a distance.

A lacy pattern, worn smooth from handling, adorned its bow. The blade was unusually long. The tip formed a clover leaf. The effect was of something both solid and delicate, simple, age-old, and intimate. This time her sleeping body responded not with a pounding heart, but with tears coaxed from a bottomless well.

On waking, she felt only caution, as though forces unseen had removed a roadblock, freeing her to choose whether or not to take the key and journey farther down an unmarked path. Along with caution came the new notion that the key was to unlock her heart.

The implications of such thinking unsettled her as she lit the day's white candle and proceeded with her routine. In what way could her heart possibly be locked? She expressed her opinions openly. She had friends in the community and participated in church socials and barn-raisings, either alone or with Amabelle. She had the opportunity to have a man accompany her. Why, in the three years she had lived in Coventry, several men had shown more than a passing interest. She just never encouraged them.

Even Austin understood that her fondness for him stemmed from her love for Phoebe, not for him.

When she was in school, she had studied in earnest, knowing that upon graduation she would have to face the stark choice of marriage and domesticity or a career and independence. Her choice had been an easy one. Yet sometimes on cold winter nights, when the heat of her body barely warmed one small space in her bed, she admitted a longing to share her life with someone, a need to care for another, and a fear of growing old alone.

No, Brenna had never considered her heart locked.

Embracing the thoughts of Jake that settled in the back of her mind, Brenna went about her business. The first thing she did was telegraph a message to her alma mater asking for information on the treatment of consumption. Any new fact, no matter how small, could be important. She came back to the shop feeling satisfied that she was taking action and looking forward to telling Jake.

Her next task was to prepare a good blood builder. She cut four ounces of iron wire, placed it in an open glass beaker and sprinkled it with wine. In a few days the metal would rust and she would have the beginnings for a strong wine of iron tonic, known to improve the blood. That, too, helped to satisfy her need to do all she could for the man Jake loved like a father.

It did not escape her that every facet of her day connected in some way to Jake. She glanced at the tall clock in the corner, just as she had done throughout the day, and thought of him again. He was coming to dinner. He would kiss her again. She knew it.

Even if she had had the time to change, she wouldn't have done so. Her Sunday best would have blatantly shown her eagerness to be with him, and with everything so new between them, it wouldn't be wise to reveal her feelings, not when they were so new to her. Instead, she greeted him at the door, wearing her customary tan work dress and black apron. She had, however, dabbed a little rose water behind her ears and checked her hair in the window's reflection a dozen times.

He stepped inside and set a divided wooden tray of tools on the floor beside the glass-topped display case. "How's business?"

"The same. How's Cosmos?"

"He had a decent night's rest for a change. Thanks to you."

"That's the cough syrup. I'm glad it's helping." She pointed to the back counter. "I'm concocting a batch of iron wine for him. It should improve his blood."

"Good." He concentrated on the glass-topped case, leaving Brenna to guess his thoughts.

"It'll give him more energy too. But it won't be ready for another ten days."

"Ten days?"

The disappointment in his voice was evident. Quickly, she added, "I've telegraphed my college for any new scientific developments. Consumption is the modern plague. I'm certain the medical community is studying it."

He seemed to consider her news, then said, "I'll tell him when I see him tonight. I know he'll appreciate the effort. I sure do."

His gratitude was hardly the first she had ever received from a customer, yet it was somehow sweeter. Unsettled by the rising emotion that came in its wake, she found it impossible to look at him without either sensing his pain or remembering his kiss. She couldn't remember the feel of his lips on hers without wanting to experience it again.

He rummaged around in his tool box. "Helping people is important to you, isn't it?" he said.

"Of course. I just wish I could do more, especially at a time like this."

A time like this. June was the time of the year when the world opened to let in the sun, to cast its long-awaited light on the inner realms. Only a few hours from now, the sliver of a new moon would mark the night.

If a *brauchere* were to perform any of the healing rituals, they would have to be done during the next two weeks. Once the moon grew to its full size, it would hold the balance of power in the fight against disease—until it died again.

A time like this. Brenna readied herself for another challenge to her claim that she couldn't perform the Old Magic, but thankfully it never came. Instead, Jake took a folding, wooden measuring device from the tray and set it on the case.

"This will be easy enough to fix," he said, "but I've got to get the right size glass. In the meantime, I'll get that cracked pane out of there. Some kid leans on it and, well, it's just safer to remove it."

Instead of the plain, high-buttoned sack coat worn by most men in town, Jake wore a loose-fitting, coffee-colored chamois jacket. "Do you mind?" he said as he prepared to take it off.

"Of course not. Go ahead."

He held her gaze a little longer than normal, then slipped the jacket from his arms and draped it on the back of one of the chairs. Brenna watched as he unbuttoned the cuffs of his gray homespun shirt and rolled the sleeves to his elbows. She had seen men working often enough before, but never had the sight of brown, muscled forearms and wide, strong hands made her think of a passionate kiss and the lustful feel of her breasts crushed against his chest.

"You know the old carpenter's rule," he said as he approached the case and knelt down. "Measure twice. Cut once."

"The rule? Oh, yes. Best to be sure. The mercantile in Whitefish carries glass. I'll make arrangements to get the size you need. I'm afraid it'll take the better part of a week."

Jake looked up. "I'm not going anywhere. At least not yet."

He laid a few tools on the floor, seeming to search for something in particular. Nothing looked new, but everything looked well cared for. "I must confess," she said, looking over his shoulder, "I never thought of you as handy."

"I couldn't make a living using these, but I've repaired more than a few wagon wheels. I even built the storage compartments inside the wagon. They're pretty ingenious, if I do say so myself. I'll show them to you sometime."

"I'd like that." Brenna recalled Sarah Zimmerman's assertion that Jake was a bank robber, a ridiculous notion. The image that grew increasingly plausible, however, was that of Jake engaged in some kind of wild behavior. With Brenna.

He slipped what looked like a short crowbar from the assortment and proceeded to loosen the nails from the frame. "Have you got some old rags or newspapers I could use for this glass? It might shatter when I take it out."

"I've got a box."

"Even better."

Brenna hurried to the back room, feelings of hope and uncertainty fueling her fantasies.

Jake worked slowly and carefully to pry the nails from the wood. The cabinet itself was an old one. Brenna must have bought it used. Everything, in fact, looked second-hand, from the massive prescription case to the small coffee mill she probably used to grind crude drugs and herbs. With an infusion of cash, a lot of work, this place could be a real success. It was spotless, well organized, and from the talk he had heard around town, a reputable place of business.

He winced as he remembered the day he had offered to cut her in on his referral scheme. He should have done a little checking first. She wasn't anything like the other medical professionals he had known. But back then, he wouldn't have believed it.

He studied the room again, looking for things he might improve. Brenna had done a lot for Cosmos, and Jake wanted to do something for her in return.

The rocking chair and the cast iron stove in one corner said this was a hospitable place. The dark, tall clock in the other corner and the organized supplies lent an air of efficiency. Colorful posters of rosy-faced children, their good health supposedly owed to Lloyd's Cocaine Toothache Drops, Perry Davis's Pain Killer, and Hood's Sarsaparilla hung on the walls.

"How's this?" Brenna said, an empty wooden box in her arms.

"Perfect."

She set the box down next to the case. That's when he noticed that the flyaway strands of hair around her face had been smoothed in place. Before coming over, he had made a point to comb his hair too. He had taken a bath and even shaved. All that so he could do some carpentry work. Who was he kidding?

"Do you need anything else?" she asked.

"No, I've got it all under control."

She seemed pleased to hear it. "Then I'm going to get dinner started."

"Go ahead. This won't take long. When I'm finished, should I just come in?"

"Oh no," she said quickly. "Why don't you call out. I'll be right with you."

"Fine." So she wasn't ready to give him the keys. How many times had Cosmos told him to be patient, that given time, mulberry leaves become silk? Jake turned his attention back to the glass-topped case, his mounting anticipation a sign that learning patience was going to be a life-time goal.

A short while later, the box of broken glass waiting by the door, Jake stood at the boundary between her personal and professional worlds. He noticed the herb chest off to his right. She had to have bought that used. Half of the porcelain knobs were chipped.

"Smells good in there," he called loud enough for her to hear.

Wiping her hands on a white bib apron, much larger than the black silk one she had worn in the shop, Brenna met Jake at the doorway. "Please," she said, extending her hand, "come in. Dinner is almost ready. Lamp chops, new potatoes, and asparagus."

"Delicious." She looked delicious. A few of those wisps of hair had freed themselves and curled along

her forehead, cheeks, and nape. There were no laugh
lines yet around her eyes, but they mirrored a passion
for life just the same, drawing him into uncertain opal-
green depths. She looked so innocent, moistening her
lips with her tongue. Watching her made him want to
kiss her then and there. Instead, he stood transfixed,
waiting for her to reveal more of herself, oddly com-
forted to see the fine spray of perspiration lining her
brow.

He followed her into the first of the two rooms she
called home. Painted pale blue, the L-shaped room
served as both kitchen and parlor. On the center of one
wall stood a black, three-burner cook stove, a cast iron
frying pan on one burner, a covered pot on each of the
others. Steam carried the tantalizing aromas throughout the room. One of his hungers would be satisfied
tonight, that was for sure.

A sturdy table and two chairs hugged the only
kitchen window. A band of dark blue fabric edged the
white ruffle that draped the window. A square of the
same blue almost covered the table. The only extrava-
gant things in the room were the lamb chops and the
glass beaker filled with white daisies. He bet that meat
had put a sizable dent in her grocery budget. He had
become a lot more conscious of such things since
Cosmos had taken ill.

"What can I do to help?"

"Nothing. This will only be a few more minutes."

"You've got a nice place here," he said. "Mind if I
look around?"

She hesitated, then said, "Not at all."

He took his time, checking out everything from the
multicolored braided rug in the center of the kitchen
area to the waist-high, half-empty bookshelves that
lined the way in to the other portion of the room.

Textbooks, every one. No—there was a copy of *The Scarlet Letter*.

The living area appeared tidy and functional. With only one small sofa and chair, both covered in faded blue and yellow calico, there was plenty of space for the orange clay pots of thriving mint and basil grouped around the lace-trimmed window. White-painted baskets of dried purple self-heal and deep blue, funnel-formed gentian grew in the darker corners. He liked knowing he and Brenna shared a knowledge of plants, though he doubted his was nearly as sophisticated as hers.

Noticeably absent were the customary tabletop vignettes of family pictures. Jake remembered the day he and his mother had had their picture taken. She had told him such likenesses were to trigger memories and someday when he was all grown up, she would be able to gaze at that picture and remember what a handsome little boy he had been. Brenna must have all her family pictures in the bedroom. He hated to think that she too had a past best forgotten.

There was no source of heat in the room. She must depend on the wood stove in the pharmacy area and the cook stove in the kitchen. He had seen the chimney, so he knew she had a small fireplace in the bedroom. Unfortunately, the door was closed. Warped too, now that he took a good look.

More than where she worked or where she cooked, he wanted to see where she slept. Having had nothing but a bedroll most of his life, he was always curious to see how indulgent others were when it came to the places where they got their rest. He glanced around the corner to where Brenna stood at the stove. Until last night, he would have figured her for a sturdy mattress and plain cotton sheets. Not anymore.

She might be the practical, science-minded druggist, but she was every inch a woman, soft in all the right places, sweet-smelling, and warm to the touch. Even from the back, with the waistband of her apron cinching her figure, just the sight of her could make a man forget himself. Especially this man.

"Sure you don't need any help?" he called to her.

"No. I'm fine. Make yourself comfortable."

He could try.

Jake walked to the corner of the room, out of Brenna's eyesight. Now, there was an odd-looking curio cabinet. Smaller than most such cabinets, the top half was open, the shelves holding an old-fashioned oil lamp and an assortment of tubular punched tins to keep her candles from the mice. From where he stood, he could see that the door to the lower half was stuck.

He knelt down and examined the cabinet. The door was warped, cupped in the middle of the top and bottom. A little more complicated than he had thought. Still, he knew he had sandpaper in his toolbox. He could fix it. He might even be able to do it right now.

There was nothing in the cabinet but a basket, probably her sewing kit. She wouldn't appreciate having powder all over it. He pulled the shaded brown basket from the dark recesses. The lid fell off.

"Well, will you look at that," he said to himself.

He was no authority on fabric, but this piece of lace was old. With care and curiosity, he drew it from the basket. It was an intricate design of delicate flowers, tiny leaves, and curling vines. As fine as a spider web, it floated between his hands like a dream.

Something that old was probably valuable. He draped it over one arm and went to the kitchen.

"Thought you might want to put this somewhere safe while I fix that cabinet door."

11

She could feel the silent scream reach her eyes.

"Brenna! What's the matter? Are you all right?" Jake tossed the lace over his shoulder. "Did you get burned?"

She knew she was trembling.

Quickly, he examined her leaden arms, her limp hands. "I don't see anything." He put his hands firmly on her shoulders and looked into her eyes.

Whatever he saw must have horrified him, for he turned away, examining her limbs again for external wounds.

"What the hell's the matter? You're as white as a ghost."

His face was a blur, though she could hear the strain in his voice.

"Brenna, talk to me!"

The piercing awareness of what she had done strangled her voice. The smell and steam of cooking assaulted her. The air began to shimmer and rise. All she could see was the bridal veil.

I didn't mean to kill him.
And then that, too, faded to black.

As he had already done a dozen times, Jake rose from the chair he had dragged next to the bed, braced one arm on the headboard and the other across Brenna's chest. He bent down and placed his lips to her forehead. She didn't have a fever. Her breathing was even.

He sat back down. Her hands, cold and damp an hour ago, felt warm now. They were graceful hands, with long, tapering fingers. He had held them and stroked them and mumbled encouragement to her, much the way he did with Cosmos. If she didn't come around soon, he would have to leave her and send for Amabelle.

He relaxed a little as a wash of pink returned to her cheeks. She stirred and opened her eyes.

"Hey," he said softly. Never had he been so glad to gaze into those beautiful pale green pools. "Feeling better?"

"The food—"

"I put the pots on some trivets I found in your pantry. Everything's fine."

She nodded.

"Are you up to eating? I can heat it up. Smells delicious."

She levered herself up and swung her legs around.

"Not so fast," Jake said.

"I'm fine now. Truly."

He was pleased to see at least the shadow of a smile, but not to hear the distance in her voice.

"You fainted, you know."

"I guess I did."

"Does that happen often? I mean, are you sick?"

"No to both." She stood and smoothed her skirt.

He felt as awkward as she probably did when she turned around to see the indentation her body had made in her featherbed and the white and lavender quilt he had used to cover her.

As though drawn by a magnet, she stepped over to the small table where he had placed the veil. Though she stared at it for what seemed an unusually long time, she didn't touch it.

"I was going to put it back in the basket for you," Jake said, "but I thought you might want to put it somewhere else while I work on that cabinet door."

"The door?"

"On the curio cabinet in your parlor. It's warped. That's why it sticks. I took a look at it while you were fixing dinner. I'm sure I can fix it. I was going to do it tonight . . ." It wasn't just her silence that was eerie. It was the faraway look in her eyes. ". . . but tomorrow might be better."

"You lit a fire, too?" she asked, noticing the flames.

"I didn't know what was wrong and I didn't want you to get a chill. The nights get so cold around here."

"I guess I owe you more than dinner."

"You don't owe me anything."

"Well, I'm sorry to have put you to so much trouble." She stepped past him, heading for the kitchen.

Jake followed. "It wasn't any trouble. Not at all. But I am concerned. I mean, what happened? You looked like you had seen a ghost."

She laughed in a way that was too forced to be believable.

"I haven't eaten much today," she said. "An empty stomach can make a person lightheaded."

Jake went straight to the pantry and picked up the

frying pan. "All the more reason to heat this up." He put the pan on the stove, still hot from a thick bed of embers. He went back for the other two pans and put them on the stove too.

"Here," he said, pulling out a chair from the table by the window. "You sit down. Just tell me what needs to be done."

"No," she said softly. She tilted her head to one side, a gesture Jake had seen Cosmos use when he was trying to solve a puzzle of some sort. But whenever Cosmos studied like that, he would furrow his brow and squint his eyes. Not Brenna. Her face showed no expression at all, except, on further examination, the bruising of some slow-healing sorrow.

"Jake, I must apologize. I'm sure this wasn't the evening you had planned. It wasn't the evening I had planned, anyway."

"Do you hear me complaining?"

"No. You're too much of a gentleman for that."

He beamed inside. "So what kind of evening did you have planned?"

At that she blushed, and he knew she shared his thoughts of passion.

He held out his hands to her.

"Oh, Jake," she said, clutching his hands. Her eyes suddenly filled with more emotion than he could discern and tears not plump enough to fall—at least not until her cheek touched his shoulder.

He rubbed small circles on her back, absorbing her silent sobs, wishing with all his heart that he could cure whatever it was that was causing her such pain.

Ah, but holding her close like this felt so good. He brushed a few silky strands of hair from her cheek and kissed her head. She smelled of roses. If he could have turned off his body's more basic response, he would have. But as difficult as that would have been when he first saw her, it was impossible now.

She turned her head, her breath warm against his neck. As though all his wishes were suddenly being granted, she tilted her head, the look in her eyes a clear invitation. He was no fool.

The small seeking movements of her lips on his lasted but a few seconds. His hunger demanded more. Yet, even as the lust rising in his blood urged him to press against her eager, yielding body, to feel her breasts crushed against his chest, he felt the stirrings of a need he had never known. With it came the awareness that having Brenna beneath him, naked and wanting his body as much as he wanted hers, would not be enough. The realization was sobering.

A small moan from the back of her throat urged him not to pull away. Making it even harder was the way she sculpted his shoulders and ran her hands down his arms.

"Jake?"

He knew of only one craving that could heat a woman's voice like that. The same craving that could darken the palest green eyes. He cupped her face in his hands and stared into emeralds. "I'm going to go back to my wagon now. I'll probably wake up tomorrow with 'fool' branded across my forehead, but Brenna—"

"No, no, no. You don't have to explain anything." She eased from his embrace but, thankfully, didn't move away. She sounded embarrassed as she rushed to add, "We should eat. After all, I did invite you."

"I appreciate all the trouble you went through, but . . . well, I'm just not hungry anymore. At least not for food."

She stepped away, though not far. "I know we

shouldn't be doing this. I just don't know what came over me."

His eyes flicked over the blush staining her cheeks and the desire still parting her lips. "Magic," he murmured, "the oldest kind."

"There you are! I've been looking all over town for you." Mayor Elton Fontaine, posture-perfect in his light-colored suit and green plaid bow tie, hurried over to the telegraph desk and nodded to Stewart McCutcheon.

"Good morning, Mayor," Brenna said.

"One of the best mornings of my entire life!" He whisked off his straw boater and bowed his head, offering her a view of his scalp. "Look! Look! Can you believe it?"

"Believe what?"

"'Believe what?'" he mimicked. "Go ahead, take a look. Take a good look."

Brenna studied his speckled pink scalp and the few, precious strands of mousy brown hair he had oiled and raked across it. The skin looked healthy. No sign of injury. "I don't know what to say."

"Just say it's amazing. Amazing!" The mayor tilted his head toward the man behind the telegraph desk. "Well, Stewart, bet you never thought you'd see that again."

"That's a fact."

"I tell you, Miss McAuley, I would never have believed it. Not in a million years. Why, if the truth be told, I was his biggest critic. But the man is a wizard! Look at me!" He ran his fingers through the wiry tufts around his ears. "Look at this head of hair!"

He readjusted his boater. "I don't know how much

longer this will fit. But you won't hear me complain. No indeed, though I'll have to set up a standing appointment with Coventry's finest barber."

Stewart finished jotting down some notes on a pad of paper by the telegraph and put his pencil down. "You look as bald as ever to me."

"Oh, pshaw. You're half blind and we all know it—though we still love you. Don't we, Miss McAuley?"

Brenna smiled toward Stewart, who simply rolled his eyes and turned his attention back to the pad of paper on his desk. "I'm afraid I can't share your enthusiasm, Mayor. At least not yet."

"Whatever do you mean?"

Much as she would like to believe that what Jake offered was the stuff of miracles, she knew better. "I don't see evidence of new growth."

"Did you get a good look?" he said, removing his hat, bowing his head again.

"I'm sorry to disappoint you."

How quickly the sparkle in his eyes tarnished. Though he hadn't moved an inch, he seemed shorter, smaller than when he had first walked in. Even his bow tie appeared to droop.

"Forgive my intrusion, won't you? I was about to ride over to Whitefish. To spy on the enemy." He gave a hollow laugh as he settled his hat back on his head, though without the jaunty tilt, and headed for the door.

"Mayor, wait." Brenna wrestled with her conscience. "Sometimes hair follicles can be spontaneously restored. It's rare, but I have heard of it."

"You have?"

"It could be that you are experiencing the sensation of growth beneath the surface."

"Beneath the surface?"

"Yes. Like germinating seeds."

"Do you think so?"

"It's possible."

"You know, I have noticed a tingling sensation. Why, I'll bet it's happening just as you said—my hair is germinating beneath the surface of my scalp, just like a seed."

Stewart piped up. "Be sure and spread the manure good and thick."

The mayor laughed and tilted his hat. "Stewart McCutcheon, our link to the rest of the world. What would we do without you?"

"Go to Whitefish."

Brenna watched in amazement as the mayor squared his shoulders and set his jaw, looking every bit the master of his domain.

"My mission exactly," he said. "I will return with a full report on our opposition as well as an aggressive plan of attack. You *have* heard of the upcoming baseball challenge, haven't you?"

"Baseball?" Brenna asked, her thoughts on Jake.

"The very same. That enterprising Mr. Darrow—to know him is to love him—has challenged Lord Austin to a regular match. Mr. Darrow spoke to me about it just the other day."

Brenna couldn't believe Jake hadn't mentioned the game to her. But then, he had a lot of other things on his mind. More to the point, she hadn't seen him since the night he came to fix her cabinet.

The mayor continued. "The game is to be played the last Saturday in August, right here in our fair town. How he arranged that, I haven't a clue. I'm simply grateful."

Stewart scratched his bald head with the pencil. "Who's he gonna get to play?"

"Mr. Darrow will assemble a team of Coventry's

finest. Don't be surprised should he come to speak with you. And Lord Austin will do the same in Whitefish."

"Now wait just a gall-darn minute—"

"You're turning red, Stewart. Look at him, Miss McAuley. He's turning red. I believe you're ill. Doesn't he look ill, Miss McAuley?"

"I'm not ill, you old bag o' wind. I'm angry."

"Now, now. I know exactly what you're going to say. How could I approve an arrangement whereby Sir Austin is positioned to root for Whitefish?"

Stewart dug his fists into his hips and marched over to the mayor, stopping only when the two were nose to nose. "Didn't you stop and think how all this is going to affect that man's frame of mind? First, he'll be rooting for Whitefish to win the baseball game, and before you know it, he'll be giving his nod to Whitefish for the cattle syndicate. I swear, Elton, sometimes I think you're one tine short of a pitchfork."

"I had those same fears until Mr. Darrow revealed the entire scenario to me. You see, Lord Austin was captivated, absolutely captivated, by the idea of playing in a baseball game. He has no devotion to either town as of yet. So while he may root for Whitefish, that doesn't mean Whitefish will win. Which means that when Coventry wins—and it will—Sir Austin will be duly impressed and his blessings will be ours." The mayor clasped his hands in prayer and closed his eyes.

"Excuse me, Mayor," Brenna said. "Did I understand you to say that Austin intends to play in this game?"

"Indeed. Both Lord Austin and Mr. Darrow must play. A condition of the arrangement as I understand it."

Brenna couldn't imagine Jake would agree to participate in a game. His leg would never be able to take the strain of running.

Stewart turned around and went back to his desk. "You darn well better know what you're talking about, Elton Fontaine."

"Don't I always?" The mayor tipped his hat to Brenna. "Cheerio!" With that, he left.

"The old fool," Stewart muttered as he jogged and stacked the papers on his desk before handing them to Brenna. "Here you go, ma'am."

Full of hope, she scanned the response she had received from her alma mater. The first tetanus and diphtheria antitoxins were being produced. Physicians were being urged to apply prophylactic drops to the eyes of newborn infants to combat blindness caused by gonorrheal infection. All of this information was encouraging to the medical community as a whole, but couldn't help Cosmos. As far as consumption was concerned, there had been no scientific breakthroughs. Vile industrial air, heredity, and lack of exercise were still considered the causes. The open-air treatment was still the prescribed. Take a sea voyage, work on a farm, ride a horse across Texas. Unfortunately, Cosmos couldn't do any of these things.

"Good news?" Stewart asked.

"I'm afraid not." Brenna folded the papers.

"Read like progress to me."

"Not enough, I'm afraid." She bid Stewart goodday and headed back to her shop to read the telegram again. Later, she planned to go up to Amabelle's. Cosmos had taken a bad turn the last few days. Jake had stayed by his side. The wine of iron she was concocting wasn't ready yet, but in the meantime, a wheat germ supplement might help restore his appetite. Besides, she might as well give Jake the bad news and get it over with.

After all her rationalization, she admitted the other reason she wanted to go up to Amabelle's: to see Jake.

It had been four days since she had telegraphed the Louisville School of Pharmacy for Women, four days since Jake had walked into her kitchen, the sins of her past draped across his arm. It felt like a lifetime since she had kissed him and confronted the aching emptiness she had denied for so long.

"How is he?" Brenna asked as soon as Amabelle came into the parlor.

Amabelle sighed and gestured for Brenna to join her on the sofa. "He has good days and bad days, though the division is far from equal."

The enthusiasm that always brightened Amabelle's eyes was gone now. Her voice, noticeably light for her age, sounded heavy. In the last few weeks even her movements had slowed. Brenna couldn't remember the last time she had seen Amabelle smile.

"I brought more wheat germ," Brenna said, reaching into the basket at her feet.

"Thank you, dear." Amabelle took the jar and stared for a moment at the shifting grains. "Last night, he told me—" Her voice caught. She took a wadded handkerchief from her sleeve and dabbed her eyes. "Last night, he told me he had instructed Jake to see to it that I receive the wedding ring he had given to his wife." She took a minute to regain her composure, but Brenna noticed how tightly she wadded her handkerchief and how she locked her lips together to keep from crying. "He told me he loves me." Amabelle burst into sobs.

Brenna gathered her friend into her arms, tears that spoke of life's cruelty spilling down her cheeks. When Amabelle finally eased back, she said, "Has your college responded to your inquiry yet? Tell me they've discovered a cure."

"There's still no cure," Brenna said, refusing to inflict the even greater cruelty of false hope.

"Nothing?"

"Medical science has made strides in many other fields, but not in this one. Not yet anyway."

"I see."

Brenna stood. "I'd like to go up and talk to him, if he's awake."

"Yes, he's awake," Amabelle said tentatively as she rose. "I was with him just before you arrived. But before you go, I need to discuss something with you."

"Yes?"

"I hardly know how to say this. We've been friends for so long. . . . "

"What is it?"

"Well, last night, after a particularly bad coughing spell, Cosmos confided to me that your mother had been a healer. Is that true?"

The pressure circled Brenna's neck like a noose.

"Yes." She saw the hurt fill Amabelle's eyes. "She was."

"Why didn't you tell me?"

"I don't know," Brenna said, the lie catching in her throat.

Amabelle shook her head in disbelief. "All these years I thought she was a widow who made a modest living doing simple nursing."

"That's the truth."

"But not the whole truth."

"I don't understand why you're so upset."

"I'm upset because you and I have been the best of friends for three years and all of a sudden I have the feeling you don't trust me."

"Amabelle, that's ridiculous."

"Is it? You told me about how humiliated you were

to get a failing grade in chemistry. I remember the day I caught you padding the lining of your coat with newspapers because you couldn't afford a warmer wrap."

All Brenna could do was nod as, one by one, painful reminders of her past scraped the veneer that all was right with her world.

"So why," Amabelle continued, her own frustration quickening her words, "didn't you ever tell me about your mother? For heaven's sake, I operate a house of recovery. Don't you think I would have been interested to know about such a healing art?"

"Yes, but—"

"If your mother had been sent to prison, or worked in a bawdy house, or was a derelict, I could understand your need for secrecy. But to hide something like that makes no sense."

"I suppose it doesn't."

Amabelle furrowed her brow, looking desperate to understand. "I'm sorry," she said. "I know my reaction is excessive. I just want to find some way to help Cosmos. When he told me your mother had been a *brauchere* and that the art is passed from mother to daughter, I grasped at the hope that—"

"That I could practice the Old Magic too."

"Yes."

"What did Cosmos say?"

"That you did not inherit your mother's skill."

"He's right. I didn't."

"How can you be so sure? Have you ever tried?"

Brenna picked up her basket, gripping the handles to keep from blurting out the ugly truth. "I'm a druggist— a good one. Isn't that enough?"

"But he's not getting better!"

"I'm doing everything I can!"

"Webley Heller died last week. Oscar Gage threw a

second hemorrhage in as many weeks. I overheard several men on the porch last evening. They're calling my home another outpost of death and taking bets on who will be next. And they're betting on Cosmos!" Amabelle covered her face with her hands and turned her back.

Brenna reached out to touch Amabelle's shoulder, wanting to soothe the pain rising and falling with each quiet sob. But Amabelle pulled away.

Brenna waited for an indication that her friend understood, but when Amabelle still said nothing, Brenna stood. "Then I guess I'll stop by tomorrow," she said, a lump in her throat.

"Yes," Amabelle said. "I don't see that there's any more for you to do here today."

Brenna nodded, not daring to speak.

Not until she was a safe distance from the house did the sting of rejection work its way to her eyes, distorting her vision. On the hard-packed dirt road, arms limp at her sides, she stared ahead as dappled shadows danced between the ribbons of white birch and the lace of green leaves. A legacy could be a heavy burden to bear.

She remembered watching her mother heal a man whose leg had been burned in a fire. His agony contorted not only his face, but that of his wife. Brenna's mother knelt down beside the bed on which the man lay, formed her hand into a fist, and turned it so the back of her hand faced the worst of the black blisters. Gently, and as close to the surface as possible, she moved her fist in a circle, all the while chanting the secret cure under her breath. The ritual went on for hours as she gently touched the surface of the man's leg. With each touch she blew softly on his wound, both giving the life force of breath and blowing the sickness away.

The man recovered.

Brenna stopped, set down her basket, and brought her hands up to her face. She studied every line, every callus. Could such ordinary hands ever hold that kind of power? She turned them over, examining the backs. White half-moons rose in each pink nailbed. She smiled at the image her mother had taught her and carefully pushed back each cuticle.

She continued down the road thinking how appropriate it was for her to have such a celestial memory. After all, today was the solstice. The sun had reached its limit. After today, it would turn back on itself and begin its long journey to the nightworld. Summer, the season of nature's liveliest and most abundant purpose, had begun. A time, as her mother would always say, when life would not be without drama.

12

Drawn by shouts and cheers, Brenna veered from her course and walked over to the cleared lot that everyone now called the baseball field. Though there were still a few hours of daylight left, the sky had darkened. A sizzle in the air said another summer storm was on its way.

"Run, Dickie, run!" half the boys were shouting as they waved their arms. "Slide! Slide!"

Feet first, the Foster boy dove to the ground, sending up a cloud of dust. Jake made a repeated scissor motion with his arms. "Safe!"

Brenna walked past Jake's wagon to where a group of younger boys, five and six years old, jumped up and down in their dirt-streaked shorts and sailor tops cheering for their older siblings. She had heard that for the last few evenings, a group of men had come out to play the game, though she hadn't witnessed it herself. Certainly, everyone was talking about baseball, more particularly, about the game between Coventry and Whitefish.

But that wasn't why she was here.

"Batter up," Jake called.

Albie Foster stepped forward, swinging the bat at an imaginary ball the way the older boys did.

"Just remember what I told you," Jake said. "Grip the bat down low and keep your eye on the ball." He stepped behind the boy and covered his small hands with his own.

"I can do it myself," Albie said, twisting free. "I been practicin'."

"Atta boy."

Jake stepped back, looked in Brenna's direction. He hesitated before waving, or at least that's how it seemed to her.

Three strikes later, dark clouds gathering fast, he dismissed the teams and ordered them to pick up the slabs of wood they used for bases and stow them under his wagon. They groaned but followed instructions, waving to both Jake and Brenna as they left the field.

While Jake was picking up the bat, Brenna walked over to where Albie Foster had just stood. Her heart still felt the sting of Amabelle's words. Jake might lash out at her with equal frustration. But there was no excuse for delaying the bad news.

"You here to play?" Jake said, offering her the bat.

"To talk."

He nodded as though he had been expecting her, then said, "I was supposed to come by and fix your cabinet."

"Amabelle told me you've been spending most of your time with Cosmos these last few days."

"And playing a little baseball in the evenings."

"I looked for you," she said, feeling compelled to let him know, yet hating the way her voice betrayed her hurt.

"Yeah, I should have said something."

"Say something now. Why haven't you stopped by?"

"I've just been busy, that's all."

She looked away, wishing she hadn't said anything.

"Now wait a minute," Jake said, shifting his weight, looking more uncomfortable by the minute. "Don't go thinking I didn't want to."

"You didn't leave me much choice."

He glanced around. "You know how sick Cosmos has been. When I haven't been with him, I've been working on the wagon. When the time comes for us to go, or for me to head out by myself, I want everything to be ready."

She heard clearly all that he didn't say. "So all your praise about our fair town and your talk of staying was merely to bide time while Cosmos recovered, or until he died. I suspected as much the moment I recognized him."

"Yeah. Something like that."

A person's bearing was always influenced by the weight of the baggage he carried. Even a man like Jake, accustomed to holding the attention of a crowd whether he was on a stage or on a baseball field, couldn't always hide his feelings. This very moment, with his dark eyes probing hers so deeply, he looked as anxious as she felt.

"I heard from my school today," she said, wanting to put an end to the tension. "The news isn't good."

"I see." He looked off to the side and swung the bat.

"But I've read about a doctor in Germany. Peter Dettweiler. He prescribes what he calls 'continuous fresh air treatment.' Instead of encouraging his patients to climb mountains and ride horses, he has them sit outside on protected verandahs for most of the day in what he calls 'cure chairs' that recline."

"You're saying I should carry him out to the porch every day?"

She thought of all the stairs. "No."

"Because if you think it'll help, I will."

"I don't know what will help!"

He groaned. "Any more good news?"

"Jake, I'm sorry. I wish—"

"I know, I know. I wish too."

The silence that followed urged her to say good-bye, but she didn't want to leave. He made no move to go either, and instead fiddled with the bat.

"You ever swung a bat?" he asked.

"No, though I've been curious."

"Here," he said, handing it to her.

Brenna wrapped her hands around the narrow end and held it over her shoulder the way she had seen Jake do.

"Hold your hands closer together. One wrist on top of the other."

"Like this?"

"That's it. Now hold it tighter."

She squeezed the wood till she felt her arms grow rigid. "Like this?"

"A little stiff, but okay. Now tilt your body to the side. Draw the bat back over your right shoulder. And swing."

She followed his example.

"No, no, no. You look like you're chopping wood." He stepped behind her and reached his arms around so that his hands covered hers. "Let me show you."

Her back against his broad chest, her body encircled by his arms, the heat from his skin steaming through her clothes mingling his scent with hers . . . Brenna lost all interest in the game.

She turned her head slightly, her lips so close to his. "Jake," she whispered.

He locked his gaze straight ahead. She would have thought him disinterested if he hadn't, at the same time, moved his arms closer together, shrinking the circle in which he held her. He swallowed hard, leaving Brenna to wonder if he felt as nervous, and as eager, as she did. His lips brushed her cheek and lingered.

They were standing in an open field at the end of Main Street. In broad daylight. She clutched the bat tighter, knowing that without it, there could be no explanation should anyone see them like this.

A clap of thunder censured them.

She dropped the bat. In the tangle to retrieve it, they came face to face. She saw a storm of a different kind brewing in his dark eyes. How she longed to ride it out with him.

Slashed by lightning, the clouds opened.

"Come on," Jake said, grabbing her arm. "Let's get out of here."

Pelted by raindrops, they ran to his wagon.

Brenna grabbed Jake's hand for support as she hurried up the portable wooden stairs that lead to his home on wheels. He followed right behind her.

Dripping wet, Brenna smoothed back her hair and briskly rubbed her arms. She stood in the narrow passageway searching through the shadows to soak up the sights of Jake's world.

The set-up was a tribute to efficiency. A short, narrow bench on one side of the aisle probably served as a work surface. Scratched and stained, the wood appeared to have a story all its own. Beneath the bench, all along the floor, were built-in wooden lockers, scuff marks indicating how difficult it had to be for a grown man to maneuver in the small, intimate space. She looked over at Jake to see him blocking the doorway.

Empty bottles peered between the slats of wooden

crates stacked halfway to the ceiling. Hanging on a peg-board arrangement of large hooks were two pots and a frying pan. A limp, cotton mesh sack held a few pieces of tinware. Jake's white shirt hung on another peg, as did his red vest.

She shouldn't be here.

"Not what you expected?" he asked as he raked his own wet hair from his forehead. "Or maybe you never even thought about where I live."

"I've thought about it." A thousand times.

The wagon creaked with every step Jake took toward her. His wet shirt clung to his skin. "And?"

"And it's much neater than I expected." Much more personal, too, with baseball cards and newspaper clippings about winning pitchers nailed to the wall.

He grinned. Despite his intent to leave one day, he was clearly glad to be with her now.

He glanced behind him at the open door and at the dark spot on the floor where the rain was blowing in. "I've got a big oil cloth poncho. I can hold it over our heads and walk you home. Or I can shut the door."

She scanned his broad shoulders, his lean torso, and the magnificent arousal he was powerless to conceal. She pictured him unclothed, knowing he would taste of salt and sun, and the clean tang of summer rain.

But there was a time and place for everything. No one had raised an eyebrow on learning that Jake had come to her shop to repair a cabinet and she had offered him dinner in return. For Jake to entertain her in his wagon, however, was scandalous.

"I think you had better take me home," she said.

He didn't look surprised, just disappointed. "I'll get the poncho."

In years past, she had felt curious about the force that drew men and women together. Her feelings now went far beyond girlish wonder. Jake Darrow was not simply an attractive man. He had the power to touch the wax Brenna was made of, to soften the wall around her heart. She knew by the yearning that squeezed her heart this very minute that, scandal or not, the day was coming when she wouldn't be able to walk away.

Warm despite the chilling rain, Brenna huddled next to Jake, dodging puddles and avoiding curious glances as he escorted her home.

He said good-bye at the door and headed back to his wagon, but not before gently pressing his thumb to her bottom lip, opening her mouth, and caressing her with one last look so filled with lust she melted.

Several days later, Brenna made arrangements with Mrs. Dinwittie to let Phoebe spend the afternoon with her. Phoebe had wanted to see Ralph Newton's barber pole and had run around it a dozen times trying to trace the red and white stripes. They had stopped in Inga's Bakery for a raisin cinnamon scone, then hurried to the livery to see the horses. It would have been a perfect afternoon if Ralph's customer, a visitor from Missoula, hadn't sworn at Phoebe when she peeped into the shop. Or if the rowdy boys hanging around the livery hadn't laughed and called her pig-face. Phoebe had hidden the tears but not the hurt.

Outside, Phoebe squinted against the bright sun. "Can we go see Mr. Belinus? I like Mr. Belinus."

She had been up to see Cosmos every day this past week. She had brought the iron wine, a weight enhancer made of malt, and more opium cough syrup. She told him the news she had received from college. He seemed interested in the idea of sitting outside and resting instead of exerting himself.

Amabelle had been cordial, but cool. Instead of sitting down and discussing each patient's progress over a cup of tea, she had prepared a list, noting who was low on what medication. All Brenna could do was hope that in time, the affection she and her friend had always shared would return. She often saw Jake there, too, though circumstances had never allowed them a moment alone, a situation Brenna found frustrating at best.

Earlier in the week, he had come to her shop and sanded down the door on the cabinet where she kept the veil. She had been so eager to see him. She could tell by the look in his eyes that he shared her feeling. But Libby Newton, the barber's wife, had come to the shop right after Jake arrived and had stayed until Jake left, three full hours. Then yesterday when Jake came back to replace the glass that had arrived from Whitefish, Rhoda McCutcheon, Stewart's wife, just happened by and stayed until Jake left.

Well, Brenna planned to spend a few moments alone with Jake today, one way or the other.

After stopping at her shop to pick up supplies, she took Phoebe's hand and headed up the hard-packed trail to Amabelle's House of Recovery. If Jake wasn't here, he was probably in his wagon, or on the ball field. She'd find him.

"Look! Look!" Phoebe slipped her hand from Brenna's and ran on her short, stubby legs up the flower-lined path to the porch.

Cosmos sat in one of the large, bark-covered rocking chairs, a colorful Indian blanket across his lap, another around his shoulders. He and the men in rockers on either side of him turned at the sound of Phoebe's squeals.

"Mr. Belinus! It's me! Phoebe!"

Cosmos opened his arms wide as Phoebe fumbled her way up the stairs. Though he lacked the strength to lift her, he held his chair steady as she climbed up. She planted a big kiss on his cheek, then settled in his lap. "My little princess," he said to her. "Gentlemen, if you haven't had the pleasure, may I introduce Miss Phoebe Halliwell, a princess of the first order and my dearest friend."

Each man bowed his head, causing Phoebe to giggle and bounce. Brenna feared that Phoebe's weight and movement might be hurting Cosmos, but he said nothing. Instead, he repositioned the blanket around his shoulders to cover Phoebe, seeming content to let her snuggle against him.

Brenna climbed the stairs and went over to him. "Good afternoon, Mr. Belinus. How are you feeling today?"

His sunken blue eyes sparkled. "I am in the presence of a beautiful princess. How could I feel anything but grand?"

"And you, gentlemen?" she said to the others.

"I got a letter from my sister back East," Mr. Drury said. "She writes that some sanitariums are feeding patients vegetables and nothing else. And others are feeding a dozen eggs a day. What do you say to that?"

"I'd say the medical community is trying everything it can to find a cure. As for the food, I believe in the balance Miss Sweet provides."

Cosmos smiled. "Miss Sweet is an excellent cook."

Mr. Drury scoffed. "You'd say that if she served you bacon swimming in grease."

"Yes, Malcolm, I probably would. Just as you would find a hard biscuit made by that new girl a delicacy."

"Yeah, I guess I ain't ready for the grave just yet. If I could just get rid of this cough."

Brenna leaned against one of the massive cedar timbers that supported the overhang. She said to Cosmos, "It appears the out-of-doors is agreeing with you."

"Indeed. My room is on the first floor now. And every morning after breakfast Jake escorts me out here to the porch where I can observe the wonders of nature and drink in her beauty." He coughed. And again. Harder.

Phoebe slid from his lap and ran behind the chair, reaching her small hands through the slats to pat him on the back. "There, there," she cooed.

Brenna reached into her basket for a bottle of cough syrup as Cosmos slumped forward, blood running from his mouth.

"Phoebe, run! Get Miss Amabelle! Quick!"

Exhausted from fighting the disease that grasped his breath and what little energy he had managed to find, Cosmos finally slept. Brenna and Amabelle had propped him up with pillows, in case another coughing spell gripped him.

With Amabelle's permission, Brenna sent one of the hired girls to town to let Mrs. Dinwittie know that Phoebe would be spending the night with Brenna up at Amabelle's. It was either that or have one of the hired girls walk Phoebe back to town. Brenna wasn't comfortable with that idea; Phoebe was too upset.

Nearly midnight now, Phoebe slept in a bed she and Brenna would share in a spare room down the hall. Amabelle dozed on and off in a chair next to Cosmos's bed. Brenna and Jake sat in facing chairs in the parlor just outside Cosmos's room. Aspen logs crackled and popped in the massive fireplace, filling the room with warm dry heat. The rafters creaked from the wind of another storm that had rolled in. The windows rattled with the rain.

"I'm just glad you were here when he collapsed," Jake said for the tenth time that night.

She nodded, too tired to talk about it again.

The strain around Jake's eyes was visible. "You don't think he's going to die tonight, do you?"

"No."

He glanced toward the door to Cosmos's room. "Then why is Amabelle in there sitting next to him? Why are you still here?"

"Amabelle loves him." Brenna yawned. "And I just want to be here in case he has another spell tonight."

"Why tonight? Because most consumptives die during a full moon? That's what I've heard. Is that true?"

"I don't know. Besides, the moon won't be truly full for another four days."

"And then?"

She sighed with a feeling of hopelessness. "Oh, Jake, I don't know."

A log collapsed, shooting sparks up the chimney. Brenna went to the bar in the corner, removed the leather-covered stopper from one of several carafes and poured herself a glass of sherry. "Jake?" He shook his head, lifting the glass of bourbon in his hand.

She returned to her chair and sank into the warm, butter-soft leather. She couldn't remember when she had last felt so weary in both body and mind. The only reason she hadn't already gone to bed was Jake. Here they were, sitting in front of a fire on a stormy summer night, though not at all the way she'd planned.

He had to be tired, too. One of the girls had gone to fetch him from his wagon. From the window in Cosmos's room, Brenna had seen him struggling to run.

She heard the chink of the ice in his glass as he

slowly raised it to his mouth. She watched him swallow and close his eyes. She imagined the whiskey spreading its warmth and wondered if she held even the smallest place in his thoughts. She imagined the taste of his lips.

He leaned forward, his hand rubbing his knee. With a haunted look on his face, he said, "That veil I found in your cabinet. That's a bridal veil, isn't it?"

"Yes."

"You were engaged?"

She couldn't answer right away, then finally said, "No. The veil belonged to my mother, and her mother, and on back for several generations. I had packed it away years ago and was just surprised to see it."

"So you weren't engaged to some man who broke your heart?" His voice sounded strained. "The way you reacted that night I came for dinner . . . I've thought about it a lot. I even talked it over with Cosmos."

"You did?"

He set his glass down. "He said it was a miracle that a woman as beautiful as you wasn't married. I agree with him."

"Thank you." She stared at her glass. "I've been infatuated a time or two. But never in love."

"Never?" He walked over to her chair and held out his hand, an unmistakable invitation in his eyes. Framed by the glow behind him, he looked every bit the flame and she felt every bit the moth. She took his hand.

With fire, wind, and rain all around them, it felt only natural to experience the passion intended for a man and woman. No sooner did their lips meet, than Jake's tongue sought the depths beyond. Eagerly, she opened to him.

Amidst muffled coughing from the darkened rooms all around them, the need for each other built as intensely as it had before. But this time his hands didn't stroke her back or sculpt her waist or cup her breasts. This time she didn't rake her fingers through his hair or fan them across his chest. This time, they just held each other tightly, knowing their future was somehow at stake.

Hours later, asleep in a bed that would soon be occupied by another invalid come for the cure, Brenna dreamed. This time, it was not Jake who appeared in the shadows. It was Hannelore, her mother. Shrouded in mist, she held the brass key—a means to keep Brenna locked in an old way of life. Across one arm hung the bridal veil—symbolic of the ritual Brenna couldn't bring herself to break. Suddenly, Hannelore disappeared, leaving Brenna to stand in her place, the key in her hand, the veil on her arm. The shadows stirred, circled her, danced.

Her heart pounding, Brenna spun around, desperate to escape. Until she heard her mother whisper her name. Filled with love, her soothing voice was not so much a sound as an awareness, a lullaby soothing Brenna's heart. Brenna stood still and listened.

"The key is the secret. The veil is the truth. Above all, it is the presence of light that creates the shadow."

13

Austin Halliwell raised a brow as he scanned the poster Elton Fontaine had just given him. "You Americans make much ado about celebrating your freedom."

"Oh my, yes." Standing next to Austin, the mayor reached in front of him and pointed to the boldly lettered list of events. "As you can see, we begin with a sunrise salute to the flag. The procession begins at eleven on the corner of Main and Ashland. Nearly every one of our school's thirty children, ages four through twenty-one, will march to the door of the church where I shall read the Declaration of Independence." He stopped short. "Oh dear, that doesn't offend you, does it?"

"Though many of my countrymen are still certain your enterprise will fail—they've not been able to reconcile that tea party incident and its aftermath—I, for one, wish America only success."

"Oh, thank goodness. Well then, as you can see, following my reading, we will have an oration by Lester Bodyk. Lester has been East and has spoken on the new telephone and has agreed to expound on the notion that such devices will eventually link the entire country. I must admit that not ten years ago I would have called such an idea the vision of a fool. Ah, but our world grows by the minute."

"This slow race. What is that?"

"That's three hundred yards. For the slowest horse."

"I see. More races, more orations, food, dancing, and fireworks."

Elton beamed. "The whole Flathead Valley will meet here and everyone will have a glorious time. You'll see."

"Yes, I suppose I will. Now, I presume you have more serious plans for Coventry's future. Or is this to be a town of endless picnics and parades?"

"Oh, no." Elton grabbed a neatly typed list from his desk. "I have our plans right here."

Austin scanned the list Elton Fontaine handed him. "My, my. When laid out in such a manner, Coventry's attributes do indeed appear impressive."

"We're so glad you agree." He looked to Stewart on his left and Ralph on his right. "Aren't we, gentlemen?"

They both nodded.

Austin walked around Elton's desk and sat in his green leather chair, then read aloud. "Central geographic position, accessibility by land and water, magnificent climate, pure water, inexhaustible forests of raw timber, matchless hunting and fishing, superior stores, and fine public spirit and enterprise."

"And," Elton said with emphasis as he tidied the framed newspaper article proclaiming his election, "we have placed an advertisement in the *Missoula Gazette* for a good plasterer and brickman, someone to open a good dressmaking and milliner shop, and someone to establish a good sawmill that can furnish lumber in any quantity."

"Quite ambitious."

"Yes, and I'm drawing up plans to modernize our steamboat facility to bring in more people from Missoula." He immediately retrieved the folded sketch from one of several tall wooden filing cabinets. "Here they are. Right here." He placed the pen and ink renderings in front of Austin. "And that, of course, means we must enlarge our hotel to a degree that will astonish the oldest inhabitant—which is exactly our goal." He looked again to Stewart and Ralph. "We're quite confident, aren't we, gentlemen?"

They nodded.

Austin appeared to study the plans. "Correct me if I'm mistaken, but I understand your town to be floundering financially. How do you justify such ambitious plans?"

"Justify?" Elton blinked nervously. "Well, I suppose our success depends, I mean I thought it obvious. That is to say, I thought—" He looked at Stewart and Ralph. "We felt certain that once you saw our plans, that is we hoped, that . . . that you would select Coventry for your syndicate." He removed his handkerchief and wiped his brow.

"I see." Austin folded the plans and rose. "Well, gentlemen, I am impressed with your grand vision." He rounded the desk and took his hat from the rack by the door. "Tell me, have your fine citizens considered the formation of a cricket club?"

Elton winced. "As a matter of fact, I did suggest it to the local blokes, but, well, Darrow is instructing the young fellows in the game of baseball and organizing a nine for the men, and—"

"Ah yes, Darrow. Colorful chap. I presume you know about our upcoming match, Whitefish versus Coventry? I must warn you, Whitefish is approaching the competition with all seriousness."

"We practice every day." He turned to Stewart and Ralph. "Don't we?"

"Every day," echoed Stewart.

"Rain or shine," added Ralph.

Austin positioned his gray fedora with a jaunty forward tilt. "Excellent! How I do love a rousing tournament. So invigorating. So manly."

Elton worried his lower lip as though in a quandary. "I keep meaning to ask Miss McAuley how she feels about the upcoming game, but she . . . "

"Yes?"

"Well, I can only assume she favors the idea. She's been seen on the playing field with Darrow. I believe he was instructing her in the holding of the bat. At least that's how it appeared to me—though I wasn't the only one to witness it. Several of us have observed them together, haven't we?" He looked at his friends.

They said nothing.

Austin arched a suspicious brow. "I think perhaps I will inquire first-hand as to Miss McAuley's preferences for the game. Thank you, gentlemen."

"Cheerio!" Elton called after him.

When Austin had gone, Stewart crossed his arms, the frayed sleeves of his jacket hiking past his ink-stained cuffs. "What in the name of all that's good and holy did you have to go and say that for?"

"I don't know what you mean." Elton hurried to his leather chair, sat down, and immediately touched every item on his desk.

"Suggesting that Miss McAuley and Darrow are carrying on. That's what I mean."

"Carrying on? Did I say that? Ralph, you heard me. Tell Stewart. Did I say they were carrying on?"

Ralph rubbed his clean-shaven cheek. "Sounded that way to me."

"Well, I merely thought it prudent that Sir Austin be made aware of the true source of his competition."

Stewart gripped the edge of the desk and leaned forward. "Prudent for you, you old fart."

"Prudent for Coventry."

Ralph scrunched his face into a question mark. "All things being equal, do you really think Austin would choose Whitefish just because Miss McAuley no longer favored him?"

With his eyes bugged wide and his voice an octave higher than normal, Elton said, "But all things are not equal. Whitefish has two hotels, a flour mill, and three pubs complete with ale and darts. And the citizens of Whitefish play cricket. Don't you see? Our only ace is Miss McAuley."

Stewart folded his arms again. "When she finds out that you've planted seeds in Austin's mind—"

"Now hold on," Ralph chimed in. "Elton wasn't the only one who saw her on the field with Darrow. So did I."

"There!" Elton said to Stewart. "You see?"

"Inga Swenson saw them, too," Ralph said, "and so did your wife."

Stewart narrowed his eyes. "What are you saying? You ran and got Mrs. Swenson, then dragged my wife into this so they could take a look?"

"As a matter of fact—"

"Why, you old biddy. The two of you ought to be ashamed of yourselves. Miss McAuley is one fine and decent woman."

"She's also a businesswoman and a loyal citizen of

this town," Elton said. "She knows the pressure we're under. She'll understand."

"Meaning you plan to tell her about your little conversation with Austin?" Stewart said.

"I plan to let time take its course, that's all."

Ralph scrunched his face again. "But she did appear—Oh, how shall I say it? Enthralled?—to be in the arms of that Darrow fellow."

Stewart groaned. "I'm leaving." He stomped out the door and down the wooden sidewalk.

"What we need," Elton said, "is a love potion."

"Why, Boldizsar, that's beautiful!" Brenna eyed the large glass bowl layered with strawberries, peaches, and vanilla pudding that the waiter placed on the table between her and Austin.

"No, no, my good man. Don't leave the bowl here. We are not pigs come to the trough." Austin pressed his checkered napkin to his lips. "Once you have presented the dessert—which I must say looks delicious—take the bowl to the buffet and prepare individual servings. And, by the by, a dollop of whipping cream is in order here."

Boldizsar grunted as he clamped his thick fingers around the bowl. "Anything else, Your Majesty?"

Austin laughed. "Oh, how I admire the irreverence of you Americans."

Brenna had tried hard to pay attention to Austin, but while he talked about the glittering social life of London, she thought about Cosmos and the other men at Amabelle's. When he retold the story of the hardships he had endured growing up the youngest in a wealthy family, all she could think of was Jake, an orphan no one wanted. She hadn't seen him all day.

When Austin stopped by her shop earlier to ask her to dinner, she had given him an excuse about needing to catch up on her paperwork. She couldn't understand why he looked so disappointed; after all, there had been other evenings when her schedule didn't accommodate his.

But she knew she wasn't fooling anyone, least of all herself. Austin was a fine and decent man, and she considered him a friend. But from the night he gave her that beautiful pin, she knew he hoped for more than friendship. Though he had never actually asked, there was a time when she had given serious thought to the idea of marrying him. Now she wondered how she could have ever considered it. It was only when he said he wanted to have dinner in order to discuss Phoebe's welfare that she agreed to go.

When she had finished her dessert, she said, "Austin, you mentioned wanting to discuss Phoebe."

He nodded, his face instantly serious. "Indeed I do. I understand she spent Saturday night last with you up at Miss Sweet's House of Recovery."

"Yes. We had gone up to deliver some medicine and while we were there one of Miss Sweet's patients threw a hemorrhage. We stayed until I was sure he was out of danger, but by then it was too late to walk back to town."

"Yes, yes, I know, my dear. I wasn't questioning you. Mrs. Dinwittie told me you had informed her prior. My concern was only that my Phoebe is becoming a burden on you."

"That could never happen. I've told you that."

"You don't know how relieved I am to hear you say it. There is so much I've been wanting to tell you—to share with you." The words tumbled out. "You see, the myth of Phoebe's mother having died in childbirth is just that—a myth. Pamela simply couldn't bear the sight of the child. She never even held her. Not once."

"Oh, Austin, no!"

He reached for his handkerchief and turned his head while he dabbed his eyes. "We were both shocked, Pamela and I, that is, when Phoebe was born. We were bewildered. Shattered. You see, neither of us had ever experienced an event so traumatic—a Mongoloid."

"I'm sure it must have been hard for everyone."

"We both felt such aching disappointment, and dare I admit it, such wounded pride. All I need do is close my eyes and I can still hear Pamela crying." He folded his hands in his lap and stared at them for a moment. "She blamed me, of course."

"Why?"

"She said I lacked the manliness of my brothers. She was right in that regard, I suppose." His hand shook as he reached for his wine glass. After a generous sip, he set the glass down. If he was hoping the alcohol would make the telling easier, he had to be disappointed, for his eyes misted as he spoke. "I refused to lock her away. She was barely four weeks old, so small and helpless, when Pamela left. We divorced the following year." He took a deep breath, though it didn't leave him looking any calmer. "I am a divorced man. I hope you won't hold that against me."

"Of course not." Brenna reached over and placed her hand on his. "More importantly, look at Phoebe. She's a beautiful, loving little girl."

Austin beamed. "Indeed she is. We learned to cope, my Phoebe and I. Unlike others of her kind, Phoebe can walk, run, feed herself. She knows her colors and she can count to ten."

"That must be because you've worked with her."

"She has never been a venturesome child, always

clinging to either me or her grandmother, God rest her soul. But since coming to Coventry, my little Phoebe has shown a flicker of independence." He held his head erect and smiled, but Brenna could see the pain still so close to the surface. "She absolutely sparkled the day she told me that you had made her an apron all her own and that she helps you by folding towels."

"She's a joy to be around. I know some of the children tease her, but—"

"Not only children. Their parents, too! They call her stupid. They say I have no right to inflict upon decent citizens the disgust of having to look at her. All of this from people who pride themselves on their lack of racial and religious prejudice."

"Try not to be too hard on them." Brenna said. "When people aren't acting out of love, they are acting out of fear."

"Maybe so. But as God is my judge, I never intended a life of pain for a child of mine."

"I know that, Austin."

He sighed again. "In her innocence and total acceptance of life, Phoebe has brought me undreamed-of joy. You don't know the good it does my heart to see the two of you together." He squeezed Brenna's hand.

An alarm went off in Brenna's mind, but it was too late. Austin was holding her left hand, stroking her bare ring finger, gratitude in his eyes, optimism in his smile.

Brenna eased her hand away. "It's late and I still have a number of things to do in the shop."

"Forgive me. I promised you an early dinner." He rose and pulled her chair.

They stepped outside and stood for a moment under the hotel's new blue awning, remnants of another evening shower dripping on the boardwalk. He took her arm. "So tell me," he said as they dodged the fresh puddles dotting the street, "what do you think of my upcoming baseball match against that Darrow chap?"

Brenna unlocked the door to the pharmacy. Austin followed her inside. "I think the whole town is looking forward to the game," she said.

"Yes, but what about *you*?"

"Oh, I'm looking forward to it, too."

"I don't suppose you know how to play. One of the chaps at the barber shop insisted that women's teams, 'bloomer girls,' I think he called them, play up and down your country."

"Well, I don't know anything about the bloomer girls, but I do know a few of the rules of the game."

"But you've never actually played?"

The strain in his voice made her wary. "No."

"Have you ever tried? I mean to say, have you at least swung a bat? Or held one in your hands?"

She folded her shawl and set it on the glass-topped counter. She had no intention of inviting him in for a cup of coffee, not when the conversation made her this uncomfortable already. "Austin, what are you trying to say?"

"Nothing of great consequence, I assure you. But I do care deeply about your reputation."

"What are you talking about?"

He laughed, but with much effort. "Oh, nothing. Nothing at all."

"Austin?"

"Well if you must know—oh, dear." He cleared his throat and straightened his posture. "Who would have ever thought that I, Austin Roderick Halliwell, a man of lineage, would have such difficulty asking a woman to marry him?"

Brenna stood speechless.

"It would be the perfect union," Austin said, talking

faster and faster. "I find you to be a compassionate and intelligent woman, the perfect wife for me, the perfect mother for Phoebe. Furthermore, as I know I've told you, I am not the most wealthy or even the most manly looking of my family, but I am sincere in my efforts, financially comfortable, and I assure you, I am healthy."

"But, Austin, I—"

"You see, Phoebe adores you, as do I. And I've simply fallen in love with your country, its wild West, its entrepreneurial spirit. I have contacts in Amsterdam whom I would trust to select an appropriate ring. In the meantime, I could help you renovate—" He stared at the glass-topped cabinet. He walked over and touched it, slowly running his finger along the new glass. "Oh dear. You've already had it repaired."

"Yes."

"By whom? If I may ask."

"Jake Darrow did it."

"Darrow? But I thought he was a salesman."

"Austin, I think we have other things to discuss."

"Yes, of course, but this Darrow chap ... He appears quite handy."

"He is. He said he had to learn how to use carpenter's tools in case he had to fix the wagon."

"I see." Austin looked around. "Perhaps you would let me order one of those fancy show globes you've been admiring. It would give me pleasure."

"I've already ordered one."

Austin went to the window and glanced at the sky. His silence made her as uncomfortable as his words. "Appears we're to enjoy a clear evening for a change. I had best be heading back."

He looked far from the confident man he portrayed. "Understand, I don't expect an answer from you now. A woman needs time to consider something as important as marriage. But I will sleep better knowing that you are at least contemplating the idea and hoping that you find it to your liking." He gave her a shaky smile. "You will think about it, won't you?"

"Austin, don't go. We have to talk about this."

"Not now. Please. If I pressed for an answer this minute, I fear I might be disappointed. And I would rather have hope than tears on my pillow tonight." He bowed. "Good night, Brenna, dear."

The afternoon had been a rainy one, but by the speed of the clouds rushing by and the wake of a clear blue sky, Jake knew the night would be perfect.

He hauled out the steel washtub and set it on a patch of weeds near the wagon. Next to it, he set a wooden crate containing sacks, small and large, of rock salt, ginger root, and melon seeds, as well as bottles of black cherry water, sweet almond oil, bundles of roots, chunks from what had once been full bales of tea leaves, and slippery elm bark. Seeing as people around here favored things English, he would comply.

He needed to whip up another batch of elixir and he needed to do it fast. Though Miss Sweet had protested, Jake had paid her another month in advance. He had also ordered both a catcher's mask and a mitt. That didn't leave much folding money on his hip. From the news around town, the Fourth of July promised to draw one hell of a crowd.

Not caring that his faded denims would get wet, he knelt on the ground and rummaged through his inventory. The world had come a long way since people ate the flesh of vipers to cure snakebites and raw potatoes to cure impotence. But given a convincing pitch, they would still believe anything. Just offer them a viletasting concoction or a box of colored pills and they would hand over the money. This time, however, he had to come up with a formula that Brenna would endorse, something without even a drop of alcohol.

He walked around the wagon and glanced down Main Street. People were still milling around. He could see the Foster boys out there helping their dad paint the front of the butcher shop. He could see Miss Zimmerman directing the two men on ladders who were nailing red, white, and blue bunting to the front of the library. Inga Swenson was standing on the boardwalk, washing her bakery window with a mop. He hadn't seen Brenna all day, not since she and Phoebe left Amabelle's yesterday morning.

He couldn't think of Brenna without feeling his groin tighten. He had spent half the night thinking up excuses to be alone with her. He glanced at the tub and the crate. If she watched him as he threw everything together, she wouldn't have to spend time analyzing the finished product and she could state up front that every ingredient was harmless.

He drew a dipper of cold water from the barrel strapped to the side of the wagon. He splashed the water on his face and headed for Main Street.

Brenna's hand lingered on the bar she had placed across the door. She had watched Austin disappear into the hotel at least ten minutes ago, his shoulders slumped, his head down. She would never forget the disappointment in his eyes. It would have been so easy to just say yes. The man offered financial security and support for her own ventures. Though he never mentioned the word "love," Brenna knew he cared for her. A woman her age would have to be crazy to turn him down. Yet that's exactly what she would have done tonight had he stayed. But would she have made the right decision?

She released her grip on the black iron bolt, not aware until then that she had been squeezing it. The one and only ingredient in Austin's proposal that had her questioning her decision now was Phoebe. The little girl needed a mother's love and Brenna already loved her.

She was about to turn away from the door when she saw Jake coming down the boardwalk. He called out something to the Foster boys and waved. He nodded to Inga Swenson and gave Sarah Zimmerman a big smile. The damp ovals on his Levi's told Brenna he had been kneeling on the ground. Perhaps that was why his leg appeared to trouble him more than usual.

She released the latch and opened the door when he was still a few yards away. He must have interpreted her eagerness for what it was, because he smiled with his eyes as much as with his lips.

"Evening," he said. "Are you busy?"

She stepped back to let him in. "Nothing that can't wait. Why?"

He peeked out the window. "Come over here," he said, taking her hand and guiding her a few feet away from the door. "They can't see us over here."

Suddenly in his embrace, she wrapped her arms around his neck in a pose now familiar. She parted her lips and pressed her pelvis to his, admitting her intense delight in the hard evidence of his pent-up need— because she felt the need too.

The sounds coming from outside were those of horses and wagons slogging through the mud. Nothing close enough to worry about.

She didn't resist when he slipped his hand around her neck and freed the knot of her apron, letting the black silk fall, or when he covered her breast with his mouth, or when he slipped her hand from around his neck and dragged it down his chest, past his waist.

He didn't resist when she clasped his manhood tight, but moaned as she stroked its full length.

Added to the sounds outside now were those of children laughing and heavy boots on the wooden walk. Though still not close, they broke the illusion of privacy and the spell of desire.

"Oh, Jake," she murmured as she drew back only a few inches. "We can't let this happen."

"Sure we can. It's what men and women have been doing since the dawn of time." He reached for her, his hands already formed to cup her breasts, but she stepped away.

"No."

"What is it? What's the matter?"

She sought the kind of smile that would pave a painless path for the truth. "Well, maybe you could, but I . . . I can't. Not like this."

He looked so uncertain. "I've really misunderstood something here, haven't I? I mean, you said you needed some time, but that's not what you meant, is it? You're waiting for something more, something like marriage. Am I right?"

At least love. Silently, she nodded.

"I should have known. I mean, you have every right."

She waited, listening with an intensity so hard it hurt, but he didn't say anything else, so she took a chance and asked, "What do you see for your future, Jake? Have you thought of putting down roots somewhere?"

"And give up the open road?" His smile looked anything but genuine. "Cosmos and I, we have a route we follow. South in the winter. North in the summer. A new adventure around every turn." He raked his hand through his hair, looking for all the world like a man who couldn't wait to escape. "I just can't see myself chained to one place." He sighed, relieved no doubt to have spoken his mind.

"I see."

"I'm sorry, Brenna. I really am. I thought you understood."

"There's no need to apologize." From somewhere deep inside she drew a precious ounce of dignity, just enough to mask her embarrassment at being so needy. "Well, I'm obviously glad you came by, but I'm sure you had a reason—another reason—for wanting to see me." She tied the apron strings around her neck, tied them tight. "Is it Cosmos? I went up early this morning to see him, but he was still asleep."

"No. Nothing has changed in the last few days. Except when he hemorrhages, the blood measures more than it used to."

"Yes, Miss Sweet told me. Two tablespoons. Twice what it has been. I'll go up again later this afternoon." She forced a lightness to her voice. "In the meantime, just what was that other reason you had for stopping by?"

"Well, I was hoping you would come down to my wagon."

She laughed, trying to conceal her pain. "Your wagon? I don't think that's a good idea."

"Hold on a minute. I have a legitimate reason."

"And what is that?" she said, hating the fact that he had to make light of the situation.

"My new elixir. I want you to see for yourself what ingredients I'm using."

Brenna shook her head. "I don't want to get

involved with that. I can't endorse your product and you know it."

"You couldn't endorse the old elixir, but this one is different. No alcohol. You'll see." He took her hand. "Come on."

"No, Jake." She pulled her hand away, though what she still wanted was to embrace him with all the passion they had shared a moment before.

"I'll only keep you a minute."

She almost laughed, so painfully true were his words.

He continued. "I have everything set up. I was hoping you would stay to watch the brewing itself, but if you can't, well, I'll just have to accept that. But if you would just look at the herbs I'm using. If you would just—"

"All right. I'll go."

Together, they headed for the door. Once again she had to free her hand from his, but this time she didn't dare let herself think about embracing him. She was not the kind of woman who would give her body before she gave her heart. And she wasn't about to give her heart to a man who wouldn't give his in return, a man like Jake. She would have to accept that.

14

There had been more than a few times in his life when Jake had been ashamed of himself, but never more so than now. With the sweet taste of Brenna still on his lips and his hands impatient to touch her, they walked side by side along the wooden walkway, stopping while Sarah Zimmerman commented on how well the play was coming along and what a shame it was that neither Jake nor Brenna had tried out for parts. Inga Swenson asked not once, but twice, if they could see any streaks in her windows. The Foster boys and their father wanted to talk baseball. Through it all, Brenna spoke with a steady voice, agreeing with everyone that the upcoming Fourth of July celebration would be the best the town had ever seen, and making sure to mention that she was on her way to examine the ingredients Jake planned to use in his new elixir.

She declined to take his hand as they stepped down from the boardwalk. He doubted any of her neighbors knew just how much she was hurting. But he had a pretty good idea.

"Here it is," Jake said as they approached a table made of a door propped between two upright barrels.

He watched her as she loosened the drawstrings of each sack and smelled, touched, and tasted the contents. She didn't say anything. She remained silent as she examined the bottle of sweet almond oil, though he nearly moaned when she dipped her middle finger into the white-gold liquid, and brought it to the tip of her tongue.

He told himself that she was silent because she could find nothing wrong with his operation. But he knew there was more to it than that. She wouldn't even look at him unless it was unavoidable, and even then, she kept her eyes down.

Why did things have to get so complicated between them?

"No bezoar stones?" she asked. "No unicorn powder? No moss from the skulls of criminals?"

"Nope. Just what you see here. Herbs, flowers, fruits, vegetables, bark, and oil."

She looked some more. "If no alcohol, what will you use for a carrier? Water?"

"Better than that. Tea."

"I see. Clever. What are you using for bottles?"

"I've got two crates of eight-ounce shop bottles in the wagon. Cork stoppers, nothing fancy. Want to see them?"

"I see bottles all the time. Why would I want to see yours?"

There was no mistaking the edge of bitterness. "Yeah, I guess you're right."

He watched the soft curve of her jaw set into a hard line and he wondered if she regretted her words. "As long as these ingredients are the only ones that go into your new elixir, I don't see any reason for me to object."

"Thank you." He gave his best smile, but she never looked his way.

"Do you have enough?" she asked. "Bottles, that is."

Had he only imagined the quiver in her voice? "I guess that depends on how much I can sell."

"I have several crates of shelf bottles in a variety of sizes. Some with cork stoppers, some with glass. If it turns out you need them, I can spare a few."

He felt about as small as a flea and even less desirable. "I hope I sell so much I have to take you up on your offer—but I'll pay you for them."

"When's your next show?"

"Fourth of July. I understand the whole valley will be in town."

"That's right." She stared down Main Street, catching a glimpse, as he did, of the citizens who were counting on her to snare old Austin Halliwell. Jake had heard the talk. He knew exactly what was going on. She'd be better off with Halliwell, anyway.

"Brenna, please. I know you're upset with me and I don't blame you. But you want something I can't—"

"I'm not upset with you. I'm upset with myself. What each of us wants out of life is no one's fault. Nor is it anyone's fault if our dreams collide, though I don't really know what it is you want out of life."

He hated himself for the tears brimming in her eyes.

"I saw all this coming," she said, "and still I chose to believe only what I wanted to believe."

"You saw what coming?"

"You." She took one of those deep breaths, the kind that steadies a troubled mind. "Well," she said, scrutinizing his paraphernalia one more time, "Now that you have what you came for, I'll be on my way."

"Wait a minute. It's not like that and you know it."

"I deal with facts, Jake. Remember? Not magic. Not miracles. Just facts, accurate observations, and deductions."

"Hippocrates," he said, recalling the principles of science upon which modern medicine was based.

"That's right. Good luck with your new elixir. I hope you do well."

He thought about stopping her, but there wasn't anything left to say. She believed in science. He believed in the dollar. And up on the hill was an old man who believed in what neither of them could produce: a miracle.

He knew one more thing, too: She believed in love.

". . . And for the support of this Declaration, with a firm reliance on the Protection of Divine Providence, we mutually pledge to each other our Lives, our Fortunes, and our sacred Honor." Mayor Elton Fontaine solemnly bowed.

Standing next to Amabelle, Brenna clapped till her hands were red. Along with nearly five hundred others standing in front of Coventry's one small church, she had a lump in her throat.

"Every year he reads the Declaration of Independence, and every year I cry." Brenna caught a tear forming at the corner of her eye. "Who would have thought he could elicit such emotion?"

They walked through the crowd, past horses with little flags flying from their bridles and haversacks of bread and butter dangling from the saddles, past wagons decorated with red, white, and blue bunting and loaded with quilts and picnic baskets, toward a row of towering conifers and Sarah Zimmerman's lemonade stand.

"Wasn't he magnificent?" Sarah said, pouring from a cut glass pitcher into two of the dozens of mix-and-match mugs arranged in front of her.

"Yes he was," Brenna said, then sipped the tart beverage. "When I first met him I didn't think he had the ability to run an entire town. I'm happy to say I was wrong."

Amabelle downed her lemonade almost at once. "I don't want to rush you, dear, but I know you'll want to be up front for Lord Austin's oration."

"We have plenty of time."

"No, you don't," Sarah said. "Look. He's being escorted up the steps now. Isn't it grand? To have a true English gentleman giving the Fourth of July oration?"

Brenna shaded her eyes as she looked toward the sun-drenched white church, the American flag draped horizontally across the door, families in their Sunday best. She expected to see an eagle soar overhead, so perfect was the setting.

"Hurry now," Sarah said, making a shooing motion with her hand. "He'll be looking for you." She winked. "Perhaps this will be the last year each of us is serenaded with that awful ditty: 'Stirred with a spade, by an old maid.'"

Amabelle set her glass down. "Perhaps."

Brenna felt the comforting touch of Amabelle's hand on her arm. The two had spoken every day this week, cutting through the clutter of chit-chat to their thoughts on friendship and love. Amabelle had apologized for jumping to conclusions about Brenna's ability to practice the Old Magic. Brenna had confided her heartache over Jake.

"Look," Amabelle said, "Phoebe is climbing the steps."

Unable to reach the handrail, Phoebe struggled to keep her balance. Brenna cheered in silence, holding her breath until Phoebe reached the last of the three steps. Despite her lack of intimate emotions for Austin, she couldn't help but feel something for him as he smiled and leaned forward, his hand outstretched to his little girl.

Amabelle tapped her arm. "Don't force your heart to accept what it doesn't want. Don't even try. The pain would be truly unbearable. For both of you."

Brenna said nothing, listening instead to the drumroll of a six-piece fife-and-drum corps and the precise enunciation with which Austin delivered each word of his oration to America. He spoke with passion about the valiant homesteader and his woman, the Madonna of the Plains, who came to arid land and made it bloom. He spoke with equal fervor about the cattlemen and their need to accept the loss of the free range and build their domain in a way that would bring no harm to their neighbor. He spoke of Coventry and his hope that it would thrive into the next century and beyond. Above all, that it would grow into the oasis of culture and refinement he envisioned.

The entire town cheered, many of them turning to Brenna and smiling. Austin extended his hand, motioning for her to join him. But she didn't want to join him. And she wouldn't have joined him, except that Phoebe was looking at her, too, bobbing up and down, flat-footed, and holding out her little arms.

Off to the side, Jake watched the whole scene. They weren't his definition of a perfect family, an Englishman who flip-flopped from snob to bleeding heart, a sweet little girl who was destined to a life of ridicule, and a beautiful, compassionate woman who wanted to be loved.

Damn it all!

He tugged the points of his red vest and walked away.

Try as he might, Jake couldn't block out the shouts and laughter drifting up from the town. They were cheering the men and boys who were climbing greased poles, chasing oiled pigs, or lumbering along in the slowest horse race.

He hadn't gone to the sunrise salute, but he had heard it. Lacking a canon, someone had exploded gunpowder on the blacksmith's anvil. Immediately, a flurry of shotgun blasts had echoed all down the valley. Fourth of July. Small-town celebrations. Evergreen boughs hanging on every store. Heaps of rockets and firecrackers. Hokey, that's what it was. He didn't need it. He sure didn't want it.

What he needed was to get the hell out of Montana. If it weren't for Cosmos, he'd ride out this minute. He'd keep riding till he no longer pictured Brenna McAuley every time he closed his eyes.

Amabelle Sweet's House of Recovery wasn't that high in the foothills, but it was high enough. He was out of breath when he finally reached the meadow.

On a beautiful day like this he expected to see every man out on that wide porch, rocking and soaking up sunshine. The porch was empty.

He gripped the railing and climbed the steps. Thank God, Cosmos's room was on the ground floor now.

Inside, the ever-present coughing mixed with the unusual sound of laughter. The laughter wasn't the deep, full-bellied kind, but it was laughter just the same. And it came from Cosmos's room. Then he heard a man's voice.

"Don't you go handin' me a line, you old geezer. You're a laying here a dying just like the rest of us. Meanwhile, your partner's down yonder peddlin' a cure-all that bears your name and likeness. And you have the gall to say you ain't a confidence man? Horse feathers!"

The laughter that followed had an edge to it, but not enough to make Jake worry. "What's going on here?" he said as he stepped inside and went straight to the bed.

Weaker than ever, Cosmos lay against the pillows, his skin, even his lips, as white as the cloth. As soon as he saw Jake, he raised his bony hand. It trembled. "Son, come meet my friends."

Jake nodded to the men, most dressed in suits two sizes too big, a few in nightshirts, heavy robes, and slippers. Jake had met all of them shuffling around over the past two months. "I see you're having your own Independence Day celebration." To Cosmos, he said, "You feeling all right?"

"As good as I have a right to expect." Cosmos smiled, accentuating the folds of loose skin that had once covered full, robust cheeks. The copper-brown stains on the front of his nightshirt told Jake he had had another hemorrhage, though apparently a small one.

Reality was either painful or ugly, and sometimes both. Jake had seen enough of it to know.

The man in the most ill-fitting suit of all leaned against the dresser. He looked to be about forty. His collar floated around his neck. "So you're the one he's been a braggin' on. He says you can sell a snake right out of a new skin."

"He taught me everything I know."

"I'm not surprised you'd be so quick to brag. He never said you was modest."

One of the other men, younger, thinner, slapped his hand on the dresser, but the weak effort produced no sound at all. "Hobble that lip of yours, Wallace."

"Hobble your own lip. I'm just having me some fun." Wallace pinched a gold chain draped across his gaping vest and pulled out a gold pocket watch. He walked over and handed it to Jake. "Here you go, hot shot. Let's hear your pitch."

"Sorry. This isn't the time or place." He tried to hand the watch back but Wallace wouldn't take it.

"Go on," Wallace said, a hard gleam suddenly burning in his eyes. "Show us how good you are."

"Please," one of the other men said to Jake. "We won't see any of the show in town. Just a taste of what we're missing—that's all we ask."

Jake glanced over at Cosmos, who looked like he was about to fall asleep. "All right," he said, "let's see what we've got here."

He examined the watch. It was heavy, probably eighteen karat. The lid was engraved with a lot of swirls and what looked to be two hearts. It was hard to tell. The surface had been worn smooth.

He cupped the watch in the palm of one hand. He had a show to do tonight. The rehearsal would be good for him. "Step right up, gentlemen, for you are in luck. I'm here to make you a once-in-a-lifetime offer on a product you won't find anywhere else." He made eye contact with each man as he spoke. "I know how important it is for you to keep to your schedule and I have just the thing to help you accomplish your goal." He held up the watch. "Have a look at this fine time-piece, gentlemen. Solid gold. Eighteen karat."

He could see the men nodding, agreeing, whether they were aware of it or not, with his appraisal of the object and his assessment of their need. All except

Wallace. His eyes had narrowed to slits as he watched Jake handle the watch. His lips formed a sneer.

"Open it," Wallace said. "Go on. Open it."

Jake held it to his ear. No one made a sound. "Still ticking."

"Open the god damned thing, you healthy bastard!"

"Hey!" one of the other men said. "That's enough of your talk. Knock it off."

"That's all right," Jake said, glaring at Wallace. Every audience had its troublemaker. "I can handle it." He snapped the latch. He looked down. Inside the cover was a wedding picture.

"That's my wife," Wallace said, his voice gritty.

"She's a lovely woman," Jake said, holding the watch up for the others to see.

"She wrote me a letter. Said she couldn't take care of the house and the kids by herself and since it didn't look like I was going to ever get better, she had to do something. I done told her six months ago to go ahead and take in boarders. But did she do that? Hell no. What she did was go and get herself another man. A healthy man!"

Wallace walked over, grabbed the watch from Jake's hand and threw it on the floor. "A healthy man like you, you son of a bitch." He stormed out of the room, leaving a shroud of silence.

Jake stood there, humbled by the thought that another man would envy him, limp and all.

The fireworks would start within the hour, but with this crowd, that was time enough. Wearing a clean white shirt, black string tie, and his lucky red vest, he stepped to the edge of the stage. "Step right up, folks. Step right up."

Crowds of people moved aimlessly up and down the street, crossing from one side to the other. There were kids hunched over from too much candy and ginger-pop. There were men hunched over from too much whiskey, and women who were just plain exhausted.

Jake held up a bottle of his new elixir. "Here it is, folks. Just what you've been waiting for. Celestial Compound. It will give you that boost of energy you need. It will guarantee a peaceful night's sleep. It's all new, totally effective, and totally safe. You can ask your own druggist, Miss Brenna McAuley."

"Miss McAuley has approved your product?" a woman in green asked.

"That's right, ma'am. She witnessed every ingredient."

"Then I'll take one."

"You won't regret it," he said, handing her a bottle and taking her dollar. "Your family will love you for it."

In the next few minutes, he sold two bottles to the woman in orange in the front row. He wondered what Brenna was doing now. Was she enjoying the festivities?

"Here you go, sir," he said to the man in the cowboy hat and handed him four bottles.

Half an hour later, Jake had sold nearly all his supply and was feeling confident. After the incident with Wallace, Jake was also feeling fortunate. His leg might be crooked, but he was otherwise healthy, except for the pain in his heart.

The crowd had shown no signs of dwindling when he spotted Halliwell working his way to the front.

"I say there, Darrow. I've heard a nasty rumor about this compound of yours."

"And what's that?"

"Word has it that Cosmos Clarion, the namesake of

your miracle concoction, is, even as we speak, lying on his deathbed at Miss Sweet's refuge." If the pause that followed was for effect, it worked. The crowd turned to Halliwell. "Do you deny it?"

The woman in orange, the one in green, the man in the cowboy hat—they were all looking at the bottles they had just purchased. "No," Jake said emphatically. "I don't deny it." On the heels of a unanimous gasp from the audience, he added, "I boast of it—not that he is ill, but that he has lived so well for so long. The man is nearing seventy-five years old." The mention of such a ripe old age drew another gasp.

He reached to the table behind him and grabbed one of the few remaining bottles. He stepped to the very edge of the stage and spread his legs in a defiant stance. Holding the bottle for all to see, he said, "Good people, have I ever claimed that this elixir, powerful as it is, could stay the hand of God? No. Of course not." He saw that he had their attention. "Living on the land as you do, you know that we cannot enjoy spring unless we first endure winter." Now they were nodding.

"As Halliwell said, Cosmos Clarion, my esteemed partner, is up at Miss Sweet's place. And it's true that despite the elixir that bears his name, the man is—"

He hadn't expected the words to choke him, but they did. And he hadn't expected his eyes to water.

When he found his voice again, he said, softer, "The man is dying."

He didn't look to see who was listening, who was nodding in agreement, who was walking away. It suddenly didn't matter. "Though Cosmos Clarion has known great hardship in his life, he has endured heartaches far worse. He knows what it is to suffer the loss of wife and child, the loss of home and job. It was his own pain that led him to the patent medicine trade.

And his own desire to bring comfort to others in pain, particularly children, that led him to formulating the elixir that bears his name." He stared at the bottle in his hand, only vaguely aware that his hand was shaking. "But even he, good people, even he must die."

Austin spoke up. "Then explain if you can, Mr. Darrow, why you found it necessary to lie. You told these people that Mr. Clarion was back in Missoula and planned to join you soon."

"Because that's what I wanted to believe." Jake was powerless to control his thoughts, and they drifted back in time to the railway station in Kansas City, to that Friday on the edge of winter when Cosmos chose him, a dirt-streaked, snot-nosed kid with a crooked leg, to be his friend.

Austin's voice called him back. "Could it be, then, that you merely want people to believe that your elixir here is non-toxic?"

Jake stood silent.

"Excuse me," Brenna said, making her way to the front. Standing next to Austin, she addressed the crowd. "Ladies and gentlemen, please," she said as she held up her hands, gaining their attention. "You need not question your purchases. I inspected every ingredient in that elixir myself. It is harmless." She looked up at Jake, her pale green eyes brimming with compassion.

The sudden crackle and boom of fireworks drew everyone's attention. The children hurried toward the rain of the glittering skybursts. Their parents followed, pointing to the soaring rockets with their high-pitched whistles and their thunderous booms. Those who remained heard Jake say simply, "Thanks for coming, folks. That's all for tonight."

Half of him wanted to find a place of quiet solitude and face, now that he could, just how profoundly his

life was about to change. The other half wanted to jump
down from the stage and take Brenna in his arms. But
Brenna walked away with Austin, leaving Jake to hear
the deafening whistles and whines of the celebration
going on all around him.

The seventh night of the seventh month was a night
for lovers, Brenna had always been told. On one side
of the heavens sat the star of the spinning girl. On the
other sat the shepherd boy whose job it was to keep
the newly spun stars in formation. All year long the
spinning girl and shepherd boy gazed at each other,
forbidden to express the love in their hearts. Only on
this one night were they permitted to come together.

Restless for hours, Brenna lay against the crisp
white sheets, cooled from the night air. The full moon
had been waning for five days now, but it still cast
enough light to pierce her room with midnight shadows.

Jake didn't love her, but that didn't prevent her from
loving him. She didn't know when it had happened,
that giving of her heart, but it had. All these years she
had felt something missing from her life. Her profession
had kept her busy, and in many ways, fulfilled. She had
a lot of friends, particularly Amabelle. Phoebe held a
special place in her heart. But as good as career and
friendship and motherly love were, they were no substi-
tute for the love between a man and a woman, just as
there was no pain like the bone-deep loneliness she felt
now.

She turned on her side and drew one of the pillows
lengthwise against her body. All these years, fear had
kept her from opening her heart. Or maybe it had protected her heart until the right man came along.

*   *   *

Wearing an undershirt, faded jeans, and scuffed boots, Jake stood in the doorway of his wagon and stared at the stars. Cosmos wasn't long for this world and Jake knew it. He'd known it for a long time. The difference now was that he accepted it. Finally.

Cosmos had already told Jake to do whatever he wanted with the wagon. Keep driving it across the country or sell it and take up baseball. Jake laughed out loud, but the sound fell to the ground and the clumps of weeds already trying to hold the wagon wheels in place.

He had always known he could never play baseball. He accepted that, too. Finally. He could keep driving across the country selling his own brand of elixir. He was good at it. It just didn't make him happy. The only reason he had stayed with it all these years was Cosmos.

He glanced toward Main Street, plunged in darkness, and still exhausted from Friday's celebration. Since when did he have a right to be happy?

He didn't know how long he stood there staring at the street, but it was long enough for his eyes to gather the light of the moon, enabling him to see his hand as he pulled the door shut behind him. He made his way down the stairs, along Main Street, to the boardwalk in front of Brenna's home.

15

Brenna rose from her bed and stood still and quiet in the streaks of silver-white light. She had heard no sound, seen no movement. But she had felt the heat.

Jake was near. As much as her heart longed for his embrace, it warned her that without his love, she would feel nothing but pain. Though she walked slowly through the room and into the shop, the sound of her bare feet on the wooden floor composed an urgent melody. Her last rational thought was that her love for him would have to be enough.

She needed both hands to lift the bolt and slide it back. She opened the door to find him, as she knew she would, standing in the murky shadows, waiting. She stepped aside to let him in. The moment of choice passed.

He closed the door and bolted it. He took her in his arms so swiftly, so tightly, she cried out, only to have the sound smothered by his kiss. In the fevered press of his lips on hers, she heard the beating of his heart. And in his ragged breath, she felt the very same agony that had robbed her of sleep since the day she saw him drive into town.

"Do you know how much I want you?" he said.

She pressed her finger to his lips, begging him with her eyes not to say any more. She didn't want to hear some weak excuse for coming to her so late, or worse yet, an apology for the lust that had driven him to her, not when she felt such love for him. Instead, she took his hand and led him to her bed.

He would be gone soon, in a few weeks, a few months at most. Knowing time was short, she slipped her unadorned cotton gown from her shoulders.

"Let me help you," Jake said, easing the fabric from her body.

She welcomed his touch. For others more fortunate, this act of mating would signal a pledge of lifelong devotion, like that of her parents, and their parents before them. She would have to be content with memories, and the hope that he would give her at least a little place in his heart.

Tomorrow night her bed would creak in its familiar, singular way, but not tonight. She climbed to the center where she knelt in the restless tangle of warm sheets and old quilt, waiting.

Just as he had observed her, she now watched as he sat down to remove his boots, and as he stood to strip off his shirt. He hesitated before tugging off his jeans, but only for a moment. The bed groaned with his added weight. Her flesh pebbled instantly at his touch.

Caught in his embrace, she tilted her head and parted her lips. Like the pulling of the tides, natural rhythms guided her hand to his hard sex. She stroked him again and again as he moaned against her mouth. If there was to be only this one time, she wanted it to be beautiful.

Earlier that night, she had kindled the fire with dried twigs of rosemary, lemon, and lavender. Now, a draft of cool air from the window entwined with the heat and aromas and worked themselves around her body like cords binding her to him, whether he knew it or not.

She resisted the growing impulse to whisper words of love, and instead yielded to the joy of being held in his arms. Guided by his embrace, she lay down beside him. His hands caressed her. Each firm stroke pressed her flesh against his until her every curve and every swell found its mate. Jake's hands were gentle when they parted her thighs, his fingers tender when they coaxed open her delicate folds. The sudden heat Brenna felt awakened a power in her she didn't know she had. She arched against his hand, yearning for more.

"God, you're beautiful," he murmured, his kiss following the trail of moonlight along her body.

She felt beautiful. She felt desired. She heard his breathing quicken, felt the pressure of his rigid shaft. Touching her lips to his chest, she tasted salt and sun, and inhaled the fragrance of passion.

Jake mounted her. Balanced on the edge of ecstasy, Brenna's fears unraveled like loosely knotted strands of silk, meant to relax at his command.

Even though this was her first time, she hadn't wanted the intimacy of his words, no matter how reassuring, no matter how flattering. Without his love, they were hollow.

"An enchantress," he whispered, then covered her mouth with his.

She had counted on silence to shield her heart from sorrow, yet she cried out when he thrust inside her, piercing her inner veil, blending pleasure with pain. Flickering light showed the concern in his dark eyes. Lest he have second thoughts, she spread her hands on his buttocks and pushed him deeper as she lifted her hips to draw him in. Behind them, flames leaped in pagan rhythms. Wild, ancient spirits danced in her mind, screaming for the moment of abandon. When the passion grew beyond endurance, she surrendered. His own shudder followed, leaving them both covered with sweat and panting.

In the quiet aftermath, she closed her eyes as he silently stroked her shoulders, her arms, her hips and thighs, as though seeking parts he might have missed. It wasn't necessary. He owned her heart.

Hours later, but well before the fingers of dawn could point, he left as quietly as he had come, as surely as she knew he would.

Brenna knew something was different the moment Mrs. Dinwittie and Phoebe stepped through the door. Phoebe, as always, beamed with adoration. Mrs. Dinwittie, usually so prim and pinch-faced, actually smiled, though it clearly pained her to do so.

"Miss McAuley, I just wanted to say that it has always been a pleasure doing business with you."

"Thank you."

"Yes, well, on an entirely different matter, if it wouldn't be an imposition, might you be able to keep Miss Phoebe this morning? Of course, if that presents a problem—"

"It's no problem." Brenna winked at Phoebe, who was standing next to Mrs. Dinwittie.

"You see, I have a pressing matter to attend to, a personal matter, that is—"

"I don't mind at all. Phoebe, do you want to help me wash a new shipment of bottles? And then we can have lunch."

Phoebe stepped forward. "A picnic?"

"Sure." The bittersweet memory of last night started to fade. "Don't worry, Mrs. Dinwittie. Phoebe and I will have a wonderful time."

"Yes, you do seem to have a way with the child." Mrs. Dinwittie furrowed her brow and glanced around, looking everywhere except at Brenna.

"Is everything all right?" Brenna asked.

"For some of us, yes, I suppose it is quite all right. Will you excuse me?" With that, she left.

As soon as Mrs. Dinwittie had gone, Brenna knelt down and opened her arms. Phoebe filled them instantly, giggling against her neck. Easing back, Brenna said, "Well, you certainly are happy this morning."

Phoebe nodded rapidly.

"Do you want to tell me why?"

"'Cause you're going to be my new momma!"

Struggling to control the panic she felt, Brenna said, "Who told you that?"

"Poppa told me and Mrs. Din."

Brenna stood. "When?"

"This morning."

How could he do this? "We have to go see your poppa right now." She took Phoebe's hand and headed for the door.

"Poppa left."

"When? Where did he go?"

"He went to Whitefish. After breakfast."

"No!"

Phoebe trembled. Her voice shrank. "He didn't eat all his toast."

Calming herself, Brenna stroked Phoebe's round cheek. "It's all right, Phoebe. Everything's going to be all right. When is your poppa coming back?"

Phoebe shrugged.

Brenna stepped outside and scanned the street, up and down, both sides. No sign of Austin. She had to talk to him, tell him the definitive "no" he hadn't wanted to hear. She had to tell him before his presumption caused any more damage, though it had already done the worst. She looked at Phoebe, at her tiny brown eyes wide with hope, and felt a rush of anger and another, far greater, of sadness. How could Austin set that child up for such bitter disappointment?

Phoebe tugged on her skirt. "Are you still going to be my momma?"

Brenna breathed in slowly, not wanting the anger she felt toward Austin to come through her words. "Phoebe, I think there has been a misunderstanding. Your poppa and I have some things to talk about."

"But are you? Are you going to be my momma?"

She looked at the trusting face of the child no one wanted to touch. She didn't know what to say that wouldn't hurt, and yet to say nothing was to give false hope.

"Miss McAuley!"

Brenna looked up to see Mayor Elton Fontaine scurrying down the boardwalk. "I heard the news." Panting, he removed his straw boater and fanned himself.

"What news?"

"I just came from Stewart McCutcheon's. Mrs. Dinwittie just wired an agency in New York City." He stopped to catch his breath. "An employment agency."

Oh, no.

The mayor continued. "It appears she has been dismissed, or expects to be shortly."

"Please," Brenna said, glancing down at Phoebe, then back to the mayor. "I don't think you should be saying such things—"

"Yes, yes, you're right. Of course." He lowered his voice. "But the wire did say that her present employer would be getting married shortly and would have no further need for her services. Oh, Miss McAuley, we are all so happy for you! For everyone! For Coventry!"

He reached out, apparently to pat Phoebe's head, but drew his hand back, an uncertain look in his eyes. Phoebe didn't look surprised at all. Brenna nearly cried.

"Look!" Phoebe pointed to a wagon racing down the crowded street. The man holding the reins jerked them back and steered the horse toward Brenna. Like everyone else on the boardwalk, she tried to fan away the cloud of dust so she could see the cause of the commotion.

Booker and Alice Griggs. As always, she looked hard-worked and he looked ready for a fight.

The wagon had barely stopped when Alice cried, "It's Dooley!" She climbed over the front seat to the bed. "You gotta help him!"

"What is it? What happened?" Brenna rushed to the rear of the wagon, stepped on the hub of the wheel and climbed up. Inside the wagon, on a threadbare quilt stained with vomit, lay one of the Griggs's eleven small, scrawny children. He didn't move.

Drawn by the commotion, Inga Swenson rushed over. So did Sarah Zimmerman. The mayor was trying to answer everyone's questions. Booker Griggs stood next to his horses, not saying a word. Phoebe was staring at him.

"How old is Dooley?" Brenna asked as she knelt down next to the boy. "Dooley, can you hear me? Can you talk to me, Dooley?"

"He'll be nine next month. God willing." Alice bit down on her lip as she wrung her hands. "He's poisoned, ain't he?"

His pulse was slow, as was his breathing. His tongue looked thick and hung from the corner of his mouth. His breath reeked of alcohol, and something sweet. "What did he drink and when?"

Alice twisted her neck to look to her husband and cowed when he glared back. "Nothing. Just that medicine you made for the mister's stomach."

Booker Griggs, gastroenteritis, elixir of triple bromide with laudanum. She had followed the formula, measured the ingredients precisely. She was sure of it. But that wasn't the issue. She had made the elixir for the father, a man of considerable weight, not a small, skinny boy. "How much of it did he drink?"

Alice hesitated. "I don't know. Honest. He just retched and retched and couldn't stop." She smoothed his hair. "He's poisoned. I just know it. Maybe he got hold of some bad roots or something. I just don't know."

"Mr. Griggs, when was the last time you medicated for your stomach, and how much was left in the bottle?"

He looked inconvenienced to say the least and spoke through gritted teeth. "Don't rightly remember."

Brenna leaned over the boy's face again. If she was right, he was drunk. "There was nothing in the medicine I made for your stomach that would smell sweet. Your son drank something else. What was it?"

No sooner were the words out of Brenna's mouth than she spotted the empty bottle of Jake's new Celestial Compound in the corner of the wagon, tucked in a pile of rope and rags. Alice saw it, too. "Is that what he drank?" Brenna asked, praying the answer was no.

Booker stepped to the side of the wagon, reached in

and grabbed the bottle. Alice screeched like a frightened bird. "No, Booker, don't! Please!"

Smashing the bottle on the boardwalk, he shouted, "The devil's brew! That's the cause of all this!" He glared at his wife, then walked away.

Alice leaned over her son, her cracked red hands soothing his brow. The crowd buzzed with "the tragedy of the poor Griggs boy" and "the shocking truth" about Jake Darrow's elixir.

As the crowd grew, Brenna had several men carry Dooley inside. "Bring him in here," she said, directing them through the shop and into her bedroom. "Mrs. Griggs, why don't you sit right here beside your son. I'll get you a pan of cool water and a cloth. You can apply compresses to his forehead." She couldn't say it would do Dooley any good, but performing the ministrations would probably help his mother.

Alice sat down on the chair Jake had used to take off his boots and drape his clothes. "Is he dying?"

"No. He's drunk." Brenna examined his vital signs again. They were still slow, but steady. "When he wakes up, I'll give him some willow bark to ease the headache and settle his stomach. But he'll still be sore. He probably won't want to eat anything for a while. What he does eat should be bland."

Alice whimpered softly and buried her face in her hands. "My poor baby."

"Help me get his shirt off. I'll rinse it out and hang it to dry."

With that accomplished, Brenna brought Mrs. Griggs a glass of lemonade and a soft cotton throw. "You need some rest yourself."

"No, no, I'm fine."

"When Dooley wakes up, he's likely to be confused. It would help for him to open his eyes and find you here."

Nodding quickly, Alice said, "Oh, yes. You're right. I'll stay right here."

"He won't wake for several hours. So why don't you lie down, too."

"He ain't gonna die?"

"Not from this."

Alice sipped the lemonade. She had to hold the glass with two hands, they were trembling so.

"Mrs. Griggs, I have an errand I must run. I'll be back shortly. I'm going to have Sarah Zimmerman stay with you. Do you know Miss Zimmerman? She's our librarian."

"No, but you go on. Me and Dooley, we'll be fine."

Brenna looked around before she left Alice and her son. The room bore no trace of the lovemaking she had enjoyed less than twelve hours ago. Except for the memories of passion and need.

Back in the shop, she held out her hand for Phoebe and said, "I'm sorry, Phoebe. We won't be able to have our picnic today."

"Because of that boy?"

"Yes. We have to go to Mr. McCutcheon's telegraph shop first, then we have to find Mrs. Dinwittie."

"You aren't going to be my momma, are you?"

Brenna knelt down and cupped Phoebe's face in her hands. "No, Phoebe. I'm not."

"Why did Poppa say it?"

"I don't know."

"Did he mess up?"

"Yes," she said, her voice catching. "He messed up. But even though I'm not going to get to be your mother, I will always love you. Always." She prayed that both their hearts would accept what had to be, especially when Phoebe reached out, touched Brenna's cheek, and wiped away a tear.

*   *   *

Brenna found Mrs. Dinwittie in the back of the church, silently rehearsing stage movements and gestures. Brenna explained that she would not be marrying Austin and that she had tried to stop Stewart McCutcheon from sending the wire, but that it had been too late. She also explained why she wouldn't be able to keep Phoebe for the morning.

Mrs. Dinwittie lifted her eyes to the one stained glass window as she clutched her hands to her heart. "I have been given a second chance. And I shan't waste it. Oh, no indeed."

Phoebe tugged on Brenna's skirt. "Is Mrs. Din happy now?"

"I think so."

"Are you happy now?"

Brenna couldn't speak.

Opening her arms in a grand gesture, Mrs. Dinwittie said, "Well, Miss Phoebe, I believe we have a picnic to prepare for. What will it be? Boiled eggs and sandwiches of cold mutton? Yum."

Phoebe shook her head. "Just bread and grape jelly."

Mrs. Dinwittie looked startled, then quickly smiled. "Grape jelly it is!" She took Phoebe's hand. "Off we go now to find Cook and place our order."

"I know how to make it myself. I'll show you."

This time, Mrs. Dinwittie looked at Brenna. "You have done wonders. You know that, don't you?"

Brenna still couldn't find her voice. She nodded to Mrs. Dinwittie, kissed Phoebe on the cheek, and hurried away.

Back at her shop, she checked on Dooley and explained to Mrs. Griggs that she had to go up to Amabelle Sweet's place. She said not to worry if cus-

tomers came in. She'd leave a pad and pencil on the
counter.

No sooner was Brenna out the door than Sarah
Zimmerman stopped her. "Is it true?"

"Is what true?"

"That you've turned down the chance to be the wife
of Austin Halliwell."

"Where did you hear that?"

With a knowing arch of her brow, Sarah said, "I *am*
the librarian, you know."

Brenna would have preferred to speak with Austin
first, to give him a piece of her mind. But he was gone
and wouldn't be back for days. She knew that if she
denied the rumor, or refused to comment, the town
would create its own version of what happened. As far
as the rumor was concerned, the only person she was
concerned about was Phoebe and she had already told
the child the truth. "Yes," she said to Sarah, whose eyes
widened instantly, "I am not going to marry Austin
Halliwell."

"Oh, the man must be devastated, simply devastated.
What did he say?"

"He doesn't know yet."

"You don't say!"

"Sarah, I need your help."

"Anything." Sarah looked down at the book of
poetry she had crushed to her chest. "Comfort and con-
solation. That's what that poor man will need."

"I don't mean about Austin." Brenna explained the
situation with Alice and Dooley Griggs and that she
needed to get up to Amabelle Sweet's place, claiming a
patient was in distress.

"You can count on me," Sarah said. "I'll stay with
the Griggs till you get back."

Brenna moved quickly. She stopped at Jake's wagon,

but he wasn't there. She hiked up the trail, weaving in and out of the shadows created by the dense forest of pines. She didn't know what she was going to say to him. Dooley Griggs was drunk and everyone in town knew Booker Griggs didn't approve of whiskey. So where had the alcohol come from? Jake's new Celestial Compound, that's where. And she had endorsed the product. Assured people it was harmless. How many bottles had he sold? How many others might mistakenly give it to their children?

She came to the meadow, strewn with so many white daisies the clouds appeared to have fallen. Jake couldn't have put alcohol in his new elixir. There had to be some other explanation.

Every rocking chair on the porch was occupied and in motion. Like magic, Jake appeared in the doorway. He was carrying the wooden tray of tools he had used at Brenna's. He looked out toward the meadow, shaded his eyes, and all but dropped the box on the porch. Knowing there was no chance of their having a private conversation inside the house, Brenna stood on the wagon-wheel path, green-gold grass waving all around her, and waited.

Gossip traveled fast, especially in a small town, but he couldn't possibly know why she had come. No man in his right mind would walk so fast knowing what she had to say. And yet, the closer he got, the more anxious he looked. She stiffened and hardened her gaze. She didn't dare let the arresting sight of him distract her from why she had come.

He stopped right in front of her, not a trace of contrition in either his stare or his stance. "I didn't think you'd have the nerve to look me in the face. Not so soon, anyway."

"So you know why I'm here?"

"One of the hired girls from town just brought the news. Everyone's talking about it."

"Well? What do you have to say for yourself?"

"What the hell do you expect me to say? Make the idea of scraping for a living sound romantic? It's not. Rattle off the advantages of riding all across the country in a wagon with me? There aren't any. Or maybe I should just say that you are one hell of a woman and I'm glad I could be of service."

"What are you talking about?"

"Come on. It all makes sense now. Can't blame you for wanting to sow at least one wild oat before you condemned yourself to a life with that Englishman."

She might have been angry had she not noticed the sadness in his eyes, had she not realized he was telling her what little he had to offer a woman, but that offer he would, that he too longed for an intimacy of more than bodies.

"I've got to admit," he said. "I always thought I was pretty good at reading people. But I never have been able to get a handle on you. But last night I thought . . . hell, it doesn't make any difference what I thought."

"I'm not marrying Austin."

Jake looked wary. Caution, or maybe disbelief, tempered his words. "You aren't?"

"The second vine of gossip hasn't climbed the mountain yet, so you'll be the first up here to know. I never told Austin I would marry him. The night I tried to tell him so, he refused to listen."

How quickly hope could bring light to the eyes. "Then how did the rumor start?"

"I'm not positive, but I think Austin started it himself. He's gone to Whitefish, so I won't know for sure until he gets back."

"The man's got confidence. I'll give him that."

"He told Phoebe I was going to be her new mother."

"Oh, Brenna, no."

He opened his arms, but she stepped back. It came as no surprise that Jake would so readily try to soothe her pain. Having seen him with Cosmos, she knew he had a tender heart. But she hadn't come up here for comfort, and knowing what else she had to say, she didn't dare take it.

"I've always dreamed of having a daughter. I can picture her dark, angel hair curls, her smile. I picture myself making her clothes: soft flannel sacks to keep her warm while she sleeps in her crib, then little dresses with embroidered butterflies."

Jake took her hands and brought them to his lips. "I know how much you care about Phoebe. That little girl has one of the biggest hearts I've ever seen. What are you going to tell her?"

Brenna needed a deep breath to relay the scene without breaking down. "We've already talked. I told her there had been a mistake, that her father had gotten things 'messed up,' as Phoebe always says. I told her that I wasn't going to be her new mother."

"How did she take it? Is she all right?"

"It's hard to say. She is so accepting of life. I don't think it occurs to her to question whatever comes her way." The tears she couldn't contain filled her eyes and spilled down her cheeks. "It's so unfair."

This time she let Jake hold her. In his arms, she sobbed against his chest. A few moments later, he handed her a handkerchief. "Need this?"

"Thank you." She wiped her eyes and nose and wadded the cotton in her fist. She gazed at the mountains beyond, hoping that the sorrow still churning inside would subside.

The view, as everyone always said, was healing.

Wave after wave of rounded peaks, blanketed in feathery green spires, gradually softened to the gentle foothills on which she and Jake stood, her back to his chest, his hands on her shoulders. Daisies, with their prophetic petals, danced like fairies at their feet. Jake broke the quiet. "Why aren't you going to do it? You love that little girl. Why aren't you going to marry her father?"

"Because he's not the man I love."

He gently squeezed her shoulders. "So you didn't come to tell me you're sorry about last night."

She turned to face him. "No, I'm not sorry."

"Good, because I haven't been able to do a thing all day without thinking about you. In fact, you know what I want to do right now? Right here in this meadow?"

She remembered seeing his body above her, feeling him inside her. The daisies blurred, but only for a second. "Jake, I didn't come here because of last night. Or because of Austin. I have to talk to you. It's serious."

"What is it?"

"Booker and Alice Griggs brought their son Dooley into town a little while ago. He's not quite nine years old. He was drunk. So drunk he was unconscious."

Jake raked his hand through his hair. "Is he going to be all right?"

"Yes. His mother is with him now, but she's so distraught, I asked Sarah to stay in the shop until I got back."

"What's this have to do with me?"

"Jake, it was your new elixir that Dooley drank. I saw the empty bottle. You told me you wouldn't put any alcohol in it."

"He could have drunk something else."

"No. Booker Griggs is dead set against alcohol. He

wouldn't allow it in his home. He would, however, allow a health tonic. Especially one that I endorsed."

"You're saying that everybody at his place shares his way of thinking? What about hired hands?"

"He doesn't have any. He has children. The point is, you said you wouldn't add alcohol and you did. God only knows how many children there are in this valley who could be in danger."

"Now wait a minute. I sold a lot of bottles, but only four—*four*—contained alcohol. Look, I never intended to deceive you."

"Then why did you? You said you wanted to make an elixir made of herbs and tea."

"That's exactly what I did, at first. But I had some customers who just wouldn't buy unless I fortified the product."

"With alcohol."

"Come on, don't look at me like I'm some kind of criminal. I added an ounce of ethyl alcohol and another of quinine to four bottles. Four. That's all. And I sold them to grown men, not nine-year-old boys."

"Quinine?"

"You know how people think. The worse the taste, the more potent the medicine."

"You didn't add anything to make it sweet? No sugar? No honey?"

"Not a chance."

"It's just that Dooley's breath had that sickeningly sweet odor."

"Then he drank something else. Most folks still brew a little something on their own, don't they? Especially out here."

Fragments of information started to take shape. "Perhaps I owe you an apology."

"Yeah, well I guess I owe you one, too. I got you to

endorse a product you wouldn't have—but I swear to God, I didn't plan to add the alcohol." He shrugged. "But it came down to that or no sale."

"I don't agree with what you did, but I understand."

"I wouldn't have sold it to a kid, though, not for any amount. I hope you know that."

He took a few steps off the path and snapped the stems of a handful of daisies. "Here," he said, offering them to her. "Pretend they're roses. I feel like celebrating."

"Because I'm not angry about the elixir?"

He glanced at all the men rocking away on the porch. He smiled and waved. "Because you aren't going to marry Halliwell."

Something far more dangerous than mere mischief danced in his eyes. He had to be thinking about last night, just as she was, wondering if it would happen again. But was he longing for it the way she was?

"Some things aren't meant for an audience. And some things are." Seduction in his smile, he pulled her into his arms and kissed her.

In the middle of the day, in the middle of an ordinary meadow strewn with ordinary daisies, Brenna felt the magic.

"They're watching," he said a few moments later as they headed up the path, "and you're blushing."

16

Two hours later, Brenna was back at her shop. Dooley Griggs was conscious and sitting up in her bed. His mother was sitting on the edge of the chair next to him, her hands a tangled knot of worry.

"You got a pretty home, Miss McAuley," Alice said, her voice as thin as wire. "Pretty things, too."

"It's kind of you to say so. Thank you."

"All this room just to yourself. I don't reckon you'd want it any other way."

"It's all right for now." She thought of Jake and how he had kissed her in the meadow. He planned to come to her shop as soon as he finished some repairs for Amabelle.

Alice pulled her lower lip between her teeth. As she did, she hunched her shoulders like a turtle retreating into its shell. "You can't never tell about a man. Some ain't what they seem. You know?"

"I suppose that could be said for all of us at one time or another."

"I suppose."

Brenna stood at the foot of the bed. "Dooley, what did you drink that made you so sick?"

The skinny boy looked to his mother, then said, "That snake oil man's elixir. I drank the whole bottle. Every drop. That's what done me in."

Brenna noticed that Alice had started to cry, silent sobs that racked her shoulders. As gently as she could, Brenna said, "Mrs. Griggs, whatever Dooley drank was sweet. We both know that. The elixir Jake Darrow sold your husband was bitter."

Alice looked up, panic on her face. "You sure?"

"Yes. Mr. Darrow's elixir contained quinine. Anyone taking it, especially a child, would have found it unpleasant to say the least."

A long moment of silence paved the way for the truth.

"Was it brandy, Mrs. Griggs? Some kind of wild berry?"

Alice nodded, her gaze far away. "Blackberry."

"Does your husband make the brandy?"

"Don't say no more, Ma! Don't!" Dooley moaned as he scurried from the bed and put his arms around his mother's neck.

"It's all right." Alice began rocking back and forth, patting her son on the back.

"I won't touch the jar again. I promise on everything good and holy."

When Dooley eased back, Brenna said, "Why don't you come with me to the kitchen, Dooley. I'm going to fix you some bread and jam. Then I'd like for you to just stay there for a few minutes while I talk to your mother."

Alice wiped her nose on her sleeve and said to her son, "You go on. Do as you're told. We'll go find your pa later."

Reluctantly, Dooley followed Brenna to the kitchen. A little while later, Brenna returned and sat on the edge of the bed.

"I made the brandy," Alice said outright, "but I reckon you already know that."

"I suspected. Does your husband know?"

"Oh lord, no. Booker, he's dead set against alcohol." She looked up, a plea for understanding in her otherwise vacant eyes. "See, my nerves, they get workin' on me now and then and I just, well, I need to calm down. And so I have a sip or two and then I feel better. I bought that elixir too. I used to buy health tonics and such when we lived in Butte. Now, they used to soothe my nerves good. But this one, well, it just didn't do the job, you know what I mean?"

Cupping her chin in the palm of her hand, her bitten-down nails scraping her cheek, Alice said, "I should have never blamed that medicine show man. I was raised to know better." She stood and smoothed back the loose strands of coarse, salt and pepper hair that had managed to escape the knot at the back of her head. "If you'll tell me what we owe you, I'll see you get it."

"You don't owe me anything, Mrs. Griggs. I didn't do anything but give Dooley a place to sleep for a few hours. But you should keep an eye on him. Don't let him eat anything heavy or spicy for the next few days." She paused. "And you should think about your own health too."

"Yeah, I'll do that. I sure will." Alice looked around the room one more time before heading for the door. "You sure got a pretty place here."

Jake looked at the forlorn faces of the boys on either side of him and shouted to the men on the field. "Shape up out there! Whitefish is going to beat our sorry butts." And Jake was going to lose two hundred dollars.

If anyone had ever told him the day would come when he would want to be somewhere other than on a baseball diamond, he would have laughed. But he had been out here every afternoon for a week now, working with the men who would represent Coventry in the game next month. Francis Foster was probably a good butcher and Smitty McGill was probably a fine blacksmith, but they weren't baseball players. Not by a long shot. Neither were the others. He ought to be going over plays with them, coaching them, forcing them to hustle. But even with a bet he could never pay hanging over his head, his heart just wasn't in the game.

Brenna, the green-eyed enchantress, had cast her spell on him. That luscious body of hers was enough to drive any man crazy, and it nearly did every time he got near her, even if it was just in Miss Sweet's parlor. But there was so much more about her to admire.

She had been coming up to examine Cosmos every day for weeks now. She made sure he had his opium cough syrup, throat lozenges, comfrey tea, and iron wine to build his blood. Jake was grateful beyond words for the concern in her eyes, the compassion in her soothing hands, and most of all, for the attention she paid to the old man. She'd sit there and listen to stories Jake had heard a hundred times. She'd laugh and hold his hand. But Cosmos was dying just the same. No amount of science or tender care was going to change that now. To make matters worse, he had started talking about the Old Magic again, convinced it was here after all.

Jake felt a tug on his sleeve and looked down to see Albie Foster, a band of freckles across his nose. "I been workin' on catchin' things like tomatoes and rocks and anything else Raymond throws at me. And Dickie's been hittin' 'em, too. Ain't we ever gonna get to play again?"

"Sure you will. As soon as your pa and the others wrap up this practice."

"But they practice every day."

"They need to."

A few minutes later, Albie said, "Are you gonna marry Miss McAuley?"

Jake started. "Where'd you hear that?"

"Just around."

"Around where?"

"You know, just around."

Dickie had been standing next to his younger brother and now he joined in. "Ma says everybody knows Miss McAuley ain't gonna take up with the King of England. That's what Pa calls him. You know the man I mean?"

"Yeah. I know," Jake said. "What else did your ma say?"

Dickie shrugged. "Just that now the whole town's gonna go to rack and ruin and everybody's gonna have to move to Missoula."

"The whole town, huh?"

"Yep, 'cause Ma says we lost our ace."

Albie scuffed his toe in the dirt, then said to his brother, "Tell him what else Ma said. You know . . . about her."

"Ma said by standing up for you the way she did, Miss McAuley let the whole town know you're the one she's sweet on."

All week long Jake had heard from one person or another how Brenna had staunchly defended him after the incident with Dooley Griggs. She had never mentioned the brandy specifically, just that she could prove Dooley had gotten into something other than Jake's elixir.

Dickie continued. "Ma said it's too late to run you out of town."

"Run me out of town? That sounds pretty severe to me."

"Ma says you lied about that old man, the one who's picture is on the bottles of the stuff you sell. And then you al-a-nated Miss McAuley's affections away from the king. But don't worry. Ma's not going to push for getting you run out 'cause she wants to move to Missoula."

Muttering to himself, Jake said, "I guess I should take comfort where I find it."

"Hey, that's exactly what Ma said you been doin'."

The beautiful crack of a solid bat against a well-thrown ball drew everyone's attention to the field. Dickie and Albie jumped up and down, waving their arms. "Run, Raymond! Run!"

Along with the others, Jake watched the splendor of the human body, physical strength and speed welded to sheer determination and heart. But for the first time in his life, he couldn't get excited by it.

"Good afternoon, Brenna dear," Austin said as he stepped into her shop. "I arrived in town not a quarter hour ago and I have been urged by everyone from blacksmith to barber to come have a word with you. I dare say, their sense of urgency has me concerned."

Brenna affixed the "closed" sign to the door and shut it. "Sit down, Austin."

"This appears serious."

Brenna pulled a chair from against the wall and angled it to face him. "It is," she said as she sat down.

Austin sat in the chair she indicated for him. "Yes, well, before you start, let me say that while in Whitefish I made arrangements to purchase two hundred head of Black Angus cattle. I think that number sufficient to start. What do you think, my dear? Shall we buy more?"

His sad eyes reflected lost hope, despite his words. Brenna knotted her hands to help calm her voice. "I'm angry with you, so angry I could swear—"

"Brenna!"

"You listen to me! The only explanation I can come up with for what you did was that you confused my love for Phoebe with love for you."

Austin started to rise, but Brenna stared him back down and said, "This whole town knows how much I love that child. How dare you tell her that I was going to be her new mother. How could you be so cruel?"

"But she adores you, too."

"I know that." Brenna stood and walked away, pacing the floor. "When I had to explain things to her, I thought my heart would break right along with hers. Oh, Austin, how could you do such a thing?"

Austin stood and folded his arms across his heart. "But I did ask you to marry me."

"But I didn't say yes!"

"I see. I suppose such things are handled differently in your country."

"A lame excuse." She paced some more. Calmer now, she said, "For all of your fine qualities, and you have many, you cannot go around trying to manipulate people to do what you want them to do or to feel the way you want them to feel." She stopped right in front of him and looked him in the eye. "If by having dinner with you or by accepting that pin, I encouraged you to think that I felt something for you other than friendship, then I'm sorry."

"But I would be a good husband. I would—"

"Austin, stop."

"I would protect you. I would cherish you. I would give you every financial advantage. And I would give you children of your own, healthy children, I assure you."

"Please. It's no use. My mind is made up."

"I see." He nodded and swallowed hard, leaving her to imagine his thoughts. "Yes, well, I had best make my way over to the hotel and see my daughter, though I don't imagine she'll be too pleased to see me."

He lingered at the door. "It's that Darrow chap, isn't it?"

Brenna said nothing and waited for him to leave.

"So this is where you live?" Austin asked.

Jake looked toward the open door of the wagon and squinted into the setting sun. "Yeah," he said, with no effort to be friendly.

"Do you mind?" Austin said, sticking his head inside.

"I sure as hell do." The floor creaked as Jake quickly headed toward the door. He bent his head to clear the opening and stepped down the stairs, pulling the door behind him. Austin had retreated several steps, but continued his scrutiny of the brightly colored wagon. "What do you want, Halliwell?"

"Am I to believe that two grown men can travel and live in this . . . this box?"

"I don't care what you believe."

"You take offense so readily, Mr. Darrow. I meant no harm."

"Yeah, well, I have a knack for sniffing out trouble. And right now, you stink."

Austin chuckled. "Trouble? I suppose if you were to find our wager, two hundred dollars as I recall, to warrant some anxiety on your part, then perhaps that would explain your rather rude manners."

Austin's thin, tight-lipped grin made Jake uneasy, but he'd be damned if he'd show it. "You haven't seen Coventry's team play yet," Jake said as he reached beneath the wagon and pulled out a wooden crate of several baseball gloves, a bat, and ball. "If you had, you'd know I don't have a thing to worry about."

"Whitefish is practicing in earnest as well. I think it only fair to let you know."

"Oh, yeah?" Jake released the two S-hooks and chains that held a drop-down side panel on the wagon. One by one, he placed the pieces of equipment on the paint-chipped, makeshift table. "You mean they've given up cricket?"

Austin moved closer and studied the items. He lifted one of the gloves. "I must agree with my fellow countrymen when I say that I find this game of yours to be slow and wanting in variety."

"Guess you haven't talked to any of your fellow countrymen lately then, since as of last month England has four professional baseball teams. Four."

Austin put the glove down, but not before trying it on and flexing his knuckles. "I find that hard to believe."

"Believe what you want."

"Yes, well, isn't that what we all do?" He ran his finger along the edge of the table and scrutinized the dirt he had collected. "Whether it regards the potency of an elixir or the affections of a woman."

"So that's what this visit is about."

Reaching into the inside pocket of his suit jacket, Austin retrieved a long, slim billfold with a gold monogram in the corner. With an air of indifference, he thumbed through the contents and withdrew two bills. "My portion of our bet." He laid the money on the table.

"The game's not till next month."

"I'm well aware of that. But since I'm about to make an investment in equipment for my own team, I need more than your simple assurance that you are capable of covering your portion of our wager. In fact, I insist."

Jake looked at the hundred dollar bills and mentally counted every bill and coin in his pocket. After settling things with Miss Sweet and paying for the new gloves, he had less than fifty dollars. "Save your worrying. When the time comes, I'll be able to cover my half. Besides, I'm going to win."

"I take that to mean you are not in a position to cover your bet at this moment." He retrieved the money from the table and slipped it back into his billfold.

"That's right."

"I suspected as much."

You pompous ass. Jake would have said the words out loud, but the man was right. Jake had made a wager he couldn't cover. Halliwell had every right to call the shots. "So what now?"

"We have an opportunity to make this wager truly interesting."

"Good morning, gentlemen. What can I do for you?"

Elton Fontaine nudged Ralph Newton, whose Adam's apple bobbed when he answered. "We, that is both of us, would like a few words with you."

"About what?" Brenna stepped down from the platform and joined her neighbors, who suddenly appeared uncomfortable.

"You tell her," Ralph said, folding his arms tight across his chest.

"Tell me what?"

Elton drew himself up. "Miss McAuley, there is no delicate way to ask, so forgive my being blunt, but did you, or did you not, turn down the marriage proposal of Lord Austin Halliwell?"

"Is that why you're here, to pry into my personal life?"

In a chiding voice, Elton said, "I believe we have a right to know."

"Since when does my personal life concern you?"

"Since Lord Halliwell showed an interest in you, that's when."

Brenna turned to Ralph. "And you go along with this?"

"Gosh, Miss Brenna, don't be mad. I gotta watch out for business, that's all. If Halliwell don't set up shop in Coventry, could be I wind up diggin' in the mines again. I like it much better with folks crowding outside my window just to watch me give haircuts."

"He's a celebrity," Elton said with certainty.

"In case you've overlooked the obvious," Brenna said, "I have a business in this town too. I have just as much at stake in Coventry's future as the rest of you."

"Exactly," Elton said. "Which is why we're hoping you will see your way clear to mend your breach with Lord Austin before he does something foolish—like set up housekeeping in Whitefish."

"Are you finished?" Brenna said, heading for the door.

Elton looked down his nose. "In the three years you have lived in our fair city, not once have I seen this side of you, and it's none too attractive, I must say."

"If you'll excuse me. I have work to do."

"It's that Darrow fellow, isn't it?" Elton said. "The man has stolen your heart."

"You leave Jake out of this."

Elton turned to Ralph. "What did I tell you?"

As though summoned, Jake appeared in the doorway.

"Good morning, everyone," he said as he entered. "Miss Brenna," he added with a smile.

"Thief," Elton mumbled, then led the way out.

When they had gone, Jake asked, "What was that all about?"

"You and me and Lord Halliwell."

"He's the big catch and you're the bait. You knew people would be upset, at least some of them." He walked over to the glass cabinet and smoothed the edges he had sanded when replacing the glass. "You could be making a mistake, you know, turning Halliwell down. The man has a lot to offer."

"If this town is counting on the benediction of one man to make it a success, then we might as well pick up our sidewalks and move right now."

"I wasn't talking about what the town might lose."

Hiding a smile, she was caught in the gaze of the man who had held her in the moonlight, whose kiss summoned the spiral of an ancient passion, and whose touch made her feel both cherished and newly born. "I know exactly what I'm giving up."

Jake looked away, leaving Brenna to wonder if he had given any thought at all to what his life would be like with her, or without her.

"What the people in this town need," he said, staring out the window, "is to see themselves as winners. If they want to prove to the world that their town is worthy of investment, they've got to prove it to themselves first." He turned to Brenna, a flicker in his eyes.

"They've got to win that baseball game against Whitefish."

She started. "Baseball?" she said, as though it were a foreign word.

"Yes," he said almost reverently. "That field is a place where character is forged and memories are made." His eyes took on the mesmerizing quality he displayed on stage. "Just picture it: Bottom of the ninth, the score is tied, two outs, bases loaded, you're the batter, and the count is three balls, two strikes. It's all up to you. The fans are screaming, but you can't hear them 'cause your heart is pounding in your ears. Your hands are sweating. You know the pitcher has the arm of a locomotive and now you see he's also got the eyes of the devil. So you step up to the plate, grind your toe in the dirt to anchor your stance. You swing the bat a few times to get the feel and to force your stomach back down where it belongs. Then you grip the wood, fist over fist, get into position, and stare straight into those devil eyes. You strike out now and your name is mud. But if you connect, if you score the winning run, then you're a hero and everybody wants to be your friend." He sighed as though he had just relived a memory. "Until the next game, and then it starts all over again."

"How often do the heroes of the game make that kind of connection?"

"Three times out of ten. Not very good odds, are they?"

"Hardly worth trying."

"To find out what you're really made of? Deep down inside? Oh yeah, it's worth it." He leaned against the counter, taking the pressure off his leg. "I've seen some of the men on the Whitefish team. They're good."

"What about our team?"

He rolled his eyes. "We try hard."

"Do you think we'll ever be good enough to win?"

"Maybe once in a blue moon."

"You won't believe this," Brenna said, glancing toward the herb chest. "There's a blue moon the last day of this month."

Then she gasped as her revelation hung in the air. Jake, his unreadable face guarding his emotions, walked over to the herb chest. She followed him, arguing with herself for what seemed like a thousand times while he focused on drawer after drawer, knob after knob. Finally, he lifted the slender white tails of the bow on one of the knobs and let the satin slide off his finger. "Is this it? Your moon chart?"

"It's a ribbon. That's all."

"Why is it on this particular knob?"

She didn't answer him.

He examined the ribbon again, the knobs, the drawers, and then looked at Brenna. "What's the mystery?"

"It's really nothing mysterious. The ribbon is just to remind me that this is the last night of the balsamic phase." *A time for letting go.* "Tomorrow brings a new moon."

He looked at the cabinet again. "Is that why the knob next to the ribbon is chipped? To mark the new moon? Or is that just coincidence?"

The power of her long-buried memory warned her to keep quiet.

"I don't claim to know everything about you," Jake said, "but I know you well enough to know that you're motivated to help people."

"A lot of people keep track of the moon. It doesn't mean anything."

"But you're different."

"Not of my own choosing." The walls were closing in. She had to take deep breaths.

"Talk to me about it. Please. Start with your mother. What was she like?"

She had never shared her past, preferring instead to keep it locked away.

"Spiritual. Responsible. Filled with insight." Each word lifted a small weight from Brenna's heart. "She had a sense of humor, too. And she loved to cook." Brenna had been taught that words themselves had power. She knew the proof of that now. Defining her mother out loud was healing.

Jake walked over to where the chairs were lined up against the wall and angled two of them so that they faced each other. Brenna followed and sat on the one he held for her. He went to the door. "I'm going to close this, if you don't mind."

She nodded.

"What was it like when she died?" he asked as he returned to his chair and sat down. "Do you remember?"

"In vivid detail." She told him about the summer afternoon and about the sudden pains that gripped her mother's heart. "I helped her to the bed. I had never seen her in anything close to panic. Until then."

"Go on."

"She had often cautioned that women were not to act beyond their stations, not to be seen engaging in the unbecoming activity of recordkeeping. That's why I was so surprised when she told me to remove two particular bricks from the bedroom wall and to reach inside."

"What did you find? Gold?"

"A book. A small, leatherbound book. Very old. I brought it to her, but she wouldn't touch it. I'll never forget the look on her face. Part sorrow, part pride. She told me the book belonged to me now. I opened it. It was her book of chants, page after page filled with ways to fight the hopelessness of the terminally ill. She was so worried that she wouldn't have time to teach me how to use it."

"But she did."

"She tried. I've often wondered what my life would be like if I had been given just one more year with her."

"Your father—where was he?"

"I never knew him. He died when I was small."

Jake nodded. " You were too young to live alone, too young to go away to school. What happened?"

"A neighbor took me in. But her pity only made matters worse. I would often wander back to the house I had grown up in. Usually at night. On the way over I would imagine that my mother would be there. We would have a few hours to sit and talk. She would braid my hair or tell me a story, or we would go out to the garden. But of course, those fantasies were only in my mind."

"Anyone ever ask you to try to heal someone?"

"Once."

Brenna looked around the pharmacy, reliving the steps she had taken to get here. "Then I heard about a pharmacy school for women in Louisville. Kentucky was a long way from Virginia, but I didn't really have a home anymore. So as soon as I was eighteen, I left."

"And then?"

"It's a long story, Jake."

"I'm not going anywhere."

She wished that were true. "It isn't the kind of college most people think of. It's located in a drugstore in the heart of the city. Joseph Barnum, God bless the man, owns the drugstore. He had suggested to several of the women who worked for him that they might want to enroll in the Louisville College of Pharmacy.

He even approached the state on their behalf. When Kentucky flatly refused to admit women, he opened up his own school, the Louisville College of Pharmacy for Women. Unless things have changed, he still doesn't have a lot of equipment, but he has the basics. The Polytechnic Society is right next door. We were given access to their library. Anyway, three years after I enrolled, I graduated, moved to Coventry, and here I am."

Still eager to run from her memories, she walked over to the prescription counter.

Jake followed her. "What about that one time? When you were called upon to use the Old Magic? What happened?"

She turned abruptly and looked him in the eye. "I failed and the baby died."

17

Jake was all too familiar with that feeling of profound loss. It had made him value the pain in his leg. It kept him alert, helped him to avoid the trap of ever assuming that all was well. Memories had always guided his survival. He wasn't at all surprised to see they had served Brenna in the same way, though she sought pain in order to soothe it.

He moved to stand beside her at the counter and braced his arms on the polished surface, facing the herb chest with its white satin ribbon and its puzzle. He reached over and covered the knot she had made with her fingers. "What about the bridal veil? You said it belonged to your mother. I keep thinking about that night I came to fix your cabinet. Everything was fine until you saw that veil. I still don't understand why seeing it made you sick."

"I wasn't sick. I was terrified."

"Was it really your mother's?"

"Oh, yes. She inherited it from her mother, and her mother before that. It's my legacy."

"Why would an heirloom terrify you?"

"I had swaddled the baby in that veil, lowered him into a basin of warm water, recited the chant. All my efforts to heal were wrapped in that symbol of love." She took a deep, courage-building breath. "But the convulsions wouldn't stop. The mother begged me to do something, but I had already done everything I could."

"How old were you?"

"Twelve. My mother had been dead only a few months."

"And that was the first time you had tried to practice the Old Magic?"

"First and only."

He continued to stroke her hands. "That's all in the past."

She turned to him and frowned. "The passage of time doesn't erase pain. It merely preserves it. Besides, it wasn't simply the veil itself that upset me. It was seeing it draped over your arm, just as I had seen it in my dreams."

With one finger, he followed the maze of her fingers. "Dream about me, do you?"

"Not willingly. At least not at first." She smiled and relaxed her hands, entwining her fingers with his.

Now wasn't the time for him to tell her how she had captured his heart, but he would. "Did your mother's attempts to heal always work?"

"In the sense of a cure? No. Not always. Sometimes her role was to prepare her patient to cross over, to die. And sometimes, many times, the phase of the moon at the time of the illness wouldn't permit her to even try to heal."

"So, she wouldn't have tried to force something before its time."

"That's right."

"Even if she had a personal stake in the outcome."

"Especially then."

He studied the knobs again. "So, when she gave you the knowledge of the Old Magic, she knew the time was right."

"She had no choice. She was dying."

He squeezed her hands. "We always have a choice."

Brenna grew quiet.

Jake had never been one to believe in the power of the mind to heal. He professed as much, every time he stepped on stage, but that was only to make a dollar. Yet he could see how Brenna's thoughts had crippled her ability to be the person she was destined to be, for if anyone knew of her ability to heal, it was Jake.

He didn't say a word when she walked over to the herb chest.

She placed her finger on the knob next to the one bearing the ribbon. "Notice the chip in the porcelain at the bottom of the knob. This one is for the start of the new moon." She moved to another knob, fourteen from the one with the ribbon. "The chip at the top of the knob is for the full moon. Fourteen more knobs, then another chip. Every day I move the ribbon."

"I see."

"This method is far from exact. The number of days between a new moon and a full moon varies slightly month to month. So I watch the sky and make adjustments."

"But if you had to be precise?"

"I could be."

Taking a calculated risk, he frowned and said, "You once called me a charlatan. Remember? A fake? A fraud?"

"I know what you're thinking. But this is different."

"I don't think so." He studied her with a kind of

detachment that multiplied the few feet separating them. "The first time I saw you was during my opening show here in Coventry. Remember? You marched up to the stage, hell bent on exposing me as some kind of fraud out to swindle everyone in the valley. You nearly shut me down. And all the while, you were quoting your noted authorities and hiding behind a mask of reference books. You're the charlatan in this town. Not me."

She didn't answer him.

"You've been healing with pills and salves and lozenges and all the rest. But you've been healing with your heart, too. Look at Phoebe. It's been your patience and encouragement that have helped her gain some confidence in herself. That's healing. Look at me. I never thought I'd see the day when I'd willingly make an elixir without alcohol—too hard a sell. But you've changed my attitude. That's healing."

She seemed to consider his words, but still said nothing.

"Maybe you've always known what you're really made of," Jake said. "Maybe you've never had to stare in the eyes of doubt. But if that's not the case and you're facing the monster now, don't you want to find out just how good you are?"

The quiver of her lip made her smile look shaky. "You're not suggesting I play baseball, are you?"

"If I thought it would help, yes."

"I don't know. . . . "

He shook his head. "We all have our own testing fields."

Slowly, she walked along the herb chest, touching various knobs, stopping now and then to close her eyes. Maybe she was thinking. Maybe she was praying. Jake didn't know. He just knew she was facing the monster he himself had still managed to avoid.

"Pretend your mother is here right now. What would she advise you to do?"

Brenna stood silent. When she finally spoke, it was with fledgling confidence. "She would tell me it was time to accept, to embrace, what she had given to me."

"Would she be right?"

"She would say that no matter what I did, or where I went, the desperately ill would find me. And she would remind me of my duty to my ancestors, to her . . . to me." She paused. "And she would be right."

Brenna turned to the herb chest and ran her fingers over the knobs.

"Tomorrow's new moon begins the time for healing," she said. "The ritual for the wasting-away disease must be done on three successive Fridays, all before the full moon." The simple act of saying the words seemed to empower her. "I will perform the first ritual on the night of Friday, the eighteenth, the second on the night of Friday, the twenty-fifth."

He didn't dare get excited yet. "What about the third ritual?"

She fingered the knobs again. "This month has two full moons. The second, the blue moon, will rise on Thursday, the thirty-first. I will begin the third ritual one minute after midnight. It will then be a Friday and the full moon will not have passed."

"Will that work?"

Her green eyes sparkled with confidence. "Yes."

Jake rushed around the counter, eager to wrap her in his arms.

"Stop!" Brenna said, holding up her hands. "Preparation for the rituals has its own requirements and they must be met."

"Just name them."

"A fee must be paid."

"I'll pay whatever you ask."

"One dollar."

"Come on, I'm not as rich as Halliwell, but I can afford to pay you more than a buck."

"One dollar."

"You're passing up an opportunity to get rich. You know that, don't you?"

"One dollar is all I require."

"Okay. What else?"

"From now until after the third ritual, I cannot allow you or anyone else, other than Cosmos, to touch me."

"Okay."

"I'm glad you understand."

"I'm not saying I like the idea, but when you love someone there are a lot of things more important than physical pleasure."

He knew she wasn't free to embrace him, but he expected his declaration of love to bring more of a response than a simple nod.

As though her soul had entered a dark night of death and rebirth, Brenna fell into a dreamless sleep and woke feeling refreshed. Hiking the path up to Amabelle's the next morning, she thought about Cosmos and the rituals she was ready to perform for him. She thought about her mother and how proud she would be to see her daughter following in her footsteps, at last. With each thought, she silently thanked Jake.

One of the qualities she admired in Jake was his love and devotion to Cosmos. To hear him express it out loud yesterday was a tribute to Jake's compassion. He cared for her, too. Gratitude was a natural emotion for her to feel. So was love. The idea of not being able to touch him for two weeks, not even to hold his hand, disheartened her. But she cared for Cosmos, too. Jake was right. Sacrificing physical pleasure was not too dear a price to give someone else a chance at life.

She entered the meadow with a clear and bittersweet truth. If, for whatever reason, the rituals didn't work—if Cosmos's faith wasn't strong enough, if proper payment wasn't made, if doubt found its way into her heart—she risked contracting the disease she sought to banish. If the rituals did work, Cosmos would recover and then he and Jake would leave.

As she approached the porch and eight men who had already aged a lifetime, she was aware of more than the creak of rocking chairs and the ceaseless sound of coughs. She sensed the hope in Amabelle's heart as her friend ran down the steps, arms open wide, to meet her. Amabelle and Cosmos loved each other. Perhaps he would choose to stay in Coventry. If Cosmos stayed, perhaps Jake would stay, too.

"Brenna dear!"

"No!" Brenna backed up.

Amabelle stopped abruptly. "Oh, I'm sorry, dear," she said, her fingers tapping at her heart. "Jake told me I'm not to touch you. I wasn't thinking."

"It's all right. I'm not used to the restriction myself, but it is necessary."

Amabelle locked her hands at her waist, a gesture Brenna recognized as insurance she wouldn't lapse into the familiar embrace the two were used to. "From the moment Jake told Cosmos, his spirits have improved. Truly, they have. Oh, Brenna dear, I'm so glad you've agreed to perform the ceremony."

"It's not that I didn't want to," Brenna explained as

the two of them headed for the porch, "I didn't believe I could."

Pausing at the bottom of the steps, Amabelle folded her hands and touched them to her lips. "And now?"

"Now I know I can."

"You do look different somehow. Do you feel different?"

"Yes. Strong."

Brenna greeted the slow-moving men on the porch, each one wrapped in a shawl or lap robe, even on this warm summer day. She made a note of who had the dry, persistent cough that typified the first stage of consumption, and those who suffered the more severe, mucous-filled cough and hoarse speech of those in the second stage. These were the men whose ulcer-filled mouths made it difficult for them to speak and eat. These were the men whose complexions had already paled to white parchment, offering a thin, translucent canvas for the bright brushstrokes of fever that spiked throughout the day and night. Cosmos was the only one in the third and terminal stage, Webley Heller having already died. But there would be others.

With Amabelle right behind her, Brenna stepped into Cosmos's room. Emaciated now, he looked like little more than a cadaver. His hollow cheeks made him appear harsh, his white lips ghostly. He stared at her, his sunken eyes morbidly bright.

"I'm ready," he managed to say.

Brenna smiled softly and came to his bed. "So am I."

Jake had been standing at the window and came to the other side of the bed. He must have stayed awake most of the night, for his eyes looked tired and he walked with more effort than usual. Despite that, his smile was warm and filled with encouragement. It was hard for her to believe that there had once been a day when she wanted more than anything for him to leave.

He brushed what little hair was left from Cosmos's forehead. "Two weeks ago all the other men were crowded in here sharing stories and tales of woe. He was too weak to sit outside, but he was still holding on."

"Still am," Cosmos said. His lungs rattled with every breath. "But hurry. Please."

She took his hand, sagging flesh on brittle bone. "We will begin our passage tomorrow night, you and I. In two weeks' time we will reach our destination, on the night of the blue moon." Gently, she stroked his hand, feeling the tremble no one else could see. "I will need your strength as much as you will need mine. Above all, I need your faith. Can you make the journey with me, Cosmos? Are you truly ready?"

He nodded. "The fee."

From the foot of the bed, Amabelle said, "I'll pay it. Whatever the amount."

"It's been taken care of," Jake said, taking a money clip from his pocket and removing only one of several bills. He handed it to Brenna, who slipped it into her apron pocket.

Cosmos raised his hand, a pained expression on his face.

"What is it?" Jake said.

He coughed, too weak to release the thick phlegm that gurgled in his chest. "The money. Not enough to protect her."

Jake looked at Brenna. "Protect you from what?"

"From the disease striking back at me. But it is enough."

"Well, I'm not taking any chances." Jake withdrew his money clip. "Here," he said, offering it to her.

"Let me contribute as well," Amabelle said. "I can't bear the thought of seeing you suffer like this, too."

"I have been paid," Brenna said.

Frowning, Jake said, "I'm not a charity case. I can pay you. I want to pay you."

"I have a greater chance of being struck by the illness if either his faith or mine lags for even a moment, though I have no fear of that happening. The money is secondary, and a dollar is enough."

Jake raked his hand through his hair. "God almighty, do you think I would have pressured you into doing this if I thought you'd be risking your own life?"

"It never was your decision." The concern in his eyes made her fall in love with him all over again. But regardless of the anxiety he might feel, she had accepted her destiny and there was no turning back. "Stay with him," she said. "Tomorrow begins the test of his last hope. Tonight he may be restless."

The moment Mrs. Dinwittie released Phoebe's hand, she ran toward Brenna. From behind the prescription counter, Brenna called, "No, Phoebe! Don't come any closer."

Phoebe stopped in her tracks, her arms at her sides, her mouth open. If her eyes had filled with fear, Brenna could have relieved it. Instead, they filled with hurt, then emptied with the ready acceptance of rejection. "Let me explain," Brenna said, never imagining how unbearably painful this moment would be.

Mrs. Dinwittie stared at her with disdain and wrapped her arms around Phoebe when the child ran back to her. "I think I've seen all the explanation I need.

In turning down Lord Austin, you've turned down this poor dear as well."

"I would *never* do that! I'm preparing for a healing ritual. I can't allow anyone to touch me. Oh, please, Mrs. Dinwittie. Don't go. Let me explain."

"Ritual? What are you, some brand of witch?"

"Not in the sense that you mean it."

Mrs. Dinwittie gasped.

"You don't love me anymore!" Phoebe covered her face with her hands and shouted through her fingers, "Stupid girl. Stupid girl."

Running from behind the counter, Brenna cried, "No, Phoebe! That's not true!" She stopped short of the child, who clung tightly to Mrs. Dinwittie's skirt, burying her face in its folds. "I do love you," Brenna said, dropping to her knees and sniffling through a sudden rush of tears. "I love you all the way to China."

Phoebe looked up, confusion in her eyes. She let go of Mrs. Dinwittie's skirt, grinned, and took a step toward Brenna.

Quickly, Brenna stood and held up her hands. "But you have to stay there, Phoebe." She backed away, her heart aching with every step. "Just for a few more days. Then I'll explain everything. You can help me fold the towels again. And we can go up to Miss Amabelle's for a picnic."

Mrs. Dinwittie stepped forward, grabbed Phoebe's hand, and glared at Brenna. "How dare you manipulate this poor child's affections. Come, Phoebe," she said and quickly scooted out the door.

"Don't go yet! Please! I have to explain to her."

There was no soothing the gut-wrenching pain that gripped Brenna's heart. She stood in the doorway, bracing herself against what she knew was only the beginning.

Rumors would spread quickly. They always did. Making choices always involved giving up something, even if it was an old way of life. Brenna's only regret in accepting her destiny was having hurt Phoebe.

The afternoon passed without a single customer, a sign that either business was getting worse, or the gossip was already spreading. She knew the answer as soon as Elton Fontaine marched through the door just before closing.

"Miss McAuley, do you have any idea what people are saying about you?"

"That I can't possibly stay in business with prices this low? Or that I must be daft for turning down Lord Austin?"

"They're saying you're a witch. Well, not everyone is saying it, of course, but some are, admittedly only a few, well, one to be exact."

"Mrs. Dinwittie? Because I told her I was preparing to perform a ritual?"

"Then it *is* true!"

"No, it is not true. I said I was going to perform a ritual, not cast a spell."

"Miss McAuley, I have, at great expense to this town, placed a half-page ad in the *Missoula Gazette* touting the wholesome character of our citizens, hoping to encourage businessmen to establish themselves in our fair town. For you, our druggist, to be accused of unsavory activity is serious. Very serious. Of more immediate concern is the reaction of Lord Austin. I shudder to think what will happen when he finds out. You simply must do something immediately to squelch this hearsay."

This was not how Brenna had envisioned telling the mayor and her other neighbors about her past and her new identity. "I can't stop people from talking or from listening or from believing what they will."

"No one around here is stupid. Merely cautious." Elton held the brim of his straw boater with both hands and rotated it like a clock. "What we must do is avoid even the appearance of witchcraft. This ritual of yours. You could cancel it."

"No. I can't."

"This is not a trivial matter."

"Nor is attempting to heal a dying man."

"Why, that's blasphemous!"

"If you would just let me explain. Please. Sit down."

"No, no, no." Rubbing his chin in contemplation, Elton said, "This is Darrow's doing, isn't it? You two are in cahoots to promote some new miracle elixir. I doubt you're even aware of it, but you changed the day he rode into town. Indeed you did. And I, for one, would like to have the old Miss McAuley back."

A deep awareness controlled her voice. "The old Brenna McAuley is gone."

"So I see." He glanced around. "You've built up an impressive business. We've all been so proud of you, your being both young and female. Perhaps it is those very same qualities that are leading you down the path of destruction. But since I have no hope of talking you out of this ritual you are so intent on performing, I can only warn you to be prepared for the inevitable backlash."

"I appreciate your concern."

"Yes, well, just who is this dying man for whom you are willing to give up your reputation?"

She reached for the bottle on the counter behind her. "Cosmos Clarion," she said, holding the label for him to see. "He is a patient at Amabelle Sweet's House of Recovery. He is in the final stages of consumption."

"Cosmos Clarion himself? Darrow's accomplice?" Elton groaned. "Oh, no. A conspiracy right here in Coventry. What could possibly be worse?"

Brenna thought about what Jake had said to her yesterday. "We could lose the baseball game with Whitefish."

"Oh, no," he groaned again. "We are doomed."

"Or our team could pull together and practice. Not every now and then, but every day. Don't you think they'd like to find out what they're really made of? Deep down inside?"

Elton rubbed his chin.

"Jake has been coaching them," Brenna said. "He knows a lot about the game."

"Yes, well it would be in Darrow's best interest to see us win."

"What do you mean?"

"The wager between Darrow and Lord Austin. Haven't you heard?"

She shook her head, the tinkling of alarm bells in her ears.

"Oh my, yes. As I understand it, if Coventry wins, Lord Austin pays Darrow five hundred dollars."

"Five hundred!"

"And if Whitefish wins, Darrow leaves town. Immediately. Alone. And promises never to return." He paused. "Miss McAuley, you look pale. Are you all right?"

"Yes, I'm fine." She wasn't going to jump to conclusions. Jake might not have told her about the bet simply because the opportunity hadn't arisen. This conversation with Elton was much the same. He wasn't in the frame of mind to listen to an explanation of *brauche*. She would tell him another time. No doubt Jake had reasoned something similar. The man certainly had other, more important things on his mind. Still, she would speak to him about it at the first opportunity. In the meantime, she wondered how dear a price it would be for him if he were forced to leave town. As far as she knew, he never intended to stay.

Elton went to the door. "So what exactly are you saying, Miss McAuley? That you have learned of some new medical developments? Something wired from that school of yours?"

"It's more like I've finally accepted an old development, a legacy from my ancestors."

"A legacy, you say?"

"My mother was a healer, as was my grandmother, great-grandmother, and on back."

He frowned. "Not the mumbo-jumbo type, I hope."

"I don't know what you mean by that, but the rituals do involve chants."

"Don't you see, Miss McAuley, that kind of activity will only fuel criticism."

"Only until people understand. As you yourself said: The people of this town are not stupid."

"Oh how I wish you had restrained yourself a bit longer, at least until Lord Austin had made his selection."

"I couldn't wait. Cosmos Clarion is dying."

The dream state came effortlessly. This time it was Brenna herself who emerged from the dappled shadows into a circle of light. Stardust in her eyes, a cup of moonbeams in her hand, the brass key encrusted with all her earlier dreams dangled from a cord around her waist. The veil swirled around her, a spiral of white lace, too delicate to hold a breath, yet strong enough to spirit away the ache in her heart—if only she could catch it.

She reached, but the veil disappeared.

Late the next afternoon, Sarah poked her head in to say that all was going well with *A Midsummer Night's Dream,* though she admitted a few of the cast members were growing less impressed by the day with Mrs. Dinwittie's overbearing direction. "Still," she said, "All's well that ends well."

"I'm glad to hear it."

"You won't believe what that Mrs. Dinwittie said about you at rehearsal last night," Sarah said. "She claims you have taken up wizardry. I told her that if you were engaged in any kind of suspicious activity, I would know about it. After all, I am the librarian." She glanced over her shoulder, although there was no one else in the shop. "It's not true, is it?"

"What I practice is called *brauche.* It's a form of healing. Some call it 'magic healing' or 'Old Magic.'" Brenna explained the old German healing art, with the hope that Sarah would understand, but when Sarah left, she still looked confused.

Brenna closed the shop early. She needed time to sit quietly and review the chants, to feel the strength growing in her hands.

With the late afternoon sun warm and comforting, Brenna knelt in front of the cabinet in her parlor. It was time to go to Cosmos. Unlike the day she opened the door for Phoebe, her heart didn't pound in fear, nor did she feel caged by her past. Jake had sanded the door. In opening it, she could feel his kindness and the knowledge that he truly was her destiny—whether he would be part of her life or not.

She pulled the basket from the dark recesses and lifted the lid. Memories of what had been and hopes for what could be mingled as the cloud of lace billowed in her hands.

It was time.

18

Focused on the thin cradle of moonlight, Brenna stood by the bed and absorbed the heat from the small white candle on the nearby table. The door behind her was closed, though she didn't need to see into the hall to know that Jake and Amabelle were standing there, anxious over what was about to take place.

Jake had met her at the end of Main Street, saying he knew he couldn't touch her, but that he didn't want her walking up the foothills alone. When she laughed, saying she had walked the path alone many times, he admitted that he simply wanted to be with her, from the beginning of her journey to the end. Now, he waited on the other side of the door, his trust in her hands.

Amabelle had met her on the porch. Her eyes red and puffy, she had claimed lack of sleep, then stammered about friendship and the future and the love of a lifetime. She, too, waited on the other side of the door, her hopes with Brenna.

Only Cosmos had smiled. Even now, hours later, as his pale skin stretched over his pain, he lay peacefully beneath the white veil spread over his chest.

Brenna curled her hand like the frond of a fern and passed her fist slowly over his chest, saying as she did, in a soft, spellbinding voice, "Do you have consumption in your marrow? Do you have consumption in your bones? In your flesh? In your skin?"

Cosmos nodded, too weak to speak.

She repeated the gestures and the words. Again, Cosmos nodded.

She stood there, quiet and still, her eyes on the moon, until moisture in the atmosphere settled on her hands, and finally, the air began to shimmer.

She curled her hand again, and passed it slowly over the veil, this time saying,

"Consumption out of the marrow,
Consumption out of the bone,
Out of the flesh
Out of the skin
Fly in the wind
Let no human body find you again."

She repeated the chant, again, and again, until she had no feeling in her body, no thoughts of her own, only the rhythm of the words.

Hours later, she drew her hand to her lips, opened it, and with three short breaths, blew some of the illness away.

Outside the room, Jake and Amabelle waited. They stood on the porch, pacing in the darkness, too tense to sit down, too uncomfortable to be confined in the parlor. Though the air had cooled enough to warrant a light wrap, it still smelled of the brief evening shower that had skittered across the valley earlier. Now and then, the summer breeze carried fragments of Brenna's soft voice and the power of her words, "Out of the marrow, out of the bone . . . "

Jake leaned on the railing and stared into a night so black it brought to mind every nightmare he had as a child. "I could have paid more. You know that, don't you? I wanted to pay more."

Amabelle looked at Jake. "But she said it was enough."

"Enough? One lousy dollar?"

"She's never been one to let money rule her life. Oh she's responsible, of course. She does a fine job with that little shop of hers. But you know, she only has two dresses and they're the same two she had when she moved here. For a lady, especially an attractive, unmarried lady, that says a lot about her, don't you think?"

He nodded. "Does she want to get married? I mean, has she ever said anything to you about it one way or the other?"

"I can't rightly say. Oh, we've discussed it, as women do. But she has never claimed marriage as a priority."

"But she's beautiful and intelligent and kind. She'd make any man a wonderful wife."

"I couldn't agree with you more. I don't think she's been waiting around for just any man."

At that, Jake fell into silence. He wasn't about to ask if Amabelle knew what kind of man Brenna might be waiting for. She probably wanted a man who could stand on his own two feet, in more ways than one.

Just then, Amabelle reached over and patted his hand.

It seemed a long time before either of them spoke again. Finally, Jake said, "I want you to know that as sick as Cosmos has been, he has been happier these last few months than he has been in years. It's because of you."

"I'm fifty-two years old," she said, her voice catching suddenly, "I've waited so long."

Jake slipped his arm around her shoulder and felt her tremble. "I've been happy in other areas of my life," she said. "I have my work; I know I'm doing something worthwhile. I have good neighbors, though none of them are in shouting distance. When I wasn't much older than Brenna, I resigned myself to the life of a spinster and decided to make the best of it." She sighed. "And then he came along."

"She'll help him. You'll see."

Thank God she didn't ask him how he knew, because then he'd have to say something about faith, and he didn't have any.

Jake and Amabelle moved into the parlor, vacant now except for the mounted heads of predators far less fearful than disease. They sat in overstuffed chairs facing what was left of a roaring fire and eventually fell asleep.

The sound of a door being opened roused Jake instantly. He turned around to see Brenna coming from Cosmos's room. He jumped from his chair. "Are you all right?" He hurried toward her. "What about Cosmos?"

Amabelle woke too and followed Jake across the parlor. "Oh dear, look at you. Come, sit down." She reached for Brenna's arm, but Jake pulled her back. "Oh, I'm sorry," she said, her eyes still heavy with sleep, her voice full of confusion. "I keep forgetting."

Brenna stepped aside, allowing Jake and Amabelle to peek inside. "Don't go in yet," she said. "He's asleep."

"What happened to your voice?" Amabelle said. "It sounds like sandpaper."

Brenna leaned against the wall, her arms limp at her sides. Perspiration trickled from her forehead, pasting loose strands of hair to her unusually pale cheek. She smiled. "I talked a lot."

"Well, I want you to come right down the hall with me and take one of the empty rooms, and I want you to get some sleep. Then I'm going to fix you a nice breakfast."

"Thank you."

No one moved.

Careful not to touch Brenna, Jake closed the door. "Is he going to make it?"

"I don't know. I have no history of my own to draw from."

Amabelle frowned. "But, dear, you must have felt something."

Jake saw the fire leap in Brenna's eyes. "Yes," she said without hesitation. "I felt the heat." As though the memory itself drained her even more, her shoulders sagged and her eyes grew heavy.

"Which bedroom?" she asked Amabelle.

"Right this way, dear."

Jake shoved his hands into the pockets of his jeans and watched as Brenna walked down the hall. It was all she could do to put one foot in front of the other. Had he done the right thing by encouraging her to perform the ritual?

Brenna took a few steps, then looked back over her shoulder. "Thank you." His answer sparkled in her tired eyes.

It had been nearly a week since Brenna performed the first ritual and still she felt the heat in her hands. It increased when she lit her morning candle. And it flared every time she entered Cosmos's room.

She walked in and set her basket on the floor near the bed. "How are you feeling this morning?" She lifted his hand, listening with her touch for a sign that his blood was gaining strength.

"Like I have new bones." The ulcers in his mouth still made it difficult for him to speak, but he continued. "My mother was chosen over her sisters because of the size and tenderness of her hands."

Brenna pulled a chair closer to the bed and sat down. "She had a strong stomach, too, I'll bet."

"That she did. She saw all sorts of ugliness. You will, too." He coughed and grabbed the bowl nestled by his side. The inevitable retching left him little energy to speak. "My lungs still sound broken, don't they?"

Brenna took a clean towel from the nightstand and dampened it with water from the pitcher. Wiping his face, she said, "Healing takes time."

When he had settled against the pillows again, he said, "My mother knew how to measure. Do you have the knowledge?"

"My mother showed me once, and I do have the calculations written down. But I've never actually done it."

"But could you? I need to know."

She considered his request. "Yes, I'm sure I could. But if the outcome isn't good?"

He managed a smile. "Healing takes time."

Brenna stood, studying as she did, the length and width of the bed. "I'll get some thread."

Half an hour later, she had stretched and cut a length of thread measured from his head to his heel. She then stretched the thread from tip to tip of his outstretched arms. It was no surprise that his breadth was longer than his length, indicating the presence of consumption. "Don't be discouraged," she said.

"I'm not. Keep going."

Folding the thread in half, she placed the mid-point at the center of his chest and stretched the doubled length along one outstretched arm. Knowing how far the disease had already progressed, she knew that the thread would never reach to his fingers. But she prayed it would reach·at least past his elbow, for if it didn't, there was no hope for his recovery.

The thread ended two short inches past his elbow.

He sighed. "I still have hope," he said, his eyes glistening. "Just as I thought."

Brenna carefully folded the thread and tucked it into her basket. "I've brought a bottle of mouth rinse. Oil of cloves." She retrieved it from the basket and set it on the table beside him. "It should help relieve the pain. Old Magic or not, you still have to eat. The directions are on the label."

She sat with him for a while longer, until Amabelle came in with a tray. As Brenna was leaving, she heard Amabelle say, "Chicken soup. I made it myself."

"Good," Cosmos said, "I'm starving." He reached for the oil of cloves.

Back in her shop, Brenna opened the box that had arrived on the morning coach. She carefully lifted the contents, a show globe.

While in school, she had heard several explanations for their use. Some said the huge glass globes filled with colored liquid were to direct the sick to the apothecary's door. Some said globes filled with red and blue liquid were to symbolize arterial and venous blood. Others said a globe filled with red liquid signaled the presence of a plague in town and warned passersby not to stop. A globe filled with green liquid signaled that everything was all right. On one belief, however, everyone agreed. The alchemists of centuries past were secretive about what they did and relied on an air of mystery and magic to maintain credibility. The jewel-toned globes they hung in their windows, as Brenna did now, said to all who passed, "There is magic here. Step inside."

In no time at all, Jake appeared at the door.

"Good afternoon," she said, struck anew by just how handsome he was and by the smile he wore like a talisman.

He walked over to the counter where she stood. "Cosmos looked good this morning, didn't he?"

"A little better every day."

He leaned on the counter. "Don't worry. I'm not going to touch you." Standing only a few feet from her, he whispered, "But when I can . . ."

The blush that rushed to her cheeks had little to do with modesty and everything to do with the fact that her thoughts aligned so closely with his.

With a look of blatant seduction, he added, "When I can, I'm going to give you a night to remember."

"July thirty-first," she said, making no attempt to hide her smile. "And you mean another night to remember."

Her reply seemed to take him by surprise. "Is it all right if we talk like this? I mean, I know I'm not supposed to touch you, but I don't want to break any other taboos or anything."

"The only taboo is touching."

"Good." He leaned over the counter and scrutinized the herb chest and the ribbon that had been moved several times. "July thirty-first, huh? I'm glad to see you're counting the days."

"One more week."

He backed away from the counter. "Who knows? Maybe then you can do some kind of ritual for this bum leg of mine."

"I can help you, Jake. But not with the Old Magic. That's for people who are terminally ill." She came around the counter to his side, aware of her teasing smile. "But a good massage could do wonders."

"A massage?"

She nodded, the pain of knowing she had hurt Phoebe still close to the surface. "You know, stroking the skin, kneading the muscles. An oil of eucalyptus and cloves would be the most soothing. Lavender oil might bring on too many . . . carnal thoughts. Still, either one would encourage deep, penetrating heat."

"You're dangerous. You know that, don't you?"

"Why? Because I know what you need?"

He laughed, but with a tinge of anxiety. "You sure as hell know what I want."

She sat in the rocking chair by the cold, wood stove and crossed her legs. Smoothing her apron over her knee, she said, "Just think about it."

"God almighty," he said, turning his back to make what Brenna knew was a needed adjustment. "I only came here to tell you that now your mayor wants to play on the team. I was just heading over to the field, but I can't walk outside like this."

"I'm so glad to hear that—that Elton is going to play on the team. I guess he's finally willing to risk Austin's displeasure."

"I don't know about that," Jake said, facing her. "He says he wants to find out just how good he is."

"I wonder where he got such an idea."

"Must have been from someone very smart."

Unspoken desire brooked the distance their bodies couldn't. "Remember the day I walked in and you were showing Phoebe how to fold towels?"

Brenna nodded. "She said you were pretty."

"You got upset with her when she asked if she could show me your secret."

Brenna remembered as though it were yesterday. "I never meant to hurt her. I love that little girl."

"You held her. You told her not to worry, that it wasn't her fault and that everything would be all right."

Brenna nodded, wondering what Phoebe thought of her now.

Jake smiled softly. "That's the moment I fell in love with you."

Slowly, Brenna stood. "You love me?"

"I told you once before, right here in this room, right after you told me about what the rituals entailed—about not being able to touch you."

She took a few steps toward the center of the room. "I thought you were talking about Cosmos."

"Oh, I do love that old man. Like he was my father." Jake followed her lead and also took a few steps toward the center of the room. "But this kind of love is different." He seemed at a loss as to what to do with his hands, so he folded his arms. "You know, one of the worst things about standing on a stage and making a pitch is never knowing how the audience will respond. They might buy. They might throw tomatoes. If they buy, I get a dollar. If they throw tomatoes, well, I've lived through worse."

"Let me relieve some of your anxiety." Brenna went to the herb chest and slipped the knot of the white satin ribbon, leaving the drawer ajar. Dangling the ribbon in front of her, she slowly walked toward him. He looked unsure of her intentions, but took the other end.

She pinched her way along the ribbon, nearing the halfway point. "This is as close as we can get right now."

He followed her lead. When there was nothing but a white breath between their fingers, she looked in his eyes. "I love you, Jake."

"Promise me you'll say it again on July thirty-first." His face was that of the confident showman, but the ribbon quivered.

"Technically, it will be August first. We have to wait till after midnight. But I promise."

"Here you go," he said, letting his end of the ribbon fall.

Not until she reached the herb chest was Brenna aware of the lightness in her body and the gentle zephyr that swirled around her, blowing away the last traces of fear. She loved Jake and he loved her. She tied the ribbon on the proper knob, knowing it was no coincidence that what had kept them apart was what had brought them together.

"So," he said as though he were eager to change the subject. "We've been thinking of calling ourselves the Coventry Comets. What do you think?"

"It's a perfect name."

"Yeah, well I guess I'd better get out there and do my job. Why don't you come out and watch us?"

She shook her head. "It's not a good idea for me to be around too many people right now—too much chance of being touched."

"Oh sure, I understand. Are you coming back up to Amabelle's this evening?"

"No. I'm going to bed early. I told Cosmos not to expect me until tomorrow night."

"The second game of the series."

"You could call it that."

"Then I'll come by for you at sundown tomorrow." He raised his hand as though warding off a protest. "I know, I know, you've walked the path by yourself a hundred times."

"Yes, I have. But I would rather walk it with you."

"Good."

She watched him leave. His leg was bothering him. When August first came, she planned to do more than tell him she loved him. She planned to show him. If he'd let her.

"Have you been busy?" Amabelle asked.

"Not busy enough," Brenna said from behind the counter. "No one is seeking to burn me at the stake, but they aren't flocking to buy toothpaste or liniment either. I can't blame it on talk. Business is simply bad."

"You look worried."

"People are just being cautious with their funds." She hoped she was right. "Jake stopped by earlier this afternoon."

"Yes, I passed him on my way in. He really has those men playing hard. I don't understand all the ins and outs of the game, but it does look like fun."

"From what Jake says, baseball is only going to get more popular, not just as a sport, but as a business. He predicts the day when tens of thousands will pay to watch a game."

"He certainly has a lot riding on the game against Whitefish."

"You've heard about the bet?"

"Word gets around." Amabelle raised a finger in warning. "But you mustn't let that discourage you."

"Does he strike you as the type who would like to settle down, in a place like Coventry?"

"I suppose that depends on the incentive."

"I suppose."

While she and Amabelle had been talking, Brenna was using a delicately embroidered handkerchief to wrap the small mortar and pestle she had been given as a graduation gift. She tied the bundle with a piece of ribbon and a sprig of lavender and handed it to Amabelle. "There. I appreciate you doing this for me. I can't bear knowing I've hurt that little girl."

"You should bring this to her yourself."

"But I would have to wait another week and I just can't. I close my eyes and see the hurt on her face and my heart breaks. Several days ago, I wrote a note to Austin and had one of the Foster boys bring it to the hotel. Without going into a lot of detail, I tried to explain the healing rituals and why I couldn't touch Phoebe, or allow her to touch me. But I haven't heard a word from him."

"He's off licking his own wounds."

"For heaven's sake, Amabelle, he's a grown man and he'll make some woman a wonderful husband. I'm not worried about him. It's Phoebe I'm worried about."

"So what do you want me to say?"

"First, give Phoebe the present. Tell her it's from me and that it's one of my treasures. Tell her that in another week I'll explain everything. Tell her that I have a lot of towels to be folded and a lot of bottles to be washed and I don't know what I'm going to do without her help. And most of all, tell her that I love her."

With a knowing look, Amabelle said, "You're going to make a wonderful mother. You know that, don't you?"

"I hope so. Someday."

"And a wonderful wife, too."

Brenna grinned. "Yes I am."

Amabelle reached to tap Brenna's hand, but pulled back quickly. "Oh, I can see why you have to cloister yourself. Touching is so instinctive between friends."

"One more week."

Amabelle held the package to her heart; a trace of

worry creased her brow. "And then the magic is over, isn't it?"

"Oh no. The magic has just begun."

"For all of us?"

"Of one sort or another."

"How I envy your faith." Amabelle whisked a sudden tear from her eye. "Now, what if Austin won't let me see little Phoebe?"

"All you can do is try."

Amabelle took a deep, strengthening breath. "Well, I consider myself a fairly persuasive woman. I don't think I'll have any problem at all." With that, she left.

The moon rose around noon the next day, though its light wasn't visible until dusk. Around ten that night, with her white candle burning softly in the shadowed room, and her veil draped across Cosmos's chest, Brenna focused on the ghostly yellow shape that was more than a crescent, but not yet a ball. She began the chant, "Out of the marrow . . . out of the bone . . . "

19

"*Have you come to measure* again?" Cosmos groaned as he levered himself to a sitting position.

"It's still too soon," Brenna said, seeing the sparkle in his eye, hearing his labored breathing. "We'll measure next week. For now, tell me how you feel." She wondered why Amabelle had changed the bedspread; the new one wasn't nearly as colorful as the other. The braided rag rug by the side of the bed, the one Amabelle had made herself, was gone, too.

"I'm a new man. That mouth rinse you made, the one with the oil of cloves, I'd like to bottle that. What do you think?"

"It's a common formula. Wholesalers everywhere carry it."

"Yes, but presentation is everything. I could put your picture on the label. We could call it McAuley's Oral Comfort. Jake thinks it's a great idea. You could travel with us and promote it first-hand." He coughed and grabbed the bowl by his side. When the spasm passed, he leaned back against the pillows. "I see I'm not yet ready for the road."

"Healing takes time," she said, aware of the effort behind his smile and of her own conviction that Jake wasn't about to leave her. He *loved* her.

He looked at her curiously. "Ahh, I said the wrong thing, didn't I?"

"Not if that's what is truly in your heart, though you'd be wise to leave room for change."

He reached out his hand for hers, and when she clasped it, he said, "You're a wise young woman, Brenna McCauley. Tell me what's in your heart."

"Hope."

"Mine too." A breeze ruffled the curtains and drew his attention. "I want out of this bed so badly. I want to walk out there in that meadow in twilight. I want to inhale without hearing that god-awful rattle."

"You will."

In less than a half hour he fell asleep. Brenna sat with him a while longer, staring out the window. The breeze could be seen only when it ruffled the curtain, or sent the daisies dancing, or started the aspen leaves fluttering on the edge of the meadow. But see it or not, the breeze was there, and with it came change.

She left the room quietly, in search of her friend. She found Amabelle in her room, crying.

She was sitting in a fragile white wicker chair, a handkerchief wadded in her hand, her eyes red and swollen. Spread across the bed was the quilt of appliquéd hearts she had been working on for years.

"You can't give up hope," Brenna said as she closed the door behind her and leaned against it, not trusting herself to move closer. "He sounded much better today. He told me he has been eating more."

Amabelle sniffed. "And did he tell you about the hemorrhage he had last night?"

Brenna shook her head.

"I had to change the bedspread, the rug. I had to scrub—"

"What are you talking about?"

"Up until now I've measured each hemorrhage by the tablespoon as I've always done. But this time . . . this time I had to measure by the cup!" Amabelle stood, her short, stout body braced for some kind of disaster. "He had just finished his dinner and we were talking about simple things, how lovely the meadow looked in those few precious minutes of twilight, that sort of thing. And then it came. All at once." She wrung her hands and looked at the ceiling as though reliving every horrid second. "I feared he would either choke or suffocate."

She inhaled deeply, visibly gathering strength. "You worked your magic twice and nothing has happened. If anything, he's worse."

"I just left him. I think he's improving."

"But the hemorrhage—"

"When growth begins, things break." Softer, she added, "It's always that way."

Amabelle's lip quivered as quickly as her eyes hardened. "I want so much to believe you, but all I've seen these last three years are men who struggle to stay alive only to avoid funeral expenses. In the end they all die. All of them." She burst into tears. Her shoulders heaved with the weight of her sobs.

Brenna stayed by the door, squeezing the knob behind her. When she finally left, it was with the uncomfortable feeling that Amabelle hadn't faced the worst yet.

"All right now. Listen up." Jake looked each man in the eye. "I'm putting Ray Foster on the mound."

Elton's mouth dropped open. "Raymond's only sixteen."

"He's got the arm, the legs, the speed, the moves, and the attitude. He's our pitcher." Jake patted the shoulder of the tall, gangly kid standing next to him. "You ready to put on a show?"

Steely-eyed, Ray answered, "Yes, sir."

"Good. Elton, give him your glove."

"No."

"What do you mean, 'no?'"

Elton frowned with indignation. "I'm the mayor of this town. I think I should be the pitcher."

"Do you want to win the game against Whitefish?"

"Of course I do."

"So do I. That's why Ray is going to pitch. I'm putting you at second base. We need your throwing arm there."

Jake noticed how many men nodded approval of his strategy and how many gave no indication of their thinking. "Look men, I'm sure you've all played a few innings for fun over the years, but now you've got the pride of your town at stake."

Elton sneered. "And you, Darrow? As I understand it, if we win, you get five hundred dollars." One of the men whistled at the amount. "And if we lose . . . what? You have to leave town? Hardly a payment to sweat over. You were leaving anyway."

"That remains to be seen. For now, we've got to practice." He selected several men, saying, "Okay, you men go over there and practice hitting ground balls. McCutcheon's going to pitch to you. Fontaine, you take the rest, spread out, and practice fielding. Ray, you come with me. I'll be the catcher. You pitch. Tomorrow these men will face that bullet of an arm of yours and we'll see what we've got for hitters."

Jake had been working with these men for weeks now, off and on, depending on their schedules, but they had yet to come together as a team. "Just one more thing," he said. "In case it hasn't occurred to you, no one wins a baseball game alone." He looked over at Ray. "Not even the pitcher. He can be one of the best and hurl a no-hitter, but somebody on his team still has to score a run for him to get credit for the game." He paused. "Am I getting through?"

Elton handed the glove to Ray, looking around to make sure everyone noticed. "Here you go, kid. Never let it be said Mayor Elton Fontaine didn't do everything he could for his town."

The men divided up according to Jake's instructions and ran onto the field. Ray followed Jake like a puppy to the pitcher's mound, but Jake's mind wasn't on baseball.

For the first time in his life, Jake had risked something he couldn't afford to lose. Making matters worse was knowing that Brenna probably knew about the bet. He wanted to go explain things to her right now, but he couldn't just walk out on the team. Besides, what was he going to say to her? "When I made the wager I was only thinking of a way to avoid having to put up the initial two hundred dollars. So don't worry. If I lose, I want you to marry me and we'll go traipsing all over the country in a wagon." And if he won, then what? "Marry me and we'll stay in Coventry and I'll do odd jobs up at Amabelle's place, or be a soda jerk." Five hundred dollars was a lot, but it wouldn't last forever. He was a loser either way.

"Coach, don't you have to play in the game too?" Ray asked. "That's what I heard."

Jake winced. "You heard right." The only thing he had going for him was the fact that Halliwell had to play also and he'd never even been on a baseball diamond.

Slipping the catcher's glove on his left hand, Jake took his position behind home plate. He couldn't crouch down as most catchers did, but he could still catch. "Okay, Ray, lift that leg, wind up, and let 'er rip."

After catching several pitches, Jake walked out to the mound. "You're letting your shoulder fly out. Keep it in. Keep it tight. Like this." Jake showed him the proper form. "Got it?" Ray nodded.

After several more pitches, Jake approached Ray again. "You're not following through on the motion of your arm. When you lift your leg and throw the ball I want you to pretend you've got to touch your left toe with your right hand."

"Touch my toe?"

"One fluid movement of the arm. But you've got to lift that left leg higher, right up to your chest and really push off on your right leg. That's where you get your velocity."

Ray tried while Jake watched. "That's good, but you've got to do better. Give me the ball and glove. You take this one and go down to home plate."

They exchanged gloves and Jake slipped his left hand into the warm padded leather. He maneuvered the ball until the seams lined up just where he wanted them. He balanced on his right leg, bent his elbows and brought his hands to his chin, cupping the ball in the glove, all while he tried to pull his left leg up, his knee to his chest. He broke out in a sweat. He quickly lowered his leg to relieve the pain.

He tried again as a deeper pain gnawed at his guts, made him grit his teeth and stare straight ahead till his vision blurred. He pictured Dr. Powers, the man he had hated all these years. *Bring that knee up higher, boy. Higher! Bend it! I said bend it! . . . filthy vermin.*

Jake let out a blood-curdling scream and fell to the ground.

Ray dropped to his knees beside him, not knowing what to do.

"Give me your arm," Jake said, struggling for his balance.

The other men came running over. "I'm going to go get Miss McAuley," Ray said.

"No!" Jake squeezed the boy's arm.

"But she's the closest thing we got to a doctor."

"I don't want a god damned doctor. You understand me?" His wagon looked a mile away but he headed for it just the same, his quickened breath drumming in his ears.

Elton came after him. "Let me help you," he said, lifting Jake's left arm and draping it over his own back.

The only reason Jake didn't shove him away was because the pain was too great. "Don't worry," he snapped. "I'll still play in the big game. Your precious town will at least have a chance to win."

"Good. That's just what I wanted to hear."

When they reached the steps, Elton eased Jake off his shoulder. "You remind me a lot of my older brother," Elton said. "A real arrogant bastard."

"Oh yeah?"

Elton nodded while he caught his own breath. "Lost his leg at Gettysburg. He was fifteen."

"Is that supposed to make me feel lucky?"

"With that huge chip on your shoulder, I don't know how you feel anything but fatigued."

Elton turned and took a few steps. "Wait a minute," Jake called after him. When Elton stopped, Jake said, "No sense in cutting practice short. Can you take over for me?"

"I believe I can manage it."

Jake almost choked on the word, but he managed to say, "Thanks."

Jake had stripped to the waist and covered his cheeks and chin with shaving lather when he heard her footsteps. "What are you doing here so early?"

"Someone slipped a note under my door after I closed yesterday. I didn't see it until this morning." She gave more than a cursory glance at his leg. "It said you hurt your leg and couldn't walk."

He picked up the razor, leaned close to the small mirror he had hung on a nail and took one slow swipe at the foam. "I appreciate your concern, but as you can see, I'm fine." He finished shaving, knowing that in the silence Brenna was watching him, examining him. Just as the almighty Dr. Powers had done. *March in place, boy. Get that knee up.* He grabbed a towel and smeared the bitter memory all over his face. "I didn't get up to see Cosmos last night. How is he?"

"Amabelle said you're usually up there twice a day."

"I had things to do."

"Like rest your leg? Jake, why won't you let me help you?"

He hobbled over to the door and grabbed his shirt from the latch. As he jammed his arms in the sleeves, he glared at her, daring her to say something.

"Look at you. You can hardly move."

With sarcasm she didn't deserve, he snapped, "I manage, for a cripple."

He waited for her to tell him to go to hell or at least stick her nose in the air and march away. She did neither. Her pale green eyes eerily fixed on his. "Why are you looking at me that way?" He all but ripped the buttons off his shirt as he fastened them. "Well?"

"When memories rise, they cloud the eyes."

"So what are you remembering? Walks in the moonlight?"

"Yours are the clouded eyes."

If it weren't for Cosmos, he'd take her in that wagon, shove all those bottles of worthless elixir aside and make love to her right there on the floor. But when a man really loved a woman he took care of her. He didn't saddle her with a man who couldn't provide for her and their children. "Look, I've been thinking about tomorrow night."

"So have I."

"Yeah, but I've been thinking that maybe it's not a good idea—you and me."

"Oh?"

He couldn't look at her eyes; they held him too tightly. He couldn't look at her mouth either. He kept thinking about how she tasted. He dropped his gaze to her breasts, her waist, her hips and his whole body ached for her. "We haven't so much as brushed shoulders in two weeks and we've both lived through it. I know I have."

She didn't look upset at all. "So I've been thinking," he continued, "that since Cosmos and I will probably be moving on in another month—"

"Are you sure?"

"Come on, you've heard about the bet I made with Halliwell."

"Yes, but why are you so sure Cosmos will want to leave? And why are you so sure you'll lose the bet?"

"I'm not sure about either one. But even if I win, I can't hang around here. What the hell would I do? Anyway, I just think it's best that you and I stop planning a future together—if that's what you were doing, I mean. It's not going to happen." There, he said it.

"I see."

"Good. So tomorrow, after you do your show for Cosmos, you'd better plan on staying at Amabelle's for the rest of the night."

"Instead of walking home, through the moonlight, with you?"

"Right."

"I see."

"I'm sorry," he said, his throat squeezing. "But it's best this way." He hardened his heart against the possibility of her tears. "Why are you smiling?"

"Because," she said, sunshine glinting off her midnight hair. "When growth begins, things break."

"What are you talking about?"

"I'll explain another time. Tomorrow night."

She left him standing there, his body clothed, his soul stripped naked.

Late the next afternoon, a storm darkened the valley. Lightning crackled. Thunder rumbled low and heavy. The clouds spilled their burden. By evening, nothing remained but a dove gray sky, a warm mist, and the whisper of magic on the wind.

Brenna walked up the foothills alone. She wasn't surprised that Jake hadn't shown up to accompany her. He had his own dark night to go through. Everyone did at one time or another. He had helped her through hers. She was determined to help him through his. Not because she was grateful, though she was, but because until Jake could heal his heart, he couldn't give it to someone else.

He was slumped in a chair beside Cosmos's bed when she came into the room. "So this is the big night," Jake said, his attention suddenly given to straightening the bedspread.

Brenna waited for him to look up, and when he did, she said, "Yes. This is the big night."

Standing on the opposite side of the bed, she stroked the wild strands of hair from Cosmos's forehead, then leaned over and pressed her ear to his chest. Rising with a smile, she said, "Are you ready?"

He nodded.

"Well, you two probably have things you want to talk about," Jake said, rising, "so I'll get out of your way." He grabbed a walking stick from beside the chair.

"Please don't go far," Brenna said. "I'd like you to walk out in the meadow with me, if you don't mind."

"He'll go with you," Cosmos said. "Won't you, son?"

"Sure." Still avoiding her eyes, he said, "I'll wait for you on the porch."

Brenna stayed and talked with Cosmos for a while, listening to stories of when he was a foreman in the three-story mill back in Massachusetts, the youngest they had ever had. He could run up and down those stairs, two at a time.

"Will you be strong tonight?" she asked.

"If it were only up to my mind, I could climb that mountain out there."

She squeezed his hand and smiled at the firmness of his grip. "I believe you could."

"Don't you worry about me. When the time comes, I'll be ready. Now, you go on. I know I'm not the only one you'll be using your magic on tonight." He winked.

Brenna pulled the door shut as she left. She stopped to talk to Amabelle for a few minutes, to calm her fears as best she could. Then she went out on the porch.

Jake was gone.

When there were only minutes left of Thursday, Brenna lit the white candle. She was sure Jake would have shown up by now, but he hadn't and no one had seen him. When she had performed the first two rituals, he and Amabelle had planted themselves in the parlor right outside the door, right where Amabelle was now. By tomorrow night the moon would have started to wane. Brenna couldn't wait. Nor could Cosmos.

Drawing on the wisdom of those who had gone before her, she prayed for guidance as she spread the bridal veil across his chest, scattering the flowers like so many daisies from the field.

She waited for the twelfth and final chime of the clock in the parlor. When Thursday was nothing but an echo, she curled her fists and brought the backs of her hands to within a breath of his chest. She gazed at the moon and inhaled.

"Out of the marrow . . . out of the bone . . . "

Again and again, she repeated the chant, till there were no words, just sounds, till the sounds became rhythms, till the rhythms danced on the wind, till the wind carried her prayer on its wings.

"Out of the marrow . . . out of the bone . . . "

High in a black velvet sky, the moon poured an endless stream of silver light until it flooded the meadow below, turning vines of honeysuckle into golden trumpets and stems of gentian into chalices of inky blue.

"Out of the marrow . . . out of the bone . . . "

*   *   *

The house was deathly still. Brenna could see Amabelle asleep in the parlor. She could hear the rattling coughs as common to the building as creaks on the stairs. She could smell dough rising for the morning bread.

She could feel Jake's heat.

She found him on the porch, his back to one of the cedar posts, his hands clamped to the walking stick in front of him. It took her a moment to adjust to the dim light and to see the pain in his eyes. "I'm glad you came back," she said.

"I never left."

"I looked for you. You were gone."

"I wasn't up to traipsing through the meadow, so I ducked into one of the empty bedrooms. It just seemed easier that way."

She could tell he had more to say. She waited.

"As you can see, I've got a lantern." He looked at the floor. "I borrowed it from Miss Sweet."

"What's it for?"

"So I could walk you home."

She waited.

"I've been thinking. With five hundred dollars, I could build an addition onto a house like yours, make it big enough for two, or more. I could probably get some work as a carpenter."

"What if you lose the bet?"

"I've been thinking about that, too, and I've got an idea. Halliwell was eager to raise the stakes once before. I think I could persuade him to do it again."

"What more could you offer?"

"I'll explain on the way home. But first I want you to know that all that noise I made before—about our not having a future together—that's up to you. I love you, Brenna."

"Are you asking me to marry you?"

He held his breath. "Yeah."

Slowly, she set her basket down and lifted the veil. Holding it lengthwise, she gathered one end and draped the other across her arm. He took the loose end.

Each fold of lace brought them one step closer together, determination conquering the pain in Jake's eyes. With the veil bunched between them like a white bouquet, Brenna said, "I will marry you, Jake."

"You will?"

"I love you."

She stepped into his gentle embrace, where she relished the liberty to stroke his hair, to trace the line of his jaw, to press her finger to his lips. The prelude lasted not a second more.

Suddenly crushed against his chest, she responded in kind to his eager mouth and the mating of tongues. What made her draw back was not any misgiving about what they had done, but the desire to do more.

She gathered the veil. He lifted the lantern.

"We'll go slowly," she said, noticing how much he relied on the walking stick.

With a self-deprecating laugh, he said, "There have been thousands of occasions in my life when I wanted to run, but never more so than now."

Halfway across the meadow, they paused. "Look," she said. "I don't know when I've seen it look prettier." The plump, butter moon was so bright it drenched the grass at their feet. "The lamp of the fairies."

"Are you saying this forest is enchanted?"

"Not always. Just once in a blue moon."

"Is this to be another silent loving?" he asked, sitting on the edge of her bed, still clothed.

"No." Gently, she eased his legs apart and stepped between his knees. Her bare flesh absorbed his warmth. "Words have the power to heal as well as hurt. I feared what you might say that night."

His hands cupped her breasts. "And now?" He eased her closer, suckling one, then the other.

She released the buttons of his shirt. "There's no longer anything to fear—for either of us." She tugged his shirt free from the waist of his jeans and pushed it off his shoulders, letting him drag the sleeves down his arms. He tossed the shirt to the floor.

"So now I can tell you over and over again just how beautiful you are." He fanned his hands across her belly, to the curve of her hips, and down her thighs. "And how much I love you." He palmed the mound of midnight curls and teased the treasure beneath with his finger.

The rush of heat beaded on her forehead and creamed the path she knew he was about to follow. His shoulders flexed beneath her hands. She tensed when he slipped his finger inside her. But only for a moment. He stroked her to that first, small moment of euphoria and held her close while she shuddered.

She didn't need anyone, not even this man she loved so much, to tell her how ripe she was for loving. She had known it for years. She had buried the need in her work, fought it in her dreams, and denied it whenever she saw a young woman glow with the presence of new life. But the need was always there.

She slipped her hand to his waist and the rigid column that spoke of his own want. She had released only one button when he stayed her hand with his.

"There's got to be a gallon of moonlight splashed around here."

It glimmered through the lace at the windows,

spreading its delicate net on the walls, the floor, and the bed. "Isn't it beautiful?" She continued to unbutton his pants.

When she had finished, he bent to remove his boots, saying, "To tell you the truth, I could use a little less of it."

Even in the shadows, she could see him wince as he tugged the left boot off. "Your leg is hurting, isn't it?"

"It's not a pretty sight." He flashed her that charming smile of his, but she saw the pain behind it.

"Let me help you."

"It's too late for that." He removed his jeans and briefs, leaning on her to free the left leg of each. He drew her hand to his sex. "But it's not too late for this."

As much as she longed for that ultimate joining, there was something else she wanted even more. "Lie down," she said softly.

20

"*Where are you going?*" he asked as she stepped over to the fireplace. "What are you doing?"

Her black hair fell like a curtain down her back. The rest of the view was even more enticing, but there was something else going on here. He could tell. She hadn't flinched at the sight of his leg. She hadn't the first time either, but, ashamed as he was to admit it, her opinion then had everything to do with her response to his body, not his heart. He remembered how the deep scar running alongside his knee and the unnatural set of the bone below had made other, less compassionate women, cringe. If he could spare Brenna from the sight, he would. Maybe they could always make love in the dark.

She struck a match and lit the wood she must have laid earlier. She took a handful of twigs from a nearby basket, snapped them, and tossed them on the fire. Fragrance flooded the room.

"What's that smell?"

"Lavender."

She sheltered the flame at the end of a long twig and brought it to the candle on the table beside the bed.

"Moonlight, firelight, candlelight. Afraid of the dark?"

"Are you?" She tossed the twig into the fire and reached for a wide-mouthed jar on the mantle.

"Of course not. What's that?" He stared at the container she held in her hand.

"Something I made with you in mind." She removed the cork.

"What is it?"

"Just a miracle."

He sat up instantly. "Put it away."

"Let me try."

"It's no use."

"How do you know?"

He pulled the sheet over his leg. "Because it's been that way since I was five years old."

"I can't align the bones. But I can make your leg feel better." She reached for the corner of the sheet.

"You want a good look?" he snapped. "Come closer. *Step right up.*" He yanked the sheet away.

Brenna glanced down at his twisted leg. "You told me it was an accident. How did it happen?"

"I told you?"

She nodded. "Shortly after you came to town."

"Yeah, well, there isn't much else to add. I was playing in the street. I fell and got my leg caught under the wheel of a milk wagon just starting its route."

She winced. "You must have seen a doctor. Some of those scars are from stitches."

He had held the memory for so long, so god damn awful long. It gnawed at his gut every single day of his miserable life. Maybe if he relieved himself of at least some of it, he could bear the rest. "Yes," he hissed, surprised at how eager he was to spit it out. "I saw a doctor. I was a charity case. Free care in exchange for testing a new splint."

"He was the one who set your leg?"

"You can understand his reluctance to show off his handiwork."

"But you can walk."

He spewed his words like bullets. "He put my mother in an asylum where she died. He put me on an orphan train." He studied her face. "Don't believe me?"

"I'd be a fool not to believe you. Men have exercised that power over their wives for years, committing them to institutions without medical or legal procedure, needing nothing more than the superintendent's approval. I'm ashamed to admit how many stories I've heard of supposedly reputable doctors doing the same with certain patients, those who complained, those who couldn't pay."

She paused, then said, "And yet I sense there is even more pain to your memory."

He stared into the fire, empty-eyed, wishing he had never let the memories come this far to the surface, yet wanting to be rid of them once and for all.

"Please tell me, Jake. Please."

He couldn't confront the rest without that squeezing in his chest that always made him want to run away. He snickered at the notion. "There's nothing else to tell."

"Trust me," she whispered.

He had never told anyone the whole story, not even Cosmos. He didn't think talking about it would do any good. But he had never known anyone like Brenna. How many times had he watched her comfort Cosmos, or hold Phoebe, or embrace Amabelle in deep friendship? Every time he saw her soothing touch on someone else, he wondered if she could do anything for him. And now, lit from behind, she looked like an angel, encouraging him to take a chance.

He had to clear his throat. "I begged my mother that day not to take me back to him. I told her that he had hurt me the last time and the time before that. But she said I had to be brave. I told her I hated her, *hated* her. She said that was all right. Dr. Powers was going to fix my leg. For free." He paused, not certain he was ready to see the ugliness he was dredging up.

Brenna's voice softened, telling him she knew to tread lightly. "But why did he commit her to an asylum?"

"Because the all-powerful doctor diagnosed her as hysterical. Subject to fits."

"I don't understand."

"Because she screamed at him. Because she pounded on his chest with her fists. And because when he swore and slapped her hard across the mouth, she grabbed his hand and bit him."

"Why, Jake?"

He could hardly breathe, his chest felt so tight. "Because when the doctor and his obedient minions prodded my scrawny body and pulled my twisted leg, I cried like a baby. I cried because I couldn't take the pain!" He squeezed his knee, knowing the torture would draw the tears back from his eyes. "All she did was try to help me."

"But you were only five years old." He leaned forward and buried his face in his hands.

Brenna understood. In the strictest sense, the Old Magic was for life-threatening disease. But a heart laden with pain warranted some kind of special help.

She set the jar on the table by the candle and drew her bridal veil from the basket. This time when she whispered, "Lie down; let me help you," he did.

She draped the white lace from his left shoulder, down across his chest, his pelvis—"It's distracting," she said with a gentle smile—and along his right leg. The heat built quickly in her hands. She dipped her fingers into the jar and scooped the green-silver liniment of rosemary and eucalyptus. She started with his toes.

She worked her fingers along the bones of his foot and ankle and deep into the muscles of his calf. She gentled her hand behind his knee, and firmed it again along his thigh. He moaned and reached for her, but she whispered, "Not yet."

She repeated the massage, then made him turn over. This time she started with his shoulders, not surprised at the tension that knotted his spine. Her movements were to calm him, not arouse her. But it was impossible to stroke him like this, to press her palms along his broad shoulders, down his sun-darkened back to the lighter flesh of his buttocks, and not have her own body respond with longing. Not when she knew how beautiful their joining could be.

"One more time on this side," she said.

When he turned over, she saw the smile she had come to love. She started at his foot again. He closed his eyes to the light of the moon, the fire, and the candle. She knew by the way he relaxed under her touch that he was going to a dark place, just as she knew he had to go alone. This time when she reached his knee, she saw a single tear fall from the outer corner of his eye and knew he was free to come back to her.

When she came to the top of his thigh, he opened his eyes.

"Now," he said, reaching for her.

Wisps of warm liniment and lavender twirled in the air like ribbons at a celebration, joining them, body and soul, for all eternity.

*   *   *

The first two weeks of August brought a waning moon, time to give things up.

Brenna had gone to see Phoebe right away, only to find Austin had taken her and Mrs. Dinwittie to Whitefish, claiming Coventry no longer held his interest. They wouldn't be back until the end of the month, in time for the baseball game. He assured the town he would not make his official decision as to the site of the new business until after the ball game, but everyone feared that for all intents and purposes, he already had.

Elton was devastated and poured his heart out to Brenna. His beautiful plan for Coventry's future had crumbled like a house of cards. How could the whim of one man wield such power? Maybe that's how things were done in England, but it wasn't how things were done in the great state of Montana. It wasn't how things were done in the United States of America. Adding to his misery was knowing that it had been his personal influence that had persuaded the town to allow that Englishman to give the address at the Fourth of July celebration. What a fool Lord Austin Halliwell had made of them all.

Brenna didn't care if she ever saw Austin again, but she longed to set things right with Phoebe. She had started out for Whitefish several times, but always changed her mind. Until the moon was new again, the time just wasn't right. Nor was the time right to get married.

Without Mrs. Dinwittie to direct, the cast of *A Midsummer Night's Dream* lost interest. Some rumbled that even if the woman came back, they had had their fill of Shakespeare. They all agreed that baseball was the more worthwhile pursuit. The men spent all their time with Jake on the diamond. The women attended classes in the library where Sarah taught them the rules of the game from an official guide she obtained while in Missoula earlier in the month.

Sarah hadn't been able to find any written proof that the ancient healing art of *brauche* was a deeply religious practice, but Brenna wasn't surprised. Knowing the secrecy with which it was handed down, she doubted written proof existed anywhere. But people listened to Sarah. She was, after all, the librarian. It didn't take long for the talk of witchcraft to disappear and for people to laugh at how ridiculous the notion—spawned by that Englishwoman—had been in the first place. They had known and trusted Brenna for years.

Up at Amabelle's, another patient died.

Cosmos, on the other hand, improved day by day, until by the middle of the month he could walk unaided to the front porch. He talked more and more about his idea for a new elixir and about how good the markets were likely to be in Great Falls, Helena, Butte, and Bozeman, each town farther south than the other. With no more hemorrhages and a diminishing cough, it was clear that his lungs were growing strong, just as it was clear to Brenna that Amabelle's heart was breaking.

Jake not only allowed Brenna to massage his leg, he looked forward to it. He would never be free of the limp, but by the time the end of August rolled around, he could not only walk without the support of a stick, he could walk faster than he had been able to in years.

He had been watching the white ribbon move on the knobs of the herb chest and wasn't at all surprised when the day came that Brenna announced she had rented a horse and buggy and was going to Whitefish.

"But the coach from Ravalli just brought up your big

supply order. Don't you want to get all those things inventoried and shelved?"

"I want to see Phoebe."

Jake knew how troubled Brenna had been over the last month, but he didn't want her any more disappointed than she already was. "I spoke with Boldizsar over at the hotel. He said Halliwell sent a message saying he and Phoebe and Mrs. Dinwittie would be back here by the end of the week. For the game. You might have more success with her if you wait until you can talk to her right here in familiar surroundings." He tapped his fingers on the glass cabinet he had repaired. "I have to go to Whitefish myself on business. Let me scout around and get an idea of how he feels about Coventry."

"You mean about me." Brenna stood by the counter, looking down at the mortar and pestle Amabelle had tried to deliver. "I tried that once before—having someone else talk to him for me. It didn't work."

He took her hands and brought them to his lips. "And was that someone as persuasive as I am?"

"No one is that persuasive."

He knew just how quickly, how smoothly, she would slip her arms around his neck and just how she would angle her head to kiss him. He wondered if she were aware of just how much he loved her.

"Let me do this for you," he said.

"I don't know, Jake. You and Austin haven't exactly been the best of friends."

"No, but we have a bet between us."

"Yes," she said warily. "The bet." She removed her hands from around his neck. "I've given your idea a lot of thought these past few weeks and . . . "

He saw the concern in her eyes. "You don't think it'll work."

"If he agrees to your terms and you win, there's no need for concern. You could do a lot with a thousand dollars."

"*We* could do a lot with a thousand dollars."

"Yes," she said with a smile that acknowledged their conversations, whispered and otherwise, about a wedding ring, an addition to the house, and rooms full of children. "But if you lose—"

"If I lose, I'll have a job, at least for a year."

"But you'd be working for Austin and at half the going rate. You'd be miserable for both reasons. And knowing you, you'd be giving him your very best."

"My very best is what I give to you. But you're right. I would give him an honest day's labor and then some."

"For a whole year!"

"I've put up with a lot worse for a lot longer."

She looked hesitant, then said, "There is one more alternative. You could leave the bet as it stands. If you win, you would get five hundred dollars, which is still a lot of money. And if you lose . . . if you lose, I could leave Coventry with you."

He shook his head. "I love you for offering, but I would never ask you to give up all you have here—a home, friends, a place in the community. I know how important those things are, though I've spent most of my life denying it.

"Besides," he added, "much as I hate to admit it, Halliwell isn't a fool. When we made that bet he had just come from seeing you and getting the bad news that you weren't going to marry him. That had to hurt. But he's had plenty of time to think things over. He's got to know that simply getting me out of the picture wouldn't mean you'd marry him instead."

"You're right. I wouldn't."

"And I don't think he'd care one way or the other if I

stayed here or took off. I understand he's only going to be around six months out of the year anyway."

"He could insist simply on principle."

"Maybe. But I see how he cares for Phoebe and I can't believe he'd do something mean just because he could."

"He does love her. And he does have a kind heart." Brenna's hands began that upward slide to Jake's neck, then stopped abruptly. "Wait a minute. If you don't think Austin would insist on your leaving town if you lost the bet, then why do you want to raise the stakes at all?"

"Because that way, whether I win or lose, I get something to use to build our future. Right here. Where I found the magic."

Ted, the bartender from The Royal Crown Pub, pointed with pride to the field, cleared of every weed and stump that had been there just two months ago. The well-worn path between the bases indicated the diamond was getting a lot of use.

"Tally-ho!" Ted said, pointing now to the rear door of the church and the men marching single file toward them. "Here come our Whitefish Filets now!"

Jake groaned. Not only did the town have a decent field, and what appeared to be regulation white-canvas bases, but the Whitefish Filets had uniforms, real uniforms. White, long-sleeved, pull-over shirts laced up the front to a flat, spread collar. Knickers and caps of blue and white railroad ticking. Each player had a glove too. A kid at the end of the line carried at least four bats and wore an apron that bulged with any number of balls.

"I must say," Ted said, "they do make an impression. Wouldn't you agree?"

"I'm impressed, all right."

"Oh look. Here comes Lord Austin now."

Austin shaded his eyes, then approached the other two men. "Well, well. What have we here? A scouting mission?"

"Not exactly." Jake felt his hopes of winning the game disappearing by the second. "Nice uniforms," he said.

"Yes, they are rather nice, aren't they?" Using his fingertips, Austin brushed the cuff of each sleeve. "I wired a man named Spalding who expedited the order for me. Have you heard of him? Nice chap."

"Yeah, I've heard of him." Jake couldn't remember if every player on his own team had shoes. "But then, a team has to have a lot more than pretty clothes to win a ball game."

"I couldn't agree with you more. Did you see our home plate? White marble."

The crack of a bat drew both men's attention to the field. "Bravo, Rob!" Austin shouted. "Another home run."

Turning to Jake, Austin said, "So what brings you to Whitefish? May I remind you that if you've come to peddle your wares again, you must get a permit."

"No, I'm not selling anything this trip. But I have come to talk to you about business. And about your daughter."

Austin arched his brow with what appeared more than simple curiosity. His voice tightened. "Theodore, would you excuse us?"

"Certainly." Ted ran toward the field.

With both men watching the practice session, Jake said, "First, I'd like to make you a business proposition. I've given a lot of thought to what your new business will need and I—"

"No, no, no. First, let me hear what you've come to say about my daughter. Then I'll decide whether or not I wish to discuss business with you."

So Austin knew how to throw a curve ball. Jake thought a minute. "It might be better if we sat down somewhere."

"I prefer to watch my team—oh, how thoughtless of me. Your leg. I forgot. Of course we can sit down." He looked around. "The steps of the church. How would that be?"

"Fine." He shouldn't have said anything. Now Austin was going to see him as nothing but a cripple. This wasn't going well.

There were three wide steps to the bright red door of the church. Both men sat on the top step. On either side of the steps were three white-painted barrels in descending sizes, each filled with red geraniums to match the red door. Jake didn't see an inch of chipped paint anywhere.

"I don't remember the church looking this nice," Jake said.

"I organized a garden club."

Jake groaned. Didn't the man have any vices?

"And now that we've dispensed with protocol, what is it you wish to say about Phoebe?"

Jake leaned forward, his palms braced just above his knees, hoping to look more at ease than he felt. "Brenna, Miss McAuley, is concerned about her."

"At one time I believed that to be true. However, I now believe her attention, and her affection, have been placed elsewhere."

"Come on, Halliwell. You don't believe that. Brenna has a big heart. She's got enough love for a lot of people, including a little girl like Phoebe."

"A little girl like Phoebe. What exactly do you mean?"

"Why didn't you let Phoebe have the present Brenna sent over? She got that mortar and pestle when she graduated. It's a symbol of achievement. That's why she wanted Phoebe to have it."

"You haven't answered my question, Darrow. What do you mean by 'a little girl like Phoebe'?"

Now what? Dance around the obvious or lay the cards on the table? Try to help Brenna or force himself to remember things best left forgotten?

"Well?" Austin said.

Jake's past for Brenna's future? If there was anything he had learned from Brenna it was the value of getting things out in the open.

"What's she got left? Seven more years? Eight at the most?"

"How dare you." Austin stood and glared down at Jake.

"Frequent respiratory infections, a heart murmur, maybe even a hole in the chamber."

"I've had enough of this!" Austin stormed down the steps.

Jake knew when pain tightened a man's walk. Why couldn't Austin be some kind of obnoxious brute? With the poor man staring into space, Jake continued. "Her jaw is small; her teeth get crowded. Anyone who watches her for any length of time can see she has poor muscle tone. Can't lift her weight against gravity; can't even play hopscotch."

Austin turned around, a grimace on his lips, pain in his eyes. "We all know you're not a true man of medicine. Just how is it you know all these things about my daughter?"

"They are true, aren't they?"

"Answer my question."

"When I was old enough, I searched every asylum on

the East Coast trying to find someone I loved. Eventually, I learned she was dead. In the meantime, I saw kids like Phoebe . . . hundreds of them. Eating bug-infested food from bowls on the floor. Naked, soiled with their own waste, hosed down like animals."

"Stop it!"

"They'd try to claw their way through the back wall of the cell, screaming, scared to death of the water."

Years of worry lined Austin's face and diminished his outrage. "Your point?"

"Only that having seen how the world treats most children like Phoebe, I know that for you to have raised her the way you have, to have taught her all the things she knows, and to have refused to stick her in a cage and forget her, you must love that little girl more than life itself."

"On that we agree."

"Then, knowing her life is short, why won't you let her see Brenna? She loves Phoebe, too. You know that. And don't tell me you don't know how much Phoebe loves Brenna. Anyone can see that."

Jake could see the curtain dropping in Austin's eyes, the very same curtain he himself had used whenever he couldn't take any more pain. "Look, I didn't come here to upset you," he said, rising. "I just didn't see any other way."

"Oh, yes," Austin said, his voice fighting for control, "you mentioned a business proposition. And what might that be?"

"First, let me say that folks in Coventry see your move to Whitefish as an indication of where you plan to set up business. Is that true?"

"Oh for pity's sake. In the six months I've been in the state of Montana, I've lived half the time in Whitefish and half in Coventry. Why on earth are people interpreting this latest move as anything other than routine?"

"So Coventry is still in the running?"

"Indeed it is."

"Good. Then what I want to talk about is our bet." Jake stood and the two men headed toward the ball field. "I'll admit your team is looking pretty good. But Coventry looks even better. I want to raise the stakes."

"Get me over there behind home plate," Cosmos said, fidgeting in his chair.

"You sit down." Amabelle tightened her grip on the high handles on the back of the wicker wheelchair. "From what I've seen, I don't think home plate is a safe place to be." She looked to Brenna for support.

"We could stay behind home plate and off to the side," Brenna said. "Besides, the game is almost over." She looked around for Phoebe. She had spoken briefly with Austin before the game started and he had said Mrs. Dinwittie would be bringing her to the field. He also said he had explained to Phoebe that the lovely mortar and pestle were treasures from Miss Brenna. What surprised Brenna even more was how highly Austin spoke of Jake. Jake had told her very little of his conversation with Austin, saying only that through their common interests, they had reached a meeting of minds.

Under other circumstances, it might have been hard for Brenna to concentrate on the game. But Jake was out there. She had prayed this would be a memorable game for him. Tonight's full moon would provide the perfect background for a celebration.

At the top of the eighth inning, with the score five to five, either side could still win. By the bottom of the eighth, the score was five to six, thanks to Raymond Foster's spectacular slide, head first, into home. Unfortunately, he hadn't heeded Jake's warning to fill his fists with dirt and had broken the index finger on his right hand. Out for the game. Out for the season. A high, pop-up fly by Stewart McCutcheon ended the inning. Going to the top of the ninth and leading by one run, all Coventry had to do was hold Whitefish scoreless for three outs.

Raymond said he'd wait until the game was over to have his finger set, but Brenna insisted she tend to it immediately. Though Sarah couldn't find anything in the rule books about it one way or the other, both teams agreed to a short break while Raymond went down to the pharmacy with Brenna.

In the meantime, the other Coventry Comets huddled on the field.

"Victory is within our grasp," Elton said to Jake.

"Don't celebrate yet. We don't have a pitcher."

Elton drew himself up straight. "Put me in. I can do it."

"I'm not looking to find fault, but you missed an easy throw to first."

"That was early in the game. I was a bit unnerved."

"Every man in the Whitefish lineup is a hitter. Except Halliwell."

"But we are ahead."

Whitefish had three outs to change the score. The alternatives ran through Jake's mind. Either he put Elton on the mound or he took the mound himself. He felt good; no question about that. The way Brenna had massaged his leg last night, he felt like he could walk to the moon. So far today he had struck out, walked, taken an easy tour around the bases on Ralph Newton's home run, and bunted for the sacrifice. He hadn't had to run yet, but in order to pitch, there was no getting around the need for a good knee.

"All right," he said to Elton. "You're on."

When Brenna and Raymond returned, the Comets took the field, with Elton on the mound.

The first batter hit a blooper over the third baseman's head, sending the batter to first base. Standing in center field, Jake groaned. Elton walked the second batter on four pitches, all high and outside. Now Whitefish had the tying run on second base, the winning run on first, and no outs.

Jake signaled time-out and walked to the mound.

"I'm not doing all that well, am I?" Elton said.

"You're giving it your all. I know that."

"At this rate my all is going to give them the game." He slipped the glove from his hand and held it out for Jake.

In that brief moment, Jake knew that this would be as close as he would ever get to playing in a big game. He took the glove.

Before leaving the mound, Elton said, "You know that brother of mine I told you about, the one who lost his leg at Gettysburg?"

"What about him?"

"He's a champion swimmer now. Just thought I'd tell you."

Jake lobbed a few warm-up pitches over the plate, shaking out his arm, loosening up his wrist. He told himself that with a little more time he could fire a ball so fast it would go right through the catcher. He was kidding himself and he knew it.

The first batter stepped up. Jake felt the sweat break on his forehead as he drew up his left knee, not as high as he wanted, but high enough to get the pitch off.

The batter swung, hit a high pop-up fly. One out.

Jake nodded to his team, acknowledging their cheers. Cosmos was waving. Brenna was clapping. The boys he had been coaching were jumping up and down and screaming.

Sore as hell, he faced the next batter. He glared at the man, making sure he could see the fire in his eyes. Two fast balls and two strikes later, the batter glared back. He would expect a curve ball now, or maybe a breaking ball, but not another fast ball. No pitcher in his right mind would throw another fast ball.

Jake did, his fastest ever.

The batter stood there with his mouth open. Strike three. Two outs. The crowd went crazy!

All Jake had to do was get one more batter out. Just one more. But his leg was throbbing.

Rob "The Robber" Gillikin strutted up and tipped his hat to acknowledge the roar of the Whitefish crowd. Shoulders a mile wide and muscles like mountains, he had already hit two home runs. Jake hungered for the sweet taste of a strikeout, though the odds were against him.

Rob tapped his bat on the plate and spit on the ground. Jake studied him, maneuvering the ball against the glove until the seams lined up just the way he wanted them. His first pitch had to be his best. If it was, it would also be his last. The fire raging up his leg threatened to topple him. He felt his balance give.

Quickly, he recovered and scanned the crowd. Cosmos, who languished at death's door only a month ago, now waved from his wheelchair, Amabelle by his side holding his other hand. Jake saw only Brenna's back, her arms opened wide to embrace Phoebe, running awkwardly toward her. No shortage of miracles on the sidelines. No indeed. Jake rubbed his knee. Maybe this place was magic.

The second baseman inched closer to first. Jake

glared at The Robber. The boy smiled. Ready for the wind-up, Jake raised his left leg as high as it would go. The pain caught in his throat.

Get it up there, boy. Higher! I said higher!

Suddenly, fired like steel thrust in a furnace, he bent his knee, brought it to his chin, and sent the ball spinning like a locomotive.

The crack of the bat told the world The Robber had connected. The line drive headed right between Jake and second base. Reflex took over. Jake stepped to the right, stretching his right arm out as far as he could. He screamed from his gut when the ball slammed against his bare hand—where it stayed.

Out number three. Game over. Whitefish five. Coventry six.

They had won! Jake limped off the field to the cheers of the Coventry crowd, the pain forgotten.

"Admirable effort," Austin said, handing Jake one thousand dollars. "My heartiest congratulations."

"A pleasure doing business with you." Jake put the money in his pocket and shook Austin's hand. No reason for a victory so sweet to have a bitter aftertaste. No reason at all. "Just curious, but if you'd won, would you have been as eager to collect?"

"You mean would I have been desirous of your services for a year? Absolutely. We may have had our differences, but I find you to be an honest, hardworking man, someone who enjoys the respect of your town and who has your town's best interests at heart. I would have welcomed your employment."

Your town. Jake liked the sound of that. Better yet, he liked the idea that Halliwell might still give him a job. He wanted to ask outright, but the words wouldn't come. "By the way," he said instead, "that was some slide you made into first base. Didn't look like it was the first time you'd done it."

Austin laughed. "I admit to considerable practice. And these long arms of mine do come in handy now and then." He grinned from ear to ear. "I did hold my own out there, didn't I?"

"Like a pro."

With a dismissing wave that belied his pride, Austin said, "Oh, I'm certain the professionals must achieve more than one hit per game, but I certainly did have fun. Even our rehearsals have been stimulating. So much so, in fact, that I've taken steps to relive the moment, in a manner of speaking."

"Thinking of playing again?"

"Yes. Do you recall the conversation in which you advised me of the new baseball teams being formed in England?"

"Yeah, I do. Why?"

"I've decided to buy one."

"What?"

"You sound incredulous, as well you might. Nevertheless, it's true. Of course, I'm still obliged by the family company to set up a cattle syndicate here in Montana. I've been assured by a round of experts that after that dreadful winter of two years ago, I can buy at most reasonable prices. Still, I do have a bit of my own money put aside, having made a bet here, a bet there. I intend to pursue the purchase of a baseball team when I get back to England. I hope to sail by the first of October."

Incredulous? Hell, Jake was dumbfounded.

"As a matter of fact," Austin continued, "I had intended to speak with you about my new venture. Would you care to join me? Move to England? Be my coach?"

"That's a dream job offer."

"So you'll take it?"

Jake hesitated. "I can't say just yet. I want to talk it over with Brenna."

A wistful look passed Austin's eyes. "Of course. I understand. Just so you know there are no hard feelings as far as she is concerned, let me be the first to wish the two of you a lifetime of happiness."

"Thank you." They shook hands again.

"I'm off to the hotel now," Austin said. "Win or lose, I promised the team a steak dinner. I say, I am most eager to get this baseball rolling. I've wired that impressive rookie, Cy Young, to see if he'd care to join up. What are the chances you could let me have your decision by tomorrow afternoon?"

Jake nodded, still numbed by the nearness of his dream.

"Excellent."

Austin started to walk away, then turned back. "Lest you think my only concerns are for commerce and sport, let me assure you that I never forget a kindness." He smiled softly. "You were right about Phoebe, you know. Right about her bleak future as well as her overwhelming love for Miss McAuley, which I've no doubt is returned a hundredfold. I must say it did my own heart good to see them embrace."

"Mine, too."

"Yes," Austin said, letting the word trail. Then he walked away, leaving Jake with a pocket full of money and a head full of ideas.

While Brenna dutifully faced the wall, Jake spread the money all over her bed. This time he didn't mind the flickering light from the fire or the soft illumination from the moon. "You can turn around now," he said.

She turned, a vision in her long white gown. Her eyes widened, but there was no gasp of either surprise or pleasure.

He took her hand and led her to the display of his worth, spread out in every conceivable denomination. "I won the bet! Remember?" He scooped a fistful of bills and offered them to her.

"Of course, I do." She accepted the bouquet, then carefully returned it to the bed. "You were wonderful out there this afternoon. I was so proud."

"There's enough money here for us to do anything we want. Well, almost anything. We could live anywhere in the world. Europe. England. Have you ever wanted to live in England?"

"No."

"Have you ever thought about it?"

"This is my home." She looked him in the eye, giving him that uncomfortable feeling that she was looking not at him, but through him. "I thought you liked Coventry," she said. "Was I wrong?"

"No. No, I like this town a lot. I like the people, the mountains, the weather. I like everything about it—especially its druggist." With a grand sweep, he brushed most of the bills aside, sending them fluttering and falling like leaves. "I love its druggist." He slipped his arms around her, relieved to feel her hands slide around his neck.

"Does that mean you'll let me massage your leg again?"

"Only if I can return the favor." He drew her closer and kissed her with the passion of a man determined to prove himself worthy.

The bed creaked softly with their weight. Jake brushed aside more bills, smiling as he did.

Brenna clutched one in her hand. Holding it between them, she whispered, "A woman wants more from a man than this."

"I know that." He pinched the end of the bill, intending to fling it away, but she held it tight.

"She wants to know that he accepts her, truly accepts her, flaws and all."

"You don't have any flaws."

"Please see them, Jake. I don't have the energy to hide them, or the desire to try."

Her pale green eyes drew gold from the fire flickering behind them. Was her steady gaze saying that she accepted him, flaws and all?

Brenna continued. "She wants to know that he will understand her, at least that he will make a genuine effort—the way you understood, even before I did, how vital it was for me to accept the legacy of my ancestors."

He glanced over to the table where the bridal veil lay in its open basket, no longer locked away.

She released her end of the bill and used her fingers to stroke his face, to trace the outline of his lips. "She wants to know that what she brings, whether it's the ability to raise children or keep a house or pursue a profession is appreciated."

"Brings?"

"To their marriage."

He crumpled the bill and let it fall to the floor. He knew what he would tell Halliwell tomorrow. "Tell me you've set a date. I'm an impatient man."

"I've been thinking of the middle of September, the next new moon."

"Two more weeks." He smiled. "And then you're mine."

Her eyes pulled him deeper into the spell she'd woven around him. He bent to kiss her. "Just one more thing," she said, pressing her finger to his lips. "She wants to know that he will love their children—no matter what."

"He will."

Jake walked into Elton's office to find him embroiled in heated conversation with Stewart, Ralph, and Austin. He wanted to talk with Austin alone, preferably when the man was in a better mood.

"I don't believe you gentlemen understand," Austin said. "I simply cannot base such a critical decision on anything other than sound business principles. For the sake of my financial investors, I am forced to set aside all personal feelings."

"You've picked Whitefish?" Jake said, scrambling to form a new plan. Brenna wouldn't move to Whitefish. Her home was in Coventry. She'd made that clear. But if the cattle syndicate was to operate from Whitefish, she'd have to move. Or he'd have to do something else for work, something that kept him off the road. He wasn't going back to selling elixirs.

"Worse than that," Elton said with a sigh.

"Now, now." Austin said.

Jake looked at the men around him. "Well you couldn't have picked Coventry or all these men would be smiling."

"You're right!" Elton raised a fist to the ceiling. "And it's all my fault. Telling the world about our valley's abundant resources . . . "

"I spoke with a government official only this morning and have selected a location on the river," Austin said, "midway between here and Whitefish. A lovely site."

"What are you talking about? There's no town between here and Whitefish."

"There is now," Elton said. "Or at least there will be. Only a few weeks ago, the government of the United States determined it an appropriate site—more appropriate than Coventry—for an official post office. I learned of the decision only this morning. I suspect political shenanigans, but who am I to question our government? The point is that even as we speak the new area is drawing attention like a magnet. Before long, it will be the hub of commerce."

Jake waited for more information. "What's the place called?

In unison, the others said, "Kalispell."

"So what does that mean for Coventry?" Jake asked.

He followed Elton's gaze around the room, seeing the already faded Fourth of July posters and the drawing of the proposed expansion to the dock. "It means," Elton said, "that we either pack up like gypsies and move or we die a slow and lingering death. Either way, Coventry is doomed to be a ghost town." He lowered his arm and sighed.

"What about Whitefish?" Jake said.

Elton smirked. "At least they're to suffer the same fate."

"Come on," Jake said. "It's not the end of the world. Packing up and moving to Kalispell may not be what this town wants, but maybe, just maybe, it's exactly what this town needs—a chance to start fresh. New stores, new houses—ones that are built to last. You can determine the best spot for a lumber mill. You can fashion a dock just as big and fancy as you want—for industry and passengers alike."

In the eyes of those around him, he saw the power of his words. He felt the power in his own heart. "What you've been given, gentlemen, is the opportunity to find out what you're really made of. The question is, What are you going to do with that power? Deny it? Run from it? Or seize it!"

Austin stepped up. "Well, my good man. Now I have a question for you. My offer to bring you to England still holds. But I will double the salary—no, I will triple it—if instead you will move to Kalispell and head up my new syndicate."

Jake extended his hand. "You just hired yourself a manager."

As they were sealing the deal, Brenna and Phoebe walked in.

Elton rushed to her, smiling from ear to ear. "We're moving to Kalispell! All of us!"

"What are you talking about?"

"Let me explain," Jake said, and told her what had happened.

"The entire town is to move? And you are to manage Austin's syndicate?"

"That's right," he said. Her voice had trembled a little when she referred to moving, but there was no mistaking the pride in her eyes when she referred to his new career. "I'm going to organize a baseball team there, too," he added.

"Splendid!" Austin said. "I've no doubt Whitefish would relish a rematch."

"I meant a team for the kids, girls as well as boys."

Austin slapped Jake on the back. "Here, here, old chap. To those of us blessed with lovely daughters—" He beamed at Phoebe, who rushed to his arms. "Your innovative ideas are pure music."

They all stood there awhile longer, talking about their visions for Kalispell and about Austin's plans to leave for England.

"What about Phoebe?" Brenna said, her eyes shining.

Austin tousled his daughter's hair. "Well, I thought to take her with me, of course. Mrs. Dinwittie has already informed me of her intent to find other employment. I mean, what alternative is there?"

Brenna hesitated, then said, "She could stay with us."

"I'll be gone for five, perhaps six, months. I couldn't ask the two of you to take charge of her."

Jake took Brenna's trembling hand. "We'd be delighted."

Every seat in Coventry's small church was taken.

From where Brenna stood in the rear, she could see Jake and Cosmos clearly. Cosmos had gained weight, not a lot, but enough to restore at least a resemblance to the mesmerizing face that graced the labels of the old Clarion Compound. He was having new labels made for his new elixir: Amabelle's Brew, a freshly steeped, completely alcohol-free tea blended with herbs selected for their genuine healing properties. He would sell it from Amabelle's new House of Recovery, the one they would build together in Kalispell. He wore an old jacket, still too big for him. The silver stars and bolts of gold lightning on the lapels reminded Brenna he was a man with his own kind of magic and always would be.

Jake looked far more handsome than he had on the day she met him. He wore his black suit, a new white shirt, and at Brenna's request, his red brocade vest. He also wore the smile that had at one time haunted her dreams, and now enchanted her nights.

She had bought a new dress. The design was simple, but the pale green matched her eyes. In her hands, she carried daisies and lavender tied with white ribbon. In her heart, she carried her mother's love.

With sun streaming through the windows, Phoebe walked down the aisle first. Amabelle followed her.

As the organist hit the first notes, Jake caught her eye. He tugged on the points of his vest, letting her know he was ready to take the biggest step of his life.

Seeing clearly through the lace, Brenna stepped out of the shadows.

Let HarperMonogram
Sweep You Away!

Chances Are by **Robin Lee Hatcher**
Over 3 million copies of Hatcher's books in print. Her young daughter's illness forces traveling actress Faith Butler to take a job at the Jagged R Ranch working for Drake Rutledge. Passions rise when the beautiful thespian is drawn to her rugged employer and the forbidden pleasure of his touch.

Mystic Moon by **Patricia Simpson**
"One of the premier writers of supernatural romance."—Romantic Times. A brush with death changes Carter Greyson's life and irrevocably links him to an endangered Indian tribe. Dr. Arielle Scott, who is intrigued by the mysterious Carter, shares this destiny—a destiny that will lead them both to the magic of lasting love.

Just a Miracle by **Zita Christian**
When dashing Jake Darrow brings his medicine show to Coventry, Montana, pharmacist Brenna McAuley wants nothing to do with him. But it's only a matter of time before Brenna discovers that romance is just what the doctor ordered.

Raven's Bride by **Lynn Kerstan**
When Glenys Shea robbed the reclusive Earl of Ravensby, she never expected to steal his heart instead of his gold. Now the earl's prisoner, the charming thief must prove her innocence—and her love.

And in case you missed last month's selections . . .

Once a Knight by **Christina Dodd**
Golden Heart and RITA Award-winning Author. Though slightly rusty, once great knight Sir David Radcliffe agrees to protect Lady Alisoun for a price. His mercenary heart betrayed by passion, Sir David proves to his lady that he is still a master of love—and his sword is as swift as ever.

Timberline by Deborah Bedford

Held captive in her mountain cabin by escaped convict Ben Pershall, Rebecca Woodburn realizes that the man's need for love mirrors her own. Even though Ben has taken her hostage, he ultimately sets her soul free.

Conor's Way by Laura Lee Guhrke

Desperate to save her plantation after the Civil War, beautiful Olivia Maitland takes in Irish ex-boxer Conor Branigan in exchange for help. Cynical Conor has no place for romance in his life, until the strong-willed belle shows him that the love of a lifetime is worth fighting for.

Lord of Misrule by Stephanie Maynard

Golden Heart Award Winner. Posing as a thief to avenge the destruction of her noble family, Catrienne Lyly must match wits with Nicholas D'Avenant, Queen Elizabeth's most mysterious agent. But Cat's bold ruse cannot protect her from the ecstasy of Nicholas's touch.

Harper Monogram